THE
Scribe's
DAUGHTER

STEPHANIE CHURCHILL

Cover designed by Stephanie Churchill

Stephanie Churchill
Visit my website at
www.StephanieChurchillAuthor.com

Printed in the United States of America

First Printing: Aug 2015
This edition: Dec 2019

ISBN: 978-1-7199-3432-9

For Sharon and Paula

This book wouldn't exist without you.

1

I NEVER IMAGINED my life would end this way. Not today. And certainly not in this place. Yet here I was. It was midday, and had I the ability to tilt my face toward the sky I would have been blinded by the early summer sun, a silent observer of my murder. As it was, I could do no such thing. The beefy arm around my throat immobilized me, and as I clawed at it ineffectively, I felt my life drain away bit by bit, with each unsuccessful gasp for air.

It had all started as a misunderstanding. Yes, I had stolen the apple, of that there was no doubt, but the fact that I stood in the middle of paradise, embraced in a powerful death grip by this clay-brained slab of meat, had come about only by mischance.

The merchant was a tawdry man, odious and duplicitous, with a false sense of his own appeal to those of the opposite sex. However unsavory these traits made the man, they served my purposes perfectly. I had come to the market, specifically to this sheltered niche between a crumbling stone wall and a wagon just a stone's throw from the fruit seller's stall, for breakfast. I knew full-well the man's reputation for lewdness as well as the opportunities it had provided me in the past, and I was certain another chance at thievery would present itself if only I was patient. I wasn't disappointed.

She was a very young and very unfortunate wife of a fishmonger from the quay. She didn't know she was unfortunate, but I smiled to myself, knowing that her naiveté heralded my success. The merchant noticed her immediately, and this was my cue to act. Stepping out from the shadows, I snaked my way across the mud-packed alleyway and lightly brushed past a barrel filled to overflowing with apples, sending several cascading to the ground. It wasn't enough of a commotion to distract the merchant away from the poor girl cornered behind a crate of berries, yet it was all I needed. Bending casually as I breezed past, I picked up one of the orphaned apples. It was as I did so that the man happened to look up, saw me take a bite. He was angry, yes, though not sufficiently so to warrant the loss of his prey to chase me. I smiled at the man over my shoulder and waved. My theft was successful. It was the next thing I did however, the afterthought, which got me into trouble.

It would have been wise to keep going, to be satisfied with the marginal deadening of my hunger pains, but I had to push matters, had to turn again and gesture towards the man with an insult clearly targeted at his salacious inclinations. I only wanted to anger him a little, perhaps just enough to give his wide-eyed young customer an opportunity to escape. Except that the merchant didn't see me. A city guard did. To say he wasn't impressed would be an understatement. I took off running.

It was morning, peak hours for the frenzied business of a market, and especially so today. A fleet of ships from Kavador had arrived only yesterday, bearing goods more exotic than the wares usually on offer even for a port city as large as Corium. The traders of that far away land came only a few times a year, and I hoped that the unusually large crowds would act as a screen to my flight. I also assumed the guard would easily give up the chase, thinking me not worth his effort. In both of these assumptions I was wrong.

As I vaulted the back end of a rickety hay cart, I chanced a brief glance over my shoulder only to be rewarded by the shocking sight of at least two hundred and seventy-five pounds of heaving, angry, solidly muscular guard no more than five or six strides behind me. I surged on.

Every good thing, including market districts, must eventually come to an end, and with it my best chance of escape. Like a doe that has stumbled beyond the forest edge, finding herself in an open meadow without tree, bush or underbrush for cover, I found myself on a deserted street lined with individual houses flanked by walls of finely cut marble. If I was to get myself out of what my impetuousness had started, it was time to give up on speed and agility and get clever.

Making a sharp right turn, I leapt over a low wall and landed hard, twisting my ankle and nearly falling. Ignoring the pain, I regained my footing and stride and continued on as before.

I was in a garden. And I was alone. Of the city guard there was no sign, and despite my dubious luck so far that day, I hoped I had finally eluded him. Taking a moment to catch my breath, I scanned my surroundings and bent to rub my throbbing ankle. A footpath passed just ahead of me and continued in a straight line for several meters before curving gently around an overgrown juniper tree. Neatly trimmed grasses nestled between each flagstone of the path, and for a precise meter on either side, unrelenting as objects of perfection, decisive and meticulous, likely a good representation of the qualities of the wealthy owners. Zinnias, coneflowers, daisies, hibiscus, begonias and dozens of other flowers in all the colors of the rainbow populated the beds in fragrant profusion, undulating in cascades throughout the garden.

I breathed in the potent fragrance, and for a moment relaxed. Unfortunately, it was a day for miscalculations. A shadow loomed, and before I realized it, the guard came at me from behind, beginning his stranglehold. I was trapped, and I was dying in a beautiful garden.

"You think this is the end?" His breath reeked of moldy onions. "You think this is your penance?"

He tightened his hold and my vision dimmed, black spots forming before my eyes as the world spun and blurred even as it faded. It was only a matter of moments before I passed out.

With his free hand, he brought up a finger and traced it down my cheek. "No, this is not how you will die," he hissed before releasing the pressure. I gulped in a lungful of sweet air before he continued, "I know a special place for boys like you. A place you will fetch a fair price. A place you will be valued..."

He licked his lips in anticipation, and I felt his excitement as he contemplated what his luck had brought him, that he would sell me for a hefty profit, would then be entitled to a first go at the new merchandise. The thought distracted him. It was all I needed.

I turned my body slightly, enough to put my left foot behind the man's right leg. With my left elbow I jabbed at his midsection, pushing, tripping him backwards over my foot. It was meant to throw him off balance, and it did the trick nicely, distracting him enough that he released completely his grasp of my throat so I could slip away. While it was tempting to turn and kick the man savagely between the legs, wisdom took hold and I fled, finding a place to hide until I was absolutely certain the guard had given up his search and left.

I now took some time to walk the garden path, to appreciate the beauty around me, to see with my own eyes the things kept hidden away behind walls as a protection from me and others like me - the poor, filthy and worthless. The smell of the place was heady, almost sickly sweet with the syrupy smell of blossoms, a far cry from the refuse-infused scents of the streets and alleyways near my home in the heart of the poorest district of Corium, the city of my birth.

I was nearly to the far side of the garden when I came to a marble-edged pool. Having just run across what seemed like half the city, I was hot and very dirty. It looked like as good a place as any to wash myself, so I sat down on the edge and bent towards the water, discovering a face reflected back to me on the calm surface. I wasn't impressed by what I saw. The eyes that met mine were green, and though they were framed by long lashes, they were entirely too close together. The lashes swept smudged cheeks displaying a smattering of unfashionable freckles. A stray wisp of equally unfashionable copper brown hair had escaped the confines of a felt cap and blew gently in the light wind. All in all there was nothing remarkable or noteworthy about the face staring back at me, and the fact that I owned it was not a matter that concerned me greatly. With a sniff, I cupped my hands and splashed them into the water, disturbing the reflection and sending out ripples across the placid pool. What was a reflection anyway? It mirrored the exterior of things only, and that darkly so. Depth and dimension of a thing was proved out by time, touch and exploration, by revelations that gave lie to the deceptions that the surface sought to make real.

After scrubbing my hands and face, I straightened and stood, and only then did I notice them watching me. Several young serving girls tended to the preparation of what appeared to be the makings of a garden party. The appearance of a bedraggled boy into their pampered midst had elicited their curious but wary attention.

"Hello," I said to them. My smile was pleasant enough, but my very presence was an affront to them and my greeting wasn't returned. Before long the girls returned to work, though the leader of the crew kept half an eye on me all the while, thinking I might cause trouble. That's what my kind was good at, after all. Little did she know that I had no immediate plans to cause mischief, for whether they understood it or not, these servant girls and I were on the same side of the vast gulf that separated the haves from the have-nots. Though they worked in a wealthy household, they themselves were not a part of it and never would be.

My scalp itched, and as I reached up under the band of my cap to scratch, a gust of wind came up and whipped it from my head, blowing it towards the silk-draped pavilion the girls had just finished erecting. A cascade of long copper-brown hair fell from confinement, blowing freely about my face and neck. Six pairs of startled eyes opened in shock as the realization struck. This boy in bedraggled trousers and a patched shirt was no boy, but rather a young woman, skinny and dirty, but a woman nonetheless.

I retrieved my cap, but when I turned, I nearly collided with a woman blocking my path, staring down her long patrician nose at me. "Gutter rats in our haven," she scoffed as she stepped closer. I stood my ground. "How dare you invade this place with your pestilence, you vermin infested son of a..." she paused then, considered my long hair and delicate facial features, and her mouth twisted into a sneer, "...or should I say *daughter* of a muddy street cur and a mongrel..."

Likely she would have continued on in this vein for some time, but I wasn't about to let her. Without thinking what I did, I slapped her face. What happened next was unintentional, but I won't pretend not to be pleased by the outcome. The slap so discombobulated her that she staggered backward, her momentum stopped only by the pool. With a startled cry, she tumbled into the water. I didn't even bother to wait for a reaction; it had been two days since I'd eaten a meal, and despite the partial apple I'd nearly inhaled not long before, I was hungry. Let the old carp in the pool fend for herself. It was how the rest of us lived.

◆ ◆ ◆

Our home was both a place to live and our place of business. It fronted a small side-street in the busy market district and was divided into two rooms: the front for the display of my sister's wares and for each of us to conduct business, and a small back room out of which we lived and worked.

Upon my return, I found my sister Irisa engrossed in her newest project, an assortment of metal objects arranged in an intricate pattern on the floor before her. She sat there motionless, head cocked sideways, with one eye squeezed shut. She studied the metal pieces with her other eye, and her mouth was screwed up into a pucker as though she was sucking on a lemon. I knew better than to interrupt her bizarre meditation, for though I didn't understand how, she found inspiration with this method. I danced around her, trying my best to sidestep the display.

It was early evening, the time most merchants closed their shops for the day, so I closed ours as well. If we had attracted any business during my absence today, likely we would never have known with my sister left in charge. She was so intent on her newest creation that most anyone could have walked off with the entirety of our earthly possessions, and she wouldn't have noticed. It was probably best that we owned nothing worth stealing.

I placed a small sack of food on the back table, my newest theft since leaving the garden, then undressed. The cooler air of the darkened room pricked at my naked skin, a delightful contrast to the hot and dusty city streets I had just escaped. Taking a bucket of water from the corner, I washed more thoroughly than I had been able to do at the garden's pool then pulled on a simple cotton chemise, choosing to neglect the rest of my attire and dripping wet hair in favor of eating. Rummaging through a small box in the corner, I found a knife and cut up the dried meat, cheese and bread I had retrieved from a neglectful merchant. Likely it was meant to be his evening meal, but I supposed I needed it more than he did based purely on my estimation of the circumference of his girth compared to mine.

When my portion of the food was gone, Irisa appeared beside

me. She glanced at me briefly, taking in my transformation from thieving boy back to young woman of seventeen, flashed me a bright smile, then quickly ate her portion and returned to her work. We remained silent. There was nothing to say, for life rarely held any marvels worthy enough to warrant the waste of speech.

Next I intended to begin mending the handle of a bucket, for I was a tinker, and mending things was my trade; but before I did so, I wanted to make some tea, so set a pot to boil over the small fire. This task was interrupted by a familiar knock sounding on the back door. I flung it open to reveal a short, rotund and balding man whose only remaining hair clung to the sides of his head like a wooly mountain sheep. He strolled casually through the door as if his presence was expected, even eagerly anticipated.

"Swine." I said the name flatly, though I couldn't help that my mouth twitched at the corners. It was hard to suppress my amusement over his acceptance of my taunt. His real name was Sveine, but Swine was what I always called him. His face registered irritation, but he didn't correct me. He never did.

He waltzed further into the tiny room with an air of importance, his eyes sweeping the shadowed corners out of habit. If he noticed my sister or the work she was doing, he made no indication. Irisa looked at him and went back to work. She knew she needn't bother with his visit. While he made his usual survey of the room, I turned back to the small fire, stoking the burning coals to coax the paltry flame into a more vigorous blaze. The water was starting to steam, and, once it started to boil, I would add a handful of leaves to make tea. So far Swine had not spoken or made any indication as to the purpose of his visit, though I was pretty sure I knew why he was here.

"You have money you be owing me. It is most needful that you, ah..." He paused, searching for the right word. I kept my back turned to him, stoking the fire to hide my mirth. "...provide me with payment..." Another pause. How this man maintained a bustling trade I would never understand. "...at your quickliest... no, this is not right..." I think he was getting exasperated. I continued tending the fire so I wouldn't have to turn around, revealing my face which was red from stifled laughter. He continued on a while longer in the same halting speech, words sputtering forth in fits and starts like a geyser. I had stopped paying attention. The water was finally boiling nicely, so I added a handful of leaves to brew.

I noticed the silence and realized that Swine had asked me a question.

"You listening? Do my talking you mind?"

I turned back to Swine, all the while considering the iron poker I held in my hand, considering the relative merits of poking him with it. Disregarding the notion as unnecessary even while wholly satisfying, I set it down and replied, "I don't mind that you are talking so long as you don't mind that I'm not listening."

He sucked in his breath and stared at me, beady eyes flashing. "Monies due soon. You remember. I am not the fool to take your impudence."

I was impressed. Impudence was a big word.

"I don't think you are a fool. But then, what's my own humble opinion against hundreds of others?" He was a filthy little man, and I was tired of the exchange. Somewhat to my surprise, rather than turn in disgust and leave me in peace, which was the way conversations like this typically ended, he moved towards me, his mouth turned up at the corners in a disgusting leer. I resisted the urge to retreat a step, held my ground instead.

He stood there for several moments, his eyes raking over my body, and I discerned calculation behind his leer. He made no move to touch me, but already my mind was racing, trying to remember where I had put the knife in case I needed it. I eyed the discarded poker and knew I couldn't reach it. My hands were behind me, so I felt around until I found a newly sharpened quill resting on a small ledge. It wouldn't kill, but it could inflict sufficient pain and permanent damage if used in strategic locations.

"Way of other kinds to provide payment. You consider..." He paused and flashed repellent yellowed teeth, took another half step towards me. This time I did involuntarily react, backing further against the wall. Putrid sack of pig dung that he was, he outweighed me considerably, and I had no delusions about who would be the loser if he forced himself on me. He reached out tentatively as if to touch me then reconsidered. I wretched away from him so violently that he startled.

I have no idea what he expected or how he thought I would react to his overture, but clearly my recoil was beyond his comprehension. He stood a little taller, puffing out his chest in annoyance. His face was red, rage filled. "Monies due!" he spat and swung about, charging through the open door into the alley.

I shouted after him, "Do you have to leave so soon? I was just about to poison the tea!" It was a great parting shot. Honestly, I was a little disappointed not to get even the smallest glance back.

I shut the door, then turned and rested my head against it for a moment. Noticing that my hands had started to shake, I closed my eyes, inhaling deeply then letting it out slowly again.

My mother died when I was eleven, leaving my father alone to care for me and my sister. Since Irisa and I were old enough to tend to all of the necessary household duties, our lives continued on in the usual way. Father earned a meager wage as a scribe-for-hire in the marketplace, selling his services to anyone who had both need and money. Correspondence and simple business contracts were the meat of his trade, though sometimes he took on a job that required travel outside the walls of Corium.

After my mother died, the frequency of these trips increased, though I thought little of it until one time, three years later, when he left on another journey. For all I knew, this occasion was no different than any other, except that this time he failed to return. He had always been extremely closed-lipped about his work, and Irisa and I knew better than to ask questions before his departure, so his disappearance was a mystery, and one which had no hope of being solved. It was easiest to presume him dead.

Between the two of us, Irisa and I managed to earn enough money from our individual trades to pay rent on the hovel where we worked and lived, and in a good month there was enough left over to buy a little food and a few other necessities, though more often than I wanted to admit, our food was acquired by thievery. My sister was the elder of the two of us, by two years. She made beautiful things from whatever scrap material she could find; bits of leather, rope, cloth pieces, etc. From small purses to shoes and jewelry, there was nothing that she had not tried. Her work was rather ahead of its time, so her clientele tended towards the eccentric or fashionably inept. Perhaps she was a visionary, but I cared little and would have been happier if she had crafted the practical over the imaginatively dramatic. We were born of the same parents, but two more different creatures would be difficult to find.

In the best of times we had not been close, being as dissimilar as oil and water. Irisa was quiet and easy to dismiss, while I was decisive, spoke my mind. Our father and mother had applauded Irisa's unassuming nature, as her demureness was a model of what a well-bred lady was meant to be. But we were not well-bred ladies, and secretly I think our father was pleased with my spunk, though he never admitted it.

It was clear, even from our earliest years, while both of our parents still lived, that Irisa would always need someone to take care of her, provide for her, and the evidence of the years since our father's disappearance bore this out. My sister was soft-hearted, concerned for those who had even less than us, always sharing what little she had with others. I admired her compassionate side but thought it more prudent to balance a giving nature with practicality -- if we starved to death, we would be of no use to anyone. I was happy to share, but I would not starve myself in the process.

Despite our differences, we had managed quite well together. No matter what I thought about her work, it was Irisa who earned the largest share of our money, while my thieving fed and clothed us. My father would not have been proud of what I had become, and those few around me who knew what I did thought me a criminal. Yet when survival is at stake, which of my accusers would not be hard-pressed to do as I have done, to steal, to thieve, to act not as a lady but as a street rat, willing to do anything short of the unthinkable? Steal, yes -- but I would rather die than whore myself. In this, Irisa and I were agreed.

My breathing calmed, I shook off my unease and retrieved

my tea. I poured a measure for myself and took some to Irisa.

She studied me for a moment then said, "Kassia, you shouldn't be so reckless." It was something she told me all the time. Ever the cautious one, my sister. But cautious didn't keep us fed. It was an old argument and I didn't want to argue with her. Not now. I was too tired.

I gave her an empty look then took my tea to a spot near the fire and sat down on the hard-packed earth floor. The enormity of our situation hit me again, and I fought back desperately against overwhelming feelings of despair. Swine was a problem, and he would never leave us alone; at least not until he was paid one way or the other. Irisa and I had been very fortunate these last several years; we had always managed to pay our rent. Until now. But how to come up with the money this time? These thoughts consumed me long after the paltry fire had smoked itself out and the night crickets began their song. I pulled a blanket around my own shoulders and sat hunched before the barren hearth, attempting to divine answers from the ash. Late into the night I came to a decision. If I refused Swine's offer, I was left with only one choice, no matter how unpalatable.

◆ ◆ ◆

Seva the Smith stared at me from across the aged boards of the table. He flicked his hand and a young girl, no more than ten years old, skittered over to him with a wine vessel, filled his cup, then looked to her father for permission to refill mine. He nodded not unkindly, and she filled my cup then retreated once again into a shadowed corner. Seva's eyes hadn't left me the entire time. I dropped my gaze, thinking that a demure pose could only aid my cause. The enormity of what I had just offered pressed down heavily on me, and I needed to find courage from somewhere. The wine in my cup seemed as likely a source as any other, so I grasped it with both hands and took a long, deep drink, wishing instantly that I hadn't. It was sour and watered more than necessary.

The long hours I spent before the dying embers of my fire the night before had clarified my thoughts, leading me to the decision that had brought me here early this morning. I hadn't dared put it off, for once I decided the matter, the deed wouldn't grow any sweeter for the waiting.

Shortly before my father left for his fateful last journey, Seva visited my family, offering my father a marriage contract for my sister. That my father was poor and couldn't provide a dowry didn't matter to him, he had said. He was a practical man and cared little for such things. Acquiring a mistress for his household was the most needful thing because his wife had recently died, and he needed someone to tend to domestic matters.

It was surprising to me that Seva cared nothing for a dowry, for who cared so little for such things? But it was possible that no one else would have him, and he was desperate. With a busy smithing trade and a young daughter yet at home, it was true that he needed domestic help. My sister could meet those needs in addition to his other less tangible needs; she was a very beautiful girl, and likely the thought of having her in his bed was dowry enough.

Though my father never discussed these matters with us, Irisa and I had both known that one day the subject of our marriages would come up, although neither of us relished the prospect since we knew we couldn't set our hopes too high. It was because of this that I uttered an involuntary gasp of relief for my sister's sake when my father respectfully but unequivocally refused Seva's offer, stating that he had higher aspirations for his daughters. It seemed an odd reason, one that did not match our circumstances, but I was happy for Irisa's sake nonetheless. Rather than appear humiliated, Seva took it with good grace and left without making a scene.

That was three years ago, this was now, and here I sat in Seva's hall, waiting anxiously for his answer, trying to appear calm while under his pointed stare. He had not appeared to take open offense at my father's refusal, but I had no reason to believe that he had not taken private offense, and that he would refuse me now because of it. I didn't know how I would answer if he asked why the offer was for me rather than for Irisa, as it was Irisa he had wanted before.

I sat under his thoughtful gaze, thinking on what my next course of action would be should he refuse, how I would stand and thank him, turn and walk gracefully to the door without losing my composure, when he spoke. "When?"

I was caught off guard by the bluntness of his question. He had been staring at me, unspeaking, since I had finished presenting my offer, and I was not prepared for his instant acceptance. I blinked at him, scrambling for an answer. Even several months from now would be too soon, but I needed him, so stammered, "A few weeks, er....I can be ready in a few weeks." Why it would take weeks instead of days was anyone's guess, but he didn't seem bothered by my excuse.

He nodded his chin brusquely. "So be it." And it was done. I was to become the wife of Seva the Smith, a man who looked to be older than my own father. I gave him a wan smile as he rose from his stool and came around the table toward me. I wasn't sure what he intended to do, and I admit that I stiffened a bit as he put his hand on my arm and kissed me lightly on the cheek.

At just that moment I heard a noise and looked across the room to see Issak, Seva's oldest son, standing in the doorway. Issak was not much taller than me, broad shouldered and muscular. He wore his fair hair long but kept it neatly braided. His face was nothing to be remarked upon in general, but his eyes -- they were the color of a storm tossed ocean, grey with flecks of blue and green, piercing and intense -- drew my immediate attention. His expression was hard to read, and I couldn't tell if he had overheard our conversation.

"The lady here has come with an offer of marriage, and we have reached an agreement," said Seva. I swallowed deeply but did my best to hide my dismay. Seva stepped away from me and returned to his wine, took a deep drink before continuing. "Issak, this is Kassia..." Issak nodded as if this was already known to him. "...your newly betrothed."

I blinked. "But I thought..." I didn't know what to say. I looked to Seva, then to Issak, then back to Seva again. It was all rather confusing.

"Do you disapprove of my son?" His face was hard and scowling, eyes flashing as if in accusation that I would even consider backing out of our agreement.

"Not at all, it's just," I floundered, too dumbstruck to say more.

"You would rather have an old man like me? I have enough children," he sniffed, "and enough help." He waved at the young girl in the corner who still waited patiently, wine flagon in hand. That he had "enough help" was in direct disagreement with what he had told my father three years ago, but perhaps his situation had changed, and I was not about to question him on it. "Issak is a fine man, will make you a good husband." Seva studied me up and down in the way a farmer would appraise livestock. I stood there self-consciously for several moments before he spoke again. "Yes, you will give him many children, I think." I couldn't decide whether to blush or be indignant. Issak had remained where he was during the entire exchange, and I wondered what he made of this new development in his life, but he had nothing to say on the subject. Instead he remained still and silent as a lump.

◆ ◆ ◆

Golden flakey crusts shaped in nearly perfect ovals lined one shelf, and delicate pastries filled with fruit and sweet honey lined another. The baker's booth was busy as usual this morning, and not surprisingly so. This particular baker had made a name for himself, not only by baking the best goods in all of Corium, but also by claiming to have come to the city after having worked in the palace of some distant king. If this truly was the case, I wondered what advantages he thought Corium gave him over the palace he previously knew, but it was never good to ask questions when you didn't really want to know the answers.

This bakery was a favorite of mine, though I tried to space out my visits. Developing a pattern, to allow anyone to take notice of what days and times I visited, could only end in disaster for me. Thieving only worked if it was not anticipated. I lingered just around the corner from his bustling trade and quietly watched as a very round woman with her unruly brood of children approached the counter. Along with her money she brought sheer chaos, and it put a smile on my face. As the woman negotiated for her day's supply of bread, her children played a game of chase, dodging and dancing around, heedless of the coming catastrophe. The woman herself was oblivious to her offspring, intent on getting a good price for the daily bread.

As if on cue, one of the little urchins knocked into a shelf of pastries, tipping the boards so that they began to tumble, rolling to the ground in a doughy avalanche. I cast a furtive look over my shoulder and made my move. My arm snaked out, and I snatched a handful of the baked delights in the space of a single intake of breath, stuffing the buns quickly into my bag. As if nothing had happened, I sauntered off with no one the wiser. Irisa and I would start the day with food in our bellies.

After making it a fair enough distance away, I pulled out a pastry and began to munch, sidestepping piles of kitchen scraps and other not so easily identifiable refuse. If one was not careful, it would be easy to step in the contents of night waste buckets that were continuously and recklessly emptied into the streets at various hours of the morning. It was wise to look both to your feet and your head when navigating the city in the early morning.

The city was alive and humming already at this early hour. Goodwives hung dripping laundry over the sills of top story windows, chattering to one another while they worked, carters hauled their goods, merchants called out to passersby in an attempt to drum up trade; these were the songs of Corium, and when an added voice joined the chorus, I nearly didn't hear it.

"Kassia!"

I stuffed the last bit of pastry into my mouth then turned to locate the source of the familiar voice. A pair of bright blue eyes met mine from a height just below my chin. I instinctively reached out and ruffled the boy's hair which was blond and softer than the coat of a mink. He was a petite little thing, smaller than most his age so that he appeared to be lighter than air; but I knew this to be a false impression, for I had first-hand knowledge of his strength and endurance, his courage and willingness to involve himself when injustice asserted itself against those he cared about.

Like me, Cai was an orphan, or at least in all the ways that mattered. He was the son of a temple prostitute, and though his mother still lived and was well fed, clothed in luxury, she had no use for this offspring conceived in her temple service. From all outward appearances, Cai did not seem to suffer for it, for like me, he was a survivor, and we were kindred spirits.

He was also a charmer, and now as I looked at the sweet face upturned towards mine, a smile lighting his eyes, I saw he wanted something. I knew it and he knew I knew it, and yet it worked every time. I reached into the sack I carried and freed a pastry. As I handed it to him, he snatched it before I could reconsider and scampered off.

"Cai," I called before he could get too far. He stopped and turned long enough to hear me tell him not to let the guards see him with it. He winked and continued on. There was a recklessness about him which connected with me, and the reason that he and I bonded more than Irisa and I ever would.

I continued on towards home, but my progress was slowed as I neared the main avenue which led from the wharf district to the palace. Finally I could make no more progress, held up by a crowd of people watching the passage of several milky white stallions led by grooms in brilliant livery. Behind the horses came wagons loaded down with crates, barrels and other supplies.

As I looked around, trying to discover the purpose for this display, I spied Issak in the crowd watching the procession. I had no idea whether or not he had seen me, but I thought it would be rude not to acknowledge him. So I slowly approached him, unusually timid in my movements. It had been several days since I had agreed to the marriage contract with his father, and I had not seen Issak since.

"Good morning, um...." I said uncertainly. I wasn't sure what to call him. He was to be my husband, but we knew nothing about one another.

"Call me Issak... please..." he added quickly, almost shyly. His gaze was fixed on me and I grew uncomfortable, looked quickly around, noting that the procession was gone, that the crowds had scattered and that no one paid us any heed. I nodded but had no idea what more to say to him, knew only that it would be awkward if we remained silent, merely staring at each other like the strangers we most assuredly were. Before I had time to come up with a topic of conversation, Issak spoke again. "Would you be free to visit again soon? If we are to be husband and wife, I would show you my trade, and there is much we should discuss."

"Yes, that would be... yes..." I fumbled. *Much we should discuss indeed.* We exchanged a few other pleasantries then made excuses to part ways. I started out for my house again, realizing that I had never discovered the purpose of the small fortune in horseflesh and wagonloads of goods. Likely a visiting dignitary was here to see the Emperor and brought tribute. It happened often, so I put it from my mind, having plenty else to think about, not the least of which being how to adjust to living life as the wife of a blacksmith. I wondered how much different it would be from being the daughter of a scribe.

Two days later, I made good on my promise to Issak and was surprised to discover him to be an agreeable enough companion. Though I still viewed our upcoming marriage as a necessity only, it had become clear to me that my future was perhaps not as dismal as I had originally anticipated, and that perhaps my father wouldn't have been displeased by my choice. Though plain in his interests and average in intelligence, Issak was a decent and hard working man, and there was no doubt that I could certainly do much worse. Life with him would likely not be exciting, but for someone in my position with few options, I counted myself lucky.

◆ ◆ ◆

I had never considered myself to be anything but plain. My sister Irisa on the other hand, was anything but. In fact, she was beautiful. While my hair was copper-brown, hers was blonde. I had green eyes, she had blue. Her skin was porcelain and free of flaws. She was everything our culture believed to be ideal. But she was not interesting. Not even a little bit. In fact, she was rather dull. She preferred the company of my father's books to the adventure of the market, another testament to her taste toward the introspective, the abstract, and things of no practical use. Despite my opinion regarding her abilities, or lack thereof, by all outward appearances she would naturally be considered a worthy marriage prize, despite her lack of dowry.

For this reason I found myself these last days, swimming in a morass of thoughts tinged with bitterness, that it was I, and not her, who had to marry in order to save our skins, and that not entirely figuratively, from the likes of Swine. But it would have been ignoble of me somehow, to offer my sister in marriage to another man when this plan was mine and not hers, though to my dismay she had readily agreed that it was a wonderful idea when I told her about it after the fact.

So wrapped up was I in these thoughts that I had not become immediately aware of the man standing before me, a man dressed in rich robes of brightly colored silk. Despite the garish colors, my eye was immediately drawn to a large golden sun medallion hanging by a delicate gold chain around his neck. His robes and jewelry taken together made quite an impression, and I wondered for a moment, if perhaps the man was a member of a traveling circus, for his fashion preference was not typical of Corium's aristocratic circles. I would have asked him which one he was, a juggler or an acrobat, but decided that his build did not lend itself to acrobatics, and the wealth of his jewelry did not suggest a travelling troupe. So I kept these thoughts to myself and offered him a greeting, smiling pleasantly in my usual way, waiting for him to speak. For several moments he regarded me keenly but said nothing. Growing a bit unsettled, I decided to watch him back. It only seemed fair.

Heavy brows sheltered dark eyes, watchful and intense, hinting at a life of experience, eyes that saw much and noted all. I could only look at them for so long before I grew uncomfortable and had to look away. His black beard was medium-length and somewhat unkempt, hiding a protruding jaw. His nose was wide and flat and rested between cheekbones which were just as broad. In no way would I have considered him to be an attractive man, yet something about him kept me from fleeing his scrutiny to go about my business in some other place, anywhere else not here.

I was just about ready to ask him what he wanted when he spoke. "You are Kassia Monastero?" I was caught off guard by his voice which was higher in pitch than his heavy features would recommend, crisp, clipped and quite pleasant to listen to.

I nodded, imagining not for a moment that the confirmation

of his query would satisfy him or send him away.

"I have work for you." He looked quickly behind him, and satisfied by what he saw or didn't see, he reached inside the voluminous satchel slung over his shoulder and pulled out a soft leather sack, placing it carefully on the counter between us. Loosening the strings, he emptied out two metal armbands onto the surface of the worn wood in front of him. He said nothing more, simply watched me, waiting for a reaction as though I was supposed to recognize the items in front of me. I could have feigned delight, but quite frankly I was confused. I had never seen anything of their like before. They were made of silver and were decorated with an elaborate filigree pattern on each end, but it meant nothing to me. Curious about them but having no idea about why he brought them to me, I began to inspect them, immediately noticing one thing. The band I had selected had once been broken in several locations. The breaks had been repaired with a poor weld to hold the pieces together, but it was shoddily done.

After finding nothing else of note and uncertain as to what else he expected of me, I set the band back on the counter and looked at him with raised eyebrows, inviting him to speak. Once again he made a quick inspection of the area immediately behind him before saying, "You will clean the bands and reset the joints so that they are smoothed and unseen."

Bemused that he would think me capable of such a task, for my beggarly little shop was clearly no smithy, and anyone with eyes to see would know this, I shook my head in refusal and said, "I'm not a metal smith. I tinker and fix. Clean these, yes. I can do that. But fix these joints?" I shook my head again.

He wasn't swayed, stating again that he wished me to do this for him. I re-explained my inadequacies, trying to hide my irritation all the while, but he would have none of it. When he pushed the bag and its contents towards me with an air of finality, I put my hand up in defeat, sighing. "Leave them. I will have to learn the skill first, so it will take time. And," I added as a cunning afterthought, "it will cost you." Yes, this would do nicely. "And..." I added yet again, "...you will pay me half up front." He began to speak, but I held up my hand to silence him.

"And I can't...won't...guarantee my work." That last part was calculated to be the quietus, the end, the death knell of his plan. He would surely balk at paying the exorbitant price for potentially shoddy work. He was asking a non-metal-smith do his metal-smithing after all. I straightened my spine and crossed my arms, my eyes narrowing in smug satisfaction at my own brilliance. I was about to replace the metal bands into the leather bag to hand back to him, thinking he had finally seen sense, when he dropped a coin purse on the counter between us.

"This is more than enough to cover the entire fee."

I couldn't hide my shock. Through an opening in the top of the bag, I could see the glint of gold. Undoubtedly my mouth dropped open. Never before had I seen so much coin. I looked up at him, wondering if he was an idiot, but saw that he was in earnest.

As I stood there gaping, a sound came from behind me, from the back room where Irisa worked. "Kassia, do you know where... Oh!" Irisa appeared next to me, but startled by the man and the bag of coins before me froze, eyes wide with surprise. The man studied her for only an instant before a smile touched his lips and eyes in equal proportion. My sister had that effect on men.

"Your sister?" He asked in inquiry, clearly confirming what he already seemed to know.

I nodded with a nasty upturn of my lip.

He missed my sneer altogether, looked at my sister only, and nodded appreciatively, then dropped another small bag on the counter. Again, I shook my head, slowly this time, but rather than in defiance it was in utter wonderment. Reckless it may have been to agree, but our problems were now over; I had just taken up a new trade.

2

"KASSIA, COME HERE." My father always calls me Katava except when things are serious, and then he calls me Kassia. I know whatever he has to say to me is important, so I go to him.

My father is standing right in front of me, though my mind will not let me see his face. It is obscured as if blocked out by shadow. But I know it's him. His voice lets me know this by its resonance and timbre, always touched with sadness.

He is kneeling down to meet me at eye level; still I cannot see his face. His fingers... they are long and slender, the nails neatly manicured. Ink stains his palms and fingertips, and as a young child, I think it strange. As he kneels there, he fumbles with a small object tied to a leather thong. He opens his hand and lets dangle a strange medallion made of silver. I reach out tentatively, but I do not touch it. My father smiles, and with this reassurance I give in and allow myself to feel it. Its shape is a maze of lines that make no sense, and its texture is cool to the touch. He lets me admire it for a moment before he reaches around behind my neck and ties the ends of the leather there, so that the metal hangs down the front of my dress.

He places his palm over it, and holding his warm hand there, he says, "Kassia, you must keep this safe. I give it to you to protect. Wear it always, and do not let anyone see it. Trust no one with it; it is very precious. Do you understand?"

He speaks with warmth and kindness, yet there is also urgency in his tone, a thinly veiled desperation, as though the importance of his instructions cannot be fully masked by fatherly love. I nod my understanding. I am only six, but his words are chiseled into my soul.

◆ ◆ ◆

As I lay on my bed, my hand reflexively sought the metal disc hanging from my neck, an action so habitual that most of the time I didn't even realize I was doing it. It was still too early for the city to be awake, and stillness reigned over the world outside my door. I startled a little when a cat howled on the other side of the boards and the thin layer of mud making up the back wall of our ramshackle house. The cat hissed and something toppled over, but the noise ended and everything faded into the silence of a city at rest once again. I had already been awake for several hours, my thoughts turning and spinning, wrestling with all that had transpired in the past several days, as well as all that was ahead, the task for which I had been hired, and the journey I was about to take.

After my mysterious customer left, I began to feel guilty for accepting such a ridiculous sum as payment for an undertaking so far outside my skill set. However, it was the solution to all my troubles, and having this newfound wealth provided a more appealing alternative to marriage -- independence, and the chance to leave Corium, to start a new life where the memories of my parents wouldn't haunt my dreams. My musings had led me to a decision: if I could do it without mortal offense, I would disavow my promise to marry Issak. He was likeable enough, but the need which drove me to his father's door was now satisfied by the surfeit of coin tucked safely away.

I had also spent some time pondering how I would accomplish my chore. Issak was a smith, and I was not. Betrothal to him still had its uses, for a time at least. My guilty conscious gnawed at me, but I consigned the feelings to the deepest, darkest recesses of my mind and visited him daily to learn what I could of his trade, comforting myself with the notion that it was all in the name of survival. I barely knew Issak, so surely he wasn't any more attached to me than I was to him? There were plenty of suitable young women in Corium; certainly his father would be able to find plenty of other candidates? In fact, it was probably a kindness to sever all ties with Issak before he became bound to me forever, considering my deplorable character.

Though Issak was initially surprised at my increased interest in the smithy, he very quickly took to my attentions, happy to tell me as much as I wanted to know. I was a quick-study, and he was a good teacher, so I picked up on the basics of smithing very quickly. The more

I pressed him for information, the more comprehensive was his instruction.

Besides the process, I faced another problem: I needed a place to work, and I needed privacy. A smith used very specific tools for his trade, and I had none of them. Hammers, tongs and swages were easy enough to acquire in the market, and I planned to search them out in the coming days, but the forge itself wasn't so easy to replicate. Using Seva's smithy would have been the easiest solution, but no matter how deceitful I was behaving, I wasn't so far gone that I could bring myself to let Issak do the very work which would enable me to free myself of him, not to mention the myriad of questions over why I needed the work done in the first place. Much to my surprise, Issak provided me with the solution to this problem over the course of our time together. Prior to moving to Corium, his father had lived in a small village near the mountains, working in a mine outside town. The mine had its own blast furnace where the ore was smelted, as well as a small smithy where Seva worked. Now, as far as Issak knew, the small mining camp, including the smithy, was abandoned.

I knew where to go, and I understood the basics of smithing, but so far everything Issak had taught me centered only on iron and steel. I needed to know how to work silver. "What makes a blacksmith different from a..." I pretended to grasp for an example. "...a silversmith, for instance?"

Issak looked up from his work and gave me a half smile. I was sitting on a stool in the corner where I wouldn't be in the way, and had been watching him work, silently appraising the steps he took to fashion large chain links, painstakingly, one at a time. It was only the earliest weeks of summer, yet already the air was stifling. I couldn't imagine what it would be like in the peak of summer, when the forge super-heated the already sweltering air, suffocating the inhabitants as if inside a tomb. Beads of sweat wet his forehead, though he didn't seem to notice, wiping it away without thought.

Rather than answer my question immediately, he pulled me off my stool, took me by the hand and directed me to an anvil, placing himself squarely behind me. Drawing in close and reaching around my waist, he grasped one of my hands and moved it to pick up a small hammer, the other a pair of tongs. With slow, deliberate motions he mimicked the striking of hammer on metal, all the while turning the piece with the tongs. The metal had been set aside long before and was cold and rigid, but the demonstration was a useful answer to my question. Admittedly I didn't catch much of what he said, for it took all of my focus to ignore his body pressing up against me and his breath tickling the loose strands of hair against my cheek.

In all the days spent in his shop, I had learned much about Issak's work, but I had also learned much about Issak the man. He loved his trade, enjoyed following in his father's footsteps to fashion useful things from metal. More than that, I had also discovered him to be an exceedingly honest man. With each passing day, I had to work harder to ignore the shame I felt over how I was using him, and now, as he stood behind me, it would take no more than for me to turn around to face him and my resolve would be gone completely. I determined not to succumb to this weakness, valuing my end goal above all. Summoning up images of my sister living far away from Corium in a small cottage surrounded by grazing sheep, I forced out all thoughts of Issak and the feelings stirring within.

"Issak, Rand has come for his buckles." The spell was broken; it was Seva. Issak pulled back from me a little, and I turned to see Seva standing in the doorway, watching me as he spoke, his eyes alight with pride. Learn the trade, I told myself. Avoid entanglements. And so my lessons went.

Now in the early morning of my departure, I fingered my necklace one last time and tucked it away before rising from my bed and leaving quietly, stopping first to pick up the tools I had concealed in an alley not far from the city gate. The streets were fairly quiet at this hour, and I expected my going to be unnoticed. My thoughts drifted, therefore I was surprised to find, as I rounded the corner, a small figure huddled near the crates hiding my stash.

"Cai, what are you doing?" I was shocked and a little irritated. I thought I had done an excellent job shrouding my actions in secrecy.

He blew off my question, intent on getting his own question

answered. "Kassia, why are you hiding smithing items here?"

"How do you know they're mine?" I asked defiantly, as if diversion would throw him off.

He wasn't unbalanced.

"I saw you hide them. What're you doing?"

The boy was too smart for his own good, so there was no sense in lying to him, but I did anyway. "I have to...um...deliver them...to a customer..." I avoided his eyes.

He looked at me skeptically. "Kassia, I saw you and Issak together. He was teaching you." I bent to scratch at a spot on my ankle to hide my blush, thinking of Issak's method of demonstration. "You are going to do some work. Why doesn't Issak just do it for you?"

The keenness of his perception coupled with the confident way he pressed his point frightened me a bit, and I didn't want to let him know he was guessing near to the truth. So I confessed. At least a version of the truth not likely to get him or me into any trouble.

I cocked my head to the side, eyes narrowed challengingly, "I was hired to do something for a client, and Issak doesn't have time, so it only makes sense for me to do it, which is why he taught me what is necessary. The work needs to be delivered to a place two days' journey from here, so Issak suggested I do it there." I hoped this was enough to keep him from asking any more questions, though I was dubious of success. If anyone could weasel the truth out of me, it was Cai, and I felt guilty enough without admitting anything more to him.

He looked slightly doubtful, but seemed to accept my explanation, so I was relieved. Standing to his full four and a half feet height, he grinned impishly. "I'll come visit you soon, to see how you are doing and to see if you need anything."

He trotted down the alley past me, and I called after him, "Cai, how can you come visit me if you don't know where I'm going?"

He stopped and turned, his face a picture of pure innocence. "Why, Kassia, you are going to the abandoned mine outside Heywood, aren't you? To use the forge?"

My jaw fell open, leaving my mouth an empty void echoing with a half-stifled grunt of stupid surprise. I didn't even want to know how often he had watched me and Issak, listening to our conversations. He returned my startled expression with a mischievous look of his own before racing off. I watched him go, still confused and shaking my head. Finally I realized how ridiculous I looked, standing there gape-mouthed at the end of a dark alley all alone, so composed my features, retrieved my stash and made my way back out onto the street.

I was no more than a few feet out of the alley when a familiar voice called out. "Out of city gates you be heading, for going out and trip to take? You not going for time of long?"

The man really needed to learn to speak more coherently. I paused and turned, trying my best to look less murderous than I felt.

"No, not long," I said, forcing a limp smile.

"Good. Yes? Monies due? Or...you remember alternative?" He took a step closer.

I didn't move, stiffening my spine to meet his stare. "Yes, Swine. How could I possibly forget? But I hate to disappoint you; my sister has your money."

Any disappointment he may have felt wasn't discernible behind his oily smile. While I don't doubt he would have accepted the alternative payment, he wasn't really in the business of flesh-peddling. Cold hard cash was what made his world turn, and since it was available immediately, he didn't balk from it.

"Sviene is happy to be hearing this." He really did look happy, the lumpish sway-bellied pumpion. "If you have need of help for something, you tell, yes?"

I let my face light up, as if something had just come to me. "Yes, Swine, there is something you can do for me, now that you mention it."

"Yes?" He was suddenly wary. His face blanched of color, and I wanted to believe he was about to wet himself from shock. Most people knew better than to take his offer of help at face value. He sensed a trick, but what could he do? I just smiled sweetly at him while he waited uncomfortably for the hammer to drop.

"The next time you shave..." I paused briefly and leaned in, lowering my voice as if about to divulge a confidence. He cocked his head, suddenly curious. "...could you stand a little closer to the razor?"

I turned and walked away before I could gauge his reaction. I knew it would take him some time to work out the meaning of my statement, and I didn't have the time to enjoy watching the process. Drat.

♦ ♦ ♦

Corium is a jewel of a city. A crown jewel in fact, and the most beautiful city in the entire known world. I had nothing with which to compare it however, as I had never traveled much beyond the city walls. Sitting upon a small finger of land on the tip of an even larger peninsula jutting into the sea, Corium guards a major river highway leading into Mercoria, the empire ruled by our good Emperor Ciasan.

Emperor Ciasan is tenth in a long line of rulers of the same name to rule Mercoria, and his name, Ciasan, means "strength" or "power". While the name may have been fitting for the nine who came before him, it was not fitting for this Ciasan, for Emperor Ciasan the Tenth had never been strong, even in his youth, and he had never been accused of being any good, either in temperament or ability. Known to be less than graceful in movement, his citizenry had taken to calling him Emperor Fumblesneeze early on in his reign, though quietly and in whispers, because no Emperor, good or otherwise, has ever taken well to such name-calling.

His son, Ciasan, Jr., waited in the wings to take the throne of his father, though Prince Ciasan was very unlike his father. Exceedingly intelligent and cunning, he displayed all the traits one would expect in an Emperor, and there were many who anticipated his rise to the throne. There were an equal number of people who dreaded it, for they feared his ascension and the retribution which would be wrought on those who had taken advantage of his father's weakness, carving out for themselves a healthy portion of power and influence by collusion and deceit.

The Emperors of Mercoria have ruled from time immemorial out of the Grand Palace of Coria, a glittering marble edifice that clings determinedly atop a massive rock overlooking the busy harbor off the Bay of Bos. Walls made of bleached white stone branch out from the palace and encompass the entirety of the city, blinding with brilliance all who stare at them for too long. Boasting the largest market and largest seaport in the known world, Corium is the busiest hub of commerce and trade in all the southern seas. People from all over Mercoria and beyond dwell within its walls, though the city has long since overrun the ancient precincts, spilling its citizenry into the peaceful farmland beyond.

To the north and east of the vast city is a range of mountains. Though the resources have long since been stripped away, the mountains nevertheless remain as a physical barrier, protecting Corium on the north side, in perfect partnership with the sea -- a barrier on the west and south. Most people no longer have use for these mountains, but it was towards these geographical giants that I was headed, for dotted along the soaring slopes were abandoned or failing mining towns beyond counting; towns like Heywood, where Seva used to earn a living.

It would take me many days to travel to Heywood on foot, so I decided to buy a horse. I didn't particularly look forward the prospect, as I knew next to nothing of horses and fully expected to be taken advantage of, but I saw no way around it. Any well-seasoned traveler knows that horse traders can be found outside any major city gate. I was not a seasoned traveler, so I had to be told this by an unassuming older gentleman who had stopped by the side of the road to pull a rock from his boot. He smiled a gap-toothed smile at me, patted me on the head, called me a dear, and pointed me in the right direction.

Despite my lack of knowledge, I determined to play the part of competent horse aficionado as best I could. Using a healthy dose of bravado often proves quite useful if you expect anyone to think you know what you are doing, even if you don't; however, in order to be most effective, it is helpful to have at least a little knowledge concerning the object of your bravado. Unfortunately, when it came to horses, I had not even a thimbleful. Having no other choice and nothing to lose, I entered the stable.

Trade was brisk, as it was early in the day and there were many people coming and going from the city. Some were there to purchase, but most were only leasing, for owning a horse outright was an expensive prospect and not always the most beneficial for lifelong city dwellers with no place to lodge such a large beast. I could have leased a horse, but if my plan worked out, Irisa and I would be moving away from the city soon enough and wouldn't need to worry about future stabling.

Putting on my best "I'm here to buy a horse, and I know exactly what I am doing" face, I examined the first offering then worked my way down the aisle, sizing up the candidates. My examination included legs, teeth, ears, and an occasional nostril, and all the while I bobbed my head in concentrated analysis, taking mental notes of my findings. Finally making it to the end of the first row, I looked back at all the animals I had just examined, confident that I had absolutely no idea what I was doing.

I turned to examine another row and nearly collided with an anvil of a man blocking my path. His arms were crossed, and he looked down at me through narrowed eyes from a height approximately equal to the tallest peak of the distant mountains. I tried my best not to look flustered, though in truth I felt like I had just been caught out doing something criminal. Before my hands could give away my unease by fidgeting, I clasped them behind my back, hoping he hadn't noticed.

"You need help?" The suggested politeness of his question was in stark contrast to the scowl on his face, and his eyes held nothing but suspicion in their depths.

I took a deep breath and explained to him with as much confidence as I could that I wanted to purchase a horse and had just been examining what was on offer. As he listened, his face never once changed, registering neither surprise nor doubt. When I finished speaking, he appeared to weigh all I had said while taking in my appearance -- from my plain attire to the wisps of hair escaping the braids on my head. He also noticed, I saw, the coin pouch at my belt, weighed down with more than a few coins, though this was done quickly, his gaze flicking from pouch then back to my face without missing a beat.

"Those are boarders." He gestured over his shoulder at the

mounts I had just been viewing. "Follow me." My cheeks flushed from awareness of my own stupidity, but the man had already begun to walk away. Grabbing my two small packs, I quickly followed him. He led me to a fenced paddock out back, stopping before a line of horses loosely tethered before a pile of hay. My heart slowed to an aching stop. It didn't take a large endowment in the area of equine education to know that I couldn't afford one of these magnificent beasts, each of which was certainly more splendid than my needs warranted. I didn't hide my disappointment in the least, and the man noticed without a doubt.

"Not those..." he said, noting where my gaze had fallen. "These..." He pointed off to my right where a much more reasonable selection stood by, using their tails to swat at the hungry flies feasting off their succulent flesh. He smiled with smug satisfaction, proud of his little deception. Funny man.

After walking up and down the line of more reasonable horses, he hand-selected one, never once asking why I needed one or how I planned to use it. It was clear by his demeanor that he thought me nothing more than another sucker to pluck, that the coin in my purse was all he was after. Even with my less-than-thimbleful of knowledge of horses, I knew a nag when I saw one. I had entered this barn not caring if I bought a nag or an Imperial war horse, but I lied. I had more pride than that.

Before even having a chance to respond to his ridiculous asking price, I heard a loud guffaw and turned to see a very tall, dark man dressed in exquisitely expensive clothing leaning against the fence behind the yard of horses. He had been watching our entire exchange with great interest. Tossing the reins of his own spirited mount to an attending groom, he effortlessly leapt the fence and joined us. Funny Man scowled, obviously suspecting that his ruse has just been found out.

Exquisite Man cast an appraising eye on me, his gaze quickly taking in my drab attire before turning his attention to the merchant. Exquisite Man lifted his chin ever so slightly, and with a look of sheer distain brushed past Funny Man to run a hand over the rumps of a number of horses on the tether before settling on one. He lifted its back leg in examination before turning once again to Funny Man. "She'll take this one."

Funny Man was not in the mood to be bullied about by my would-be-rescuer, so rather than be put in his place, he puffed out his chest and countered. Back and forth they went, on and on. I eventually lost interest and sat down on a crate near the wall behind me. My thoughts wandered wildly enough that I lost track of what transpired, and before I realized what had happened, I was startled by the approach of Funny Man leading a horse in full tack. Instantly confused and wary, I craned my neck around the pair in search of my hero, but he was nowhere to be found. Funny Man shoved the reins into my hand, saying nothing, then spun around in disgust and walked away. I looked at the reins then back at the horse. The horse didn't seem inclined to explain what had happened, so I shouted out a feeble, "What do I owe?"

He never did answer me, merely waved his hand in my general direction as if in dismissal. I stood there staring off after him for a long moment before realizing my good fortune. Exquisite Man. I had no idea what he had done, or more importantly why he had done it, but I was richer by one horse because of it.

Back out on the street a large crowd had gathered and it was difficult to pick my way through the throng. Frustrated at my lack of progress, I tossed a question to a passerby to ask what it all meant. The woman appeared to be mesmerized by the goings on and didn't even look at me when she answered. "It's the prince. He just arrived."

"The prince?" I had to shout a little louder because she was already walking away from me.

I was just barely able make out her words as she replied, "Prince Casmir..."

The name meant nothing to me, but as I pondered her words, the crowd parted just enough for me to see a man sitting astride a milky-white stallion. He was expensively dressed. Exquisite Man. A prince.

◆◆◆

Dreams are cozy illusions when they want to be. Sometimes they can terrify us with diabolical realism, leaving us shaking and sweating with fear; sometimes they pierce us with the wistful longing that comes from seeing the face of a long-lost loved one. Sometimes dreams are plain and simple, comforting us with the familiar and ordinary, the daily and routine. Other times they are downright comical, with abstract and distorted images, fragments of true things paired with the unimaginable, things that exist one moment and morph into something else the next. I woke from such a dream my first morning on the road. It was raining, but the rain was viscous and smelly. No matter what I did, I couldn't escape it. Nearly suffocating from my dream, I struggled to escape the fog of sleep, immediately becoming aware of something warm and rough moistening my cheek. My eyes snapped open, and I looked up to see the very long tongue of a horse reaching towards my face, preparing to make another wet swipe. Reacting as anyone else would, I rolled quickly to my side and sat up, swiping at the spittle on my face with a dry sleeve. I scowled at the horse, though she merely blinked her doltish brown eyes in return.

Telltale shades of brilliant pink painted the sky to the east, illuminating wisps of clouds just above the mountains, announcing a new day. According to what I had pieced together from multiple sources, I expected to reach Heywood by late afternoon, if everything went smoothly. I rubbed my eyes and tried to stand, immediately regretting my choice. I was not a horsewoman, had never even been on a horse before in my life until yesterday, and today my body reminded me of that fact. The muscles of my legs screamed at me for their abuse, the delicate skin of my inner thighs joining in with their own accusations, rubbed raw by an entire day of constant friction from the jostling of the saddle. I didn't even want to look but imagined I'd find raw, angry-red patches where once the skin was a healthy pink. I winced and forced my attention to the fabric of my newly purchased dress, a dress that more accurately matched my new status of fine-horse-owner. I packed away the few items I had used for sleep, and after several miserably failed attempts and even more shouted curses at the sky, I finally managed to mount my horse and set off, ignoring the pain in my legs and hoping I wouldn't be permanently infirmed.

My journey didn't progress as problem-free as I'd hoped.

It was midday, and I was already tired and sore from the last day and a half of riding. Just staying atop my horse was taking a large portion of my already waning concentration, so that when a hungry fly began to take interest in me, pestering me mile after long mile, I inevitably became distracted and irritable. Several times he landed on my ankle, and every time I lashed out with my foot, shaking it off. As the fly continued to land, bite and annoy, it happened. I was attempting to pass by a particularly portly merchant and his overly large brood when the fly decided to strike again; however, this time, rather than paying attention to where I aimed my lashing leg, I carelessly flailed. My toe connected with the side of a hay cart on the other side, and the heel of my shoe snagged in the cart's railing.

Because we were moving more swiftly than the lumbering cart, and because my foot was stuck, I was pulled from the saddle slowly, off the back of my horse's haunches. Fortunately, the fall forced the exact movement necessary to free my foot, and as I fell, I managed to land safely on my rump, albeit with a rather painful bounce. It could have been a disastrous fall. My head could have been kicked, my leg could have twisted oddly and broken... But for some reason nothing was injured other than my pride, though that injury was enough.

I won't pretend that no one noticed, or that the few who did, didn't laugh, because everyone did notice and everyone did laugh; however, there was one kindly soul who took it upon himself to restrain my horse and then offered me a hand up. Since it was obvious that I had come to no serious harm, he let me be, and I limped over to the side of the road to let everyone pass, and so that I could take a moment to gather my wits, catch my breath then figure out a way to remount. If it was possible, my legs pained me even more than they had when I first woke up that morning, stiff and raw.

By the time I reached Heywood, the sun had just descended below the peaks of the mountain ridge to the west. It was too late to go in search of the abandoned mine camp beyond town, so I decided to find an inn.

The main street was flanked on either side by a handful of sturdy wooden buildings as well as one or two stone-built ones, all of which were serviced by a centrally-located circular stone well. A few painted wooden signs indicated shops, though it was difficult to make them out in the dying light of dusk.

I knew Heywood was in decline, but I was still surprised by the vacant feel of the town. It wasn't yet so late that everyone should be homebound, but I shared the street with no one, the sound of my horse's footfall the only noise to compete with a barking dog and the wail of an infant from somewhere behind closed doors. The air in this village at the foot of the mountains was crisp, and except for the scent of wood-smoke, it was delightfully clean. I felt rather than saw pairs of suspicious eyes follow my progress down the street, so I pulled my cloak more tightly about my shoulders. Travelers were likely not uncommon here, for there were still a few who sought their fortune in the mines that were supposedly empty. Despite this, I wondered how unusual it was for these villagers to see a young woman astride a reasonably good horse enter their town alone.

When I reached the middle of the small village, I spied a squat, stone-built inn with low-hanging eaves of thatch. A trail of smoke billowed from an opening on the roof, and raucous laughter interspersed with bellicose conversation emanated through the door. It occurred to me that I should have changed out of my fine dress into my older, plain one, thinking for the first time that I may not be entirely safe here, but it was too late to do anything about that now.

I ignored the warning voice in my head and dismounted, preparing to enter the inn and negotiate for a bed for myself and stabling for my horse. Before I could do so however, I sensed the presence of a person standing just behind my shoulder, so turned. He was a mountainous human, and he was grinning widely. I took a step back, momentarily caught off guard and unable to go further because my horse was behind me. The urge to shift to the side to put a little more space between the Mountain Man and me was overwhelming, but I was thwarted when my horse intentionally turned her head, blocking my way. That she did it on purpose was clear to me when she bared her teeth in a mischievous smile.

Returning my focus back to the Mountain Man, I studied him

more closely, to take his full measure. His grin was still firmly in place, and he towered over me. He was nearly as wide around as he was high, with no neck to speak of, though his girth seemed to be attributable to muscle rather than soft flesh. With his hands on his hips, he looked like a mighty sailing vessel about to take to the wind. His hair was brown and tousled, with bits of straw poking out here and there, but his shirt and trousers were both clean, despite being too small. He was an odd sort of fellow, yet his eyes were clear and bright without even a hint of malice in their depths, putting me somewhat at ease.

"You need bed for night?"

"Um..." I hesitated, "...yes?" For some reason I felt reluctant to admit this, though my purpose in dismounting outside an inn had to have been obvious.

I startled when the Mountain Man started laughing. Not just any kind of laugh, but the kind that boils up from deep within, starting first as a low rumble then finally bursting forth and overflowing like the tide rolling in, crashing onto the rocks, leaving flotsam and jetsam or... *sea foam*, I thought, as I wiped away a dribble of spittle that had landed on the bridge of my nose. Instinct told me to move away, though I knew what would happen to me again if I did. Of all the horses in the world, I was stuck with one with a sense of humor.

Finally, Mountain Man's laughter began to roll to a stop, and I glanced quickly around me to see if anyone else had seen this spectacle or was concerned in any way for my welfare, but saw no one. I laughed a nervous laugh then switched my gaze back to Mountain Man, giving him what I hoped was a pleasant smile as if to express my complete and utter comfort standing so near a huge man laughing a cavernous laugh for no apparent reason.

"You come," he said, still chuckling at his own private joke, and began to walk away, waving his hand in a gesture that suggested I follow him. "I have place for you. You no stay here. They steal horse."

I had no argument for that, so I followed him, figuring that my horse would give me a shove in that direction anyway had I refused. I thought I heard a horse-like snickering from behind me, but I didn't dare turn around. The last thing I needed was to see a look of satisfaction in those equine eyes.

◆ ◆ ◆

"Kassia..."

Irisa hisses loudly in my ear and I startle awake, rolling over to see her urgent face a mere finger breadth from my own. The room is in utter darkness, and I rub my sleep-heavy eyes hoping to clear my foggy vision. She woke me from an excellent dream involving a dapple-grey pony running through a field of blooming Rose of Sharon shrubs, my mother's favorite flower.

"You need to get up! Hurry!"

I am still foggy with sleep, and even my sister's urgent pleas, wrought through with hysteria, don't make me want to get out of my bed. It took me a long time to fall asleep last night, and I don't think that what Irisa wants me to do is worth the effort.

A swift kick lands on my shin, and I sit bolt upright, howling in pain. I shoot her a look of liquid fire, but she is unmoved. She hisses, "Something is wrong with Mama. You must hurry. Run and fetch Jeah. She will know what to do. HURRY!"

She has my attention. No longer fighting sleep, I quickly dress and slip out the door into the thickness of night, picking my way down the alley and around the corner to the house of Jeah, the matron of a cloth shop, and a dear family friend. The incongruity of how she also happened to be an expert on the use of medicinal herbs never mattered to me; most important was that it was to Jeah that my mother always turned when Irisa or I ever had need of a tincture of some sort to soothe a fever or heal a wound.

I pound on Jeah's door and am rewarded within minutes by the appearance of Jeah's husband peeking through a crack in the door. I explain my need, and he nods, opens the door more fully to admit me. He disappears, and soon Jeah is there. I explain the situation to her, and she unquestioningly accompanies me back to our hovel. Irisa lights a single oil lamp, and it casts a spectral light over the scene of my mother, delirious with fever, thrashing about on her pallet and wailing in pure agony.

Jeah is a peaceful woman, exuding tranquility with every

breath, often able to ease aches and pains with little more than a soothing word or a gentle touch. But right now Jeah mirrors terror, and despite her best effort to hide her fear, she isn't quick enough that I don't notice it. Uncharacteristically oblivious of the fears of two frightened girls before her, she pulls a vial from the small pouch at her waist. Uncorking it, she gently lifts my mother's head and pours the contents of the vial directly down her throat. Within moments, my mother's thrashing ceases, and she falls limply back into Jeah's strong arms.

My face is ashen and my hands cold and sweaty, but I say not a word, reach out for my sister's hand. She takes it immediately and squeezes it tightly in her own grip. Jeah motions to her husband who had slipped into the room unnoticed behind us. He effortlessly picks up my mother and carries her from the room, through the door, and into the night.

Jeah sits back on her heels and takes a deep, calming breath. Her eyes are closed, and she wipes the sweat from her face with her sleeve. She turns towards Irisa and me and offers a weak smile, fabricating a reassurance that she is not feeling herself. With a measured consideration she asks, "Where is your father?"

Irisa speaks up, her voice soft and trembling, nearly breaking from the strain, "He's traveling."

I add, "We don't really know where he is. He's been gone for several days." I look down at my hand clasped tightly enough in my sister's so that nearly all the blood has drained, making my flesh appear pale and waxy. I hear my heart beating loudly in my ears.

Jeah considers our words before continuing, "Go back to sleep, dear ones." She reaches out and caresses my cheek. "I will see to your mother and will send someone to check in on you tomorrow."

With that, she stands and leaves us to our confusion and distress. Without a single word, Irisa blows out the oil lamp and returns to bed. I remain standing, staring into the dark night, shivering despite the mild night air.

◆ ◆ ◆

"What is your horse's name, dear?"

The words were sweet and full of compassion, but they barely penetrated my brain. I was still shaking from my dream, a dream that came all too often, shaking me to the core each time I had it, for every time it came, it gripped me with an intensity that left me bereft and desultory for many hours after waking. Piecing together my present reality was nearly impossible, and it made my head hurt. Before the question was asked, I had only begun to remember how it was that I was now sitting at a table being questioned by this quiet and unassuming woman.

Mountain Man, whose name I later learned was Emik, led me away from the horse-thieving inn, to this house. He had thrown open the door then announced to the room at large that he had returned, and that he had brought company. I knew better than to follow the hulk of a man into an enclosed place, but I did so anyway.

The house was clean and cheery, with a delightful fire dancing in a hearth set into the back wall. The room itself was lofty, its ceiling reaching to twice the standard height of an ordinary house. Just above and to the right of where we had entered was a long, low loft with a ladder tucked away into the dark corner of the room.

Once my eyes had adjusted to the dim light, I spotted a woman standing over a cooking pot hung above the fire. She raised herself from a stooped position and made her way over to me, introducing herself as Adyna, Emik's mother. She invited me to sit down, and upon giving me something to drink, Emik explained what I needed. Adyna agreed most readily, and we agreed on a price. After being satisfied by a simple meal of heavy black bread softened with a thick pottage, I was sent off to bed in the low loft where, lulled by a soft bed and a full belly, I promptly fell asleep.

Now in the dim light of the early morning, the question came again: "Your horse, does it have a name?" She asked more quietly this time, as if she sensed my mood. Her gentle prodding brought me back to the present, to my breakfast and the matronly woman who had spoken. I looked up, blinking in a state of mild confusion, doing my best to focus on the question put to me.

"Oh..." I paused, having no answer for her. "Rose of Sharon.

Er, Rose... or Sharon..." I waffled, still a bit dazed.

"Your horse is named Rose, dear? Or Sharon?" The woman looked perplexed, and rightly so, though she was polite enough to take my answer with good humor as seemed to be her nature. It was in fact, no fit name for a horse, but I had said the first thing to come into my head, still assaulted by the images of those flowering shrubs and the running pony from my dream fighting for dominance over the remembrance of my mother's agonized screams still ringing in my ears. My head hadn't stopped throbbing, so I buried my face in my hands, trying and failing to shut out the bright light of morning.

Adyna must have sensed my distress, though she had no way of knowing its source. Likely she equated my distress with the reason I had so strangely appeared in her town, possibly assuming I was running from something, a guess not far off the mark. I was running from something. Wasn't everyone? Mercifully she left me in peace, and by the time I had finished my meal, my mood had lifted and I felt like it was time for me to offer my gratitude for her hospitality and depart.

When I asked after Emik, Adyna assured me he would be back soon, if only I would wait a few more moments. I need not have worried because as if on cue, Emik rounded the corner just then, a small satchel slung over his shoulder. From it he pulled out two small partridges which he handed to his mother; the satchel he handed to me. "For you. Now you have food for rest of day." His face was open and cheery, as if nothing imaginable could stomp on his joy.

Adyna offered me a quick hug before I could protest the gift, saying "You look like you are in need of a kindness." A lump stuck in my throat. To say I was astonished wouldn't go far enough. The fact that a seemingly well-to-do young woman, someone apparently their social better, was traveling alone would be enough to make even the most reticent person curious, yet never once had Adyna or Emik asked me why I was in Heywood or where I was going. Instead they had offered me food and a night's shelter for a pittance, then took it a step further, beyond necessity. Adyna had sensed a need in me, a need for kindness, though she had no idea why I might need it. She didn't know I was a thief, that I stole my bread to survive. I was also a soon-to-be-oath-breaker, having already used Issak to get what I needed before leaving him in the lurch, breaking my vow to him. Adyna and Emik had no idea what manner of character I was, yet they showed me love regardless, openly and without restraint. By their kindness they had heaped burning coals on my head, almost beyond what I could bear.

With constricted lungs I offered my thanks to the pair, then with less trouble than the day before, mounted my horse. Well wishes were piled atop an insistence that I return to them if ever I found myself back in Heywood, and I departed. Turning my attention away from where I had been, I fixed my mind on my goal: finding the mining camp. The boom days were long over, the forge long out of use. It would be abandoned, as Issak had said, and I didn't expect to find anyone there. Why would I?

◆ ◆ ◆

My dream was long-forgotten, replaced by a hopefulness brought on by fresh air and sunshine, and the miles passed with pleasure. That Rose was a quality steed was proven out by the way she effortlessly made the last leg of the journey, with a spirited step and a proud arc in her neck. She was on an adventure, and she demonstrated it with ears that faced forward, upright and keenly aware of everything in her path. Never mind that she was also sly and mischievous, traits I didn't expect to find in an animal.

We were nearly to the mining camp, and I needed an accurate read of my location, so I dismounted and climbed on foot up a short but steep rise for a better view. Once satisfied that the next turn was the correct one, I turned to descend, only to discover a surprise: the road was exactly as I had left it, minus one horse. After a short search, I found Rose not far off, merrily munching the sparse grass carpeting the clearing. I grabbed her reins with a huff but she merely blinked her large, brown, horsey eyes unconcernedly, oblivious of the glare I fixed on her.

Not long thereafter, we reached our destination. Not wanting a repeat of what had just happened, I tethered Rose securely under the shade of an ancient oak then surveyed the camp. The smithy was central to the camp, a sturdy stone building with a large chimney on one side, surrounded in efficient order by lodgings, kitchens and storage, all enclosed by a mossy, rotting wood palisade. The place looked and smelled derelict, and it was clear that no one had lived here for some time. Assuming the forge was in even marginally good condition, I could finish my work and be back home before Irisa managed to give away everything we owned.

At one end of the settlement was a small stable. Its thatched roof had seen better days, and I would have to investigate its sturdiness before committing to stabling Rose there, but since the structure was still standing after all these years, it would probably be sound enough for a few days more. I opened the door to the small hut used as lodging, and disturbed a mouse which scurried for shelter. Particles of dust danced in the air, lit by the ray of sunlight which streamed through the doorway behind me. The air was stale and deeply earthy, mixed through with the scent of the rotting straw used as fill for the mattresses which were now more or less decomposed mushroom food. I stashed my few domestic possessions here and poked my nose into the remaining buildings before venturing into the smithy itself, the place I would undoubtedly spend the most time.

I cracked open the door, and peered inside. Rather than the clouds of dust and signs of disuse I expected to find, this room was clean, orderly and not at all abandoned, a conviction further solidified by the scent of fresh smoke that permeated the air, maybe only a day old. My heart thudded and my mind reeled with wild scenarios.

And then it happened.

A sudden cacophony of cracking and crashing caused me to nearly jump out of my skin, and I turned just in time to see the timbers of the stable collapse into a heap before becoming engulfed in a large dust cloud, throwing me into an immediate fit of coughing. I covered my face with my sleeve and waited for the dust to settle. When it did, a pile of rubble stood where the stable once was. I laughed a little to myself, thinking that I should be more careful before moving into the worker's hut for the night. Turning away from the newly formed rubble pile, I went back into the smithy to unhinge a shutter, allowing in some daylight, when something hard and unyielding made direct contact with the back of my skull. It was the last thing I remembered.

3

"IRISA, TAKE THESE things to Jeah and don't tarry." My father hands my sister a bundle of papers bound with a securely tied cord and scoots her out the door. Once she is gone, my father turns to me and kneels down to meet my eyes.

"Katava, do you understand why we must leave this place?" I do not, but I know my father craves my assurance, so I merely nod my assent. "There's a good girl. Quickly now, retrieve your things. As soon as Irisa returns it will be time."

I do not know why we are moving, not truly, but I figure it has something to do with the death of my mother, even though my father has never admitted as much. I am only a child and have no way to fully comprehend my father's desperation to move, that it is essential for him to escape the sights and sounds familiarly connected with my mother. My grief is too selfish for that. I only understand that in leaving these familiar things, I will be leaving behind the very essence of my mother: the places she cooked, told her stories, braided my hair, the places we laughed and cried and lived our daily lives. I will never again be able to stand in the corner of the room and look at the spot on the wall where together we carved our initials in the long hours of my sickness, when a common childhood illness nearly took my life. I could take my pitiful possessions to any new home, and I could take the phantoms of my memories, but I could not take the floorboards on which she walked or the window sill where she set her potted plants. My childish mind thinks simple thoughts, and I need the comfort of tangible reminders. But all of it will be taken from me, and I am powerless to stop it, powerless to stop anything that happens to me.

My father knows none of these fears, and I do my best to hide them from him as I have always done. From my father's perspective, I am a child putting on a brave face. He smiles down at me with such pride that I cannot bear to let him see my grief. I hide behind a mask and will be strong because it is expected of me; because it was my

mother who soothed my tears and calmed my fears. No matter what
happens to me in the future, that way is now lost to me.

◆ ◆ ◆

Perhaps it was morning when I awoke, but it was pitch-dark
in the room I found myself, so there was no way of knowing. Had I
been able to free my hands from the bonds which tied them to a post at
my back, I wouldn't have been able even to count my fingers. I would
however, have been able to scratch the itch burning into my skin just
above my shoulder blades. As it was, all I could do was shift
uncomfortably, trying to distract myself away from it. I wondered if it
was possible to go mad from an unscratched itch. At this point, I
thought it entirely possible.

Issak had assumed incorrectly that the mining camp was no
longer in use, and I never thought to question the theory. Obviously I
was mistaken and mentally berated myself for my carelessness. How
big a mistake it was would only become evident once I discovered the
identity of my captors and the reason I was being held here. I hoped I
was still at the camp, but whoever thumped me could very easily have
loaded me onto a cart or a boat and taken me miles and miles away.
Modern footpads were so unpredictable.

Next my thoughts turned to Irisa, and I wondered how she
was getting on, alone in Corium. How would she fare without me if I
ended up dead? Would she fritter away all our money on the sad-eyed
beggar children dotting every corner of the city or would she be wise
and resist her compassionate urges? Would Swine get paid regularly,
and on time? I was assailed by images of my sister working in a brothel,
but slammed shut the door to my imagination before it became too
overwhelming. There was nothing I could do for her from here. I was
powerless to protect her.

I was wrested out of my depressing reverie when the door
flew open, flooding light into the room. The sudden assault on my dark-
adjusted eyes made me flinch, and I banged my head on the post behind
me. When the waves of pain subsided, I looked up with a scowl,
prepared to see the face of my captor. What I found was a surprise.
Rather than an evil degenerate, a miscreant of the worst degree, I found

a regular-looking young man leaning casually against the doorframe, dressed in a clean shirt, trousers and solid boots. His arms were folded across his chest with confidence as he eyed me silently for several moments, studying me with both curiosity and amusement. He was mostly lean and wiry, though his arms and shoulders were overly muscular, as if he was used to wielding a pick or the hammer of a smith. Longer than fashionable dark hair fell nearly to his shoulders, while several rebellious locks hung over his forehead, partially covering one eye. I supposed that he thought this gave him a mysterious look.

I glared at him and spat with venom, "How dare you?" thinking he might stagger backwards from the force. I was mistaken.

His eyes danced, a smile quickening his lips. "How dare I what?" he asked, clearly amused.

His eyes weren't glowing red, so I knew he couldn't be a malignant spirit sent to taunt me. "How dare you tie me up like this! I demand to be released this instant, or else..."

He eyed me up and down, clearly noting my compromised position. "Or else what?" he asked slowly, quietly, not rising to my bait.

He had me there. I really wasn't in any position to bargain. We both knew it, and it infuriated me even more.

"Or else... I will..." I began uncertainly. He raised his eyebrows in anticipation of my scathing threat, narrowing his eyes as if he had me, but I didn't finish. Taking a different tack, I said, "You sure are smug, aren't you?"

He took this change of direction in stride with a continued smile, nodding his encouragement that I continue. When it was clear that I had nothing more to say, he released a broad grin then turned to someone behind him and nodded. Brushing past Smug Boy, a beast of a man entered. He was most certainly a relative of Smug Boy, for his features were nearly identical, only older; probably his father. Footpaddery clearly ran in the family.

Beast Man crouched down next to me, his eyes soft and kind, his mannerisms graceful and lithe despite his bulk, for he too had the muscular arms and broad chest of a smith, with the scars lacing his skin adding to my conviction. In his hand he carried the small leather bag containing my silver arm bands. He opened it and pulled out one of the bands, balancing it gently on the flat of his palm. "Where did you get this?"

He had asked earnestly, and I didn't see any harm in answering him honestly, not being in a position to defy him anyway. "In Corium," I said simply. Beast Man remained still, his silence compelling me to elaborate. "A man visited my shop not long ago and paid me to mend the seams." The admission sounded ridiculous coming from my mouth, and I shifted my gaze to the dirt at his feet. These men were clearly smiths, and it seemed laughable to me now that I would make an attempt at their trade.

"What did this man look like?"

I don't know why he needed to know, for the answer didn't concern him in the slightest, but again I was uncharacteristically compelled to honesty. "He wore brightly colored silk." I paused, trying to recall his face. "He had dark, watchful eyes. Intense, like he was always on the alert. He had a very short unkempt beard over a protruding jaw. Broad cheek bones, heavy brows." Nothing about my description moved my captors outright, though Beast Man did blink a few times. "He kept looking over his shoulders, like he was ashamed to be found there, or to see if he was being followed." As an afterthought I added, "Oh, and he wore a large golden sun necklace."

At the mention of the sun medallion, Beast Man's eyes widened, and he rocked back on his heels slightly. Once sufficiently recovered from his surprise, he narrowed his eyes again and scrutinized me, then stood, turned on his heel and gestured with his head for Smug Boy to follow him out. Without so much as a glance in my direction, Smug Boy did as instructed, pulling the door closed behind him. I was left alone again in the darkness, left alone to ponder whether or not my horse and the arm bands were lost to me, yet thankful that I had gotten my payment from my mysterious customer up front. All that was left to me now was to plan how on earth to get myself out of it all.

◆ ◆ ◆

It seemed like hours before Smug Boy and Beast Man returned. I hadn't been fed even so much as a crumb during the entirety of my captivity, nor had I been given water to wet my parched throat. My head hurt, and I was feeling edgy, like a caged animal longing for freedom, waiting in a state of agitation for an unprotected piece of flesh to present itself as a target. I flexed my imaginary claws in anticipation.

My mind had sorted through many ideas related to escape, the wildest of which involved gnawing off an appendage, though I had quickly dismissed the notion as impractical and entirely too painful. Smug Boy finally did return, yet this time there was a complete lack of smugness in his carriage. He simply looked tired, and I decided that "Smug Boy" wasn't an appropriate name for him any longer. He pulled a knife from his waistband and cut my bonds. I kept my mouth shut and sat unmoving, waiting to see what he would say, but when he was finished, he just stood and left. I rubbed the back of my head and stood, following after a short hesitation.

I emerged into the fading light of dusk, noting immediately that I was still at the mining camp. The sun must have only just disappeared behind the mountain peak high above, as its bright halo was still readily visible. It would be full dark soon enough. Had I been here a full day? Two? It was hard to know.

A ring of people waited just outside the door, with Beast Man at its center. He gestured at Smug Boy with his thumb and without preamble, said simply, "This is Jack. I'm Rem, and this," he said as he waved his arm generally at the others who stood around him, "is everybody else." That was it. Nothing else. No explanation, no apology.

A myriad of thoughts ran through my mind. I was angry and defiant, indignant over my treatment and upset about the lack of explanation. I wanted answers. Yet none of these thoughts turned into actual words. "When do we eat?" was all I said. It's not what he was expecting. "When do we eat?" I asked again, my irritation more evident this time. "You had me locked up in that... that place..." I waved blindly behind me, gathering momentum, "...for who knows how long. No food. No water. I'm half starved! Does the Emperor know that you treat your prisoners this way? I'm sure his lawyers would have something to say." I placed my hands on my hips with resentment. Rem and Jack only stared. No one else spoke. A fly buzzed irritatingly near my face, and I blew it away with a puff of hot breath.

"You were only in there for about one turn of the clock," Jack said carefully, as if speaking to one slow of wit. He flashed a smile, dimples pitting his cheeks.

Only an hour? I felt like a muttonhead, but still chose to counter his good humor with a scowl. If I was honest, I'd admit that it was in fact, all rather amusing, but I was too proud to let on. "That's no excuse. I have rights," I said weakly. My argument was losing steam, and all knew it.

They ignored my last remark and chose to move on. I was rather glad for it, truth be told. "What's your name?" Jack asked.

"Kassia."

"Kassia, would you like to join us for our meal?"

It seemed we were friends now. "Why yes, thank you for asking," I said sweetly.

"We'll have some lovely roast partridge tonight." Emik's partridges. The corner of his mouth twitched.

Jack led me from the mining camp, up a small rise and into a dense forest, thick with undergrowth. We followed a narrow game trail until it opened into a small clearing where several wattle and daub huts covered with leafing branches squatted on the far side. If one was not looking for them specifically, it would have been easy to overlook their existence, so naturally did they blend into the foliage of the forest edge.

It was to one of these huts that Jack led me, to sit near a fire over which two small, succulently golden birds roasted on a spit. They were sizzling and dripping their juices onto the flames below, tended by a young woman who took my measure with a look I couldn't identify then looked away. I ignored her, looking round the small camp instead. Before long I noticed one of my bags leaning against the nearest hut, the top open, its few contents partially spilling out the top.

Jack noticed the direction of my gaze then smiled and shrugged, loosening a shock of hair to fall into his eyes as he did so before unconsciously brushing it away. I pursed my lips and turned back to the fire, taking a seat, preparing to make an acrimonious remark about his manners in general as well as his use of a certain blunt object on the back of my skull, when he forestalled me.

"Who are you?" His lightness was gone; he was all business.

I eyed my bag again and felt my anger returning. "You know, I should be asking you who you are," I said rancorously. "I came here peacefully, minding my own business, and you attacked me! I wasn't bothering you in the least." I said this last bit with a puerile huff, to further my point, then raised my hand to feel the back of my head where a small lump had formed. "Why did you have to hit me?"

"Which question do you want me to answer first?" His snarkiness was back.

"What?" I snapped, not looking at him, distracted by a small trickle of blood that was oozing from the split in my scalp where I had been hit. It didn't improve my mood.

"'Who are you' or 'why did you hit me'? Because knowing which question you want answered first will determine how I answer you."

No, he most definitely was Smug Boy. Jack Smug. I stopped examining my head wound and turned to glower at him. We weren't starting off well. "I don't care. You choose," I said shortly. I didn't see why he had to be priggish with me. I was the victim here, after all.

"Well, my name is Jack, as you already know, and you met my father, Rem. We're smiths by trade, though our land is now closed to us, our homes and all our possessions taken." The naked intensity of his announcement stilled me. His irreverence was gone, replaced by blunt anger. "We eke out a living by venturing into small towns and villages, doing odd jobs then sharing with each other and living communally in these woods. We hunt and fish, surviving however we can." He paused to take the food offered to him by the woman who had been tending the roasting birds. I took a portion as well, and we each began to eat as he continued, "My family, specifically my father, used to serve King Nikolas of the Kingdom of Agrius in the days before he was overthrown. The violence of the coup threatened our lives and we fled, found safety here in the Sidera Mountains where we've lived a life of exile ever since." He growled the last part, and it seemed as if the firelight caught his eyes, fueling the passion with which he spoke.

Likely Jack took me for a pampered brat, bred in finery and without want because of who he perceived me to be, because of my clothing and the fine horse I rode. I think he wanted me to know that my complaints were meager compared to how he and his father and friends had been living. He couldn't have guessed farther from the truth, so I kept silent, and he probably assumed that by doing so I either wasn't following him, or that I didn't care. In truth, it was both. Despite my father's extensive tutelage on history and politics, he never taught us about the mysterious land of Agrius or its deposed ruler, King Nikolas. I might have wondered why he had neglected that part of my unusual education, but at the moment I didn't care. It had been a long day, a lifetime even, since I had left Adyna and Emik. I was tired, my head hurt, and I wanted my stuff back so I could finish my work and get on with my life.

Jack wasn't deterred by my disinterest, so he continued. "Because of the valiant bravery of his personal guard, King Nikolas managed to escape, along with his son, Prince Bedic, his new wife, and other members of the household. My father and I and all these people here were some of the lucky ones." He had slowed his narrative a bit at this last part, softening his voice so that I had to listen closely to hear. "We later learned that there were brutal reprisals from the new regime on those unlucky enough to be left behind. I was a very young boy at the time, so I don't remember it at all, but I do remember the screams. My father says the city was on fire, that death and destruction was everywhere."

It was full dark now and the little community of exiles had mostly given in to the night and had gone to bed, but one or two other fires were still burning, and murmurs of subdued conversations rose and fell like gentle waves of the sea. Our fire popped, releasing a hiss of sparks which rose skyward in an updraft, drawing my gaze with it. A gust of wind forced its way through the clearing, and the trunks of trees creaked and groaned in reply. I wrapped my arms around myself, suddenly chilled, but not entirely from the wind. The incredible nature of Jack's story had worked its dark and somber tendrils into my imagination, and I was feeling the effects, realized that I had been hanging on his every word despite myself.

Jack continued, matching his volume to suit the melancholy of his tale. "My father had served King Nikolas faithfully, like his father before him. He was the palace silversmith and made many fine things for the king and his family." Jack paused only momentarily, and I glanced quickly at him, noting the wistful sadness in his eyes. Doubtless Rem had recounted all the tales of his youth in an attempt to regain for Jack at least a measure of what he had lost, as if in the telling of the tales, the memories would be kept alive. Likely Jack felt the emotions of his father as if they were his own. "He's an artist, unparalleled in his talent, but he lost everything, and now we are merely wandering tradesmen, getting work whenever and wherever we can."

"Why can't you go home now?" I asked, in spite of myself. "Surely it's been long enough that you'd be forgotten by now?"

He shook his head. "We have nothing to go back to. Our homes are gone! And Bellek has spies," he spat out the name Bellek, as if it was an abomination, "and a long memory. He doesn't forget that easily. Besides, my father is a rather vocal opponent. We'll never be safe as long as Bellek sits on the throne."

What did I know of such things? Up until now, my life had been fairly uncomplicated. Even so, something about Jack's story sent a shiver down my spine. It could also have been because the wind was worsening, and that the tongues of flame of our small fire danced ferociously, suggesting diabolic goings on. It would have been entirely atmospheric if lightening struck ominously overhead, but nothing of that nature happened.

I wanted to shake this eerie feeling so tried to think of a way to change the subject. "Where is my horse?" I felt a little guilty that all this time had passed, and I had yet to ask after her.

It took a moment for Jack to respond, still seemingly lost in the private world of his memories. "Oh, your horse is stabled over beyond." He pointed into the darkness. "Don't worry. She's been tended to. What do you call her? She is a magnificent beast!" The topic revived him, and he looked almost boyish as he asked the question. In my experience, men are capable of standing together in a line, never facing one another but rather staring at a fixed point somewhere in the middle distance, doing nothing beyond quaffing ale and discussing horses for hours on end. When I told him her name was "Rose" his thoughtfulness turned to astonished disbelief, as if he had expected something entirely different, like "Asenthia, the Goddess of Thunder" or the like. I was preemptively irritated and rolled my eyes at him, dismissing the mockery I knew was coming. Yes, I had named my horse after a flowering shrub, but that was none of his business.

"It's the best I could do," I said dismissively, and when he seemed about to interject another comment, I quickly added, "You never answered my other question. Why did you hit me?"

He gave me a sheepish look and ran his hands through his hair. "About that..." He rose and retrieved something from inside the small hut then sat back down, opening his hands to reveal the leather pouch containing the arm bands. "As I already explained, we live life on the run. This place isn't well known, which is why we work here, so when anyone shows up we get suspicious." He said this as though thumping me on the head should now seem reasonable to me. I glared at him. "It was a precaution!" he said in obvious defense. "You could have been from Bellek, and we had to be sure. A lot of lives depend on our caution. After we secured you in that storage shed and started trying to decide what to do about you, my father found these in your things." He loosened the strings of the pouch and dumped out the metal bands.

"Obviously you know what they are," I suggested, "otherwise Rem wouldn't have asked me specifically about them. Why?" It was clear to me now that he and his father attached some sort of significance to these bands. It was entirely possible they knew more about the object of my assignment than I did.

"My father made them." My eyes widened into giant orbs of astonishment. "They were commissioned by King Nikolas as a gift at his son's marriage, to be presented at the celebration feast. They bear the sign of the Royal House of Sajen," he pointed at the filigree designs on the ends of the rings. "Unfortunately, they were never presented due to Bellek's malicious timing." He looked at me expectantly, as though everything should make perfect sense. My obvious incomprehension didn't pass unnoticed.

"The coup happened during the wedding ceremony. You didn't know?"

"No, I didn't know. This is the first I've heard of your precious Agrius or King Nikolas or Bellek or any of it." He had asked innocently enough, and he didn't deserve my sourness, but fatigue made me overly self-conscious when my ignorance was revealed. I wondered if my head was done bleeding, so checked and found that it was. I closed my eyes and rubbed my temples, trying to ease my headache. It was all so much to take in.

He continued, unfazed by my bad attitude, "The man who brought you those bands in Corium? His name is Figor. He was Prince Bedic's friend. My father thinks he may have been instrumental in the coup because he now serves as an advisor to Bellek on the Council. He must have traveled to Corium with Prince Casmir, Bellek's son." Jack looked as though he had just tasted something rancid. "Kassia, you showed up here with a mystery, do you know that? My father is puzzled over why Figor still had those armbands and why he gave them to you."

Jack could have continued talking for all I knew, but I didn't hear him. I was still preoccupied by something he had just said. "Prince Casmir is from Agrius? He's King Bellek's son?" Jack nodded in confirmation. Fabulous. It was all getting better by the minute. Whether I wanted it or not, I was woven into Jack's story by at least two threads. Not only was I in possession of the silver arm bands which were originally made for Prince Bedic, the former heir apparent of a kingdom I'd never heard of, I was also in possession of a horse purchased for me by the current heir apparent, the son of the king who had usurped the throne. Was Casmir's intervention in the horse paddock that day pure happenstance? Would the bands have had any significance to him? If Jack could have seen my face clearly in the darkness, he would have seen all color drain from it as I processed these revelations. But because I didn't want him to know his words had shaken me, I uttered an audible snort of derision and rose from the fire to find my bed. It seemed preferable to admitting my fear.

◆◆◆

53

"So, what became of Nikolas, his son, and the merry band? Obviously you're not with him anymore, so..."

I had slept well on a bed of spruce boughs covered with soft fox pelts, awakening to a clear, bright morning, refreshed and energized, ready to get to the work at hand. Had I wanted to allow it, it would have been a simple enough thing for me to conjure up the same ominous feelings Jack's story had evoked last night, but it was easier to go on as though none of it touched me, keeping from him what I really thought or felt and covering it instead with flippancy.

Jack scowled at my continued lack of respect, though to his credit, he smothered any caustic retort that may have been hovering on the tip of his tongue. "No, the king isn't with us," he said drily, "or the Prince. The King went into hiding, and my father later learned that his security was short lived. Within the span of a few months the spies of Bellek located him... and murdered him in his sleep." After a moment he added, "Prince Bedic simply disappeared, so he probably faced the same fate."

My defenses slipped. It was one thing to hear of coups and daring escapes through fire ravaged cities. That wasn't personal. Cities were big places, and fire impacted masses, so it was easier to detach from it. But assassination was altogether a different animal. King Nikolas and Prince Bedic, though I didn't know them, were people, individuals. Each of them represented a life snuffed out prematurely, and this impacted me more than any of Jack's other news. It was hard to pretend I wasn't affected, and he must have sensed my discomfort. Thusly pacified, he changed the subject. Our conversation the night before had been all about politics and Jack's history. Now he wanted to know about me. Because he had shared so much about his life, it felt odd to keep secrets from him any longer, so I told him everything, except for the part about Issak, of course.

He seemed genuinely interested about me, was shocked when he found out who I was and that I was an orphan living alone with my sister. My expensive horse and showy attire had thrown him off. He laughed appreciatively when I told him how I had told off Swine, but when I got to the part about Figor's arrival, he turned serious.

"Kassia, did Figor purposely seek you out?"

"Yes, I think so..." I thought back, and in my mind's eye I looked up, seeing a man standing before me, watching me as would a person who has discovered something curious. While his presence had startled me, I hadn't been thrown off my stride until "...he asked for me by name, and there's no reason he should have. I was just an average merchant trying to do a fair business, not someone that people sought out specifically because of my specialized skill. If he'd simply wanted a tinker, he'd have looked closer to the palace. The matter grew stranger once he told me what he wanted me to do for him -- and then he paid me in gold without flinching." I glanced up to see if he was following me. He was. "All other thoughts fled from my mind. I just assumed he was mad, but I wasn't about to turn down the money." I shrugged.

At the mention of the gold, Jack flashed me a look, but he said nothing; instead he stood and paced slowly around the fire, massaging his scalp and tousling the hair on his head as he wrestled with his thoughts.

The same quiet young woman who had made our meal the previous night was by the fire, watching us over a steaming pot of water. I hadn't noticed her speak since I had arrived, but she seemed keenly aware of everything that passed between Jack and me, and that she had followed all our conversations. I mentally dismissed her and disappeared into my own head for a time, blankly watching the fire as Jack continued his silent brooding. Long moments passed before he finally said vacantly, "There's bread to eat, if you're hungry." Without indicating where this bread might be found, he strode off across the clearing, leaving me alone with Fire Woman.

By the time I found some food and finished eating, Jack hadn't returned. So with nothing else to do, I explored, first going in search of Rose and finding her snugly stabled in a cozy byre along with a handful of other animals. My mischievous horse greeted me with a soft nicker when I stroked her neck and rubbed her velvet nose. Someone had already seen to her food and water, and without seeing much else I could do for her, I left her to her ease.

The morning was half gone when Rem found me. "Kassia,

can we talk?" I peered up at him from my crouched position in the dirt at the base of the shady tree where I had made several lovely drawings with a slenderly tapered stick. A shaft of sunlight slanted through the canopy of leaves overhead, highlighting a pair of bees working in a patch of wildflowers near me. The same sun beat down in Corium, but the mountains cooled the air, aided by a gentle breeze carrying the wafting seeds of thistle and dandelion. I had only been gone from Corium for three days, but already I had grown accustomed to the peace of this forested retreat, away from the dust choked streets of that crowded city. I wondered if perhaps Irisa and I should move to the mountains instead of a cottage in a meadow.

"My schedule is pretty full at the moment, but I suppose I could spare a moment or two." My sarcasm was lost on Rem. He obviously had weighty things on his mind, so I made a mental note to tone down my fabulous sense of humor.

Rather than lead me back to the settlement as I had anticipated, we walked to the old mining camp. Smoke rose from the chimney of the old smithy in lazy ascent, eventually dissipating into the clear blue sky overhead. He opened the door, and I was greeted by a force of warm air. Jack was working the bellows, fueling the fire that burned in the oven. The shutters were thrown open wide to let a cool breeze blow through, but it was still very warm, though not as stifling as Seva's smithy had been. My thoughts turned to Issak and I flushed.

Rem indicated that I take a seat, and then crossed the room to retrieve one of my silver bands he had already started working on.

"Kassia, I think it's extremely significant that Figor sought you out." The man was a genius, but I kept my face neutral lest he think I had him figured out. "Figor is a very powerful man and is highly esteemed by Bellek. How he managed to ingratiate himself onto the Council I can't say; but what's more important is why he brought you these..." He let his words trail off unfinished as though he intended to solve the mystery here and now. I remained quiet and let him have a moment, but before long he continued, "Kassia, I believe you are a special young woman." He was deadly serious, but it was all I could do to restrain my laughter. His assertion was ludicrous.

I wasn't completely successful in hiding my doubt as I replied, "Rem, I can see the truth in the notion that this Figor person sought me out specifically, but I think it's highly unlikely that it involves anything more than..."

Rem quickly cut me off. "Charity?" Rem looked at me skeptically, shaking his head.

"Well, no," I said, though in fact, that's precisely what I was about to say. The word sounded much more unlikely coming from his mouth than from mine.

"Because he knew you needed the work and didn't want you to starve to death?"

"No!"

"Then what?"

He had me. I had no idea, and that was the problem. But I wasn't about to admit that there was anything special about me. I was the daughter of a dead scribe. My father was a scribe, and I was a thief. Then I had another thought. "Maybe my father knew something. Maybe he came across something during his work as a scribe, something valuable to Figor, or to Bellek, or Casmir, maybe Ciasan even... something scandalous or... treasonous..." I shuddered at the thought. "If Figor or Casmir or Bellek thought my father knew something they wanted, if they wanted the information or wanted him silenced because of it..." I thought about his disappearance, and it took on an entirely different meaning. "I don't know why they would have waited so long, but maybe they thought I also knew of it, that my father shared the secret with me." Or my sister. My eyes widened and I leapt off the table, making for the door.

"Kassia, where are you going?" Rem started after me, alarmed at the speed of my flight.

I yelled back over my shoulder as I sprinted away from the camp towards the settlement to retrieve Rose, "To Corium. I need to get to my sister."

Jack was quicker than his father and caught up with me, grabbing my arm to stop me. "Kassia, wait!" His grip was painful, and I couldn't break free.

"Jack, let me go. You don't understand," I plead. "If I am as special as your father thinks, no matter the reason, so is my sister! I doubt that Figor expected me to leave Corium, but my sister is still there, and he could get to her. She isn't very capable. If anyone was to threaten her or take her..."

"Kassia, we don't even know Figor's intentions. If he was interested in harming you or your sister for any reason, he would have done so. Why would he give you a pile of money if he meant to harm you?"

Jack released my arm, thinking he had calmed me, but as soon as he did, I turned and took off again.

"Kassia! Stop!"

Something about his voice froze me. Reluctantly I obeyed, turning to hear him out.

"Come back and let's talk about this. We don't know what you would be dealing with, going back to Corium unprepared. Let's just say for a minute that Figor means you harm, that he found you gone and decided to go after your sister... Kassia, if that's the case, they already have her. But if not, if Figor doesn't care about her, she's still at home, still going about her business and unaware of all of this."

Jack had closed the distance between us during his persuasion and was now near enough to place his strong hands on my upper arms, not to restrain but offer reassurance. His voice was soothing now, as if he was talking to a spooked horse. "We need to think through this thoroughly and make a plan before you go. There has to be a reason Figor gave you those arm bands, and if we talk about it a bit, maybe we can come up with some sort of reasonable explanation. As it is, if you go storming off like this, you could get hurt, maybe even play right into their hands."

He had a point, and without even realizing it, he had offered what I needed, a voice of reason, something I hadn't even realized I had been craving. For far too long I had been forced to be the strong one, to be the decision-maker, to set the course for Irisa and me whether I wanted to or not. It felt nice to have an ally, someone I could finally trust completely. My posture softened and I unconsciously leaned into

Jack's arm. "You're right. Thank you," I said simply.

He didn't immediately respond, and neither did he remove his supporting arm, content to let me relax there. After a while, "Kassia," he said. I must have relaxed into him more than I realized, for his words startled me. "At the very least," he began again, and this time with my full attention, "we can immediately disregard the notion that Figor's interest in you has anything to do with your smithing skills." He spoke seriously enough, but there was an undeniable barb hidden there, further evidenced by the smile which played at the corners of his lips. I was not amused.

◆ ◆ ◆

I have often wondered if there is any such thing as "normal", though in reality, I doubt it. There is at least one thing unusual about everyone, whether or not they know it about themselves or their life. Like living with a dilapidated stair. You know to step over it, not knowing when it might give way, doing so millions of times in the course of a week, thinking nothing of it. While others may fix the stair, you don't even recognize that it's dilapidated. It's part of your life, blends in with the background of all the other sights and sounds of your day in a way that makes it invisible to you. It's unusual, but it's familiar. I didn't pretend to be normal, because I knew without a doubt that my life was unusual. But in my unusual, familiarity was to be found, and there is comfort in familiarity.

It was dark when I arrived in Corium and had Rose stabled. I was just able to slip through the small wicket gate with barely a hand-breadth of space to spare as the guard was closing it for the night. He shot me a stern look with a shake of his head at my careless disregard for the integrity of my limbs. It closed with a resounding boom behind me, and then the heavy wooden beam nestled into place across the gate's width, its iron bolt sliding into place with an ominous clank. I was inside Corium, and for better or worse wouldn't be free to leave until morning.

Jack was here, somewhere in the city, though I hoped to find him in my home rather than en route to it. Before I left the little mining camp and settlement of Agrian exiles, Rem had worked to restore the silver arm bands, and as he did so, we discussed my situation. As much as he wanted to come with me to Corium, to offer his protection and help solve the mystery, it was too dangerous. Rem had a history, and Figor could recognize him. It was agreed that Jack would come along, since Figor didn't know him. He had left the day before me to scout ahead and determine if I was walking into a trap by coming home. If everything was fine, he'd be there waiting for me. If not, he would forestall me before I could get there, keeping me from walking into a trap. I hoped for the former rather than the latter.

I made quick work of navigating the city streets which were nearly empty at this late hour. The alleyway near my home was dark and eerily quiet, though this in and of itself wasn't unusual. It was only my heightened state of awareness which made me feel ill at ease. So far Jack hadn't stepped out of the shadows to keep me from going home, so I took this as a good sign, indicating that everything was quiet at home. As I approached my door, my spirits began to rise, and I exhaled a nervous sigh, thinking that perhaps I had been a bit overdramatic about it all. I slipped the latch and pushed open the wooden door, creeping inside. The room was empty. It was pitch black inside, and the air smelled of stale ash. No Jack and no Irisa.

I stifled my rising panic as I fumbled my way across the room, stumbling over objects on the floor which shouldn't have been there. Finally grasping the wall near the hearth, I searched the place where we kept our flint. My fingers shook, and with some difficulty I lit a small clay lamp. The light was feeble, but it was sufficient to illuminate a scene of utter chaos. All around me lay a scattered mess. Clothing and cookware, trinkets and blankets -- the entire contents of my house lay strewn about; no corner had been left untouched. It was astonishing, but what impacted me the most was seeing my father's things, his papers and documents, quills and ink pots, torn, smashed, damaged. His books were laid open; some were ripped apart and left toppled where they fell.

I stood in the center of the room taking in the mess, and a knot began to coil like a snake in my stomach; my legs suddenly became weak. Staggering towards the wall, I reached out to touch its solidity, reassured by its strength and presence. Easing myself to the floor, I dropped my head into my hands, closed my eyes, and tried to block out the world, if only for a moment.

Irisa was gone and Jack wasn't here. It was enough that my sister was gone, likely taken, but by whom, and why? Was this the work of Figor, on the orders of Casmir? What were they looking for? But for Jack to be absent as well... it defied explanation. Whatever it was, there was no one to ask; I was the only one left.

The hour was late, and there was nothing to be done right now. I couldn't stay here, but it was unlikely anyone would come in the middle of the night; I would decide what to do in the morning. Blowing out the lamp so no one could see any trace of light spilling through the cracks in the wall, I settled in to get some rest. At least that was the theory. It was a long time before I could silence my raging mind and drift off into a fitful sleep.

◆◆◆

"My sweet little Katava... You need to be more mindful of the sweep of the loop here... and here..." He emphasizes his point by tapping the quill like a woodpecker onto the parchment on which I am practicing my letters.

"Yes, father." I try to keep the fatigue out of my voice, but I don't know how successful I am. It is still early morning, the time we always work at our daily lessons before Father leaves for the market to work. He thinks we need an education, and it bothers him not a bit that we are girls or that poor children are never educated. Every morning we sit at this small table learning to read and write, studying history, governance, literature, poetry, and a little music. Sometimes we do more of the same in the evening, when father poses questions of philosophy, history, or statecraft.

"Father?" I venture hesitantly, uncertain if I will receive a direct answer.

"What is it, my sweet?" He is checking Irisa's work, not looking at me.

"Father, why do you work in the market? Why don't you work in the house of a great lord? Why wouldn't one of them want to hire

you? Then maybe we could live somewhere else." I look around sadly at our miserable surroundings. Father's hand freezes momentarily and his quill bobs almost imperceptibly. His eyes dart down to the hard packed floor, though not quickly enough that I don't see the shift in his eyes, like when storm clouds sweep in to cover a sunny blue sky.

"Katava, it is enough," he whispers quietly. His eyes flick up to mine for only the most fleeting of moments and he turns back to Irisa, continuing on as if I had never spoken. I am rarely brave enough to ask questions of my father, particularly questions about his former life, the one he left before he came to Corium. He is an expert at maneuvering conversation away from that topic. I force my fingers to return to their work, concentrating on my loops as father showed me, but my heart is not in it.

◆ ◆ ◆

I managed to awake before dawn, though the short night made it difficult. More than anything, I wanted to roll over and pretend none of it was real, that I'd awake later to a house filled with the smell of a cooking fire, the sounds of my sister singing softly to herself as she worked. It was an exquisite delusion, but one which would only cause more pain if it was allowed to linger in the halls of my imagination. I fought hard against the waves of lethargy dulling my senses but was pulled from its grip by a noise. It wasn't a precisely cultivated intuition that had awakened me; I wasn't alone. I shot out of bed and came face to face with an intruder.

"You know, you could have at least made me some breakfast," I nodded towards the now cold hearth, "or started a fire. Something useful," I said, disapprovingly.

My guest puckered his lips into a pout at my admonition, but only for the briefest of moments before a grin lit his face, and he shrugged dismissively. I returned his smile and closed the space between us with two broad strides, encasing him in a giant hug. "Cai, it's good to see you. How are you?" By way of answer he merely shrugged again. Seeing him was like the sun breaking out from behind the clouds, instantly cheering and instantly warming. I pulled a stool over to the hearth and bade him sit on it as I set about starting a fire to boil some water, forgetting altogether the urgency of my situation. From somewhere in his pockets Cai pulled a packet of tea leaves which he emptied into the water. The aroma was exquisite and my eyebrows rose in surprise. There was no telling how he had acquired them, but with Cai it was usually best not to ask.

As much as I wanted to catch up on the latest news, to pretend that life was the way it always had been, I needed to get to the heart of my predicament. If anyone knew what had happened to Irisa, certainly it was Cai. As I ladled out some tea, I asked him, "Do you know where Irisa is?" There was no need to ease into the question. The present state of affairs was obvious. I was hopeful but expected bad news nonetheless.

His face fell, and he dropped his eyes to study the chipped rim of the mug in his hands. He gave it a quick twitch, sending the brown liquid swirling in an agitated circle. My heart thudded in my chest, and I willed myself to hear the worst, whatever the news. "She went missing four days ago."

It's what I expected to hear, but that didn't make it any easier. Though I hated to admit it, Jack and Rem had been right. Setting out from the mining camp so recklessly that day wouldn't have helped anything. I would have discovered my sister's disappearance sooner, but it would have changed nothing.

"Sigmus the Baker noticed she hadn't shown up for her daily loaf and sent Tess to check up on her. He knew you were gone so watched out for her."

It was good to know that in all the vastness of Corium, someone had noticed. "Did anyone else come by looking for me? A young man, perhaps?" Cai didn't know Jack, so he might not have noticed, even if Jack had come and gone at some point. Cai shook his head helplessly. My heart sank, and I added, "I can't stay here."

"I know," he said miserably. He looked about to say more, but hesitated and kept silent instead.

I stood and began to pace around the mess, pushing aside random objects with my toe as I went. "I need somewhere to think, somewhere safe to figure things out. Maybe to Issak, though I don't really want to have to explain it all..." My voice trailed off as did my thoughts.

"Kassia," Cai said tentatively. "Kassia, you can't go to Issak."

"Why not?" I was alarmed, but perhaps he was right. Perhaps by going to Issak I would include him in whatever was going on here. He was a good man and certainly deserved better. I was reminded again of my original plan, to disavow my promise to marry him and felt instantly guilty. No, I wouldn't go to Issak, though I would have to get word to him somehow, find some way to explain my absence. Cai kept looking at me with haunted eyes, his face pale. I stopped pacing, realizing there was more to the story, something he needed to tell me but dreaded. Returning to my stool, I sat down and gripped it as if it was a lifeline. "What happened? Cai?" My question was desperate; I needed to know, but I dreaded the answer.

"Men came... He was beaten... his family..." his voice cracked, "his home burned..." He paused, and panic rose in my chest. Cai looked at the floor, afraid to continue yet unable to keep the truth from me. "He's dead." These last words were barely discernible from a sigh, so fragile and delicate were they, as if to speak them made the horror of their meaning more real.

I fought to keep my voice level. "Who? Cai, who killed him?" It was unreal. Everything. The world had gone stark raving mad.

"Men from Prince Casmir," he whispered. My stomach lurched, and I swallowed back the gorge rising in my throat. Dizziness threatened to overtake me, and I slipped to the floor, dropping to my knees grabbing fistfuls of dust from the floor with scratching, desperate fingers as an anguished cry escaped my lips. I felt my lungs constrict, then my throat. I couldn't breathe. The air had been sucked out of the room. The walls were closing in on me. Irisa had often called me reckless, and indeed I was. Issak was a good man, and I had killed him.

4

Fog clouds my vision. Ice encases my body, penetrating, cruel, piercing. I am frozen; I cannot move. Sounds float around me, muffled voices and the suggestion of activity, people swirling and hovering just out of reach. The sounds rise in volume then ever steadily begin to boil and churn. The words sharpen and focus, yet while I should be able to make out the speech, it remains just beyond my comprehension. The voices climax in a state of frenzy, are shouts now, raging and surging in intensity and speed, coming at me like daggers, attacking like angry hornets. I cannot keep the voices at bay, and they are on the verge of consuming me. I want to cover my ears and scream, but I cannot move. I am powerless.

◆ ◆ ◆

I bolted upright, rigid and tense, my body shaking with terror and confusion. The pounding of my heart flooded my ears with sounds of surging blood, my desperate dream having sent me down a slippery, sloping spiral into stark terror. The room was still dark, for morning hadn't yet arrived, and it was cavernously cold, the likely culprit of the ice prison from my dream. My clammy body dripped with sweat, even as my skin prickled with gooseflesh. My thin blanket lay bunched at my feet where I had kicked it during the night.

Cai lay near me, but he hadn't been disturbed by my dream, the peaceful bliss that ruled his days clearly having a firm command on his nights as well. I took several deep breaths and forced myself to calm down then took in the shadowy shapes around me, remembering where I was.

After telling me about the brutal death of Issak, Cai led me away from the mess of my house and all that was my former life to this partially-filled and virtually derelict warehouse. All plans of leaving Corium, including any thoughts of Jack, fled from my brain. A new purpose drove me.

Because Cai was Cai, knowing the city better than anyone else I knew, he easily located Casmir's lodgings on the steep slope between the Grand Palace of Coria and the Bay of Bos. It was a busy district, and there weren't many places we could hide where our continual presence wouldn't be noticed, at least within view of the useful parts, to glimpse the Prince and his entourage. So it was with no small amount of discouragement that we settled in next to a sheltered byre across from the kitchen entrance, hoping to observe the household. Or at least the lower orders of his household. Well, the lowest of the low -- the kitchen maids. The next two days found us engaged in surveillance, busily watching absolutely nothing beyond the comings and goings of small girls emptying buckets of refuse. It was a boring task, and we despaired that it would produce anything helpful.

It also didn't help that we were subjected to a steady rain. Corium nestled in a coastal desert of sorts, so it was not often that rain fell; but when it did, it tended to come in heavy showers that blew through quickly and just as quickly moved on. The rain which had fallen these last two days was highly unusual, persistent and tenacious. Everything was wet, and the air was vaporous. All in all, it matched my dismal mood precisely.

I had chosen to wear my thieving clothes today, thinking that a lurking boy would be less noteworthy than a lurking girl. That morning I had also made another choice, something I hadn't done in all my years of wearing it -- I had left my medallion behind, buried in a hole under my sleeping place along with my stash of gold and the silver armbands. This decision I was glad of however, for the chaffing from my wet shirt was nearly unbearable.

Cai shifted his position to better see between the fence slats, but the movement of his feet created a sucking sound in the soft mud. He looked at me warily, afraid that the sound had betrayed our presence, though I doubted that anyone had heard it over the noise of the falling rain. I shook my head to reassure him, and he relaxed, turning his attention back to the kitchen door.

The day was nearly gone by the time we admitted utter defeat. There seemed to be no point in watching this muddy yard any longer.

Even if any of the girls knew a thing about Irisa, it was unlikely that the news would be proclaimed within earshot of our hiding place. We needed a new plan and began our trek back to the warehouse.

As the rain rolled off my nose and dripped down the line of my back between my shoulder blades, I got angry and stomped in the mud. Jack was supposed to be somewhere in the city, but since learning the news of Issak's death I had given him or his failure to appear little thought. There was no reason to believe anyone would have connected him to me, but I had to consider it as a possibility. I chewed a strand of hair as I walked, puzzling out my options, finally deciding that it was time to return to the mining camp outside Heywood. If anyone had news of Jack, it would be Rem. Cai listened to my plan and nodded agreement. Tomorrow we would go, and Cai would come with me. But for now, food and dry clothes topped our priority list.

So caught up was I in my daydreams of warmth and dryness that as I approached the warehouse, I didn't immediately notice the figure standing just outside the door. Swine. His arms were crossed over his paunch, and a scowl carved deep grooves around his mouth. I was shocked to see him here.

"You be owing me monies. Back owing. Interest on top of the owing." His eyes burned holes into me. He took a threatening step forward. As he did so, a cascade of water poured from a dip in an awning just overhead, flattening his wooly hair against his neck, though he remained utterly oblivious to it, so furious was he. Blood suffused his face, mottling his skin with blotchy red patches. Usually I handled Swine with adept skill, easily out-thinking and outmaneuvering his slower mind, but this time he scared me. I glanced over my shoulder to see that Cai had made an adroit disappearance. I was glad. He didn't need to be caught up in what could easily turn unpleasant.

I threw up my hands in conciliation. "Swine, I..."

"Sveine. Name is Sveine." He spat the words, nearly choking on them in the process. He took another step towards me, blood pulsing at the vein in his neck. There was no sense in backing away. He would only follow me, and I would look like a cowardly fool.

"Irisa had your money. She was to pay you," I said, hoping he would believe me but knowing it wouldn't make any difference because he seemed beyond caring.

"So you said, but no believing you when no sister be found."

"I have your money, Sveine," I said correctly, keeping my tone light and easy, in the way one would talk to a spooked horse.

"Good." He smiled at me, but it was oily. His fury was abating, but he was still dangerous. "My men tell me rats in warehouse. Come see, said they, and here you are."

"This is your warehouse?" I looked at him gape-mouthed. What were the odds?

By way of response, he grabbed my arm, opened the door, and pushed me inside. I pushed wet strands of hair out of my eyes and stepped further into the darkness of the empty warehouse, Swine immediately at my heels.

"Where your things?"

A sickly form of relief flooded over me. He would require a ridiculous sum of money to satisfy his anger, but at least the worry of him would be dealt with. I led him to the hole I had dug for my valuable possessions -- the gold from Figor, my medallion necklace, and the sack containing the armbands -- but found it had been disturbed; my heart sank. I dropped to my knees and reached into the pit, only to come up empty-handed.

I stood, knees trembling a little with agitation and confusion, and turned to face him. He stared at me with his arms folded again. "Swine, I..."

He grabbed my wrist with a twist. I yelped in pain. "You make me fool for last of time," he hissed.

We were interrupted by the arrival of a city guard. Swine must have expected him, because he didn't seem surprised by the disruption. The guard took a look at me, and when recognition registered, pure delight lit his eyes and a cruel smile spread his lips into a thin line over rotted teeth. It was the same city guard who had chased me into the garden. He finally caught his thief.

"Has this one been causing you trouble?" He looked me up and down with relish.

"Trouble! No monies pay me after much time and trouble." Slipping into his native tongue, he blabbered on for several minutes before realizing his mistake, though the guard was oblivious to his tirade, caught up in his delight over finding me. It was only when Swine pulled the cap from my head, freeing my long tresses that the guard's delight truly began to soar. I was no boy after all, but a young woman, and I was now his.

"Swine...er, Sveine... We discussed alternative payment, remember?" I said with a pained smile then flicked a glance at my gleeful guard, knowing he'd agree with me. Though it sickened me to suggest it, it was all I could think of to do, for if nothing else, it would buy me some time to work out another plan. The guard tugged at my arm with eagerness, as if he was ready to follow my suggestion, knowing how long he'd waited for this day.

It wasn't to be. The guard was shocked into stillness when Swine shook his head with vehemence. "No, to Black Fortress she go." Swine had no interest in listening to reason, and not even the prospect of earning money as a flesh-peddler would sway his anger. I had humiliated him beyond his normal abilities to handle it. With a curt swish of his hand he ordered the guard away with me.

As we filed out, the glint of something caught Swine's eye, and he paused to pick it up. In the center of the room lay a sack, its contents partially exposed. Silver. My arm bands. A gleeful smile stretched across his piggy face when he saw the fineness of the pieces. "These be yours?" I glowered at him, and he took this as affirmation. "Payment. Maybe sell to palace. Prince Ciasan give them to lady-friend."

He was amused by his own joke, but the idea sickened me. I didn't want those armbands anywhere near the palace. I didn't know how they ended up in the middle of the warehouse like this, but I was given my answer when a single feather drifted down from the ceiling. I glanced up furtively so Swine wouldn't notice. High up in the rafters I spied a foot dangling. Cai. He had slipped in ahead of us from a different entrance and snatched what he could before we came in, but the armbands hadn't quite made it.

Swine waved his hand again for the guard to take me before he turned and waltzed away, delighted by the way things had worked in his favor. I called after him, "Swine, you have your payment now. Let me go!" So panicked was I, that I barely noticed the intimate familiarity which guided the guard's search for weapons. Swine said nothing in return, the echo of his laughter the only indication that he had heard me.

◆◆◆

Mosrad Prison was a gigantic structure near the coast, and though not as large as the Coria Palace itself, it was more menacing both in construction and in purpose. Large and rectangular, it boasted six round towers and two large gates, one for the use of its "guests", and the second for all other business. The stones of the prison were black with age, and it was said that the fortress had once been the stronghold of an ancient king of Mercoria before the coming of the Emperors. Moldy and stinking, the Black Fortress, as it was often called, was ensconced in a perpetual fog, as if the gloom which shrouded it like a distressed phantom exhausted the less enthusiastic rays of the sun.

I wasn't ignorant of what likely awaited me in prison. Though my arrest was caused by a little misunderstanding over rent, a misunderstanding which two reasonable people should have been able to settle quickly, I knew that once I entered the prison as a guest, it wouldn't matter whether I was a rent avoider or a killer of aristocratic babies, for equal treatment awaited all inside the walls.

As we crossed under the great gate, I looked up to see the large iron portcullis, its great spiked teeth mawing overhead, sending a shudder through my frame. My mud-caked shoes squelched as we made our way into a small alcove just inside the gate of the cobbled inner courtyard. We stopped at a small table, and its disinterested occupant took down my name on a scrap of parchment meant to be the prison's official log book. There were several other such pages carelessly tossed into a heap on the floor behind the clerk, a sight which made my hopes sink even further because it suggested the futility of keeping records in such a place. He barely glanced at me as my escort described with delight the reason for my arrival, and then with a curt nod sent us off. Another prison guard approached, and with a coolly detached order, dismissed the city guard. Sensing the loss of his prize, the man protested, but he received no sympathy. He moved off, but grumbled as he did so, casting disgruntled glances over his shoulder as he shuffled out.

I hated to see him go. It was like trading the devil I knew for the devil I didn't. The city guard was lewd, but he was a known quantity. I had beaten him in the past, and I knew that if I was left in his charge, I could find a way to beat him again. The man that accompanied me now was smaller, but his eyes were cold and hard as steel. His movements were precise and frugal; a man with a military disposition. I would not lie to myself regarding my chances of escaping his custody.

We entered a busier courtyard filled with many other people -- guards changing duty assignments as well as those who shirked their duties, preferring to watch the intake of new prisoners over the monotony of their lonely stations. Lined up against the far wall in the feeble light was a host of prisoners waiting, their postures suggesting that the waiting boded nothing good. No one paid us any heed, though soon enough all eyes would be on me, for now I faced a forced disrobing, aided by my helpful guard.

If the female form hiding under my male attire went unnoticed before, it was neglected no longer. The previously lifeless prisoners became instantly animated, tossing crude comments and filthy suggestions my way. To his credit, my guard remained a consummate professional, was unmoved by the whoops and calls, and made no move to take advantage of my compromised position; instead he benignly handed me a shapeless sack of a dress to cover myself. My face raged with fury and embarrassment as the whistles and calls got more colorful and more obscene. As I was led away, eager hands reached out in mostly unsuccessful attempts to grab at specific parts of my anatomy, but thankfully my guard kept me moving, and we headed more deeply into the heart of the prison.

We descended several flights of stairs, down long corridors, past countless rows of ominous heavy wooden doors. Finally we stopped, and my guard produced a key, fit it to a lock, then swung the door inwards with a muffled groan of metal, a portentous indication of disuse. We entered the deeper gloom of the cell and my nostrils were immediately assaulted by a stench so foul that I gagged. My guard nudged me ahead then affixed my wrists to chains attached securely to the wall. Something about the new circumstances changed him, for in a manner completely at odds with how he had so far behaved, he flicked a finger under my jaw, slapped me on the rump, and turned to leave. "Make yourself comfortable, sweetheart. Your valet will be by shortly." Amused by his little joke, he barked a harsh laugh and was gone, closing the door behind him with a thump of finality, leaving me entombed in darkness and defeat.

In the dim light that bled into the cell before the guard closed the door, I caught a fleeting glimpse of the filthy interior, including the shapeless forms of the other prisoners inhabiting the gloom with me. Each of us was a lump of hopeless flesh left to rot in our own filth. Not a sound was uttered. There was no word of welcome, not even in mocking sarcasm. We were islands unto ourselves, and any well of comfort from which my fellow inmates may have drawn had long since dried up.

I nudged around on the floor with my toe and kicked a pile of damp straw then immediately recoiled. In the end I chose to sit on it anyway. It didn't matter. My future was bleak at best. I was alone, and no one could help me. Cai knew what had happened, but he could never find a way to get me out. Jack may have been able to think of something, but he didn't know where I was. Neither of them knew the other. I tried to force my mind to think on more pleasant things, but when nothing presented itself, my thoughts returned with alarming alacrity to my present circumstance. I felt abandoned and isolated, let down by the few friends I had, and I didn't imagine for a moment that I was safe. Far from it. With no one to see or care what I did, I dropped my head onto my up-drawn knees and wept. The night would be dark and long, and the day that followed would be no different, for day had ceased to exist.

◆◆◆

Rough hands grabbed my arm, yanking me from the rank straw to my feet, though my mind was slow to react to this shift in position. The reluctant cell door had likely groaned loudly in protest as my visitor entered, but nothing until now had aroused me from my deep sleep, if sleep is what it was, for I had existed in a world of shifting shadows and desperate hunger for whatever passed as days in my new reality. If pressed to it, I would have guessed that at least five days had passed since entering the prison, and in those five days nothing had happened to alter the state of my dismal existence. Only the sound of rodent scratchings and the shuffle of the other dehumanized life forms sharing my cell varied the monotony. I reeled at the clamor of my chains dropping to the floor, collapsing down onto my vile bed once again only to be immediately hoisted upright with surprising gentleness before being ushered out the door.

My companion, a man dressed in civilian garb, led me from behind. Upon entering the passage outside my cell, I immediately shied away from the brilliance of the single rush light burning in a sconce on the wall, but the man gave me a gentle push to continue me along. It was just as cold out here as it had been in my cell, and I rubbed my arms with my hands to try to induce some warmth. Several flights of stairs later, we emerged into the central bailey of the prison. Though it was night, the air was much warmer than it had been below. As we crossed the bailey to the central keep, I looked up into the deep darkness blanketing the towers soaring overhead. A soft warmth of light glowed at the top of each tower, but this only furthered the menace I felt, for it suggested the insurmountable loftiness of the structure in which I was imprisoned. And though the blanket of stars lighting the sky overhead would once have cheered me, this time it only enhanced my feelings of insignificance and powerlessness. A single tear beaded at the corner of my eye, and I rubbed it away briskly with my muck-crusted hand.

We climbed the outer stairs into central keep, navigated corridors until eventually stopping outside a room at the end of a dark hall. My guard opened the door, gently shoved me inside, then closed it quickly behind me. I spun around with an instinctive need but was disappointed by the solidity of the closed door.

After so many days of inactivity, my lungs burned from the

effort of climbing all the stairs, and as I panted, I turned and leaned back heavily against the door to catch my breath. I sensed rather than saw that the room was small based on the close feeling of the air, but because it was so dimly lit, the corners were cast in deep shadow, and I could see nothing beyond the center of the room which was lit by a single lamp sharing space on a small table with several covered platters.

My hunger was raw, and I reacted instinctively, lurching several steps towards the table, making it no farther before the hairs on the back of my neck stood on end. I wasn't alone. My senses fired like a feral cat, and my eyes sought desperately to penetrate the heavy shadow in the farthest corner of the room. A man leaned casually against the wall, watching me motionless until noting that I had seen him. He paused for a moment before straightening and taking a step into the brighter center of the room.

He was an older man with neatly cropped gray hair, still dark at the temples. His eagle-eyes fixed on me with intensity, shrewd and penetrating, aligned down an aquiline nose shadowing a pleasant mouth formed into a benign shape I couldn't read. His clothes were opulent and enhanced with rich jewels encrusting the details of the embroidery at the neck, hem and cuffs of his silk doublet. The belt at his waist was wide, and from it hung a long dagger. It was this dagger which arrested my attention, for once he stepped near the lamp, I could focus on nothing other than the prominent sun emblem carved onto its hilt. The man noticed, and a smile touched the corner of his eyes. He was here with Casmir. I fought the urge to turn and pound desperately on the door to be let out, willing my gaze back to his face instead.

He let this revelation pass without comment and reached for the tall vessel on the table, pouring out a measure of wine into each of the two cups. Setting one aside for himself, he reached across the chasm between us, offering me the second cup. I didn't take it. My dry mouth had already registered the fact that liquid therapy had been offered, and it was ludicrous to turn it down, yet I stood resolute. I knew there was food under the covered platters, an immediate respite for my crippling hunger, but despite these obvious truisms, my arm remained resolutely at my side. I must have looked an obstinate fool to the man. A befouled and starving obstinate fool.

"Come, you must be thirsty." He thrust the cup towards me again, and as he did so, the ruby liquid spilled onto his thumb, leaving a jeweled droplet on his pallid skin. Still my arm remained as a stone, heavy at my side.

With a raise of his eyebrows and a resigned shrug, he placed the cup gently on the table in front of me then smiled and took a seat in the chair behind him. He picked up his own cup and leaned back to take his ease, crossing his arms while settling the wine comfortably on his forearm. He studied me for a moment before twitching a smile and taking a delicate sip. His eyes closed in rapturous delight. For just a moment he sat motionless, letting the flavor of the wine work its magic on him. I admit that I was intrigued. I had never tasted good wine, but this wine must be exquisite indeed to cause him such a reaction.

Who was I kidding? Pride would do nothing for me. I was thirsty. It was good wine. I sat and drank.

A bouquet of flavors burst on my tongue, exploding with colorful fragrance. No pride was worth missing this, I decided. The man seemed pleased by my decision and pushed a covered dish towards me, nodding as if to encourage me to take a look. I needed no further prodding from him, for my stomach had already decided on my next course of action.

I lifted the lid and discovered a thick stew of meat and vegetables swimming in a savory, brown gravy. Tearing a hunk of bread from a large loaf, I began to eat, slowly at first, though it wasn't long before I ravaged my portion and looked up, startled to see that the man had been watching me the entire time, eating nothing himself. Even his wine cup remained untouched, was still full and rested on the table where he had last set it down.

I finished off my wine and he refilled my cup, still not saying a word but still watching me with genteel patience, though there was no mistaking the hint of sardonic humor in his features. With a little less self-restraint, I finished off this second cup but refused a third when he made a move to refill it once again. I was certain I would need my wits about me because there had to be more purpose behind this encounter than to provide a prisoner with a meal. Men of his ilk didn't normally serve stew to anyone, much less to a prisoner.

"Gorgollasa," the man said. When I looked uncomprehending he added, "The wine. It's a rare varietal served only at the Emperor's table, brought in from a great distance at even greater expense. Exquisite, is it not?"

I continued to look at him blankly and he laughed, picked up his cup, and drank, retreating more deeply into ecstasy with each swallow.

I grew increasingly more uncomfortable. Gorging myself hadn't been wise. The food was rich and heavy, and I had been starved for far too many days. The wine, while consumed on a full stomach, was affecting me more than it should have, and I fought to keep my thoughts focused. I wondered if I would be able to keep everything down or if I would get sick. If it happened that I needed to retch it back up, I decided I'd aim for his shoes.

After a moment, he came to himself again. "Oh, but I forget myself." The man got up from his chair and retrieved a basin of water, offering me a soft towel with which to wash myself. When I didn't move to take it from him, he circled behind me and picked up my hands, one at a time, cleaning each of them before washing my arms and then my face, one gentle stroke at a time. My toes curled, yet I sat motionless as he worked. The water was warm and soothing, but I didn't want to show him how cathartic it was. A bit of humanity had been returned to me, though I wished it hadn't been him to give it. He was a dangerous man.

He returned the basin and wiped his own hands on another towel before returning to his chair. "You are Kassia, daughter of Amion, yes?" Now we came to it. Whatever it was.

"Yes." I saw no point in denying it. He obviously knew who I was already.

He said nothing else for a moment, sipped on his wine while he watched me intently. If he meant to unnerve me, he was doing an excellent job.

"Your mother? Where is she?" he asked finally, not looking at me as he did so. Instead he poured more wine into my cup and his. I refused to touch it.

"She's dead," I said flatly. He was toying with me. I wished he'd get to the point.

He accepted this without comment, moved on to the next question as though checking items off a mental checklist.

"Your father?" His face was devoid of emotion, but his eyes came alive with this question.

"Dead. Presumably," I said, as casually as I could.

"Presumably?" He cocked an eyebrow at me in surprise.

"He went away on business and never returned. He's dead. Why else wouldn't he come back?"

The man took a moment to consider this before continuing. "Your father was a scribe." It wasn't a question but a statement, and I didn't feel it required a response. "Did he do interesting work?" Despite the smiling way he asked the question, I felt a chill race through me, as if the temperature in the room had dropped instantly. My hands started to shake as my mind's eye recalled the chaos of my home, my father's work space and his scattered papers. Irisa's abductors had searched for something, and they looked specifically through my father's papers. I squeezed my palms together until my very bones ached, hoping the pain would overcome the tremor. I narrowed my eyes and stared at him instead of answering, unwilling to give away anything, yet he continued, undaunted: "Did he ever speak to you of his clients? Were there certain individuals to frequent your home? Special family friends? Regular guests?"

"No. He told me nothing. Why would he?" I said caustically, feigning a defiance that only partially existed.

Ignoring me, he went on. "Irisa, your sister..." He was no longer pretending to ask politely. This was now an interrogation. "Where is she?" There was something in his eyes when he asked this, a hardness, an anger barely disguised. My answer to this question was more important than anything else he had asked after so far, as if he was trying to tease something out of my reply, and that once he got it, it would determine the course of something else I couldn't quite comprehend. My head was fuzzy, and I couldn't think straight; my full belly and the added sedative of the wine were making me sleepy. The entirety of our conversation was beyond my comprehension, yet one thing was clear: I needed to proceed cautiously.

"She is away, visiting a friend," I offered. It was a lie, but I wasn't about to let on that I knew the truth, that Casmir's men had taken her. Why would he even ask this question unless there were factions at work... I could make nothing of it, had no idea what he was about, but I wanted him to think that I did, so I smiled at him, a smile dripping with knowing, a cat smile of satisfaction that showed I had taken the upper hand in a game about which I knew nothing.

A shadow crossed his face only momentarily before he regained control. He stood then, turned his back to me and paced away several steps before returning. Seemingly making up his mind about something, he came around the table and leaned his weight against it a mere handbreadth from me and forced a smile, an action which belied the tense grip with which he held his dagger's hilt. I stifled a shudder and held my spine stiff as he continued to smile down at me, pulling the dagger from its sheath. Balancing it delicately on his right palm, he stroked one finger of his left hand caressingly up and down the length of the blade before turning it over and doing the same to the other side. The flicker of the lamplight caught at the blade, enhancing the whorls and patterns of the smoky blue-gray steel. I was captivated and horrified all at once.

In one swift motion he flipped the dagger so that he held the blade in his left hand, giving me a clear view of the sun emblem on the pommel. This man was from Casmir, and he wanted me to know it. If I had any lingering doubts before, they were now thoroughly vanquished. His message successfully given, he replaced the dagger and stood, walked back around the table. Grabbing his wine cup, he quaffed the dregs and slammed the empty cup back down on the table with a force that startled me. It was the first thing he had done to indicate any loss of control. The interview was over, but he wasn't through with me yet. I was certain of it.

In several broad strides he crossed the room to the door. His hand grasped the latch, and almost as an afterthought he stopped, turned back to look at me again, his eyes cold, his smile thin and brittle. "Kassia, as you are undoubtedly aware, I am a visitor to your fair city. If I had need of a tradesman... say, a blacksmith ... where would you suggest I go?" His words dripped with malice, his smile serpentine.

My chilled spine solidified into ice. Hiding my clenched fists in my lap, I locked eyes with him, doing my best to match his cold stare. "I'm not so good with the recommendations. Can I interest you in a sarcastic comment?"

He was not amused. Pinpoints of concentrated fire burned in the depths of his eyes, and searing bolts of hatred rippled across the space between us.

"Civility is not one of your strengths, I see." His lips thinned as an inky smile spread unattractively across his face. "I am tempted to do the honors myself," he sniffed with disgust, eyeing me up and down, "but I've promised another." He paused then with an almost paternal look added, "It didn't have to come to this, Kassia."

Turning abruptly, he flung open the door and gave a curt nod to someone just outside my line of sight. He had gone, but the doorway immediately filled with the familiar form of the city guard who had brought me here. He wasn't alone; he brought a friend. The looks on their faces left no doubt as to what they intended.

With shaking knees I stood, willing my composure to ape a confidence I didn't feel. I glanced at the open doorway behind the men and began to walk towards it. Lifting my chin with an air of regality I had no right to, I said, "I'm afraid I don't have time to chat, boys. Can we postpone this until some other time?" and tried to brush past them.

It was worth a shot.

The bigger of the two men reached out with his giant paw, grabbed me by the arm, and with a staggering ferociousness hurled me across the room where I crashed face-first against a crate, arm outstretched in an attempt to break my fall. Break it most certainly did, but not my fall. Fiery jolts of pain exploded up and down my arm, and I grabbed it, vaguely aware of a warm wetness beginning to drip from a gash in my forehead down into my eyes.

Despite the fog of pain that swirled around me, threatening to send me deep into its welcoming arms of blessed obliviousness, I fought hard against its lure, knowing I needed to remain lucid enough to take in all aspects of my precarious position, hoping I could yet find a way out of this. Both men had crossed the room towards me, the bigger of the two smiling down at me grotesquely, his eyes hard and malevolently leering. My old friend, the city guard, looked at me blankly, his face wiped clean of any hint of emotion or humanity. Precarious position indeed.

I no longer remember which one of them reached out for me first, taking the front of my tunic in his fist, jerking it towards him, tearing the fabric half way down. My throat constricted, and I tried to wrench away, but one of them punched me in the face, snapping my head sideways and backwards with a force that dazed me. The fist gripping my tunic released me with a shove, and I stumbled backwards to the floor as the figures loomed large over me, desperate fingers urgently tugging at their belts.

My eyes sought a way past them, but there was nothing. The men blocked me, trapping me in the corner. There was no way out. I was powerless to prevent what they intended.

One of them seized my ankles, and a fear more debilitating than anything I had ever experienced gripped me in its paralyzing clutches. It was clear that this was about to be the longest night of my life. I wished now that I'd had more wine.

◆ ◆ ◆

Dripping water. I hadn't noticed that sound in all the many days of my confinement. Why was it so loud just now? It pulsed in my ears with a steady rhythm. Or perhaps it was my heart, beating with reckless temerity from somewhere deep inside.

Cold. Ice in my spine, ice in my fingers, ice stiffening me all the way to my toes; my skin pricked with gooseflesh. My body convulsed with shivers threatening to rattle the teeth from my mouth.

Fire. Searing currents of fiery pain coursed through my body like the waves of a sulphurous lake, burning me, rolling in undulating waves of all-encompassing power, threatening to rip me apart from the inside, tearing and scratching me with talons of violence in my vulnerability as I lay in a semi-stupor on the filthy damp floor of my cell.

My eyes closed again, though perhaps they were never open to begin with. Rolling seas... loud whispers, urgent and hurried... floating, flying... blessed obliviousness...

◆ ◆ ◆

"Kassia, come take this basket from me and put it with the rest. I see some blooms just over there." My mother is looking up at me from her crouched position in the middle of the meadow, a smile of purest bliss transforming her usually careworn features into the radiant beauty I see before me. I do not often witness this much joy in her eyes, but her smile completely transforms her now, and I can only imagine what she must have looked like in her youth when she first met my father. It is little wonder he fell for her. I do not know their love story, for neither of them ever talk about it, so I imagine my own version of their story in place of the truth, one involving beauty and mystery and perfection.

We came to this meadow outside the confines of Corium early this morning to take a break from the suffocating city, to gather flowers, an activity my mother often tells me is a necessity from time to time, in order to remember more peaceful days. She moves away to gather the purple blossoms, and as she does so, I stop to watch her. Rather than collect the flowers in her basket, she separates bloom from stem and works each into the braid that wraps itself in a neat coil atop her head, so that by the time she is finished, she is wearing a delicate and fragrant coronet fit for a queen.

◆ ◆ ◆

Tendrils of a languid stupor embraced me with comforting arms, its soothing allurement holding me fast, tying me with invisible threads to a bed made entirely from the fibers of my carefree dream.

This imaginary world was not to last long, however. All too abruptly I was awakened by a burning sensation so overwhelming that a scream burst from my dry, cracked lips. A cool hand touched my cheek, and a soft, gentle voice whispered in my ear, "There, there. Be calm, my poor dear." Instantly I thought of Jeah, just as quickly dismissing the notion. I had seen her dead and buried with my own eyes not long after my father disappeared. The burning sensation cooled, and I opened my eyes, surprised to see the warm glow of a small oil pot lamp and the face which it illuminated. I turned my head slightly to see around the woman and noticed that I was no longer at the scene of my humiliation or in a prison cell, but a small room, clean and tidy and comfortable.

My body felt like molten lava, fiery with fever and engulfed by spasms of pain that threatened to overtake me with each wave. The very act of taking a breath was enough to sicken me, so I decided I would quit. Breathing. It seemed the more sensible alternative to inhaling liquid fire. I tried to move my legs but was rewarded with a pain so overbearing that I screamed again in anguish, incapable of coping with what I couldn't control.

The same gentle hand brushed my cheek again with a soft coolness, and the same voice began making shushing sounds, as if soothing a fussing infant. When the surge of pain subsided and I settled, I opened my eyes. A sad smile met my gaze, warming the otherwise ordinary features of an old face, a woman ravaged by years. She searched my eyes for a moment, and without saying a word applied another layer of poultice to the gash over my eye, covering it with a clean cloth and tying something around my head to secure the bandage. I wondered if I would have a scar, figured I would, wondered why I thought it was important just now.

"Your arm has been reset, and your wounds have been tended," she said quietly as she replaced her medicine containers into neat rows on the shelf behind her. "Do your best to leave the bandage above your eye untouched until I return."

"Why?" The sound I forced into the word sounded somehow detached from me, as if something outside of my own body had spoken using my mouth.

Her old eyes snapped to mine, though not unkindly. There was no hiding her compassion. "Why, what?" she asked gently yet cautiously, her wariness communicating surprise and concern, though for what reason I couldn't imagine.

"Why are you helping me?"

She pondered for a moment before saying simply, "It is what I do." Her countenance softened even more, but this time sadness nestled in next to the compassion.

"My wounds..." I croaked brokenly, unable to finish my question.

She knew what I asked however, and with the cool detachment of one used to dealing with the painful wounds of the afflicted, she said, "You have a broken arm, several broken ribs, severe cuts and bruises too numerous to name, and..." her voice trailed off at that, leaving her next thoughts unspoken momentarily. "...wounds that only time can heal, a violation that is all too common to women in that place." Her eyes flashed anger before she continued, "You fought them hard," she said more determinedly and with approval. I cast my eyes downwards to the patched quilt over me. "There is no shame in it, Kassia," she added kindly when she saw me look away. "They would have overpowered you no matter what." She brushed lightly at the puffy bruise on my cheek, a colorful reminder of where I had been punched. I flinched, turned my face away, and closed my eyes, unwilling and unable to face the reality of it all. I didn't accept what she said, that there was no shame in it. There was shame in it. How dare she suggest otherwise? I was broken and damaged, and full of anger that wrapped itself in self-loathing, had already begun to take on a life of its own, uncontrollable and powerful. I was sick with it and wanted nothing more than to change the subject.

I didn't look at her as I asked, "What's your name?"

"Liri."

I hardly noticed when Liri took my hand in hers, gave it a gentle squeeze, then rose and left with neither word nor sound, the door closing behind her softly as if it were made of nothing more substantial than sugared wafers.

A single tear broke free and rolled down my cheek, indication of a turbulent sea of emotions which, contrary to my will, were rebelling thoroughly and without apology. Before another renegade tear was able to follow the first, I forcefully slammed shut the door to my heart, hiding my brokenness and shame, locking it away securely where no one could ever find it.

◆ ◆ ◆

Time crept by. What could have been days or weeks moved on with maddening slowness, and most of that time was spent fighting off memories -- memories of Issak, of his bloody, bludgeoned body. Though I hadn't seen what was done to him, the only images I could summon of him involved his brutalization. Then there were my wounds. With each ache and tremor, I saw those men, their leering faces, felt over and over again my defilement, each blow, each intrusion. I relived the violence in my dreams each night, and it was inescapable. All of these things had forged me into something new, a new Kassia, something different than I had been. The problems of my earlier life now seemed distant and far away.

I fought to discipline my mind, to stay away from the visions which continually invaded my sleep, my dreams, to stay focused instead on my present circumstances, of healing my body even if there was no hope for my mind, and of puzzling out where I was, how to escape and what to do once I had accomplished these things.

Liri came regularly to tend my wounds, and with her expert ministrations I made dramatic progress. Though my broken flesh was easily repaired, my broken bones would take more time to knit. My broken spirit...I did not want to think about it, so I shoved the notion away from me, forcing it into the deep, dark recesses of my mind.

I was still too weak to do more than take the few steps necessary to cross the room to look out my small window, but I did my best to do it each day, to see even the tiniest glimpse at the blue sky. My view showed nothing but a wall, but being so close to the outside was comforting. One day Liri set up a chair near the window so I could linger longer, and I found that the fresh air helped me think.

In addition to all the other questions that plagued me, Liri was the newest mystery -- who was she and why was she helping me? Any time I plied her for information, she replied kindly but elusively. Assaulting prisoners was a normal activity in the prison, but treating them with tender care afterwards was not. Let her keep her secrets. Everything was a mystery and would likely remain so until I could escape.

One morning quite like the others that had come before, Liri entered my room, only this time rather than her bag of ointments and herbs, she carried a small parcel wrapped in cloth. I took the bundle from her and held it, staring in confusion and fascination. She offered no explanation, merely smiled and urged me with a simple nod of her head to open it.

I obeyed. Inside was a book, leather bound and fastened shut with a sturdy silver clasp. My hands shook as I opened the cover and began to page through the contents. My father had owned several books but none of them were anything like the one I held. This book was sumptuous.

"It looks like a book describing places in great detail... an atlas, I think they are called." My words trailed off as I continued to page through it. "There are maps here, showing lands dotted with rivers and mountains..." I couldn't hide my joy. I no longer cared about the battered state of my body or the hidden wounds no one could see. I was a child again, ushered back into the presence of my father, my sister, and the happy memories of that time. I thought I had hated learning, hated being forced to it as a child, but this simple gift reminded me of all I had been given, for what my father had taught me...

...for an education unusual for a poor girl... one given in secret...

"Liri, where did this come from? Who sent this?" The question was sharp and biting, suspicion and accusation unintentionally lacing the words with acid.

Rather than being offended by my rudeness, Liri merely smiled at me and offered, "It was left here for you. Someone thought you might find it useful." Without saying anything more, she turned and left the room with a grand air of satisfaction.

I stared after her. I knew better than to pepper her with questions, having been altogether unsuccessful in the past at learning anything useful. She held her secrets closely, and I did not begrudge her of it. More than likely information was coin to her, and she was valued for her ability to hold on to it. I would have done the same in her situation.

I had a benefactor and a "useful" book. Another person in my life had given me hope.

5

RAIN POURED FROM heavy clouds, drenching the streets and rushing off roofs in torrential waterfalls. It seemed fitting to me that the day I left prison was just as rain soaked as the day I had entered it.

Two days and three nights after my gift book arrived, I found myself, as happened most nights, caught up in one of many recurrent dreams. I rode my horse, Rose, along a gentle mountain stream, delighting in the crisp air, the clean scent of pine, the rosy-aroma of thimbleberry and the honey-perfumed blue-flowered penstemon.... In a shift as abrupt as it was ferocious, a cold darkness enveloped me, the brightness of day turning to the blackest of night. Coils of ice entwined me, rendering me powerless and vulnerable. The sounds of nature silenced, replaced instead by a rising chorus of voices swirling like eddies inside my head, always unintelligible, increasing in volume until I could no longer stand the shouting. The worst of my dreams alerted Liri, because often I woke to find her at my bedside, her hand firmly in mine as I slowly recovered. The comfort of her presence usually lulled me back into a secure and peaceful sleep.

This night was different; the dream came again, but it wasn't comfort Liri had for me. It was escape. She shook me from my terror, whispering hoarsely, "Kassia, Kassia..." over and over again until I roused. "The time has come and you must go." I didn't move, still foggy with bewilderment. "Now, Kassia." With great effort I opened my eyes. Just then a loud crack of thunder shook the walls, and I grabbed for Liri. My limbs shook, my breathing ragged and gasping, and when I would question her she covered my lips with a single finger. "No, there is no time to explain." As an afterthought, she added more gently, "It's not my place to provide you with answers. Now come, there is no time to delay."

Liri helped me dress in a plain gown and sturdy shoes then wrapped me in a long wool cloak. My trepidation continually increased as the rain lashed at the roof and the wind pulled at the window shudders. I was in no doubt that I was meant to go out in that demonic squall. Freedom tempted just beyond the door, but its thrill was tempered by the anxiety lancing through me with rabid viciousness. I had to be strong enough to embrace it; there was no question.

If the weather hadn't been daunting enough, I faced a physical challenge as well. I had been in Liri's care for about six weeks, and in that time, I still hadn't regained my endurance. The very act of dressing left me breathless, and as soon as Liri was satisfied with my clothing, I braced against the wall to rest. My freshly knit ribs ached from the pressure despite the wrap Liri had tied snugly around me to help stabilize the pain. How would I be able to move quickly enough to escape?

Satisfied that she had done all she could for me, she escorted me out of the tiny bedroom, and as I entered the outer room, I realized this was all there was to the house -- one bedroom and an outer room for everything else. I had no idea where Liri had slept all this time, but when I would ask her about it, she waved my concern aside. "What was most needed was for you to heal," and this was all I could get out of her on the subject.

She turned to me as we reached the door, to fuss over a few more details of my appearance, but I got the impression that the sundries weren't important. She wasn't quite ready to give me up. "Your horse is just outside the door. There is a man waiting who will help you mount. You are to say nothing, not even a single word, do you understand?" She gave me the instructions with confidence, but I could see the strain in her eyes. Something was gnawing at her. I searched her face, but there was no evidence of anything amiss, so I nodded. "Good," she continued. "It is very early in the morning, still not yet dawn, and the streets are empty. Because of the storm, the city watch will be keeping close to their stations, and this is why you must leave now. But," she added with a maternal shake of her finger, "it also means that if they should catch you, you will be even more suspect. It is essential that you keep quiet and follow your guide." She bent to the floor and picked up a strapped satchel. "Here are your things."

She opened the door and a dramatic peal of thunder rattled the heavy wooden door frame, echoing up and down the narrow lane beyond. I looked back at Liri, suddenly overwhelmed by gratitude for the woman before me, for her tender care and unconditional love for me, a stranger. Adyna and Emik, and now Liri.

"Thank you," was all I managed, though I wanted to say more.

She smiled at me then, a smile so broad and open to make her appear years younger than she was. She clutched at my hand and reached up to touch my cheek. "Faro í fridði, yar hátin."

"Who are you?" I asked on impulse.

She opened her mouth as if to speak, reconsidered, and then closed it again. With nothing left to say, she nudged me out the door and into the cataclysm. Two horses and the darkened shape of a figure waited just outside the door as promised. The man came around behind me and took me like a child in his arms, lifting me up to the horse. As I eased my leg over, I tried to make out the man's face, but it was too dark, his hood too deep, and the rainfall too intense.

Gingerly settling myself onto the saddle, I turned to bid a final farewell to Liri but with a pang found the door securely closed and no light or any other signs of habitation coming through the cracks of either door or window. My guide was mounted by now, so I turned back to the lane ahead. Our journey was begun.

◆ ◆ ◆

Life on the road -- the rigors of heat and sun, cold and rain, danger from bandits, the hardship of not knowing when or from where your next meal would come -- these were the things that hardened travelers learned to accept, even relished to the point of pride because they were the marks of a life lived on the edge, the badges of merit. Not for me. I preferred a warm fire, a full belly and a predictable life any day of the week.

Perhaps in time I would come to accept these conditions, for we hadn't yet ridden even half way across the city. No one had told me where we were going, or how long it would take to get there, but even if the distance was short, I knew that because of my injuries, it would require every ounce of energy I could muster, probably more than I possessed, and I clenched my teeth in determination.

I did my best to distract my mind away from the rain pelting my face, the fatigue nestling into every sinew of my body, and the dull ache that throbbed in all the leftover places. I thought about blazing warm fires, fresh bread, and soft cushions, but realized it didn't help my mood so stopped, studying the muddy streets and breathing in the smell of wet horseflesh instead.

I had just begun to realize the rain was slowing to a light drizzle, thankful for the reprieve, when my guide tensed and stopped. Bells tolled somewhere behind us. He threw a glance over his shoulder and kicked his mount forward. I couldn't be sure that I heard sounds of many booted feet pounding the cobblestones of the streets behind us, but I had no intention of confirming it one way or the other. Within minutes we turned into a narrow alley, past several yards and into a courtyard to our left.

My guide threw himself from his horse and immediately came to me, lifting me gently to the ground. I was powerless to react midair, but once my feet were firmly on the ground, I instinctually recoiled from his grasp, turning abruptly to shield my face. Phantasms of prison still haunted me. If he was shocked by my reaction, there was no way to know, for his hood was still pulled tightly around his face and the darkness of early morning made it difficult to see. He took a step backward, and obedient to our avowed silence, swept his arm toward a half-door, indicating I should go in.

It was pleasantly still and dry inside, smelling of clean straw, leather and oil. Piles of hay lined the nearest wall and short rows of stalls lined the farthest one. It didn't appear that anyone knew we were here, but the earliness of the hour made that inevitable. My guide pointed at a place in the corner for me to sit and wait. As soon as he left, I was overcome by exhaustion and dropped onto the soft pile of straw, letting my bag fall where it willed. Heavy of limb and tired beyond measure, I closed my eyes, drifting into a sleep deep enough to leave me untouched by my dark and shadowy demons.

◆ ◆ ◆

The heavy scent of wood smoke mixed with the savory aroma of breakfast stirred my senses enough to lure me into opening my eyes a crack. I was rewarded by the sight of a wall, a stone one, and not even a pretty stone one. While it would have been easier simply to close my eyes and pretend I hadn't awakened, my hunger pangs offered a strong enough argument against it. Gasping pitifully, I curled my legs underneath my body and pushed up with my good arm, eventually making it to a standing position. I willed my legs to walk towards the fire burning in an open hearth in the center of the room.

I eyed my companion, hiding my surprise, and took a seat as close as possible to the flames, grateful for the radiant warmth. I watched his hands as he continued to cook, unashamed when I wondered if the pan held enough food for the both of us, certain that it didn't. My greediness must have been too obvious.

"I've already eaten, if that's what concerns you." I was embarrassed by being found out, so rather than respond, I looked away, examining the room instead, realizing he must have moved me here from the stable while I slept. "Old servants' quarters," he said lightly. My eyes darted around the room, looking for doors and windows. When he saw the haunted look in my eyes, he added, more gently, "We'll be safe here."

"Jack, I..." I began, uncertain. A lifetime had passed since I saw him last. Where did one even start? Where had he been these last two months? Had he searched me out? Had he known I was in prison all along? Why didn't he come to Liri's house sooner to take me away? I was growing angry inside, didn't trust what I would say to him. Accusations hung just behind my lips, but I let my words dangle unfinished. Jack didn't deserve my bitterness... or did he? It was difficult to control the emotions I didn't understand: denial, embarrassment and shame mixed in various portions, guilt over Issak jumbled together with the visible and invisible wounds inflicted on me in prison. Seeing Jack again made it all the more confusing. He fit into it somewhere, though it was beyond me at that moment to figure out how. All of these thoughts went through my mind in a flash, but Jack remained oblivious to the turmoil that was in my heart and head so allowed me to lapse into silence, appearing unconcerned by my failed attempt to speak.

The food was fully cooked now, and he filled a plate then circled around to settle down next to me. Resting the plate on his knee, he cut the meat into bite-sized pieces. "Thank you," I said simply, remembering my manners. I looked down at my knees, uncomfortable with the tightness forming in the back of my throat. Before any unpredictable words could follow, I stuffed a bite into my mouth and chewed slowly.

By the time my food was gone, I had recovered my composure enough to take a good, thorough look at him, and the sight wasn't reassuring. He looked desperately tired, rings of care circled his eyes, and dark shadows smudged his cheeks. The shock of hair that normally obscured one eye hung limp, mirroring the fatigue in his shadowed eyes. I resisted the overwhelming urge to reach out and brush it away. For the first time it occurred to me that his weeks in Corium had done him no favors, and I felt a tinge of guilt over my anger towards him.

So much had changed, so much had been lost since I saw him last, and it remained to be seen whether or not I was redeemable. When he looked at me, did he see the same Kassia? He shouldn't. I wasn't the same Kassia. I asked none of these things. Instead, "How did you find me?"

It was his turn to look down at his lap, his gaze fixed on his fingers as they worried a worn seam at his ankle. "I arrived in Corium ahead of you as planned, and when I discovered your house had been ransacked, I immediately thought of Casmir." He looked up at me briefly to make sure I was still listening. I was. "I thought I would have enough time to find out where Casmir was staying, to see if I could learn anything, but..." he grew suddenly sheepish, his cheeks glowing with a flush of embarrassment. "...but I got lost. Couldn't find my way back to your house."

Anger flared in my eyes and he winced, wanting, I'm sure, to defend himself but knowing he would fail miserably. I ground my teeth with frustration as he continued, "I eventually made my way back, but I must have missed you. I didn't know what else to do so waited there. One day your friend Cai arrived out of breath. I was caught off guard, but he was completely unfazed by my presence, figuring out immediately who I was. He told me all about your landlord and the arrest." Jack's voice softened to a broken whisper. "After the guard took you away, he followed at a safe distance. When he confirmed you were bound for Mosrad Prison, he came racing back, knowing he needed to find me. It was risky going to your house, but he couldn't think what else to do."

He stopped his narrative and reached up to run his fingers through his hair, pushing the renegade lock off his forehead. "You were already in the prison by then, and there was nothing I could do about it." He looked at me quickly, wanting me to agree with him. What he said was logical, but I made no reply and his face fell, his fingers clenching at his boot ties. It was obvious that a war waged within him. "Kassia," he stammered, "if only I had been there sooner." Regret was thick in his voice. "I could have done something to save you from... everything..." He said the last word so quietly that I wondered if he was even talking to me or merely voicing his own private thoughts. Then with barely contained fury, "I wouldn't have let them take you."

He startled me with the last part, but my own thoughts and feelings were conflicted, and his words only served to upset me further. While his defiant declaration was noble, it had come too late. I was already a damaged, broken Kassia. I had been the cause of a good man's death, couldn't protect my sister from her captors, and had personally suffered a fate worse than death. My anger needed a target; I needed to put the blame on someone, and Jack was accessible. No, I had no words of comfort for him right now.

"The idea that you were in Mosrad... alone with those guards..." he fumbled for words, clearly uncomfortable and fighting to express his thoughts clearly. I wished he wouldn't. "...powerless..." I wanted him to stop. "...a woman..." I wanted to scream. The gorge rose in my throat and I couldn't listen to any more.

Just as I was about to tell him stop, I shifted positions, hugging my knees to my chest with my good arm. Immediately I regretted it. My tender ribs shrieked in protest, and I gasped. Jack reacted instinctively, reaching to embrace me. He was motivated by genuine concern, but he couldn't have made a bigger mistake. On instinct I screamed at him not to touch me, tearing away with a violence that surprised even me. I staggered a few paces away and stopped to face the opposite wall. I knew I had hurt him. If I turned around at that moment, I knew I would see surprise and devastation on his face.

"Kassia..." he began slowly, his words heavy with distress, but stopped, his confidence broken. I made no move to turn back to him and he said no more. Moments passed, and I heard him cross the room, open the door. "What did they do to you?" he whispered. "If you would just tell me..." His voice trailed off.

I wanted to turn to him, tell him... Tell him what? There was nothing to tell. Nothing had happened. Nothing that concerned him. Letting anyone in, to see my scars, the pain, both physical and emotional, was a risk I wasn't willing to take. It invited vulnerability, and vulnerability led to injury, injury to scars. I had enough scars already. No, it was better to lock my heart away, keeping it from prying eyes where it would be safe. Only then could I begin to reassemble myself.

"Whatever they did to you, it doesn't change who you are."

His words hung there, weighty and almost tangible, but still I didn't turn. He stood one moment longer and the door closed quietly. I was left alone to suffocate in my own pain.

◆ ◆ ◆

I loosed my hair and combed out the tangles with my fingers, struggling to re-plait the strands and failing miserably because of my arm. A few hours had passed since Jack left after our uncomfortable conversation. I was exhausted, so took a short, dream-free nap, waking to feel somewhat refreshed. Jack returned, finding me struggling to order my tresses without comb or brush. A light-hearted spark touched his eyes, compassionate, warming and disconcerting, and I dropped my gaze to the dusty floor, self-aware.

"There's water for washing when you're ready," he said hopefully. I was grateful and nodded. Washing had become a daily ritual for me since prison; I could never be clean enough it seemed. Jack looked relieved by my easy acceptance of his offer and sat down next to me, ostensibly free of any discomfort over our previous conversation. "I'll let Miarka know. She'll have to bring it here for you though. She and her husband would like you to stay out of sight."

He anticipated my question before I knew I even wanted to ask it. "Miarka and her husband are merchants. They live through there." He pointed at the door. "They would be arrested if anyone found out they sheltered an escapee, much less one as interesting as you." He winked at me and I flushed.

"How did you find me?"

He was clearly uncomfortable but answered anyway. "After I knew you had been sent to Mosrad, I sat on a barrel and watched the prison every day."

Before he could continue I cut him off. "You mean to tell me that the entire time I was in that place, you sat and watched it?" It was inconceivable.

"Yes," he said simply.

"Every day, for all those weeks?"

He nodded. "Nearly." This stark admission stabbed me in the gut with a pang of guilt. I had judged him harshly earlier.

"I tried not to draw attention to myself," he continued, "but someone noticed me. A man approached me one day, said I shouldn't worry about you. He told me to buy a horse and retrieve yours. Then I was to find the house of a certain merchant and her husband and wait for further instructions."

I looked at him doubtfully. What seems to be too good to be true usually is, and the stranger's solution seemed woefully too good. I was thankful he had listened to the man, but I wasn't sure I would have been so trusting had our roles been reversed.

He saw the doubt on my face. "I had no reason to trust this man, but I didn't have reason to distrust him either." I tried to appear more believing but wasn't successful. It was his turn to be irritated with me. "Kassia, what did you expect me to do?" When I had no response to this, he continued, "I did as the man said. After only a few days, word came to me by way of a letter. The time was soon, and I was to be ready to leave at a moment's notice."

"How convenient."

He flashed me another irritated look. "I would say so, yes, considering that you are now out of the prison. I'd say it was very convenient. If you'd like to go back to Mosrad..." I wiped the smirk off my face. Jack was right. What other choice did we have? "The man that contacted me by the prison came again last night. He told me it was time to leave then led me to Liri's house and disappeared. You know the rest. I don't know how we were discovered, but fortunately we were close to Miarka's, so I just brought us here."

"What about Cai? What happened to him?"

"After Cai gave me his news about your arrest, I saw him a few times afterwards, but within a couple of weeks, he disappeared. I haven't seen him since."

It was curious, but Cai was a unique boy, and I knew better than to worry about him. Another question harried me. "Assuming we actually had escaped Corium last night, where were we supposed to have gone, or did the man's good ideas end outside Corium's gates? I suppose we should find your father and then maybe we can figure out what to do next." I was so caught up in my wonderings that I didn't notice Jack's irritated look transform into one of surprise.

"Kassia, the man said you knew where we were supposed to go. That you had been given instructions?"

My head snapped up at that last part. "Did this mysterious man make any mention of exactly who was supposed to have given me these instructions?" Jack shook his head. Wonderful. "Just exactly who was this man? And for that matter, who is Miarka?" I indicated the room with a sweep of my good arm, "and why is she helping us?"

Jack's face looked pained. "There's not much help there, I'm afraid. Miarka and her husband are closed mouthed about it all. They won't tell me anything useful." Why did everyone have to be so infuriatingly mysterious? He saw my dark mood and offered hopefully, "Kassia, they are in danger because of us. We should be grateful."

He was right. Liri had been the same way. There was nothing left to be done but to figure out what I was supposed to know that I didn't know I knew. Or... something...

◆◆◆

The morning of our departure arrived. I sat perched on a stool as Miarka trussed up my hair in a way that made me feel ridiculous but which was a necessary part of my costume. I was to play the part of the wife of a middle-class man, Jack, and needed to dress accordingly. It was Miarka's husband who had come up with plan for our leave-taking. He felt that if we dressed to fit the part, we could simply walk out the gates, becoming one with the crowd full of other average citizens. The plan was brilliant in its simplicity.

We had been here several days. Since none of us knew of any reason for speed, Jack felt it would be expedient for me to rest a little more before we left. Miarka took great satisfaction in treating me as the daughter she'd never had, and plied me with food and sweets, clothing me in finery and making sure I had multiple baths a day if I wanted them. She never asked questions of me or my past but was always willing to offer whatever help or comfort she could provide.

Miarka was finishing the last pin of the last plait of hair when Jack emerged from another room dressed in his new finery. He stood in the doorway momentarily frozen to the floor when he saw me, a vastly different creature than I was, for now before him sat a woman dressed in an expensive sleeveless tunic of pale blue taffeta draped over a light saffron gown of soft cotton. I dropped my gaze to the floor, pretending I hadn't seen his moment of unguarded shock, giving him time to recover.

"We should probably be going," he said matter-of-factly, fastidiously interested in smoothing the folds of his new pleated jacket. I hid a grin. If he was uncomfortable with his new appearance, this son of an exiled metal smith, he didn't show it, was more muddled by my new persona than his own.

Miarka finished off the last detail of my hair by adding a small jeweled decoration then raised me to my feet, whispering, "Faro í fridði, yar hátin." It was that phrase again, the one Liri had used when I left her home. Her manner and intonation unnerved me.

"Thank you," I said, cautiously, and then added, "but what does that mean? The woman who tended me after prison, she said the same thing."

Miarka tilted her head slightly to the left and looked at me obliquely for a moment before saying slowly, "It means, roughly, 'go in peace'."

"Faro ee frii...doy, yar hatin," I said, stumbling over the words. It sounded similar to something my mother would have said, though she rarely spoke the tongue of her youth, before she married my father.

"Faro í fridði," she said again, this time even more slowly so that I would catch the words clearly.

I repeated the phrase once more and thanked her.

We found our horses waiting, lightly provisioned for our journey. Rose nickered at me in an unexpected welcome, and I put my palm on her velvety nose. Not wanting to show me affection for long however, she flicked her head to the side as if to say enough was enough.

The morning was delectable. Fresh air blew gently from the direction of the Bay of Bos, salt-tinged with a hint of sea life. High clouds drifted lazily overhead in wisps like carded wool. Scents of baking bread mixed with the green smells of fresh produce filled my nostrils as we moved through the streets towards the eastern gate. I did my best to appear accustomed to the courtesies paid me by those we passed, keeping my gaze level, smiling, offering greetings, and nodding when appropriate.

Despite the crowds, we made excellent progress, and, as expected, were shielded by the normalcy of our appearance. The stone crenel and merlon segments atop the gate had just come into view above the rooftops immediately ahead when I stopped, frozen in my tracks. Surprised, but very aware of my tension, Jack stopped too, looking to me for an explanation.

I spun on my heel toward him. "Kiss me," I said urgently.

"What??" His eyes widened into orbs the size of full moons.

Not having time to explain myself, I locked lips with him. Initially frozen with shock, he quickly relaxed and eagerly played his part. We would have words later regarding the earnestness of his role playing, but for now I kept watch over his shoulder as the crowds scattered, making way for a contingent of guards leading an expensively dressed tall man. Though I lived a thousand lifetimes I would never forget that face or the cold eyes looking out from it.

The retinue was nearly past us, and I wanted nothing more than to end our farcical embrace when another person caught my eye. Figor. I didn't know if he had seen me, but I threw both arms up around Jack's neck, ignoring the daggers of pain from my tender ribs, and pulled him more tightly to me. Jack was nonplussed, reacting with aplomb and a bit of swagger. Before I could completely shield my face, Figor turned and locked eyes with me. It was hard to tell if he looked at me with intentionality or out of sheer dumb luck, but terror struck at my heart nonetheless. Rather than react in any way, he turned his gaze away, a small smile the only indication that he had seen me.

Overcome with relief, I dropped my arms in pain, and gasping for air, pushed hard against Jack's chest so that he staggered back several steps.

"What? What did I do?" he cried, shocked by my abrupt action.

If I hadn't been so irritated by his enthusiasm I would have laughed at the astonishment on his face. He really was clueless. I rolled my eyes then turned and pointed at the backs of the retreating guards in exasperation.

"What about them?"

Still utterly uncomprehending, he stood there, his smile half-cocked, caught up in the satisfaction of his own male prowess. I rolled my eyes again, picked up Rose's lead, and continued on towards the gate, leaving Jack behind speechless and staring after me.

◆ ◆ ◆

We arrived at the settlement of exiled Agrians at the end of the second day still having no idea where to go next. A ring of faces lined the central green as we approached. Men, women, and children watched in silence as Jack helped me down from Rose's back. Weary beyond words, I refused food and collapsed onto a pile of furs inside Jack's hut; but rather than fall instantly asleep, my mind started racing as I tried to puzzle out our final destination.

I had lain there lost in thought for what seemed like hours when a scream shook me back to the present, though I realized almost immediately that the scream was my own. Emerging from the fog of my confusion, a warm, gentle hand reached out of the relative darkness and caressed my cheek, brushing back the loose strands of hair that had fallen across my face. It took all of my effort to remain still except to crack my eyes open long enough to see Jack crouching over me. Even in the failing light of dusk, I saw lines of care and worry chiseled into his face.

◆ ◆ ◆

Morning came quickly enough, and I painfully climbed out from under a pile of blankets, forcing my muscle-sore legs to move me out to the fire in hopes of finding something to eat. It had been too long since I last rode Rose, my mischievous horse, and the delicate skin of my thighs was once again marred by blisters.

Fire Woman tended the fire, only this time rather than watch me in silent inquiry as she had done before, she simply ignored me, paying more heed to the pottage she tended than to me. If Jack paid her to cook for him, certainly he got a discount for her less-than-charming disposition. Maybe she warmed his bed.

Since I hadn't eaten the night before, I was famished and would have eaten my arm except that there was food ready at hand. It didn't appear that Fire Woman was going to offer me anything, so I helped myself to the pottage she was stirring. She barely moved as I scooped a large portion into a wooden bowl and sat down. I had just taken a big bite when Rem and Jack approached.

Rem made perfunctory greetings, distracted by the heart of whatever it was he wanted to say next. "Kassia," he said cautiously as he lowered himself gingerly onto the ground next to me. "Jack told me what happened." Jack had seated himself across from me, and now his eyes darted to Rem as if in warning about something. Rem pretended not to notice. "The man who questioned you in the prison, you say he was with Casmir?" I nodded, agreeing that this was so. "He asked you questions about your family?"

It took an enormous amount of effort to force myself to revisit that room, reliving those moments in my memory. I closed my eyes and attempted to calm my breathing, to remember things as they happened, but immediately my mind's eye met the cold, malevolent eyes of the man with the dagger. Opening my eyes again, I sought out something to look at rather than to make eye contact with Jack or Rem and found an ant crossing the dirt at my feet, watched it make a circuitous path around a clump of dirt.

"Yes, he asked me about my father and mother. I told him they were dead." The words came out woodenly, as if I was disclosing news about the price of grain. "He seemed unimpressed, as if he already knew it all. Then he started questioning me about Irisa and a fire lit his eyes. I told him she was visiting a friend. Cai had already told me men from Casmir took her, but he pretended not to know where she was. I wasn't about to let on that I knew he was lying."

The fire crackled and birds sang cheerfully overhead, oblivious of the somber moods of the humans below. "He did ask me something else, as an afterthought, as he was leaving the room... before..." I stopped myself just in time and took a deep breath. I hadn't admitted to Jack what had happened after my interrogation, and I wasn't about to let it slip now. Rem looked at me expectantly, so I continued, "As he was leaving, he made a casual inquiry about metal-smithing." A horrifying realization flooded over me. "It was probably just a reference to Issak," I said, trying to sound convincing as I worked through the logic, "but it's possible he knows about you too."

I glanced around the clearing at the quiet people going about their morning chores. I had long considered my part in all of this, but it hadn't once occurred to me that the lives of these people might be impacted as well. The knowledge of what happened to Issak should have made me more cautious, but clearly I hadn't learned my lesson. "I wonder if my escape was fabricated, if he let me go thinking I'd lead him here?" I tasted bile in my mouth.

Rem didn't seem to be moved by this revelation, probably because he'd made the connection already. He picked up a stick and poked the fire, considering my words. After some time, he looked up at Jack and nodded. Jack rose from the fire and extended a hand to me.

"Kassia," he invited.

"Jack," Rem barked, shortly. The reproof seemed harsh. "See to your responsibilities." Jack didn't react negatively, instead, turned and offered his hand to Fire Woman who had been sitting by stoically during the entire exchange. She rose obediently and allowed herself to be led away as Jack made his way over to a man leaning against the doorway of the next hut over. My eyes followed the pair.

"You should have this back." Rem dropped something into my lap, and I picked it up without thought, fingering its familiar shape. My pendant. The one my father had given me all those years ago. Cai must have given it to Jack after he retrieved it from the warehouse. "Jack kept it all this time. Wanted me to clean it up for you."

I should have been ecstatic to get it back, particularly when I discovered that rather than a leather thong, Rem had hung the medallion on a delicate silver chain, but I was distracted and looped the piece around my neck without a thought. "Yes, thanks." My eyes hadn't left Jack and Fire Woman, so I didn't notice the way Rem studied me closely.

"Kassia, you should keep that safe. Never show it to anyone, do you understand?"

Forget Jack and Fire Woman. My head whipped around, and my eyes locked on Rem. "What did you say?"

"I said you should keep that safe. Never show it..."

"Yes, yes..." I said impatiently, "but how... why..."

Rem merely shook his head as he stood, ignoring my question. "Gather your things. We need to clear out. It's time to find a new home."

6

I WATCHED AS a young girl carried a wicker basket, struggling to keep upright as she floundered, taking cautious steps towards the meager pile of baggage the family had piled near a handcart. The girl's father was disassembling the family's bower, stacking neat piles of logs just inside the forest edge, to be used the next time the community returned to this place. The speed with which the settlement packed itself in order to move was astonishing, though it should not have been. They had lived as aliens in a strange land, having fled their homes in Agrius during the tumult of the throne-taking by the usurper Bellek. It was hard to say how many times they had moved during the past years.

The girl floundered again, and I held my breath as the basket teetered perilously. Taking on an impossible life of its own, it leapt from the girl's arms, landing roughly on the ground, toppling to the side. The girl screeched as the lid popped open and a puppy tumbled out, rolling once, then twice, and stood, bounding away from her as fast as its short, bandy legs could go. The girl set off in pursuit, but the puppy eluded her grasp.

I wanted to help her, but stayed my impulse. Rem had cautioned me to keep to the periphery. The members of the community were well able to organize and pack on their own, and he worried that I might upset the balance by offering to help where none was needed. It was a kind suggestion, though I suspected something else motivated him. Despite being accustomed to the potential perils of their lives, in this case the peril was brought on by someone from outside their ranks rather than their own actions. People had been kind enough towards me, and I had no complaints, but I didn't want to test the limits of their patience so obeyed Rem and kept to myself, measuring the passage of time under a tree, well out of the way of the bustle.

It had given me time to think more about what my benefactor intended for me. While I was grateful to have been provided with a way out of Corium, I had recently begun to wonder why I had any responsibility to do what I had been instructed to do. I was free now, beholden to no one and could go where I wanted. What obligation did I have towards anyone? Only towards Irisa, I thought with a pang of disappointment. The idea of staying with Jack and his people had tempted more than once; to do this however, would be to abandon my sister, and I couldn't do that. No, if I wanted answers, if I wanted to find my sister, I had to play along and follow the path that someone else had laid out for me.

Which brought me back to the problem at hand: where exactly did this path lead? Jack claimed I had been told what I needed to know, that I had been given some new knowledge... Realization struck me like a whip to the backside. My fatigue dissolved. I raced back to Jack's hut and pulled out the leather-bound book that had been a gift during my recovery. I had no idea what I was supposed to find but was now convinced that the clue was hidden somewhere within its pages. Daylight was nearly gone, so there wasn't much hope of solving the problem tonight. Tomorrow our journey would begin, and I hoped I would be able to study the pages as we went.

◆ ◆ ◆

"You called out last night, in your sleep."

I had dreamt of Issak again. This time it was only his eyes, serene and welcoming, suggesting strength and security. Most other times I dreamt of him I had nightmares, the scenes bloody and violent, my mind inventing visions of how he had died, as if I had been in the very room when he was beaten to death. I hadn't been there of course, had only heard Cai's second-hand story about what happened. But the dream I had last night was different. It was just Issak's eyes, watching me as I walked calmly down a barren road. And the dream had been silent. No voices, no noise, no sounds to accuse or threaten.

I glanced side-long at Jack. "Oh?" I pretended not to be unnerved by the notion, having no desire to discuss Issak, with Jack least of all.

"'Issak', you said." He tried to keep his expression open and casual, but his eyes were narrowed enough to hint at something else entirely.

We travelled two abreast because the road was very narrow, lined on either side by a thick cover of hawthorn and ash, the forest floor thickly carpeted with bush and bramble. Little or no conversation rose among the exiles, for most focused on the journey, sobered by the speed of departure. What little conversation there was to be had was hushed and brief. I had given Rose her head most of the time, doing my best to perch my book in front of me to read as we traveled. I had spent the morning hours reviewing the same text I had casually perused at Liri's house, paying no mind to the twitter of birds in the trees around us or the slowly thinning air as we climbed higher and higher into the mountain heights.

I had been lost in a text describing a large lake in the east of Mercoria, on the border with Elbra, when Jack interrupted my thoughts with mention of Issak.

Jack still studied me, but I refused to grab hold of his leading question. Knowing how intense my nightmares were, it's likely he had heard many things during the nights we had been together since Liri's house. I didn't want to think about my sleep and the restless demons which kept me from peace. I knew that Jack was disturbed by my thrashings at night, for on more than one occasion I had awakened in the darkness to find him holding me, his body protectively cocooning me as I fought through my terror. Morning always found him back in his own sleeping place, and though I was grateful, I didn't want to embarrass myself by acknowledging the intimacy of his actions. To do so would have shown weakness, would have forced me to confess to my powerlessness and need.

He sensed that I would give him nothing, so moved on. "So have you found our instructions?"

I shut the book with a thud and a sigh, needing to rest my eyes for a bit, giving them a rub. "Our instructions?" I asked, picking up on his word choice and its implication. Jack looked at me blankly, clearly missing the point I was trying to make, so I clarified. "'Our instructions' you said. 'Our' is a word used to imply more than one person."

"Yes, our instructions," he repeated back to me meaningfully.

"Kassia," he began with weight, "I'm going with you. Did you think I'd let you go off on your own?"

Yes, that is precisely what I thought, not thinking it necessarily a bad thing. Jack had no personal interest in my predicament, and I had already brought danger to this innocent group of people, didn't enjoy the prospect of involving any of them further, including Jack.

"I'm already involved," he said, as if reading my thoughts. "As to this group," he indicated the string of people winding their way up the mountain path just ahead of us, "they aren't immune to dangers of their own making. It's long been a way of life, and it would never occur to any of them to blame you, to send you off alone in retribution. Is that what you think will happen?"

That was some of it, yes. Rem had insinuated as much. But it wasn't the full story. I believed him in part, but I also noted that he glanced briefly in the direction of Fire Woman as he assured me of my blamelessness. Thankfully he didn't press me further.

"In a few days we'll come to a crossroads. We'll turn west from there, to make for the valley, so you'll need to decide before then which direction our path should take us, whether into the valley or east and deeper into the mountains."

We continued in companionable silence, each of us lost in thought for some time. I considered all he had said, lulled into a drowsing state by the rhythmic plod of Rose's hooves on the hard packed road. I felt myself nodding off, so reopened the book as a distraction and began to flip casually through the pages, finally stopping on the page displaying a brilliant map. Though I wasn't certain of the meanings of all the symbols in the drawings, I found the colors and patterns delightful. My eyes were drawn towards a large object in the middle of the map, the lake I had just been reading about. It was then that my eyes popped open.

"Jack, look at this and tell me what you see."

He took the book and studied the map I showed him. After several moments he looked up at me, his expression dubious.

"So?" I prompted him, barely able to contain my excitement.

"So... I see a map."

"And?"

"And... I see a dot... with a circle around it," he said flatly, unimpressed.

I screwed up my face with irritation, and he continued, "And... it's a small circle? Well inked, bold stroke, but still very small... That's about it," he said, his manner placid and serene, not catching the fire that burned in mine.

I sighed and relaxed, feeling myself go limp with fatigue. Yes, that was 'about it', a dot and a circle. Unimpressive. There was no telling for certain if this was my clue, but we had nothing else to go on, and I didn't know what else to do about it. Someone thought I might find the book 'useful', so it had to be significant. The solution had to be here. Jack must have sensed my frustration and, having nothing else to offer by way of an alternative, gave in.

"I'll see what my father thinks." And taking the book, off he went, threading his mount past the column of travelers, drawing near his father who walked in front, leading the procession. His persuasion must have been easily done, because within a very short time, Jack was back.

"My father knows this place. Even if we're wrong, if it's not where your mysterious benefactor would have you go, it's as good a place as any. You should be safe there." Jack handed the book back to me, and I packed it away carefully, a look of triumph trumpeting my satisfaction. "When we get to the crossroads, you and I will continue north and east."

"What about your father?"

"The people have always looked to him. They need him, and he feels the responsibility for their care. He'll go on with them."

I already knew this would be so, but it only added to my guilt. Jack would leave his father for me, and together we would go on to find answers in Islay Bay on the shore of Lake Allmor in Elbra. All would be revealed soon enough; soon I would be free.

❖ ❖ ❖

After nearly a week of slow travel along the steadily rising mountain path, we said goodbye to all the nameless faces I had never met. It was inevitable that by now each of them knew every detail of what had brought me into their midst as well as what now took me away, the son of their leader in tow.

I felt a pang of regret for the somber faces watching silently as Rem and Jack embraced, pounding one another on the back in enthusiastic male bonhomie, as if Jack was doing nothing more than sauntering off on a leisurely hunt for game rather than parting from him on an indefinable mission. Fire Woman joined Rem then, standing mutely beside him as Jack kissed her hand stiffly in parting. Rem watched on, eyeing his son meaningfully as he did so, and I felt a spasm of discomfort, averting my eyes. The feeling only left once Jack and I turned and put the group behind us. Since we were both on horseback, we picked up the pace, and it was with great surprise that I found just how much the last week of slow riding had helped me build up my endurance. From then on we rode many miles each day.

On a crisp, sun-splashed morning we broke the timberline in the first range of lower mountains, and the view was breathtaking. Behind us lay the thickness of the forest canopy and ahead lay rocky crags and outcroppings interspersed with thin copses of trees scattered loosely, all dotting a background expanse displaying another range of soaring peaks tall enough to become treeless at the tops and covered in snow and ice. I knew there existed lands regularly visited by such fierce elements, having a full season devoted to the same ravaging, frost-bitten winds and snow-blinding storms as those mountains, and I shuddered at the idea that people lived and survived in such climates. Thankfully our route would not take us into the second range of mountains, turning instead due east and into a plateau land, skirting the shoreline of the Anglera Sea on its south side until we reached the port town of Islay Bay.

We were not in a blinding snowstorm, but the air was colder and moister than the warm, dry climate of Corium, and I burrowed more deeply into my thick woolen cloak, pulling the edges more securely around me as I tried to still my chattering teeth. What to me was deep, penetrating cold was to Jack nothing more than a brisk day, and he let me know it by the open amusement he didn't hide. I ignored him and pulled the cloak around my ears even more tightly, shielding my face from him.

After only a day of travelling the ridgeline, we entered the Allmor plateau, a vast tableland that stretched from the Sidera Mountains east to Allmor Lake, and this soared my spirits nearly as much as the day I had found the clue to our destination, each milestone marking progress on my journey. Even my dreams seemed affected, for the dark demons of terror hadn't visited me since the night I had dreamt of Issak, the night we left the mining camp. Despite the constant wind, bitter and biting at our backs like an asp, it was easy to believe we had put the worst behind us.

It was late in the day when we descended the back side of a gentle rise, and with heart-stopping suddenness, the land broke away to reveal a deep gorge, the waters of a cerulean blue river surging far below and emptying into the Anglera Sea which twinkled to our right with the light of a million shards of the sun. Over the side of the gorge opposite to us, multiple waterfalls cascaded the edge of land, creating an ethereal veil of mist. I looked on with awe, expecting this magical place to bear a name which suggested the mystical qualities conjured here.

"Lynchport."

"What?" The name jarred my senses.

"Lynchport," he said again, pointing at the town clinging to the cliff face as if it had talons, its buildings lined up one by one along a narrow road winding down the steep side to the flat ground at the river's edge.

I laughed, thinking the name suggested something dark about its history. "The name makes me think that they used to..."

"Hang people?" Jack cut in. "Yes, they did. Quite a lot of them actually." Jack watched me take this in, amused by the look of horror I couldn't hide.

"What, here?" I asked incredulously. "This place is too beautiful for that." I shook my head, unable to connect the image of a gruesome hanging with the utter beauty of the landscape. Rose stomped her feet in the soft earth, impatient to be standing at such a great height when the offerings of a warm stable and fodder tempted. I patted her neck in consolation, still pondering the revelation.

"It's long had a reputation for being a den of robbers, a haven for pirates and other colorful creatures. But don't worry; those things don't happen here anymore. Much." He winked at me and prodded his horse forward before I could reply.

As we wound our way down the cliff face along the narrow and twisting road, Jack explained to me that Lynchport was a busy port, making use of the protection of the mountains to the north and the natural deep water cove. Goods would be carried from here upriver to all parts of Mercoria as well as to Elbra and Pania via Allmor Lake. He and his father often came to Lynchport, to trade or to gather news, so he was well enough familiar with the place.

The waters of the busy port below sparkled, alluring me into a stupor of awe. All manner of seafaring vessels anchored in the bay below, and I was surprised to see the vast difference in size, shape and quality of these vessels, representing a diversity of traders from all over the world. Nothing I had seen so far made the place resemble a den of robbers, though neither did I see anything yet to demonstrate the opposite -- that the wealthy would find a deluge of comfort. Jack assured me that there was plenty of comfort to be found, no matter a traveler's taste. He said this last with a smirk but I chose to ignore him, keeping my eye on the narrow road ahead because I didn't trust Rose for even a moment, could imagine myself tumbling off her back and careening down the side of the cliff into the river. I wished I was riding a sturdy pack mule instead of this mischievous mount.

The farther we descended the cliff-side, the more the land broadened out, revealing variation in both quality and style of housing. The shadows were already lengthening, and as there was no other option, we decided that Lynchport was the most likely place to spend the night. We had been on the road for so long that the idea of sleeping in a real bed was quite appealing. We were far enough from Corium that our risk of being identified was small.

"I know just the place. It's farther upriver from the bay, but that way it will be quieter and away from notice."

We arrived at the inn and were greeted by two boys who eagerly took our horses to feed, water and stable in exchange for a small coin a piece. The inn was two stories tall, solid-built with heavy timbers, and bright with whitewash, a welcoming patch of flowers growing just outside the door. Jack pushed open the door and we were immediately greeted by a lively man with a significant paunch, a barrel chest, a wiry mustache and a bald head. The top of his head barely reached Jack's shoulder, but his demonstrative manner nearly knocked me over.

"Welcome to the Buxom Maiden!" he said, his arms open wide as if to embrace us.

I eyed Jack but resisted the urge to respond to the welcome. If I was to play my part, I had to go along with whatever came my way, no matter what, including allowing Jack to take the lead in our little performance.

"Sir," the innkeeper continued, "you and your..." he paused as he looked at me, a question and hint of suspicion in his eyes.

"Wife," Jack offered helpfully, putting his arm around my shoulder and giving it a squeeze with a touch too much enthusiasm, a cheeky grin firmly in place. "Just wed in fact." I resisted the urge to stomp on his foot.

"Ah, very well!" he said, his effusiveness returning. "You are most welcome here. Most welcome indeed!" He winked at me and I forced a smile. "It so happens that my best room is available for you, cozy and romantic with a nice view of the waterfall."

This time I couldn't restrain myself and shot Jack an indignant look. He didn't notice, merely continued to bargain with the innkeeper for good price on our room, a meal, and an extra blanket, all "to maintain appearances," he told me later. The innkeeper took our things and disappeared upstairs while I found a seat in the public room. For his part, Jack went to check on the horses to see that they were given a proper stabling.

A short while later we sat down together to a superb meal while Jack explained that he thought we ought to spend two nights here as it would give me a chance to rest up and would allow him to see to the repair of his horse's harness. He offered his reasons a bit too brightly, but I was inclined to go along with him. Why invite more nights on the road rather than enjoy another night in a soft bed?

A small group of men in the corner pulled out pipe and whistle and began to play a lively dance tune. Other patrons rose with enthusiasm to dance and clap along, and Jack seemed inclined to stay and partake of the fun, but when he caught me stifling a yawn, he rose from his chair and, with a gallant pose, offered me his arm. I didn't argue, took it and allowed myself to be led upstairs.

We found our room easily enough, and I was just about to comment that the "finest room in the inn" was likely nothing of the sort, but rather an excuse to take more coin when Jack opened the door. As it swung inward, I gasped. The room was larger than I expected, large enough to hold the usual amenities as well as a small brazier bright with hot coals; though even more awe-inducing to me was the wooden wash tub next to the brazier, filled to the brim with steaming water. I turned my slack-mouthed face towards Jack who had already brushed past me, not noticing my reaction. When he finally did turn to see me still standing in the doorway, he smiled a cat smile and shrugged, playing off his gallant gesture with a carefree response as though the appearance of the tub had nothing to do with him.

"When the innkeeper's wife heard we were newly wed, she insisted that you use her wash tub. I could hardly turn down that kind of offer could I?" I very much doubted that the tub had been the innkeeper's wife's idea, but I decided to let it go. If he didn't want my appreciation then I wouldn't give it to him. "She said it's laundry day tomorrow so we can only keep it this one night unless you want to help the laundry maids?" His eyes twinkled as he spoke.

Jack took my silence as evidence of belief and reached behind me to close the door. It was then that I also noticed the bed. One tiny, narrow bed barely wide enough for a broad-shouldered man to lie face-up. I had been too interested in filling my empty belly earlier to think much about the sleeping arrangements. Jack saw my discomfort, but took it only as fatigue, or as reluctance to bathe with him in the room.

Bathing raised its own set of problems.

It was only later, after I'd managed to fix up our extra blanket as a make-shift barrier between the bath and bed that I luxuriated in the warmth of the water in the washing tub, imagining Jack sitting cold and uncomfortable on the bed, waiting for me to finish. It was hard to summon up much sympathy; this was his scheme, and now he could suffer for it. I took my time, and, when I decided Jack had languished long enough and the water had cooled sufficiently, I rose from the tub, dried off and dressed. Pushing aside the blanket barrier, I intended to ask Jack where he planned to sleep the night only to find him sprawled out over the entire width of the bed, snoring softly.

I scanned the room, verifying what I already knew: that there was no other sleeping place, not even a chair. Inching my way towards the bed, I tentatively reached out and grasped Jack's forearm, shaking it gently. He didn't move. I leaned over him, grasping both shoulders, and shook him again. Still nothing. Finally I leaned in close, putting my mouth next to his ear. "Jack," I whispered. Without so much as a twitch beforehand, both of his arms came up around me, and he flung me onto the bed beside him, nestling against me in a way that left me powerless to move. Like a rat caught in a trap, I lay frozen from shock and confusion.

"Jack..." I began, embarrassed and irritated at the same time.

"Nairin..." he mumbled into my hair which was wet and dripping onto his nose.

I had no idea who this Nairin was, but she was not me. I was not her. I tried to dislodge myself from his arms, but he was too strong for me, and all I could do was lie there, staring helplessly at the ceiling, waiting for him to roll over again. With not even a blanket to cover myself, it promised to turn into a long cold night. These thoughts occupied my mind for a time, and just as I was about to drift off to sleep it occurred to me that for the first time in weeks my ribs did not hurt. I smiled.

◆ ◆ ◆

I awoke the next morning to sunlight streaming in through the thick glass of the small window, lying on my side facing the wall, and perched on the very edge of the bed, free of the heavy weight of Jack's arm around me. I sat up, noticing that I was the sole occupant of the bed. Jack lay curled up on the floor near the cold brazier, covered with the spare blanket, his cloak pillowed under his head. A pang of guilt knifed through me. I had slept very comfortably all night and was well rested but I wasn't sure Jack would be able to say the same.

Thinking to let him rest as long as possible, I slipped out of bed then quietly dressed. The door opened and closed without a sound, and I made my way to the common room below then out into the morning sunshine. A glorious sight met my eyes. The sun shone fully now, over the lip of land high overhead, piercing the cascades of tiny waterfalls on the far side of the gorge across the river and raising a veiled mist, thus painting the wall of the gorge with a myriad of rainbows that shimmered with an aura of beauty worthy of bard-song. I shook my head in disbelief. This town deserved a better name, and I wondered how the citizenry accepted it so casually.

I had no idea how much longer Jack would sleep and I was very curious about the town. Surely a little walk wouldn't do any harm? What could possibly happen?

The Buxom Maiden was upriver from the bay, and it took me several minutes to walk there. I wanted to see the ships in port, to see if they were similar to the ones that made port at home, so headed first for the quay. The largest of the ships were docked out in the middle of the deepest waters of the bay, with smaller skiffs ferrying people back and forth to land. Medium and small ships docked alongside wharfs, and sailors were busy loading and unloading, climbing, lifting and hefting cargo with ease.

I purchased a plum from a fruit vendor and bit into its sweet flesh, trying my best not to let the juices ruin my fine clothes. I was deciding what to do next when I heard a familiar voice, freezing me to the spot.

Immediately across the boarded walkway stood a tall man with a thin face, gray hair that receded slightly at the temples, an aristocratic nose which only enhanced the patrician appearance of the patterned and quilted jerkin he wore over his light linen shirt. The same wide leather belt I had seen before hung a dagger I would never forget, could never forget because it haunted my dreams; for emblazoned on its hilt was the sun emblem, the sign of the Royal house of Vitus of Agrius. I nearly choked on my plum, dropping it instead. It rolled behind a barrel and I bent to retrieve it, casting my face into shadow.

"Captain Veris, we can't possibly have the gallows ready for your use before the end of the day. It takes time, and we haven't used it for so long..." The voice was high-pitched and sniveling, reminding me of a juvenile rodent.

"I have no time for your excuses, my lord reeve. We are setting sail on the tide, and the deed must be done before then."

"That's high-reeve, and I'm not a lord, my lord... I..."

"We are returning to Prille where my Prince awaits, and I expect to be able to dispense with my prisoner here before we go. Nothing will prevent it." Captain Veris raised his perfectly gloved hand and pointed a finger at the reeve who tried to look uncowed under the hard look of this cold man. "I will not be delayed by the trivial excuses of the high-reeve of a backwater town. Prove to me that this village is called 'Lynchport' for a reason."

"Yes, my lord," the man replied miserably, swallowing hard. I could hear the dejection behind his words then heard him shuffle his feet as the group moved off.

I stood with my newly retrieved plum in hand, though it was now covered in a thin film of filth. I was just considering whether to toss it or buy a new one when the voices carried back to me, and this time the words were significant. "Sviene is a suitable name for him, no? This particular pig has been greedy for too long, and for taking my prize away from Corium, he will pay with his life." There was a pause in the conversation then, "No one is to touch the girl, do you understand? Not even in fun. She is bound for Prille under my personal care." He added meaningfully. I dropped the plum again, though this time for good. The voices were softer now, and I strained to hear more. "Her sister... managed to slip away, but... use for her... Casmir..." Their words had faded, but by now I had heard enough. Swine was about to be hanged, and Veris had Irisa. I had to find Jack.

I had not even so much as turned to leave when I sensed a shadow loom over me, felt a body presume to press up against me from behind. "Care to go for an early morning swim?" A hand snaked out and began to explore my contours. "I hear the water is quite stimulating this time of day." His foul breath was rank on the back of my neck and his hand had worked its way up my body, was now toying with the chain holding my medallion. I never had to deal with these kinds of problems when I wore my thieving clothes.

"Oh," I purred as I turned to face him, a smile sweet on my lips, "not as stimulating as this..." I pressed a knife to his groin. There was no doubt that he knew exactly what I threatened, and as his nostrils flared I could see panic wash over him, watched it throb at the pulse in his neck. He dropped my medallion, letting it dangle freely down the front of my gown. "I am no easy pickings, you bastard," I hissed venomously, my eyes hard as granite. But rather than stumble back and away as I had hoped, he gathered his nerve and made a quick swipe for the knife, though he wasn't quick enough, and my grip was secure. I felt the blade bite deep into flesh and sinew as I pulled the knife clean away. His eyes were wide with both shock and pain, and as he began to cradle his injured hand, I brought my knee up hard between his legs. Instantly the man doubled over, vomit spewing from his mouth.

Just then I noticed a dirty beggar sitting with his back against the wall only a few feet away. He stared at me in mute astonishment, and I acknowledged him with a nod of my head and a honeyed smile as I tucked away the medallion then wiped the knife clean on the backside of my attacker. Concealing it carefully away inside my sleeve, I turned and walked casually away as though nothing had happened.

To anyone watching, I appeared calm, but the reality of it was that I was reeling inside. To be touched in such a way, to hear the crassness of his insinuation, all of it worked to dredge up a slough of memories which both sickened and angered me. I felt a twinge of nausea at the thought, but swallowed it away, leaving only the phantom pains of my healed injuries.

My mind's eye imagined what happened after I left the scene: my attacker rose from his puddle of vomit only to stagger away cradling his mutilated hand against his bloodied shirt. I had seen the man's livery; he was under the command of Captain Veris, and he had seen me, but more importantly, he had seen my medallion. He would go back to his cohorts to tell an exaggerated version of the truth, and though my identity may have meant nothing to him at the time, it was possible that others would piece it together once his story was told. If finding Jack wasn't urgent before now, the stakes had just been raised.

◆ ◆ ◆

I had never been behind a waterfall before now. What appeared ethereal and mystical from a distance was something altogether different when one was on the other side. Behind me stretched a cave going back much farther than the feeble light would reveal, so I could only imagine what lay in its deepest parts. I tried to set aside all the stories I had been told as a child, of trolls and nymphs and other fantastical creatures living in places no human should venture. A cool, damp breeze tinged with earthy smells of moss and damp soil wafted gently through, and I recalled myself back to reality, grounding myself in what I could see and hear. My wait in this place could go on for some time yet, and it didn't do to dwell on wild imaginings.

After learning the vital news about Swine and Irisa, I all but ran back to the inn to find Jack. He wasn't waiting patiently in our room as I half hoped, but was crossing the common room towards me with a sour look on his face instead as I came through the main door. Without so much as a word, he grabbed me and dragged me to a far corner, his fingers digging into my arm, likely producing bruises where his grip was a vice. Astonished patrons watched on, some with looks of surprise, some with amusement and knowing smirks.

"Kassia, what are you trying to do to me?" he seethed. His face was no more than an inch from mine, and his fingers continued to dig into my upper arms in his anger. I winced in pain and he must have realized what he was doing so relaxed his grip, if only a fraction. His complexion was red and his eyes squinted. Rather than remark on this, I swallowed my retort and did my best to look contrite.

In the calmest manner I could muster, I explained everything

I had overheard and everything that had happened, neglecting for obvious reason, the knife incident, deciding he needn't worry unless it became an issue later. When I finished, Jack looked up, noticed pairs of eyes watching us. Rather than continue our conversation in public, we retreated to the privacy of our room to discuss our options, eventually coming up with a minimalist plan. No, not even really a plan. Rescue Swine then rescue Irisa. That was it. I didn't give a fig for Swine's life, but his involvement with Irisa begged explanation, and right now he could tell us more than we knew.

It was no difficult thing to discover where Swine was being held. He was Veris' prisoner, awaiting his time at the gallows and secured by chain to a post just off the main market square in a holding area close to where the gallows were being hastily erected.

It had taken an enormous amount of charm on my part, but I had been able to talk Jack into allowing me to go with him to Swine's holding place. I had no idea what he had in mind, but I wanted to be there. We both changed out of our finery and into plain attire then together set off to free the pig.

"Kassia, this is going to be easier than I dreamed." Jack's smile was broad and confident, a dimple pricking his left cheek. Two men watched Swine, one hovering near the prisoner while the other lolled at the narrow entrance to the holding area. Jack turned to me then, brushing away the lock of hair from his eye as he did so. He stepped near and pressed his hands gently to my shoulders. After a long, searching look, he said. "Remember what I told you. Wait for me behind the waterfall, but only until sunset. If I'm not back by the time the sun disappears behind the rim of the gorge, leave without me." His face softened and he paused, as if considering his next words. When the moment had grown over-long, he said quietly, "Be careful." I got the impression he meant to say more, but something held him back.

He did manage a quick squeeze of my hand before jumping the pile of crates shielding us from the street and striding over to the lazing guard at the mouth of the holding area. Though his back was to me, I imagined a broad grin spreading across his face. He talked with the man for some moments, and the two laughed over a joke.

Everything looked a picture of burghal camaraderie, just two men swapping stories at side of the road. If I hadn't been watching carefully, I would never have noticed Jack pull the dagger from his belt then bring it up cleanly between the man's ribs, just under his heart, with a quick and powerful thrust. I mentally staggered backwards, shocked by Jack's brutal action, that he could kill so effortlessly, so coldly. I had no idea what he had planned, but certainly this was not it. Yet there it was.

Jack eased the man, who had never uttered a sound, down to the ground and arranged his arms in such a way to hide the hole in his chest. With a swipe of his hand, he closed the man's eyes.

The guard closer to Swine appeared alarmed initially but grew unsure when Jack shrugged, his body language remaining friendly and casual. I imagined that he still smiled companionably, confusing the guard even more.

This time there was no conversation, no banter or small talk. With alarming speed and deadly accuracy, Jack's dagger took the guard by surprise. When the man was eased to the ground, Jack grabbed the keys to unchain Swine, who had watched everything unfold before him, his eyes wide and unblinking. Yanking Swine to his feet, the men hustled across the street towards me.

"Irisa is on board Veris' ship," he said to me as he quickly bound Swine's hands with strips of cloth. And to Swine he said, "You're going with her," pointing at me, "and you're going quietly."

Swine stared at me in even greater shock than he had been in when his guards were murdered. Perhaps he thought I stood before him as a ghost. "Hello, Swine," I said lightly, a smile bright on my face. It was sardonic but sweet, and Swine was speechless.

Jack cut in before I could say more. "If I find out later that you so much as sneeze to get attention, I will personally see to it that you live out the rest of your days as a eunuch." He gave the knot an extra tug to make certain the binding was secure.

"Jack, how do you plan..."

He didn't give me time to finish my question. "Kassia, just go. Hurry." He looked grim, and his eyes pleaded with me to cooperate. A knife of worry sliced through me, but before I had a chance to say anything more, he was away, and I watched him until he disappeared into the crowds.

Turning my attention back to Swine, I smiled thinly. "Here." I dropped a rolled up cloak over his hands to hide the binding. I then pulled up my sleeve a fraction to reveal the hilt of my knife so that he understood matters perfectly.

"Nothing to say?" He looked down at his feet. "Good boy. This isn't like you, this whole not talking thing." I gave him an infantile pat on the head. "I noticed the improvement immediately."

Spinning him around, we headed out of town and to the waterfall behind which we now waited. I did my best to ignore him. I wanted to know all he knew but realized there would be time enough later to interrogate the greasy son of a hedgepig. For now I was content to let him sit against the cave wall, his arms and legs tied, mouth gagged.

We hadn't been waiting long at all, so I was surprised and somewhat unnerved when I heard the sound of someone approaching, shuffling footsteps over the scree covered floor. I swung around to face the newcomers, hand on knife, only to discover Jack picking his way towards me. To my great relief he looked unharmed; but to my great surprise, rather than Irisa, he brought with him Cai.

7

IT WAS EARLY evening by the time we left the relative protection of the cave behind the waterfall, and wanting to use as much daylight as possible, we set aside conversation in favor of haste. It wouldn't take long for Swine's escape to be noticed, and because there were only so many roads out of town, it wouldn't take interested parties much time to determine which one we had chosen. Jack took into account the risk of our being followed when he chose our route, so chose a path that was nothing more than a game trail following the river north and then east. He hoped that its narrow width would minimize any disadvantage we had in being outnumbered by our pursuers. There was simply no room to maneuver.

We set a strenuous pace, riding straight through the first night and the entirety of the next day, stopping only to water the horses and to relieve ourselves. By the time dusk fell full on the second day, the horses were barely able to put one foot in front of the other.

The humans of our party were no less exhausted, and none of us had energy enough to hunt or fish for fresh meat, so after getting a fire started, we settled instead for dry provisions from our packs. Weariness invited immediate sleep, but the heat of countless burning questions scorched my tongue and needed escape before I could succumb.

As Swine held answers to my questions about Irisa, if not other things, he was my target. Before I launched myself at him however, I searched around for a stick.

"Swine," I said, poking him with it. He flashed irritation but quickly concealed it behind a mask of resignation. "Why did you take Irisa? Back there in Lynchport, Veris said you took her." His fleshy eyelids were heavy and drooping, giving him a houndish appearance. When he looked down, keeping his mouth firmly shut, the effect was minimized. I straightened my spine, losing patience. "You had me imprisoned because you said you didn't know where she was, you corpulent little prat..." I was very close to jumping on his head to throttle the brass out of his buckles. Yes, I wanted to hurt him, but we needed answers, so decided it wasn't the right time. Maybe I would settle for poking his eyes out after he told me a few things. "You had her the entire time! When you had me arrested, you had her!"

Jack perked up at this, the hint of barely concealed animus behind his eyes. He was looking for a good fight but held back for my sake. Swine only looked sullen. To demonstrate his willful obstinance, he stuffed a piece of hard, stale bread into his mouth, bulging his cheeks like the greasy hedgepig I had accused of being his sire.

"Well?" Jack growled, his voice pitched low with menace. "Answer the lady."

Swine maintained his mulish silence, and I lost all patience, rose over him and smacked him on the back of the head. Caught by surprise, his head snapped forward, and he spat out the bread. I was about to do it again, having had a taste of the pleasure that hurting him had given me, when Jack forestalled me. "Kassia..." he said, shaking his head almost imperceptibly. He was right. I took a deep breath to calm myself and backed down.

Swine rubbed at the spot I had hit him. There was something new on his face, a semblance of warped admiration for my waspish temper perhaps. "From the Agrian Prince he was, from Casmir. Out of Corium I was to be taking her," he finally admitted. "But it after you to prison," he added with a hint of smugness, as if sending me there had been a long-due reward for him.

I ignored his haughty posturing and grabbed on to what was most important right now. "Who was from Casmir?"

"Man who forced me to take her."

"Why? What were his reasons?" I dripped. Why would Casmir torture me in prison but have Irisa taken out of the city, and by Swine of all people? It made no sense.

Swine shook his head. When I threatened to stand up again, he added quickly, "My life. He threaten... either I take girl or he kill."

"Irisa? He would have killed Irisa?" I asked.

"Not the girl, me!" he replied, incredulous at the thought that someone had dared to threaten his life.

"What about Cai? Why was he with you?" I asked Swine, but when he didn't answer I looked to Jack.

"He found me when I went to find Casmir's ship. He didn't go along with Swine and Irisa, he was following them."

I looked over at Cai who had curled into a ball and fallen asleep immediately after we'd made our hasty camp. I'd have to ask him about his part in all of this later. "Why would Veris do this?" I wondered, partially to myself.

"It no Veris," Swine said adamantly.

"What do you mean no Veris, you..." I calmed myself as I spoke, though it took an enormous amount of effort. We needed his cooperation, and he was finally offering something without having it beat out of him first.

"Figor he was," he said simply.

Figor. The man that hired me back in Corium. This man Figor was getting curiouser and curiouser, and now I believed he was the key to everything.

◆ ◆ ◆

"It was too simple."

It was late, and we should have been sleeping. Jack sat entranced, his eyes locked on the flames of the dying fire as he spoke. Cai lay frozen as a stone in the same place he had dropped when we first made camp, and Swine was lying on his cloak motionless, presumably sleeping. I watched Jack watch the few remaining tongues of fire as they pulsed in a bed of bright orange coals, plumes of smoke drifting up and up, higher and higher, to be lost in the dome of night sky, inky with blackness and pricked through with pinpoints of light. I inhaled the comforting scent of wood smoke as I waited for him to continue.

"For a man concerned that his prisoner be hanged before he sailed," Swine shifted ever so slightly at that, "he most definitely changed his plans quickly enough since he was gone before I had a chance to rescue Irisa."

Absently my hand sought the medallion at my neck then,

pulling it free of my tunic, I felt its comforting contours, traced the incomprehensible lines with a single finger. Swine shifted positions again, and when I looked over at him saw him watching me closely.

"Sajen," he said simply.

"Swine, your mouth is moving. Sound is coming out. This is never good."

He ignored my retort and continued. "Bedic Sajen... spirit at peace," he mumbled groggily then closed his eyes again.

I was stumbling over the name when Jack spoke. "The son of Nikolas, deposed King of Agrius." It took me a moment to focus on his response because he had spoken so softly.

"Swine," I said bitingly. He eyes shot open in fright. "What about Sajen? What made you say that?"

He raised a finger and pointed at my chest. "The bennu. On necklace."

I looked to Jack for confirmation of this, but he didn't seem to be paying any attention. "Jack?"

"I don't know, Kassia." He shook his head slowly. "I was too young. If it was the symbol of Prince Bedic's house, I don't know about it."

"How would my father have gotten it?"

"It's hard to say." He shrugged. "Tokens like that are often handed out in recognition of a service done."

"But that means my father would have known the prince, at least in some way." It was an interesting thought, possibly explaining Figor's finding me in Corium. Maybe it even hinted at my father's mysterious past. If I was correct in my assumption that he had stumbled upon something important, perhaps it had been information beneficial to the old King Nikolas and the token had been given to him as thanks. There was just no way of knowing what it was, and Swine certainly wouldn't know anything about it.

Jack seemed less impressed than I was. "Kassia, there really doesn't have to be a mystery as to why your father had it. Such tokens are given commonly enough."

True. There may have been many such medallions in

existence. But I had never seen another and had always been led to believe that its possession was significant. Why would my father have told me to keep it a secret otherwise?

Jack still seemed distracted, changing the direction of our conversation. "Kassia, did anyone happen to see the medallion while we were in Lynchport? When you were out for your morning walk perhaps?" He looked at me suspiciously. It seemed I had to tell him what happened at the quay, with the guard. So I did.

"You WHAT??"

I wasn't sure if it was the knife part of the story that made him uncomfortable or the fact that I was accosted. Maybe it was both. I wasn't keen on either part of the story myself, to be honest.

"So both Veris' man and the beggar on the street saw the medallion..." Jack began carefully, trying to comprehend.

"Yes, but you said so yourself... these things," I touched the surface of my tunic just over where the medallion was now tucked safely away, "are insignificant."

"I never said they were insignificant!" He was upset now. "I said it was no mystery that your father had one!" His voice had risen in both volume and tone.

"But there have to be others in existence. I can't have the only one." I countered, half-heartedly.

Jack gave me a wilting look. "There probably are more, yes, but how many people flaunt them? Kassia, Casmir is a prince whose father came to power through treachery and violence. His people fear him. Do you honestly think anyone who owns one of those is going to be quick to parade it? Or give one to a child to bandy about? If they had any sense, they'd have kept it locked away in a box, buried in the ground rather than be handed out to be worn as appropriate jewelry!"

While there was truth in his words, the insinuation that my father had lacked sense when he gave it to me made me bristle, and I glared at him with bodkins for eyes.

He didn't seem impacted, continued without missing a stride: "King Bellek has spies, and undoubtedly the longest standing order from his illegitimate reign is for all of his henchmen to be on the lookout for something just like that. It's why my father's somewhat vocal opposition to Bellek keeps our people in such danger."

I couldn't be certain, but there seemed to be a hint of bitterness in his words, as if his father's opposition to Bellek was not wholly acceptable to Jack. Perhaps it wasn't the opposition itself so much as how he went about expressing it. It was something to be probed later; right now I was more incensed over why he was focusing this anger on me because of it.

"Jack," I seethed, trying to keep my voice level so I wouldn't wake our companions, "my father specifically told me to keep this medallion a secret. It's always been hidden, and only once have I not worn it since he gave it to me -- the day of my arrest," I spat, "until your father gave it back to me at the mining camp. As it turns out, it was a good thing I wasn't wearing it that day or else it would have been taken away from me after tying me immediately to whatever is going on."

"Well in the end it didn't matter did it?" he said snottily. "As it was he got the armbands, enough to connect you to the Sajens when he sold it to Casmir." It was an unfair accusation, and I flicked a look at Cai to make sure he was still asleep. "It just proves that you weren't careful enough! How can I protect you when you are so careless!"

"I never asked for your protection," I cut in with lethal hostility, though he acted like he hadn't heard me and kept going.

"The armbands, your interrogation and escape... It's a wonder the whole of Casmir's guard isn't on our tail."

He stood and paced away from the fire, reaching up with both hands to brush over his hair.

His anger towards me was incomprehensible. Still I was willing to excuse it. We were both exhausted beyond belief, and the added stress of our situation made us each say things that should have been better expressed or held back. It was his next comment however, that caught my breath and held it ransom.

"...never mind your dalliance with that guardsman in Lynchport..."

It was a low blow, and he knew it. Though I had never told him specifically what had happened to me in prison, he was a smart person, and Mosrad was no different than any other prison the world over. I didn't imagine Jack to be the kind of person to shoot such a verbal bolt, and I was shocked into silence, letting his words hang in the air, unchallenged. It would have been so simple for him to apologize in that moment, but he didn't. Instead he strode farther from the fire until he was completely out of the reach of its flickering light and into a place shrouded in darkness. The air took on a sudden chill, but its icy fingers didn't touch me. I had already retreated within myself, into the walls of my bastioned heart.

Miserable but not wanting Jack to see, I lay down facing away from everyone, pulled my cloak about my shoulders, and closed my eyes. A small rock lodged under my hip, and I used the discomfort to focus my attention away from my anger, considering it a more appealing distraction from the dark thoughts that were threatening to invade my mind, for I would be hard-pressed to close that door once opened. When the rock lost its power to hold my attention, I called to memory the face of my father, then I remembered my dreams of that brown pony running through fields of wildflowers, imagined myself upon its back. Happy.

◆ ◆ ◆

Dreams of the men came again. I hadn't seen their faces for many weeks, but my argument with Jack had drawn out their ghosts. My body ached with echoes of my abuse, dull throbbing with twinges deep inside, building all the way to the surface of my skin and manifesting as sensitivity at the touch of the fabric drawn tightly across my chest.

I hugged myself as tightly as I could then cracked open my eyes so that only a bit of the morning sunlight could peek through my lashes. I was trying to decide if this day was worth the effort or not, for I was numb towards Jack. Though my bed of hard ground and coverlet of woolen cloak was not as luxurious as the lovely bed at the Buxom Maiden, right now it seemed more appealing than another day of hard riding on an overloaded horse in the company of an unsympathetic companion.

Deciding there was no way to escape the inevitable, I

managed to get up and found Cai already awake. He had been fishing and had a nice little breakfast already prepared. Both Jack and Swine were still asleep, and I had no intention of waking either, so I ate in silence. As so often was the case, I felt an overwhelming need to be clean, so when I finished, I picked up my cloak and tucked my knife into its folds thinking to keep it near me in case I needed it.

I was just turning to leave when Jack spoke. "Where do you think you're going, alone, without protection?"

The sting of Jack's calloused words last night didn't hold my tongue captive this morning. I swung on him in defiance. "And what business is it of yours to be concerned?" He had yet to sit up, was still lying under his blanket with his eyes closed. Only now did they open, and I continued, "So now you are my protector?" He sat up at that. Cai eyed us momentarily then quickly dismissed himself, pretending to be interested in something far from us. My blood was up and I gave Cai's leave-taking the barest of notice. "I don't need your protection. What good has it done me so far?" I spun around and stomped off towards the stream. "Besides, I have my knife," I muttered the last bit, not sure and not caring if he heard me.

Jack set off after me, grabbing my arm from behind. "Kassia..."

I shrugged him off before spinning to face him. "I was imprisoned, Jack. Where was my protector then? I was alone and faced a humiliation you cannot even begin to imagine. Fought off two men and lost." I took two steps backwards, away from him. "They beat me, Jack, and they had fun doing it." My hands started to tremble as my sight turned inward, my voice shaking but losing none of its force. "When they were done with that, they each took turns... they..." I cut off a sob and squeezed shut my eyes, stopping the tears threatening to come, then bit my tongue so hard I could taste blood. It was the closest I had come to admitting to anyone what had happened. Knowing the tide would roll over me in uncontrollable waves if I let it, I countered with the only thing sure to stem the tide. Anger, defiance. My eyes snapped open again, fiery and fixated on his, "I live it again and again, Jack. In my dreams. They come at night, they came last night in fact, and I can't stop them. Where were you then, O Great Protector?" I spat the words. "Safe. You were safe, Jack. And free. I didn't need you then, and I don't need you now." I spun on my heels and stalked away. If he could wound with words, so could I.

My anger hadn't abated, but neither did I feel like continuing our verbal sparring. I wanted, needed, a bath. Finding a rock to hide behind, I undressed. Jack had followed me at a distance, and even though he kept to himself, his presence unnerved me. "I'm going to wash now. Keep your eyes to yourself." It wasn't as if I was particularly shy. I knew how it was between men and women, had learned to see without really seeing. But everything had changed inside that prison. Some things were best left unseen. "No watching. I'll know it if you do."

"Don't worry, I won't," he said softly. He sounded contrite, though it did nothing to move me.

The water was crystalline, blue and cold, and as I entered it, my skin pricked as if with thousands of tiny daggers. I shivered instantly, yet deeper I sank, wanting nothing less than complete immersion, seeking a cleansing that remained elusive. The piercing sharpness of the cold incited my senses at first, making me feel alive, vibrant. I closed my eyes and dropped completely under the surface of the water then floated there with the world shut out, entombed in the silence of a watery grave. After several long moments, the sharpness of the cold numbed me until I lost all sensation in my extremities, a poetic contrast to the dull heat of pain in my heart.

◆◆◆

Cai was a bright and cheerful boy, always had a smile and a good word for everyone, and I had never once seem him crabby or depressed. He loved life, and his joy was contagious to anyone lucky enough to meet him. Yet this morning he was subdued and nearly invisible, tended to the packing of our camp like a mouse in the shadows.

"Cai, thank you for following Irisa." I had come up alongside him immediately after returning from washing, wanting to distance myself from Jack. He accepted my gratitude with a nod but kept working. "No, I mean it." I stilled his hands with mine and made him look at me. "You didn't have to do that, but you did, and it means a lot to me."

He nodded again with a slight blush to his cheeks, and I wondered suddenly if perhaps my sister had an effect on even the youngest of males. "She needs looking after, Kassia. There wasn't anyone else, so I did it."

"But how did you know where to find her? Last time I saw you in Corium, you had no idea where she was."

"I didn't know where to find her. It was an accident, really. Jack was watching the prison, so I watched Swine. One day a man came to his house with someone. It was Irisa, but I didn't know it then because she was cloaked, and I couldn't see her face. When the man left alone I was curious so kept watching Swine's house. I kept watching, and after a week or so, he left with the woman, packed like he was taking a trip. It was when they were leaving that her hood slipped and I saw her face. I didn't have time to find Jack, so I did the only thing I could think of. I followed them. They were just to Swine's waiting ship when Veris captured them and took them on board his own ship instead."

"But how did you follow her if they left Corium on a ship?"

The impish light I knew all too well lit Cai's eyes as he said, "I snuck aboard, hid in the stores, even in the ballast when I had need. When we reached Lynchport, I heard two sailors talk about how Swine was taken ashore, so I snuck away again to try to learn more. That's when I found Jack, but by the time we got back to the ship, they had just set sail."

Only Cai could pull off something like this. If Emperor Ciasan ever needed a truly effective spy, he could do no better than this young orphan.

He continued on, explaining very matter-of-factly and devoid of emotion how he then happened upon Jack, and it occurred to me that he sensed my morose mood innately. When he finished, I hugged him again in wonder, and he went about his duties with a subdued sensitivity that endeared him to me even further. Even Swine was unusually docile this morning, though I couldn't resist the urge to poke him with a stick several times when no one was looking. He said nothing in reaction, just moved away from me, resigned to my provocation.

We were on the road very quickly and made as good a pace as could be expected with our fatigued bodies and horses. The hours passed by in silence. Neither Jack nor I had much desire to talk to the other, wanting to cover the miles as quickly as our overburdened horses could handle. Trees skirted with thick undergrowth lined the edges of the road with unrelenting monotony, making it difficult to get an accurate gauge of how much distance we had travelled since morning. Despite the coolness of the earlier part of the day, it was now midday, and the sun beat down from high overhead. The air had thickened, and there was little breeze to cool us.

It was clear we all needed a break, so with mutual need we stopped, but not before Jack could scout out grass and water for the horses. After several minutes, he returned and led us to a place not far off the road, behind an outcropping of rock, and into a small clearing where there was plenty of grazing for our two horses as well as a ready supply of fresh water from a brook which murmured through the trees on the far side. Others had used this place as a camp. Charred stubs of wood lay scattered inside a ring of stones in the middle of the clearing, and with a ready supply of good kindling from the old-growth trees hemming us in, Jack had a small fire started without much hassle. Cai slipped off immediately to hunt.

My body's healing was well on its way to completion, but from time to time I felt the ache of my knit bones keenly. Today was one such day. I rubbed my forearm and flexed my hand to try to ease away the ache. Cai had not yet returned with meat, so Jack and I were left with only Swine for company, and he seemed disinclined to conversation, had slipped into a catatonic state against a tree trunk on the far side of the clearing. The melodic strains of his snoring wafted over us as we sat together doing our best to ignore each another.

Or so it seemed to me until Jack chose to break the blissful state of conversation-avoidance by speaking. "Kassia, we really need to talk about that necklace of yours."

I wanted to poke something, but since Swine was sleeping, and I wanted to leave him in that state, I poked the fire instead. "What about it, Jack?" I did my best to keep my tone level, but I wasn't sure I had been entirely successful. I reluctantly forced a somewhat brittle smile on my face in an attempt to appear cordial.

"They know you now. Veris seems to know more about this mystery than either of us, and he knows you by sight. Even if he had been plagued by ambiguity before, there is none now. That necklace could only add to your problems if you keep it. I've been thinking about this a lot, Kassia, and I think I should hold on to it for you. They don't know me."

I couldn't hide my doubt. "But if they've already connected me to whatever they've connected me to, it won't matter. And besides, you're traveling with me. Any number of people saw us together in Lynchport, and anyone could have seen us taking Swine with us when we left."

"We don't know any of that for sure," he interrupted, "but we do know for certain that they know you, and that medallion has already put you in danger. Holding on to it could cost you your life."

"As it could yours." I stared at him and he stared back. "Jack, I don't know why my father gave it to me. I don't know why he didn't sell it or trade it or bury it for that matter," I said pointedly, "but I do know he gave it to me, said I should keep it safe." I was still angry with Jack, but the heat of my anger had mostly dissipated, leaving a numb chill in its place. "He also told me to trust no one with it. I'm sorry, Jack, but that includes you." It was a silly thing to say. Jack had the medallion in his possession for a time in Corium, had given it to his father later to be fixed, who in turn had returned it to me. That wasn't the real issue. The real issue was far more complicated, but I didn't want to admit it.

As he listened, Jack fingered the hilt of the sword he had stolen in Lynchport before our escape. It lay across his lap, providing a good place to focus his attention as he considered his next words. Finally he looked up, and in a voice that didn't try to hide his hurt said,

"After all I've done to help you? After all the jeopardy brought to my people in Heywood? You still don't trust me?"

His words, rather than irritate or incite me to a predictable caustic response, tugged at my conscience. My mind was muddled, and all the troubles and pain of the past several months froze my tongue.

"Kassia, do you trust me?" He asked again more insistently, not willing to let me avoid the question.

I didn't answer, continued to poke the fire. The stick I used was sturdy though short, could have been a child's walking stick perhaps. One end was charred, as if someone before me had used it for exactly the same purpose I used it now, except that the previous fire-poker probably wasn't having a conversation like the one Jack and I were having, one laced through with shadows and demons, and colored by themes related to dead parents, jewelry inheritances, deranged princes seeking vengeance, questions of trust. No, these things just happened to me, it seemed.

I laughed a bitter, broken laugh. Trust. It all seemed so simple to Jack. Did I trust him? The truth of it was that I really didn't know. I didn't think it was even about Jack, at least not specifically. Trust him with my necklace? Yes, I trusted him with that, and I knew that's what he was asking. But his probing opened up other possibilities he knew nothing about. Did I trust him with my vulnerabilities? No, I didn't think I could. I didn't think I could trust anyone with those. Ever. Did he know I lived in constant fear? That what those men had taken from me in prison was far more than anything physical? That I would never feel secure again? To admit to this, to trust someone else with this knowledge would be to submit the last semblance of power I had, and I wasn't ready to give that to Jack just yet.

My reverie was broken by sound of jangling tack. I turned just in time to see two mounted guards wearing the livery of Prince Casmir enter the clearing. The relief mirrored on their faces made it clear that they had been tracking us. Jack reacted instantly, jumped up with sword in hand ready to defend us, though neither guard seemed overly perturbed by his show of defiance. The nearer of the guards dismounted without regard for the length of steel in Jack's hand and began to advance on me, rope in hand. It was the guardsman from Lynchport, the one whose hand I had mutilated when my blade was pulled from his ill-considered grasp. He had no reason to love me, and I panicked, taking an involuntary step backward, finding it difficult to hide my fear. My mind wanted me to fight, to race at him with blinding speed, knife in hand, unconcerned with the outcome. My mind knew I couldn't stand there helpless, knew it was either him or me, preferred it to be him. But my body disagreed. I was paralyzed by fear.

Jack had no such inhibitions, but when he would have made his move, the second guard still sitting his horse snapped a crossbow to his shoulder, took deadly aim at Jack who immediately stayed his hand. "Drop it." Jack obeyed, though his eyes never left the guard who was now well into the process of binding my wrists behind my back. Jack remained frozen in place, using all the good sense the gods had deemed fit to give him.

Satisfied that his knot was both tight enough and painful enough, my captor spun me around to face him. He flicked a glance at his buddy with the crossbow. "Oy, Brac... Just how steady is that arm of yours?" He had a sneer on his face, one both belligerently confident and menacingly suggestive, and I stopped breathing. Out of the corner of my eye I saw Jack's fist clenching and unclenching, his face red and rage-filled. "Do you think you can hold him for a few more minutes while I get what's owed me?" The man stepped in close, his breath coming hot and fast.

The trees and clearing faded, and I found myself back in a dark storage room with a throbbing head and painful arm. Leering gap-toothed faces spun before my eyes, circling like vultures. I could hear their coarse laughter and lewd jests. I was exposed and vulnerable. Tears wet my cheeks.

The trees and clearing reemerged with blinding speed when the guard shoved me to the ground, and I landed painfully. My head snapped back against a something hard, and I saw flashes of hot color dance before my eyes. A shadow loomed over me.

A harsh voice pierced the horror. "Long enough for you to do what you're told. You know your orders. Don't give me cause to report what you've done and the same be done to you in return. She belongs to Captain Veris now. Best think on that."

I heard a grunt of disgust then felt a rope tighten on my ankles. Clarity of vision returned, and I had a moment to observe our captors. The one on horseback still held the crossbow steady, fixed intently on Jack. The disgruntled one, the man who now had even more to hold against me, retrieved another rope, presumably for Jack, which meant that at least for a time they intended to keep him alive. This gave me a small measure of hope.

I was just beginning to wonder what had become of Cai when, without explanation, the crossbow fired, its bolt slicing through the air and imbedding itself with a meaty thwack into the tree behind Jack. In startling succession the guard who had fired the bolt fell from his horse, landing heavily on the ground at an odd angle, breaking his neck with a sickening crunch. The other guard froze, just as astonished as me by what had just happened. It was only then that I saw Cai step out of his hiding place from the cover of the trees. He held a slingshot, and it was spinning wildly. With a flick of his wrist he let fly a projectile, hitting the other guard with deadly accuracy, dropping him to the ground.

When he was certain we were safe, Cai freed me. I stood and assessed any new injuries, rubbing the back of my head and the rope burns on my wrists, glancing over to see Jack standing near a tree, still looking dazed and confused by what had just happened.

"Jack, did you see that?" I laughed out of sheer relief, thanking Cai for his fortuitous arrival by engulfing him in a hug likely to break his bones. "Cai, where did you learn to sling like that?" So euphoric was I that I didn't immediately take notice when Jack didn't share in my delight. When I realized he wasn't celebrating, I turned to him. "Jack, I..." I froze, and my smile fell. The dazed look on his face had not disappeared, and his pallor had deepened. "Jack?" He still stood by the tree, unmoving, unspeaking, and his hands trembled. I took several cautious steps toward him, and it was then I noticed the crossbow bolt sticking out of his side.

"Kassia," he whispered, "I hate to alarm you, but we have a

problem." His breathing was quick, shallow.

I closed the remaining distance between us and dropped to my knees in front of him, eye level with the shaft of the bolt now pinning him to the tree. I reached out to touch the bolt, letting it hover just a hairbreadth from the wound instead. "A problem? By the gods, Jack..." I looked up into his face to find him smiling down at me. It was thin and colorless, but it was a smile nonetheless. I was no physician, but even I knew that arrow wounds to the gut were usually fatal. There were too many vital organs in the body that didn't react well to perforation, would bleed uncontrollably until the person died a slow, painful death.

I wasn't willing to give in to the reality of this fate for Jack. "We need to get this out."

"No, leave it," he whispered raggedly.

"Why would we do that?" I asked incredulously.

"Because if you pull it free, it's hard to say what damage you could do," he strained. "You could cause more injury to whatever this thing has lodged itself into, and I quite like my parts more or less intact." The half smile was still on his face, and he tried to maintain a sense of levity about the situation, but I could tell that he was in great pain and quickly losing his ability to stand. I hated to think what would happen if his feet buckled under him.

"You do need to break off the shaft though, where it pins me to the tree. Use the knife in my bag. Be quick..." For the first time I heard desperation in his voice.

"Kassia, I can get something from the forest, some moss to stop the bleeding." Cai didn't even wait for my approval, darted off on his errand before I could reply. I was relieved, to be honest. The notion of causing Jack any pain wasn't appealing, and I knew that this procedure would hurt exceedingly. I didn't really want Cai there to watch, and likely he didn't either. I didn't begrudge him of it. One of us had to do it.

When I returned with the knife, I found that Jack had closed his eyes, but he was still standing motionless. "Here, drink this." I handed him a wine flask I had found on one of the dead guard's horses.

He readily accepted it, and drank greedily. "Ready?" I didn't really know if I was ready, but the thing had to be done. Taking a deep breath, I sawed through the shaft as quickly as the tight space allowed. Once finished, I eased him to a sitting position against the tree trunk. Jack had done admirably well during the entire procedure, hadn't so much as uttered a groan. Smiths were made of sterner stuff than I knew.

Several moments passed. "Jack?" No answer. I moved in closer, put my face right in front of his, my hands on his cheeks. "Jack??" I called again, a little louder this time, but still with no response. My heart nearly seized in my chest. "No... no... no, no, no, NO!!!!! Jack..." I grabbed his wrist, sought his pulse with my fingers as I had seen Jeah do so many times in my youth. It was there. He lived. I sank back drained and exhausted, closed my eyes and leaned my head against the tree for a long moment before grabbing the wine flagon I had given Jack. With shaking hands, I took a deep draught of the ruby liquid, spilling half of it down the front of me in the process. I wiped my chin with my sleeve and took a deep, steadying breath.

"Kassia?" Cai had returned so silently that I startled. "Here is some moss." He kneeled down next to me. "Is he going to be okay?" His voice sounded so small, his question so plaintive that it was tempting to lie to him.

"I don't know, Cai. I just don't know." I sighed then grabbed his hand, gave it a squeeze. "But we need to remove this bolt. He's sleeping now, and there's no better time to do it."

"But he said to leave it!"

"I know," I said grimly, "but it will have to be removed at some point. And besides, he wasn't really in a good position to judge the situation when he said it. I'm not an expert, but I don't think it hit anything vital." Cai looked at me skeptically so I pointed out the fact that the shaft was lodged in his left side between his ribs and pelvis, angled towards his back and perforated just the edge of his torso. Most likely it pierced only muscle. "It will not be an easy wound to heal, and it will be painful, but assuming he avoids infection, I think he'll recover."

I hated to defy Jack, but I thought he would suffer more if the bolt was left in place for someone else to extract later. On a more immediately practical note, the natural sway from riding a horse would be overwhelmingly excruciating with the bolt in place.

Since the tip had been cut off and left embedded in the tree, I grabbed the nearer end to me at the fletchings. Bracing myself with one hand on the tree and the other on the bolt, I pulled slowly but firmly until the shaft came free. Jack didn't move or react, but he did grunt in his unconsciousness. We bound his torso, and when I surveyed the results, I knew we had done our best.

Satisfied that there was nothing else to be done at the moment, I lay Jack down as comfortably as I could and took Cai with me to search the guards for any items that might be of use to us. We considered taking their chain mail but decided that it wouldn't be worth the effort. Since there was nothing else of value on the actual bodies, we searched their horses, but found nothing more than extra provisions and weapons in addition to the horses themselves.

As we were stripping the horses of all signs of Casmir's livery so that no one would have cause to accuse us of murder and theft, Cai noticed me eyeing the sling tucked into his waistband. "Pigeons. They taste good, and a slingshot is the best way to kill 'em. You've gotta have good aim."

"Thank you again, Cai." He shrugged, as though saving lives was something he did every day.

When finally there was nothing left to be done, I turned to survey our little clearing and realized with a sudden horror that I had forgotten about Swine. I scanned the area frantically, hoping that the ponderous moldwarp hadn't chosen to run off in the midst of the chaos when I found him, curled up under the large overhanging boughs of an evergreen tree, snoring peacefully, clearly having slept through all the chaos. I poked him with a stick. "Get up, you clodpate, before I poke harder." He hopped up as quickly as his corpulent little self could manage. "We need to get Jack on his horse and I can't do it without help." He looked around at the carnage before him with confusion but did as he was told.

"Jack, are you awake? Can you hear me?" I touched his cheek

and he opened his eyes. He was still very pale, but at least there was no sign of fever. The next day or two would be a good indication of how he would fare overall. "We need to get moving, and you need to get up. Do you think you can stand?" He closed his eyes again, as if summoning every ounce of determination he still possessed, and with my help, stood.

"Swine, crouch down and let Jack use you as a ladder." He looked aghast at the notion. "Do it! If you value your miserable life..." I think he was tired of being poked with a stick so complied.

The process took an inordinate amount of time, but we eventually managed to get Jack seated more or less securely. I mounted behind him in order to keep him steady as we rode, and with Cai in the lead, our austere party set out. Within moments Jack's head lolled down onto his chest and his weight sagged fully against me. On impulse I stretched up to plant a kiss on the back of his neck and was quite surprised when he squeezed my hand in response. We had to make it.

◆ ◆ ◆

Dusk was falling faster than Swine's hairline, and there was no indication that we were anywhere near a village or settlement out here in the middle of the forest wilds. Jack had long since lost his battle with consciousness, the stress of riding thinning what remained of his mostly depleted endurance. It wasn't so long distant that I was made to flee on horseback, nursing a body still in recovery, and the memory of it made any hopefulness I may have begun to feel drain away along with Jack's endurance.

Defeat. It wasn't a word I was familiar with. Even after my unspeakable treatment in Mosrad Prison, I still maintained a desire to fight. It wasn't the same now. Something about the wound being Jack's rather than my own, combined with the fact that I also felt responsible for Cai and the paunchy knotty-pated maggot named Swine made the entire experience too much for me. I felt overcome and opened my heart to despair, let it wash over me without apology as we finally gave in to the night and made a hasty camp. I didn't even bother to start a fire, not welcoming its cheer. Once I settled Jack, I curled up all on my own, away from the others. The night was not as brisk as it had been up in the plateau land west of Lynchport, but even so, it promised to be a cold night for me, for I had given Jack my cloak. I fell asleep with tears wet on my cheeks, unashamed should anyone see me, knowing no one would, not caring if they did.

8

MY UNCOMFORTABLE AND restless night came to a swift end when morning arrived with predictable consistency. Black outlined treetops stood watch over our sleeping place in the shadow of the sun's rays filtering through the cracks in their tops. The sunbeams were penetrating and effusive, but altogether too cheerful and I was too miserable to derive much comfort from them. Reluctance weighted my limbs, yet there was a task at hand; Jack needed a healer. With great effort I arose and shook the stiffness from my arms and legs. Cai wasn't there, had likely gone in search of food. Swine still slept. Jack lay motionless where I had left him last night. I sat down near him and tucked my legs under me, studying him. He lay peacefully, a vision of serenity in stark contrast to the violence of the previous day. On impulse, I reached out and gently brushed back the hair from his forehead. He stirred but didn't rouse.

"Jack, I'm sorry this happened," I whispered so that only Jack and the air around us could hear. "I'm so sorry, and it's all my fault." A tear broke free of my lashes and rolled down my cheek unhindered. "You should have listened to me, should have stayed with your father and let me go on alone." I grabbed at my skirt and twisted the fabric between my hands, wringing it as if doing so would choke out my misery. My tears flowed in a steady stream now, but I made no move to wipe them away. "If only you knew what happened to me, you might have listened, might have known I wasn't worth the effort..." My voice was raspy and broken, constricted from the battle that raged within me, the battle which currently went in favor of my misery. "Jack, I am an orphan, have no one and nothing to call my own. Why? Why would you bother with me? I'm damaged and broken, not worth it." My nose was running freely. "And now this..." I gestured at his wound as if he could see me, as if it would prove my point.

Why was it always easier to deal with one's own misery rather than witness it in others? -- my mother's painful death, Jeah's sudden and inexplicable death, my father's disappearance and now Irisa's, Issak's brutal murder, Jack's injury -- I couldn't be blamed for what happened to my mother, Jeah, or my father, but I could take responsibility for the rest. If not for me, none of them would have suffered. These were burdens I would carry all my life, and I didn't see any way to escape it.

"Kassia!" Cai broke into the small clearing with such speed it was a wonder he didn't fall flat on his face. I was shocked out of my bleak confession by the suddenness of his appearance and drew the back of my hand hastily across my face to wipe away all evidence of the tears before he could see. If Cai noticed the redness and swelling of my eyes, he didn't let on; his excitement was too overwhelming. "A settlement! Just beyond the next hill!"

"What?" I leapt to me feet along with my heart, my tears forgotten. "How big?"

"Large enough to have a sturdy palisade with a fortified gate, but there's something odd about it."

"What do you mean, 'odd'?"

"Come see."

I glanced down at Jack, but he was still quiet and unmoving, and I knew he would be fine. Swine snored on and likely would remain that way until we woke him, as was his way most mornings. I cast a fleeting look around the camp to locate our weapons, saw that they were where they needed to be then patted my sleeve to assure myself that my knife was securely tucked up my sleeve. It was. I had long since decided that Swine was no physical threat to us. Even the sliminess of his actions the last time I had seen him in Corium had somehow paled after all I had experienced, but I still remained cautious enough to safeguard our weapons and money in case he ever got it into his head to run, taking our supplies with him.

"Okay, show me," I said finally.

We set off together, though Cai scampered ahead of me like a fawn. I was more cautious, picking my way over fallen logs and tangled underbrush, not interested in falling and reinjuring my newly repaired body. After a short while we climbed a small rise, and from a break in the trees at the top saw smoke rising from a settlement across a flat expanse of trees in a low lying area, just as Cai had promised. It was difficult to tell how large the settlement was for the thickness of the forest which came right up to the edge of the sturdy wooden palisade. Trees were usually cut back a good distance from a fortification so that attacking enemies could be seen and dealt with immediately, but not so this settlement. Cai was right; it was odd, though for more reasons than I could easily identify.

We returned to camp, and when I tried to wake Jack, he stirred but didn't fully rouse. I was immediately alarmed, so felt his cheek, relieved to find that it was warm but not hot with fever. "Jack?" I brushed my fingers lightly over his forehead then held my palm to his cheek. His lashes fluttered, his eyes opened, and he smiled weakly. "It's time to leave. We found a settlement and we hope they have a healer."

With laborious effort Jack stood, and we left our hasty camp, leaving no sign that we had been there, save for a small scorched spot on the earth which Cai kicked over with dirt. We were a fragile group, injured, fatigued and despairing, except for the ever-optimistic Cai who led us along the stream, thinking that we might find a bridge and thus a road towards the settlement.

"You don't need to be sorry," Jack whispered after a while. We had been walking in silence, and I had been focusing all my energy on supporting him with one of his arms slung over my shoulders. His whispered words surprised me. I stared at him, uncertain that he had actually spoken, but he met my look and continued, "Not damaged or broken..." He stretched out one finger and brushed my cheek, tracing a line. So he had heard my candid confession earlier. I looked away embarrassed, pretending to scan the edges of the forest for footpads or for a fabled single-horned axolot from the nursery tales of my youth. We trudged on.

Cai's optimism proved itself when not much farther ahead the road split. We took the left-hand path over a small, rough wooden footbridge, continuing along an extremely narrow trail. Eventually the path opened up and widened then elevated from the forest floor with steep banks on both sides, a curious element until we noticed that the ground on either side was saturated with standing water. Symphonic sounds of marsh-dwelling creatures filled the air, and I startled at the sound of several large splashes not far from the path, shuddering to think what might have happened had we tried to navigate this path in the dark.

The air was thicker here, moist and heavy. My thoughts turned fanciful and tinged with ominous foreboding, as if we were being watched, like the very shadows were sentient. I scolded myself for being absurd yet noticed that the horses had similar thoughts and had begun to nicker and toss their heads nervously. "Cai, keep a firm hand on them. If they decide to break away, there's no getting them back."

The path curved subtly left at first then sharply, and as we emerged fully around the corner, an imposing gatehouse greeted us. The gate was shut, and no one was about, either atop the walls or the gatehouse itself. I studied the palisade to the left and right and realized now why it didn't matter that the tree line came right up to the walls - the marsh did too. And if the large splashing sounds I had heard earlier were any indication, no sane person would ever consider attempting to gain entrance in any other way than by this gate.

I glanced at Cai who also examined the walls, and then to Swine who gave no indication that he cared. He seemed more interested in his next meal, was presently digging through his pack for something to satiate his hunger. Jack leaned on me more heavily now, and I knew his strength wouldn't last much longer. I hated that we had been forced to come here, hated the guards who had tracked us and who had shot Jack, hated that this was the only settlement we had come upon, and that our lives were dependent upon the good will of whoever lived here. I was no fortune teller, but something about the place made my hair stand on end, and it didn't take great powers of intuition to know that Cai felt the same.

"Hello?" I yelled at the deserted gate, but there was no response except for the chorus of frogs chirping around us. I swallowed back the bitterness I felt because of our need, wanting to make things better, infuriated by my inability to change the circumstances, and frustrated by the fact that help awaited behind these locked gates. The silence was heavy and leaden. "Hello?" I yelled again with more fervor, trying to repress my rising panic for Jack's sake.

I was preparing to make yet another call when a wicket in the large door of the gate opened and a man appeared. He loomed in the doorway momentarily, watching and scrutinizing before shouting: "Hver ert pú? Hvao vilto?"

It didn't sound like he was inviting us to dine, but neither did he seem hostile. Taking a wild guess, I offered up our identity. "I am named Kassia," I patted my chest, "and these are my friends," I indicated at my travel companions in turn, "Cai, Swine and Jack." He didn't need to know that Swine wasn't a friend. We could get into those subtleties once we were well enough acquainted to pass around a flagon, slap each other on the back, and assimilate blood feuds. For now... "My friend here," indicating Jack, "is injured. We need help. Do you have a healer? Then we will be on our way."

The man didn't immediately speak but stared at us menacingly, like a carrion bird hunched over a branch waiting to pick the bones of a dying creature. I couldn't make out what he was thinking, and I glanced at Cai who watched on in the same state of mind as me, curious yet anxious and nervous that we would be turned away. Finally the man raised his arm, motioned us forward. I was relieved but also apprehensive to walk into this swampy fortress of doom. For while the settlement promised a hoped-for healer, I couldn't shake the feeling that something dark and disturbing awaited us.

"Fylgiden mér," he said and continued to motion with his arm then turned to walk away. By the time we filed through, horses and packs included, our guide was far ahead of us, though the idea that we could lose him didn't prevent me from stopping in my tracks as soon as we passed through the gate. Stone-paved streets spread out in a grid pattern, wide and open, lined with people, animals and carts. This was not remarkable. Every city, village or town was the same. What was remarkable, and what had stopped me, were the earth mounds lining the streets, the tops of each reached by steep steps cut into the sides of the mounds. It seemed that nothing existed at ground level other than the streets themselves, for every structure in the settlement perched high atop one of the individual mounds.

The construction of the wooden palisade was very unusual too. While made from typical material -- stout logs stripped of bark then sharpened to points at the top and strapped together to form a wall -- the construction of the bottom of the wall was very odd. The logs overlapped in such a way to form a patchwork of sorts, leaving spaces or channels between the logs. At a height roughly equal to the tops of the mounds, small gates dotted down the length of the wall in both directions, spaced evenly as far as I could see.

I wasn't the only one who stared. Even Swine looked about him with curiosity, and Cai took in all the same unusual features of the settlement as had I. Only Jack seemed uninterested. Unintelligible Man realized he had lost his following, stopped and beckoned to us again in his foreign speech. "Komdu, komdu. pú verour ao fylgat mér áounen ég snúa pér aftur út eins og pakklátir pjófnaour sem pú ert líklegast!" Still uncomprehending the specifics of his words, I understood his meaning well enough and forced my feet to start moving again.

As we walked, I took more interest in the people of the settlement. They weren't openly curious, but many cast furtive looks in our direction as we passed, not wanting to stare too obviously. They were a small, dark people, dark haired and dark eyed. These dark features were paired with pale skin, so fair that they almost seemed bloodless, and the contrast was arresting.

Our guide paused at the base of one of the mounds. "Leyfi hesta hér." He pointed at our horses then at the empty spot in the road next to him, indicating quite clearly that we were to leave them here. "Fylgiden mér."

"Cai, he wants us to leave the horses. Stay here with them," I whispered. He looked at me wide-eyed but said nothing, nodded mutely then sank back against the wall of the mound as though willing himself to disappear into its dank earthiness.

Unintelligible Man undoubtedly noticed Cai linger behind but didn't object. The rest of us followed him through a doorway at the base of the mound. Every other mound had exterior stairs, but this one was different, and I sensed that it was set apart for some reason, even if I couldn't yet justify my suspicion. If I had any certainty that I wouldn't be overheard and understood, I would have whispered my fears out loud, but as it was, I didn't think I would find any comfort from Swine who was sweating so profusely from his nerves that he was drenched, and Jack didn't need to bear the weight of my concern. He had his own problems.

We climbed the stairs spiraling around sharply to the right. The walls were wood paneled, whitewashed, and beautifully decorated with domestic scenes.

Eventually we emerged into a small vestibule. It was dark and contained two doors, one to the left and one to the right. It was through the door to the right that Unintelligible Man entered and bid us follow.

The room was almost a letdown after my wild imaginings of how unusual I expected it to be. Domestic trappings lined the floor and the walls; a small table sat against the wall, several small stools were scattered in various locations. There was a small hearth for cooking and to provide heat, and light came in through several small windows dotting the walls to the right and left of where we entered. As my eyes adjusted to the light I noticed a young woman bent over some mending in the corner. She eyed us surreptitiously when she thought we weren't looking but continued on with her work, never once missing the rhythm of her stitches.

"Veroc hér." Unintelligible Man gestured with his finger, pointing to the ground at our feet to let us know that we were to stay. "Év min breátt aftur."

I nodded that I understood his meaning well enough and he turned, knocked on another door set into the back wall. I heard no response given, but almost immediately he opened the door and entered, closing the door behind him.

I eyed the young woman doing the mending, though she seemed inclined to pretend she had taken no notice of us. Before I could make up my mind about her, Jack swayed heavily, so I guided him to a stool. He sat gratefully, needing no persuasion, and I stood solicitously at his shoulder with my hands protectively on his shoulders. Swine didn't wait to be invited, took a second stool nearest the hearth, slumping down on it with all the drama of a convicted prisoner awaiting his final meal before death.

Our waiting time lengthened, and I grew impatient but took the opportunity to watch the girl in the corner as she sewed, noticing that her glances my way became more and more frequent. When it was clear that she had something on her mind, I pushed aside my hesitation and broke the silence.

"What's your name?" I had no idea if she would understand me, but I thought it a safe guess. She wasn't like the rest of the people of the settlement. Her coloring proclaimed it so, for she had brown hair and a honey-warm complexion.

Startled that I had spoken to her, she responded softly with "Eria," then glanced nervously at the door, all the while worrying the ties lacing her dress. She took in Jack and me together, glancing from me to Jack then back to me again, her eyes large and brown, her expression slowly changing from her initial surprise into something I couldn't quite read. "You are Mercorian?"

I nodded. "Yes, from Corium."

She accepted this and glanced side-long at the door again. "You are brother and sister? Or husband and wife perhaps?" Though softer than a summer breeze, her voice was very pleasant and resonated with a familiar lilt.

"No." I said simply, not feeling the need to elaborate.

When she glanced at the door yet again, my unease grew. "You must be careful to..." she began conspiratorially but stopped abruptly when the door opened. Taking up her sewing once again, she spared no more glances in our direction, continuing to work as if she had never spoken.

Unintelligible Man had returned, but rather than speak, he stepped aside, allowing another man to follow after him. "Böðvar," he said quietly with no small amount of awe, then bowed to the man and left quietly by the same door we had entered. A small woman followed on the heels of Böðvar, though she didn't seem much in awe of him as Unintelligible Man had been.

I assumed Böðvar was in charge, so rather than wait for him to address us, I spoke: "My name is Kassia, this is Jack and Swine. Cai is waiting with the horses. We're traveling through, but Jack was wounded by bandits. He needs his wound tended, and then we need a night of lodging. After that we'll be on our way. Can you help?"

The man didn't even seem to hear me, gave me the barest of glimpses before brushing past me to stand beside the hearth.

"We can pay," I offered, trying again to engage him in conversation, but he didn't reply and I fell silent. I focused on the feel of Jack's shoulders under my hands, summoning motivation to try again.

"He understands you and speaks your language, but he can't talk to you else he becomes ónrenn." It was the old woman who had spoken. "Unclean," she clarified when she saw I didn't understand her meaning. "Tóka will help. Come."

I wasn't sure if this woman was Tóka or if Tóka was another person we had yet to meet, but she had offered help, so I lifted Jack to his feet and we followed the woman obediently into the next room, leaving Swine to his ease.

The air in this much smaller room was thick and heavy, almost palpable, and laden with a spicy fragrance that overwhelmed. I fought to find breath and choked back a cough. The room was also shrouded in an oppressive darkness nearly as thick as the air, and the small lamp hanging by a chain overhead did little to dispel its tangibility.

Heavy furs covered all of the walls, and an overloaded shelf supporting piles of jars and parchments lined the nearer end of the room, all of which added to the closed-in atmosphere of the room.

We were alone with the woman, and when no one else joined us, I assumed she must be Tóka.

"You in Porpio á Fen now and most welcome here. Please, Kahssa... sit?" She indicated a chair piled with furs. I agreed mutely and sat as directed, then watched as she took Jack by the hand and led him to a table in the center of the room. He sat without protest on the edge of the table, and she gently pulled off his shirt, folding it neatly, and set it aside. As she moved back to examine his wound it occurred to me that never once had we told her the nature of Jack's problem, yet somehow she knew. I nudged my unease aside and tried to be grateful Jack would finally be tended.

She studied the wound for a short while then, going over to the shelf behind the table, she retrieved several long thin sticks, put them into a tall clay vessel and lit them. They began to smoke immediately, and soon the room filled even more so with the pungent, stinging scent of incense. She returned with a small jar and a towel then motioned to me to join her by Jack's side. When she had lay Jack back on the table, she took one of my hands and placed it on his forehead then placed the other directly in the center of his chest so I could hold him down while she cleaned his wound. Jack flinched but didn't try to move.

Watching her work made me uncomfortable, and seeing Jack in this compromised state unnerved me, so when she finished with this task, I pulled away my hands. Tóka scowled at me, shaking her head sharply, so with some reticence I put my hands back. She palpated the skin around his wound then followed the path the quarrel had taken from front to back by gently rolling Jack to his side.

She smeared some ointment onto both sides of the wound then turned to me. "You sit again, yes?" I nodded and sat back down on the furs. The smoking reeds were going with ferocity by now, and the fumes were sweet, almost sickly so. I covered my mouth and coughed, my head dizzy. Tóka noticed my discomfort and came to my side, placed her hand under my elbow, and directed me to the door, opening it for me.

Eria was there to greet me. She took the old woman's place at my elbow and led me to a seat near the fire. "Here," she said, and handed me a cup of something. I took it and drank greedily, spilling some of the contents out the side, down my dress. It wasn't long before the overwhelming effects of the incense faded, and soon Eria brought me a plate of food. "You should eat." There was that familiar lilt in her voice again.

"Thank you." I hadn't realized how queasy my stomach had become, but the food seemed to help. "You are from Pania?"

"Yes." She said flatly, but didn't elaborate.

"My mother was from Pania," I offered, hoping to encourage her, but this piece of information went over like a wet blanket. I cast about for a topic of conversation that would elicit some form of reaction, something that would bring back the Eria that wanted to share a secret when we first arrived. "Tóka... she is an accomplished healer?"

"Tóka has many skills," Eria replied immediately and with passion, but her eyes revealed something more alarming. What was it? Fear? No, more than fear. Absolute terror.

"So my friend Jack, he'll be alright?" I asked lightly, trying to ignore my discomfort. She said nothing and looked away, though I noticed sadness in her eyes. She busied herself by washing the table despite its spotlessness.

"Eria, what's going on? What aren't you telling me?" I took in the room with a scan. "And where is Swine?" It hadn't occurred to me before now that he wasn't here. The effects of the smoke had now mostly worn off and my thoughts were clear again. The potential implications of our situation weighed on me, sharpening my suspicions.

Eria crossed back towards me swiftly, tugged at my arm with some urgency. "You should go. Take a walk."

"Why? Where should I go?" She didn't answer, instead ushered me to the door.

"Get some fresh air. Check on your horses." Her voice was pleasant and her smile bright, but it was fragile, forced. She was clearly uncomfortable about something.

"What about Jack?" I insisted. A noise sounded behind the door to the room where Tóka and Jack were, and Eria startled, pushed me out the door, closing it behind me. I stood there in the darkness of the vestibule confused, deciding that there was nothing else to do but take her advice. Maybe I could make some sense of this place by walking, and perhaps that was Eria's intention, her way of getting me to find out what she felt she couldn't tell me herself.

I set off from Tóka's house not knowing where to find the horses as Eria had suggested, but figured the settlement couldn't be so large to make it impossible. Eventually I heard the tell-tale sounds of a stable and climbed the stairs to the top of the mound where I was met by a man who looked very similar to Eria, with coloring more akin to Pania than Porpio á Fen. Like Eria, he was also subdued, furtive and kept his eyes downcast from my curious looks. I suspected that Eria intended me to find him, but like Eria, he seemed fearful, so I didn't probe him. The horses seemed content enough and there was little else I could do, so I left them and their keeper.

I wandered around a bit longer but found nothing helpful to our situation. I was about to turn and head back to Tóka's when I recognized Cai's familiar voice calling out to me, saw Cai and Swine striding towards me. Cai looked quite pleased with himself.

"Cai, you look like a cat that's been fed cream. Why are you so happy?" I was tired, but seeing Cai reminded me how to smile.

"Kassia, I found the best shop in the entire world! They sell sweets that put even the Emperor's bakers to shame!" I doubted that, considering the conditions of this marsh-settlement but didn't feel like countering his beliefs.

"You managed to keep well occupied for the afternoon then?"

"Oh, yes!" His excitement increased as he told me his tale. "After you left me alone with the horses, that man who led us came back. He wanted me to follow him and to bring the horses. Lotur, I think his name was. Anyway, we stabled them and I came back for Swine. We've been exploring ever since." He had told his tale with animation, though he became a bit more circumspect at his mention of Swine, seeing my face sour.

Cai went on to tell me about the various merchants he had met, how unusual their wares, how most everything seemed so primitive to him. I explained that this was not surprising considering the solitude of the settlement and the inhabitants' probable lack of trade. Swine kept his mouth shut during our entire exchange, and if there was a bright spot in my day, this was it.

"And Kassia, I found out about these mounds," he indicated behind him, to a mound bearing one house, "why nothing is at street level." This caught my attention even if nothing else he said was particularly novel to me, because the mounds were a mystery. "Since they live in a marsh, every night the ground water comes up and the river rises outside the far wall." He pointed off to his right. "Every night the settlement floods and the mounds keep them safe from the water."

"This happens every night?" I was astonished.

"Yep. Those planked walkways you see connect the mounds together in case they need to cross during the flood. And the way the walls are built? The crossed logs allow the water to pass through without taking down the walls, and the gates up high let them get in and out by boat if they need to." These people were perhaps not as primitive as I had first thought.

Cai had long since sat down next to me, had grabbed my hand and held it as he talked. Swine still stood in the roadway, his eyes busily watching the merchants and villagers go about their business. When Cai finished relating his news, his voiced sobered. "How's Jack?" Despite his light manner, it was clear he had been worried all afternoon. Even Swine turned his attention back to me in order to hear my answer to Cai's question.

I explained what Tóka had done, telling him only the facts, withholding the darker, more foreboding sensory experiences, the premonitions and fears which had assailed me during my time in the house. Maybe I thought I was being foolish, maybe thought the more practical predilections of a young boy would temper what I sincerely hoped were my more fanciful illusions. Surely I was just tired and overwrought from the last several crazy months of my life? It was a short-lived hope.

"Kassia, there is something strange about this place." With that one comment my control slipped. So he sensed it too?

Even Swine seemed more oddly rattled than normal by Cai's casual comment, added a hearty head shake to give his opinion and said unhelpfully, "No money. Just exchange. No good, no, no good." He was oblivious to the dark shadows that Cai and I sensed, but as there was nary a stick to be found with which to poke him, I simply rolled my eyes and looked back to Cai.

"The people have been very helpful, even encouraging to me. The man with the sweets was obliging enough. But..." He stopped, at a loss for words. I encouraged him with a smile. "...while they seem eager to make me happy, they are also expectant about something. Like they are all watching, waiting." He gave a little shake, like a dog flinging the water off its coat. "I'm hungry." And just like that, his wariness was gone, forgotten because of the subterranean rumbles of his stomach.

I needed a moment to regain my composure, some more time to think, so I instructed Cai to go back to Tóka's house and told Swine to go along too, to keep watch over Cai. I knew Cai needed no such watching from Swine, but it seemed the easiest way to get rid of the hedgepig.

I continued to sit and watch, to think and process all that I had seen and heard, and eventually I returned to Tóka's house to find things exactly as they were when I had left. Cai and Swine were eating and sat contentedly by the fire, so I joined them and ate my share, and though we ate in silence, I was certain we all were focused on similar thoughts. Eria joined me after I finished, and in her lovely lilting voice explained that Jack remained in the fur room, his condition unchanged, but that he rested peacefully, though I was not allowed to see him. When I pressed her for more details about Jack and asked to see Tóka, she closed up and would say no more. Needless to say I went to sleep in a fitful state despite the comfortable bed of piled furs before a roaring fire.

◆ ◆ ◆

I hadn't dreamt about my mother in a very long time, because the grief of my mother's loss had been replaced by worse horrors which more regularly stalked my nights. Last night was an exception. I dreamt of her again and awoke confused and surprised by the change. While my dreams of Mosrad were terrifying, and I was glad to have one night free of them, the dreams of my mother were unsettling in a different way. Something about Porpio á Fen had stirred them up again, though perhaps it was simply Eria's connection to Pania.

After a modest morning meal, Eria took me outside onto a small porch to show me the view. Many other inhabitants were up, doing their work and preparing for their day, implying a level of domesticity not unlike any other city in the world. I could almost pretend these people were normal. I noticed a small coracle propped up against the wall of the house and she informed me that this was how they got around Porpio á Fen after the flood waters came at night. Her answer was straight forward and didn't invite any other curiosities, but I couldn't resist asking about my day yesterday as it seemed the most likely chance at solitude, and I might not get another chance.

"Eria, when I was wandering yesterday I checked on our horses." She listened with interest, her eyes watchful. "I met a man there..." I paused, thinking that maybe she would take it as a cue to explain, but she didn't. "...he looked like you."

She smiled faintly. "Yes," she said quietly. "He is like me," she started, her eyes scanning the street below as she spoke, "we are..." she started again but stopped abruptly, her face blanched of color. She had seen something down below, but before I could encourage her to continue, she turned and fled back inside. It was irritating. Just when I thought I might learn something significant she had been frightened off. But by what? I looked at the street below, spotting Böðvar almost immediately. He stared up at me balefully. Disgusted, I turned and followed in Eria's wake.

Inside Cai and Swine were seated together at the small table playing a game. It looked as though Swine was teaching Cai how to play, so I came nearer and watched for several long moments. Yes, Swine was indeed teaching Cai how to play. I gave Cai a questioning look and he responded with a grin and shrug, and though I scowled, he remained unabashed.

A hand touched my arm lightly and I startled, swung around to discover Tóka behind me.

"Jack is awake, would like to see you. You come?" She didn't have to ask twice.

I entered the fur room and was delighted to discover Jack fully awake, sitting up in the fur chair I had used the day before. His face was lined with fatigue, the skin stretched tightly across his features, but he wore a smile so bright that my heart soared at the sight of him. I crossed the room in several large strides and gave him a hug, uncaring that Tóka was here or that it was so blatant a show of affection towards this man who elicited such complicated emotions from me.

I turned to thank Tóka and discovered that she had already gone, had left as unobtrusively as she had approached me. Jack laughed softly, and I turned back to face him. The warmth of the look he now gave me brought a flush to my cheeks and I moved away to look for a stool, giving me enough time to compose myself.

Once seated, he reached for my hand, and my pulse quickened. There was so much I wanted and needed to say to him, but suddenly I could find no words. All the fears and anxieties of the last many hours drained, and I was left with nothing but a warm, comfortable, secure feeling. For now it was enough simply to rest in the comfort of his presence.

After a time we finally did talk, though our conversation was easy, the topics light. We remained in this light place for a while, but after a time Jack couldn't hold back his fatigue. When I noticed his attempt to stifle a yawn I said, "You should rest." He nodded briefly, then closed his eyes and leaned back. As he lay there in the stillness, the lines of fatigue and pain eased, his countenance softening. I smiled, brushed a gentle kiss onto his forehead and left the room quietly.

When I emerged, I sought out Tóka. "Tell me about his wound. Will we be able to leave tomorrow?"

Tóka studied me closely for several moments, considering, then smiled a smile that didn't touch her eyes. "He is most fortunate of men." She returned to her work by drawing a small measure of liquid from a bowl at her right hand and pouring it into a container on a bench near the window. A loose pouch hung at her waist, and from this she withdrew several handfuls of dry leaves, stirring then mashing it down. Her hands were strong, her movements efficient and practiced. "The bolt which pierced him chose a most favorable path," she continued, flicking her gaze to me briefly as she worked. "His life was not touched, flesh only."

I had no idea what that was supposed to mean so got back to what I saw as the issue at hand. "So... we can leave soon?"

She ignored my query, kept stirring and mashing, stirring and mashing. I wasn't sure if she was going to answer and was about to ask again when she took me by surprise with a question of her own. "Your life... It was touched, yes?" I stared blankly, completely missing her point. When I said nothing, she set down her work and came over to me. Taking each of my hands into each of her own, she placed my palms, one on top of the other, flat against my abdomen and held them there. My mouth suddenly went dry. Anger and shame merged into a hot flush which worked its way up from my chest, spread to my shoulders, up my neck and finally to my face. I snatched my hands out of her grasp and retreated back a step. She ignored my hot look, merely smiled at me knowingly before turning back to her work. "You now ónrenn," she proclaimed finally.

I was flustered and angry at her impertinence. I looked around and to my horror realized that Cai and Swine had stopped playing their game and had been watching the entire exchange. I choked back all of the vicious words I wanted to say and replied much more calmly than I felt, "What do we owe you for your care of Jack?" I wanted to get her back on track, take the attention off of me. Tóka acted as if I hadn't spoken, and it was beginning to irritate me. "I can pay, want to pay you. Just tell me how much you want, what is owing?" Maybe she didn't understand what I was offering. Swine had said that he hadn't seen merchants exchange money, so perhaps it was the money that confused her.

Finally Tóka looked up from her work again and took in the sight of Swine only briefly as if dismissing him outright before moving her gaze to Cai and then me in equal measure. With her own degree of irritation she said, "It has not yet been determined. There is one thing left to be done," before returning to her work. She really hadn't been very helpful. I swallowed drily then made up my mind to leave her a reasonable sum for her services. We would leave tomorrow, no matter what Tóka had to say on the matter.

◆ ◆ ◆

The afternoon found me walking through the settlement again, because sitting inside Tóka's house waiting for nothing to happen was agonizing in its tedium. It hadn't helped my mood that Swine and Cai had developed an unlikely friendship, and this grated on my nerves even more than the tedium of sitting. I couldn't really blame Cai; he was likely capable of befriending a wild boar.

The settlement of Porpio á Fen was not overly large, but my explorations yesterday weren't thorough. I was curious about the day to day life in the settlement, anything to get my mind off Jack, so decided to find the market, discovering it close to where I had been yesterday. Like any other market the world over, the streets were filled with mothers and their children, bargaining, playing, chasing and catching up on the latest gossip. One such mother was buying bread from a merchant, and the instance reminded me of the child in Corium who had knocked over the pastries at my favorite baker. It brought a smile to my face.

I moved on and saw other merchants, but the one that captured my imagination was a brilliant leather worker whose artistry equaled any craftsman I had ever seen. I watched mesmerized as the merchant tooled intricate and delicate designs onto all kinds of leather items - clothing and shoes, mugs, and even plates. He seemed pleased by my attention, and as I was about to leave he offered me a small token of appreciation, a knife-sized sheath. When I reached into my money pouch to pay him, he merely shrugged me off, shaking his head. Since arriving at Porpio á Fen, my presence had been viewed with a cultivated wariness if not outright obliviousness. This was the first overture of enthusiastic friendliness, and my spirits were raised immediately. I could almost forget the cloud of foreboding that had been hanging over me ever since arriving, and I couldn't help the smile that lit my face as I left the merchant.

I was still in good spirits when I left the market and rounded a corner into an area that could only be a religious site. The building which dominated the square was a tall, narrow structure made of smoothed and cut stone, tapered toward the top, and decorated with elaborate carvings and animal skulls. A porch ran the full length of the front of the structure and was reached by stairs cut into the front face. A crowd filled the square, though nothing was happening at the moment, and everyone appeared to be waiting for something.

Near to my right hand, to the side of the paved square in front of the stone building, was a small fenced area for animals -- three large blackbirds tethered to the fence, squawking their protest, three dogs, and one old, emaciated goat bleating pitifully. One of the dogs jumped up and placed his large paws on the edge of the wicket fence. "Hello there, lovely boy!" I ruffled the fur on his head and scratched his ears. He was happy and friendly, his face open and enchanting. I had always loved dogs, but neither of my parents had ever thought it wise for me to take one on as a pet. "What have you done that you must be kept here like a prisoner?" I continued to rub his ears, and he rewarded me with a sound like a gurgle of delight and a lick. I laughed, suddenly fantasizing about taking him with us when we left this place. Maybe he could keep an eye on Rose, my trouble-maker horse.

A ripple of excitement shot through the crowd, and as soon as I sensed it, I turned my attention to the commotion. A man dressed in a full-length robe of furs stepped out of the stone building and onto the porch. I let the dog continue to lick my hand while I watched. A hush came over the assembled throng as a small boy emerged from the temple behind the man who I decided must be a priest, bearing an oversized headdress made of long-braided tassels. The priest bent over, allowing the boy to place the headdress on this head. He straightened, raised both arms, and yelled something in the language of the Porpians, causing a cheer to rise from the small assembly. This cued a stream of other boys to enter the porch area from behind him, stopping in a long, solemn line facing the square below.

A hush fell, and all commotion ceased, as if a spell had been cast and every observer had been turned to stone. As these things happened, I realized that my hand was no longer being licked, so I turned to see why my canine companion had stopped. He wasn't there. A quick search revealed that he had been led through the crowd and up the long stone stairs to the top of the porch where he now stood, tail wagging, seemingly excited by all the children, and thinking that maybe one of them might play with him. I grew uneasy, but even my foreboding couldn't have been imaginative enough for what happened next. A knife flashed in the hands of the fur-robed priest, his hand and knife coming away bloodied. The dog fell and lay in a pool of his own blood, dead. The priest raised his hand for all to see, and the audience cheered loudly, but with purpose, as if it were a practiced response of expectation. I shuddered and shrank back against the wall, disbelieving what I had just seen. I was used to the slaughter of animals for food, but what I had just witnessed seemed purposeless.

The crowd silenced again as one, as if in anticipation of something they knew was about to happen. The fur-robed priest saturated his knife in the dog's blood then turned to face the line of boys. My heart nearly seized in my chest after what had just happened. This time my imagination was up to the task, and I stood frozen, afraid to watch, yet unable to look away. The priest began to walk the row of boys, trailing the bloodied knife in a horrific line along the naked bellies of each boy. When he reached the end, he turned, coming back in the same way he had gone before stopping at the third boy from the end. The boy smiled in rapturous elation at being chosen, raised his arms to the sky, then crumpled to the stones at his feet when the knife flashed again. I stifled a shriek with my fist jammed into my mouth and backed away hastily, sickened by everything I had lucklessly witnessed.

Heedless disregard for my surroundings spun me into a person immediately behind me, and looking up, I discovered Böðvar watching me with placid eyes. I was shaking too violently to notice that he had put his arms around my shoulders gently; without invitation he drew me close. His demeanor was calm and reassuring, and I allowed myself to be comforted by him. When I was sufficiently recovered, he turned me, leading me away from the scene of the slaughter.

Not too far from the temple square was another mound to which he led me, much like Tóka's on the inside but slightly smaller. Once inside, I was greeted by a young man about my own age. At a nod from Böðvar he poured a measure of liquid from a jar into a cup and pressed it into my hand then guided me to a padded bench where I sat to drink. It tasted sweet with a slight scent of pine, and I felt instant warmth spread through all of my limbs.

I noticed that Böðvar had left the room, and that the young man who had served me my drink was working on something in the corner, but I couldn't make out what it was. The longer I sat, the harder I found it to concentrate. A deep calm had settled into my spirit, though

I couldn't remember why this was a welcome thing. I swayed in my seat.

A voice startled me. "Böðvar wishes you to join him." Böðvar. He was a nice man. It seemed a reasonable thing to do. With shaking legs I stood, assisted by the young man who had spoken. Why was putting one foot in front of the other so difficult? My mind wandered. Jack. I wondered what he was doing now. Was he awake? Was he in pain? Did he miss me? "Kassia ónrenn," a voice said. I made a valiant effort to snap back to the present, to try to assemble the threads of my consciousness into some form of order, to try to make out what was being said. "Böðvar fix. You trust Böðvar."

Böðvar? Who was Böðvar? Did I know this Böðvar? The room spun, and I nearly fell when a pair of strong hands caught me, helped me to a low-lying table covered in soft fur. Why was fur so significant to me just now? Maybe it didn't matter; it looked overwhelmingly comfortable, and I lay down, willing myself to melt into the soft folds. Wanting nothing more than to drift off to sleep, I was irritated to be kept from doing so by the appearance of a face hovering over mine. I wished it would go away so I could sleep. I smiled lazily thinking of sleep. Sleep, yes, I wished for it.

A gentle hand stroked my cheek momentarily and I wondered why, uncomprehending but not caring, too comfortable. "Kassia ónrenn," the boy had said. "Böðvar fix. You trust Böðvar," he had said. That phrase stuck, and as much as I wanted sleep, something inside me forced my mind back to those words. My head felt like an overstuffed bale of cotton, but I fought against the current that kept trying to pull me into the blessed oblivion of sleep. I didn't know what this man Böðvar intended, but I wouldn't allow myself to be compromised again, in any way. Never again. Mists swirled at the edges of my vision, and I felt as though I was seeing through a long, hot tunnel of steam. Regardless of anything else that had happened, I was pretty sure that I didn't want Böðvar to fix me. I wasn't broken, was I? He said I was ónrenn, and a memory surfaced. Tóka had called me that. Said my life had been touched. But I am Kassia. I wanted to tell him this, as if it would matter. Anything that had happened to me in the past had nothing to do with these people. Their meddling was not welcome.

"No," I said, shaking my head, trying to brush his hands away. My movements were clumsy, only half controlled. "No, no," I said more urgently, flailing my arms in wider arcs. I sensed rather than saw that Böðvar had backed away from me as I attempted to sit up. An unsettling dizziness overwhelmed me, but I brushed it aside and sat up fully, swinging my legs over the side of the table. I locked eyes with Böðvar but his face revealed only bewilderment at what I was doing. I slid down to the floor and found that my legs threatened to give way at any moment, so I grabbed the edge of the table and used it to brace myself as I took several awkward steps in the direction of the door. When the table ran out, I trusted to my own wits, closed the remaining space with a slowly returning sense of solidity. I was relieved that Böðvar hadn't tried to stop me, hadn't even followed me.

The boy waited in the main room, quietly watching as I made my way to the stairs. Because he had no idea what had or hadn't happened in the other room, he made no attempt to stop me from leaving. His lack of action was passive, but his look was a hungry one. I couldn't leave fast enough.

I still trembled violently and my legs felt as if all the bones had been removed, but the outside air helped to clear my mind, and the foggy vapors slowly dissipated as I walked. Horror flooded me as I realized that I had somehow allowed myself to be led to that house. I had trusted Böðvar, though I didn't really know what it had almost cost me. Furious with myself, I spied a bucket of water carried by a man walking the other way. He shied away when I wrenched it from his hand and dumped the contents fully over my head, allowing the water to gush over me like a flood. Its coldness alerted my senses, and I woke up more completely to reality. I walked on, dripping from my impetuous bath all the while ignoring the looks on the faces of passers-by, some knowingly satisfied while others, thankfully, were embarrassed for my sake. I ignored them all as I shouldered my way back to Tóka's and climbed the internal stairs.

I breezed through the common room, ignoring those present and leaving a trail of water where I walked. I was too upset to care who saw me. The Emperor himself could have been dancing naked on the table for all it mattered to me. Without knocking or caring what I might find, I pushed into the back room intending to find Jack and was relieved to find him alone, asleep in the same chair as before. I closed the door behind me gently, not wanting to wake him, needing him to stay asleep.

There was just enough room on his chair, so I sat, shunning the stool in favor of nearness to him. I nestled in as closely as I could, laying my head against his chest, allowing my head to rise and fall with the rhythm of his breath. He was warm and his scent was comforting, so I breathed in the aroma of his skin, taking it into my lungs to become a part of myself.

A wave of emotion flooded over me as I rested there, fatigue, fear, shame, inadequacy... though I fought it down with all my might. After a while the fight eased, my defenses melting like a block of ice before the flame. I didn't know if I was worthy of love, didn't know how to navigate all that had happened to me, how to deal with the scars of my past, but I knew I needed Jack in my confidence, needed him in my life, nearly at any cost. I was not ónrenn when I was with him. Broken and flawed though I was, life shouldn't be lived alone. Perhaps this was my redemption, a place to begin the healing.

◆ ◆ ◆

I awoke with a start to discover that I was cocooned tightly in Jack's arms, and that he was awake, smiling down at me. I smiled lazily back.

"How long have you been awake?" I asked in a whisper, reluctantly breaking the sanctity of the silence that held us close.

"Long enough to get a cramp in my arm from holding you." His tone was serious, but his mouth formed its typical quirk at the corner.

"Serves you right," I returned, feigning acerbity, "for all the grief you've caused me these last few days." I nuzzled more closely against his chest, and he brushed away a loose strand of hair then stroked my cheek. I closed my eyes and breathed him in again, deeply, possessively. "How do you feel? Do you feel up to traveling soon?" I murmured, keeping my eyes closed.

"I ought to be able to travel again tomorrow. My life wasn't touched, remember?" His tone mocked the strange cadence of Tóka, and I giggled, looking up at him as I did so. What I saw there, the intensity of warmth and acceptance and longing, took my breath away. I fought the instinct to pull back, to hide behind the iron walls of my heart, the place I usually shackled my emotions and abused feelings, and while it would have been safer, I had fought too hard to get to this place; I didn't want to go back.

Jack read my conflicted thoughts, and many things could have happened next, but I was relieved when he merely moved his hand to cup my chin in his palm, drawing his thumb lightly across my lips. I thrilled at the intimacy but was relieved by his restraint.

"What have you been doing to occupy your time while I've been languishing in this sick room?" He asked quietly.

I was still drowsy and intoxicated by feelings so freshly brought to the surface that I had to force myself to make sense of his question. I had come in here to find Jack, hoping to forget everything that had just happened. I didn't want to revisit it, but I knew that it couldn't be ignored. The weight of my overwhelming burden had temporarily dissipated, but now it came rushing back.

I couldn't think coherently when I was so near him, so I sat up and tried to compose my thoughts. Tóka had provided Jack with a flagon of wine made from tree sap which he picked up and offered to me. I looked at it suspiciously but he smiled warmly, and I took a sip, finding it surprisingly refreshing. Fortified once again, I started at the beginning and explained everything to him, starting with our arrival on the first day, all of which was understandably hazy to him. I explained Cai's observations about the culture of the Porpians, the construction of the settlement, including the walls, about the flooding that occurred every night, and Swine's observations about their system of barter. Jack remained silent during my entire explanation but laughed when I told him about the new-found affinity between Cai and Swine and how they spent hours playing pebble games.

Jack had managed to encourage me back into his arms as I

talked, and he occupied his hands now by twirling strands of my hair around his fingers. "I never would have imagined anyone warming to Swine," he admitted. "Maybe the sway-backed pig has some value after all. Maybe we were wrong about him?" This earned Jack and elbow in the ribs.

It was refreshing to be light-hearted again, but there was more I needed to tell him because he hadn't heard the worst of it yet. He listened quietly as I explained about Eria's unspoken fear, about the man she intimated that I find at the stable, and the temple ceremony. He listened to everything stoically, only stiffening significantly when I related my experience with Böðvar. I assured him that Böðvar's intentions, whatever they were, had been thwarted and that he had remained mysteriously uncaring about my hasty departure, that I had made it back here untouched in body if not in soul by the experience. Jack relaxed.

Neither of us heard her enter, but just then Eria approached us quietly, gently, to tell us that food was waiting for us. With a reluctance that bordered on refusal, I peeled myself away from my nest and helped Jack to stand, surprised at his steadiness and delighted by the strength I sensed had returned to him.

"Kassia, wait," he said, stopping me from leaving and pulling me towards him. My heart thumped against the walls of my chest. "What I said the other day..." he started then paused, and I waited for him to continue, uncertain what he would say next. "...about that guard in Lynchport... I'm sorry, Kassia. It was a hideous thing to say. It's just the idea that anyone would do anything to you, to hurt you in any way... It sickens me. I would do anything to protect you, you know that, don't you? I was panicked when you told me what happened, and I said really stupid things, crazy with fear for you. Will you forgive me?"

I couldn't speak. The words were there, but they wouldn't come out. Of course I forgave him. I nodded with a soft smile, and a look of utter joy washed over his features. My heart felt like it would burst, yet it nearly seized up instead when Jack moved in closer, leaning towards me. I smiled coyly, but with a mischievous wink turned and walked away, leaving him standing there bereft of his prize.

We emerged to find pairs of eyes watch us with great interest as Jack led me across the room where we seated ourselves at the table for Eria to serve us our meal. No one spoke as we ate our food, and the tenuous grip on peace I had only begun to piece back together melted wholly away. Feelings of foreboding had taken up residence in my spirit again, drawn like a hound to the scent of my inner contentment. It didn't help that Eria kept eyeing us from her stool as we ate.

Finally the hour grew late enough, and our make-shift beds were made up. Eria left us to our rest to find her own pallet on the far side of the room away from the fire. Tóka had long since returned from wherever she had been, but she had said nothing when she came in. The look she gave me as she navigated her way into her fur-lined back room, Jack's former sick room, was odd, but I didn't care. I had no desire to speak with her or anyone else from this settlement again. I wanted nothing more than to leave first thing in the morning, shaking the dust from my feet as I went, and never looking back. We were bound for Islay Bay. Our journey had been delayed too long already. At first light we would depart.

I knew that my rebellious thoughts would not calm enough for me to be coaxed into sleep, so I pulled my pile of furs over and combined them with Jack's, knowing that if I was encircled in his arms I might find some peace. I lay down next to him, and he immediately wrapped his cloak over us, drawing me into his arms. I nestled up against him, and in this way I fell asleep. A deep, dreamless sleep.

◆ ◆ ◆

The initial hours of the night passed without remark, but I startled awake at the sight of Eria leaning over me, her face the merest of inches in front of mine. She was shaking my shoulder, and it took me some moments to awaken. Jack was roused next to me as she spoke.

"You must leave. Go, now." She was urgent in her appeal. I had been in this position too many times in the past for it not to work on me this time. It was a new way of life for me it seemed, to be awakened in the night to an urgent appeal. My instincts screamed and I came instantly awake.

"Why? What is it? Eria, tell me."

"They mean to take payment in the morning. You have to leave now before it's too late."

"What is that supposed to mean? I intend to give her money, think it's reasonable considering the kindness she has done..."

"It is no kindness." She spat the words, interrupting me. "You must go. I can't explain it now." She urged me to get up and dress. Jack woke Cai and Swine in succession and they dressed hurriedly, asking no questions, sensing innately the need for silence.

When we had gathered our meager possessions, she motioned that we were to follow her out onto the balcony, to the waiting coracles. It was a haunting sight to see, the flood waters high up the sides of the mounds, moonlight reflecting off the surface of the water, showing the mounds as individual islands afloat in an ethereal lake.

Eria got into one of the coracles and quickly demonstrated how to use it. There were enough for us, though I had no idea how she had managed to acquire so many. I found my own vessel to be somewhat unwieldy, but somehow we all managed to navigate the flooded streets of the settlement, slipping out one of the gates set up high in the wall. Once outside the walls of the settlement we navigated around trees and other floating debris, our way lighted by the full moon which shone down on the landscape with a steady glow. Eria's timing was perfect, and I regarded her with a newfound respect.

Once we made it a fair enough distance so that we no longer feared our speech being overheard, Eria stopped, turned her vessel enough to face Jack and I who had kept close to the side of my coracle. Her eyes were the size of orbs, the moonlight revealing both fear and urgency.

"Take me with you." Her words were laced through with a determination that wouldn't be thwarted.

I looked first at her then at Jack, my expression undoubtedly conveying hesitancy brought on by the unknown.

"Please," she cried. Her words, which were strained with pleading born of terror made her voice thin, almost otherworldly, the lovely lilt of Pania all but gone.

9

I SAT BEFORE another fire, gazing into its depths, allowing it to lull and mesmerize. While it could have been any one of the fires I had gazed into and been warmed by in these last many weeks, this fire was different from all the others. With each consecutive fire I contemplated, the cares of my life had grown increasingly weightier and weightier. Soon I must break under it all or be malformed beyond redemption. Was the spirit of a person meant to bear so much? I was certain mine was not.

We were now two days out of Porpio á Fen, and even though the mysteries and horrors of that place remained unexplained, at least we were beyond reach of their demons. Our going, while likely discovered, had so far remained unremarked. However, our escape had been reacted to, it seemed as though we were not being followed and were finally free.

The fire cracked and sizzled, sending an endless flow of sparks skyward in a furiously rising plume, like tiny points of light returning home to the stars. And like I had done so often, times beyond counting, I lifted my eyes to watch them ascend.

On the night of our departure from the Swamp People, the description Jack and I had taken to using for odd race of marsh-dwellers, Eria led our band of coracles into the heavy blackness of night. We followed blindly, trusting in her knowledge, all the while maintaining our silence which was broken only by the musical trickling of water each stroke of the paddle begat.

The hours progressed, soporifically, one into the next. My arms pulled at the single paddle in my hand, forcing each muscle and sinew to obey despite their continuously attempted rebellion and nearly effective pleas of fatigue. Not to go on simply wasn't an option.

I hadn't even noticed the outlines of trees surreptitiously taking shape around me as dawn awakened until I felt a shudder like a ripple move through my little vessel as it scraped the ground. The flood waters had retreated into a subterranean rest, and our journey would now continue on foot. Following Eria's example, I stepped from the boat, and rather than sink into mud and muck, my foot found purchase on the spongy surface of the dead and decaying leaves carpeting the floor of the dark and brooding forest.

I glanced at Jack, looking for evidence that he wouldn't or couldn't continue, but rather than fatigue or distress, his countenance appeared to be carved out of pure determination and grit.

We immediately set out at an unrelenting pace without pause even to ask a single question much less think about what we did. All I could do was concentrate on the next footfall, the next log to climb over, to stay upright and ignore fatigue despite the longing for a rest. I knew Jack was in constant pain. His wound had barely begun to heal, and despite Tóka's ministrations he was still physically vulnerable, though he did his best to hide the fact. All knew it, so we took turns to help him along; he didn't disparage the assistance.

After many hours of walking, I shielded my eyes with my hand and looked up at the brightness of the dappled sunlight filtering through the blanket of leaves overhead. The sun was approaching its zenith, and as it did so, Eria noticeably increased her watchfulness. She grew more alert with every step, her eyes darting from place to place like a woodland creature, senses firing in preparation for flight. I was about to ask her what was wrong when I saw them: our horses a short distance ahead.

"Eria..." I began at a whisper, touching my hand to her shoulder.

Before I could say more, Eria cut in, somewhat more loudly than I had expected, and with a conspiratorial wink, "Not everyone in Porpio á Fen is a believer in the Yðir, the gods of the marsh. We were not without help." She didn't elaborate, but a giant smile of satisfied success spread across her face. We closed the distance to our horses, and I felt relief to see Rose again. Troublesome mount though she was, I had grown attached to her and was happy to see that she had been well cared for during her time with the Swamp People.

"Eria, we must hurry," said a new voice from behind a blind

of fallen logs and piled branches. It was a hunting blind, and immediately I wondered if it belonged to the Swamp People. A man emerged into the open. "I had to leave sooner than I planned. Your going was noticed earlier than we expected." Jack reached for the dagger at his belt, but Eria noticed and put her hand on his wrist to stay his reaction.

"Jack, no. We're safe." Eria sounded relieved, almost euphoric, and as a result Jack relaxed his stance. Eria thrust herself forward, all but falling into the arms of the new arrival, the man I had seen minding the stables. "This is Buran, and he has brought your horses." She was utterly triumphant and stood beaming, as though she had been single-handedly responsible for ending the epoch-long Island Wars between Kordofãn and Umm Dul.

"I took them out for exercise," Buran offered with a shrug, "and never came back." He couldn't hold back his pride and smiled a rakish smile, one which fully explained the impulse which had sent Eria hurtling into his arms. I knew nothing about the relationship between Eria and Buran, but his smile was infectious and I couldn't help but beam back at him.

I turned to share in the moment with Jack, finding rather than gratitude, a cool indifference instead, as though he didn't want to be easily impressed by our new companion. I hid a laugh, amused by his male posturing, and checked my keenness, even if only a little. Unabashed by Jack's rudeness, Buran continued, "We need to keep going. It won't have taken them long to notice that I didn't come back and to connect it with the truth of the matter. They'll be looking for all of us now, and they'll know we have horses."

We began to divide up our packs amongst the horses, and as we did so, Buran pulled Eria aside. "The ceremony should have started," he said quietly, pitching his voice for Eria's ears alone. I was too close and couldn't help overhearing. "And they'll be as furious as an agitated nest of hornets."

He looked up when he said this last part and caught me listening. I shot Buran a look, remembering the violent scene I had witnessed at the temple, wondering in that moment what it had to do with us, but then decided that Buran's suggestion of haste was wisdom itself. There would be time for answers later. For now he was absolutely right - we needed to move, though my determination was based more on instinct than any certain knowledge. We hadn't been prisoners of the Swamp People necessarily, at least not outright, yet our status had always made me uneasy. His comment solidified my conviction that there was a connection between us and the eager anticipation I had sensed from everyone in the settlement, as if something big was about to take place, and we were to be a part of it.

Once mounted, we set off at a pace quick enough to draw out the distance between us and our pursuers, giving us what I hoped was an ever-increasing buffer between freedom and whatever it was we had been.

We slept that first night where we fell, too exhausted to eat and wise enough not to light a fire. The next day mirrored the previous day, fear pushing us on while keeping us silent. Now as I sat watching the sparks float to the heavens and listening to the sounds of nocturnal creatures stalking the darkness, I tried to imagine myself far away, in a small cottage near the sea, all in an effort to keep my mind off the questions which had followed me out of Porpio á Fen. I was afraid I wouldn't want to know the answers once faced with them.

I ached all over and wanted sleep to come, but my mind wouldn't let me. Cai had already succumbed to the embrace of slumber, but Swine, Eria, Buran and Jack were still awake, staring at the fire with me. I pulled my knees closer to my chest and took a bite of food, hoping to quell the nausea which had been plaguing me the last few days.

"Kassia, what brought you so far north of the main road, into the marsh?" Buran's arms wrapped tightly around Eria as she leaned back into him. Her voice was relaxed and quiet, the gentle lilt of Pania flowering her words. "It is not a commonly visited place, the reason the Porpians built where they did. Where are you going?"

She was watching me earnestly, and as she did so, she tilted her head to the side, waiting for my answer. Firelight caught and held in the depths of her hazel eyes, highlighting the gold specks which appeared to glow like the very embers of the fire. Jack sat on my left, his arm wrapped protectively around my waist as if he was afraid that some new terror awaited us in the night, determined not to let it have me. I smiled lazily at the thought then turned my attention back to the question Eria had asked. I wasn't certain how much of the truth I wanted to share with anyone, not after what had happened to us in Lynchport, but I decided there was no harm in telling them our first destination was Westwald on the western shore of Allmor Lake, and that from there we would go on to Islay Bay in Elbra.

"I have family in Islay Bay," offered Jack, in simple explanation.

Eria accepted this and moved on, looking at Jack and asking, "And how were you injured?"

Immediately alarmed at what he might say, I nearly rushed to answer her, to keep Jack from being too honest. I needn't have worried. He shrugged then said off-handedly, "bandits".

An owl screeched overhead, setting off a flurry of scurrying feet through the underbrush around us. The fire popped, and the leathery scent of birch tar tickled at my nose. It was my turn to ask some questions. "How did you come to Porpio á Fen, and why were you so eager to leave? Were you prisoners?"

Eria looked first to Buran who nodded his approval, encouraging her with his eyes to tell the tale. "Buran and I are from Pania, the western edge. My husband," she said, squeezing his hand and confirming what I had suspected about them, "was a captain in service to a minor lord of the west, Hinne Lubien af Dalur."

Buran took up her narrative. "Lord Lubien was..." he paused, considering his next words, "forced out of his position," he said cautiously. "His household packed up, and we left Pania, took sail across Allmor Lake, through Westwald, then south, intending to head deeper into Mercoria."

"Intending?" I asked. I hadn't thought to interrupt his narrative, but his manner hinted at something far more complex than he was letting on and I was intrigued.

"Lord Lubien sickened. We needed help, and found a

settlement in the marsh," Eria continued, her voice quieting as though she was back in the moment, remembering her entrance into the dark and sinister confines of the Porpian settlement. "Tóka healed him, and we were grateful, but it was made clear that it would cost us and we became wary, for we knew they did not deal in money."

I swallowed back my fear, remembering all too clearly the way Tóka had avoided a direct answer when I asked about the cost to heal Jack. She had eyed Swine, Cai, and then me in turn before answering vaguely.

"When they learned who Hinne really was, of his former status in Pania, the cost went up." Eria's voice was barely above a whisper now, and it took all my effort to concentrate on her words, though in reality I knew what she would say, because I had suspected what would happen to one of us after I saw the slaughter in the temple district. "Our son..." She broke then, turned her face into Buran's shoulder and wept.

"A life given requires a life taken. Their gods require it," he spat. "Lord Lubien's life was mature, the healing required the life of one young. So they took our son, they offered him to the Yðir, their gods. He was barely three." Buran's words were spoken steadily but had congealed into an elemental force, given life by hate. "Even that was not enough. Our number was large, so in exchange for the freedom of the many, they took us prisoner." Buran hugged his wife closer, and Eria looked up at us, her eyes red-rimmed and puffy.

"And Lord Lubien agreed to this?" Jack was indignant.

"What choice did he have? We would all have remained prisoners unless he agreed to it." Buran spoke in anger, but I knew his anger was not directed at Lord Lubien or at Jack. "Lord Lubien was a good man, and our son was dead," he added, more softly.

"And so were we, dead, though we lived on the outside," said Eria, her voice strengthening from the same hate that fueled Buran.

"When was this?" I asked, wondering how fresh the heart wound was.

"Three years ago," Buran answered. How ironic that they suffered a loss the same year I did, the year my father disappeared.

"Kassia, they would have taken payment from you too." Eria took in the sight of us, of Jack and me, Swine and Cai. "One of you would have been given to the Yðir as payment." Her words trailed off and none of us felt like talking any more.

After a time, Jack squeezed my shoulders and yawned. Unable to sit up any longer, he curled up in his cloak and went to sleep, followed closely by Swine and Buran, leaving Eria and I alone with our thoughts.

My body was tired, more tired than I thought possible, but my mind was still buzzing. One thing remained unexplained, though I hadn't wanted to ask about it in front of the others. Eria sensed this and watched me intently as I worked out what it was I wanted to ask next.

"When we were at Tóka's, she called me ónrenn..." At my question, the look in Eria's eyes took on an aspect that I didn't recognize, as if the word ónrenn was significant, that she knew what I would ask, and that she had an answer but wanted me to ask first. She wasn't going to make it easy for me, so I took a deep breath and plunged ahead. "Böðvar wanted to fix me, because I was ónrenn..." I paused, suddenly knowing I couldn't ask. I looked down at my lap and studied my hands, the dirty, broken fingernails on the ends of my fingers, the scratches and cuts on my palms from too many days of living in the wild.

"Because your life was touched," Eria added cautiously, prompting me to continue.

"Yes." I looked up from my hands, met her eyes. "That's what Tóka said. But I don't know what she meant."

"Don't you?"

I looked down again, avoiding the intensity of her gaze. "No." Heat rose to my cheeks. Eria rose and came to sit next to me.

"Kassia," she took my hands in her own, "they wanted you specifically as payment to the Yðir. I know this. I know Tóka." She let that sink in for a moment before adding, "But Tóka knew something about you, knew something needed to be fixed first, knew their gods would require it. A life for a life, remember?" I kept my eyes firmly fixed on my lap. "If they had taken your life as it was, they would have taken two lives..."

She let the words hang there and I closed my eyes, shut out the world as my emotions began to spin and tumble, as her words sank in and penetrated, for they had forced me to face what I didn't want to hear. The faces of the men in Mosrad rose up in my mind, their salacious stares, their violence, and my vulnerability. I wrested my hands out of her grasp and raised them to the sides of my head and squeezed, rocking back and forth where I sat and let escape a soundless sob of anger and defiance. Eria wrapped her arms around me and held me while I wrestled internally. Two lives. My life and the life growing inside my womb. Somehow I had known, should have known, but I hadn't let the reality surface long enough to recognize it, denying it with every fiber of my being.

Eria held me for a time, but despite her compassion, it was late, and after a while she left me to find her rest beside Buran. I nestled in next to Jack and pulled my cloak over the two of us, shielding us from the dark things that stalked the night.

◆ ◆ ◆

Smoke stung my throat, and I sat up with a start, coughing and rubbing my eyes. Leaping immediately to my feet, I began to yell, hoping to rouse anyone who slept on despite the smoke. The forest was blanketed in a heavy, white smoke, and it was hard to see the fingertips at the ends of my outstretched hands as I groped across the small clearing blindly, arms flailing in front of my face.

I thought I was nearly to the place I vaguely remembered tethering the horses last night when I tripped over a substantial rock. My toe was on fire, and as I sat there massaging it, a calling voice pierced my consciousness: "Kassia, wait, nothing's wrong!" A gust of wind blew through just then, temporarily displacing the smoke screen that had started all the confusion in the first place. The cause of the problem was revealed: a feeble fire burned in our camp site and from it billowed a column of smoke. I felt instantly foolish for my earlier panic but equally irritated with the two inept fire tenders hunched over their sorry excuse for a fire. Cai looked apologetic, but Swine simply looked daft. The dolts had nearly given me a heart attack.

175

Buran moved in with his usual efficiency to take care of matters, bolstering the fire into a hearty blaze without much effort. "We can't take much time to eat. Get that fish cooking," he directed Cai, "and let's move out." From there he moved to pack up his paltry gear and loaded his horse. Jack and I followed his example, though I knew Jack wondered why Buran had taken it upon himself to assume the leadership of our little group. Fortunately for our sake, he kept his thoughts on the matter to himself, for I didn't have the energy to deal with his injured pride.

By midday we slowed to a sluggish pace, and out of mutual need, we stopped for a break. Jack had made admirable progress in his recovery, relative to the conditions, but he still had so much farther to go, so it was with little surprise that as soon as we dismounted I discovered a small bloody patch on his clothing. I forced him to sit back against a tree so that I could inspect the wound and clean it. I was relieved by what I saw, that the tissue around his wound remained pink and healthy. Tóka was a good healer, and despite my opinion of her, I would be thankful for that at least, if for no other reason.

The rest of the group was occupied with various things: Eria and Cai hunted for plants that could be used medicinally, the latter teaching the former about each. Buran and Swine each napped, leaving Jack and I to our own rest. When his wound was covered with a clean cloth, I took his arm around my shoulder to help him stand. He didn't protest, but neither did he cooperate. Instead he pulled me back down next to him. He placed a single finger of his free hand under my chin, lifting my face to his, and pressed a kiss lightly to my lips.

A little surprised but not at all put off, I asked coyly, "What was that for?" By way of answer he kissed me again, yet this time he left nothing about his motives in question. I gave in fully, melting into him, and immediately a fire took hold between us, searing in its blazing heat.

It was some time before we pulled apart, breathless, and only then, looking into the intensity of his gaze, did I become aware of my heart which beat at a rate likely to send it soaring into the air. That he had stirred a fire so easily, and that I had given into it so readily and willingly was alarming, and I immediately looked away disconcerted. I had the presence of mind to know that I was fighting back the memories and emotions of that night in Mosrad and that what Jack had just done had nothing to do with those men; yet the knowing didn't stop the fear I couldn't control or escape, for the fruit of their violation grew in my womb. How long would those men wield power over me? It seemed to me now that it was a lifelong sentence, and I wasn't sure if I was strong enough.

"Kassia," he implored in a gentle whisper, searching my downturned face, willing me to look back up at him. I took a deep breath and met his gaze. I had no way of knowing if his thoughts had taken the same turn as mine, but his look was so full of compassion that I guessed it to be so. The same old persistent lock of hair hung down on his forehead, partially obstructing his eye, so instinctively I reached out and brushed it away. He caught my hand before I could retract it and turned it over, pressing a tender kiss into my palm. I closed my eyes and fought the urge to pull it out of his grasp, feeling the heat of my desire stir once again.

Shame. Would the stirring of desire forever invoke feelings of shame? Its hooks were grafted onto my soul, continuously tearing and piercing me, leaving an open wound that continued to bleed despite my desperate attempts to pretend it wasn't there. I knew that unless it healed completely, it would be forever debilitating.

Somehow discerning my internal battle, and in a voice as soft as the clouds of carded wool floating in the sky overhead, he said gently, "Kassia, you are more beloved than you know." He stroked my cheek, and I forced myself to allow him, though I still didn't open my eyes. His admission may have been an honest one, but I wasn't sure if I was worthy of its focus. A single tear broke free and rolled down my cheek. "What is it?" he asked quietly as he wiped away the tear with his fingertip.

I willed my eyes to meet his, through tears that had begun to fall a little faster. "Jack," my voice cracked, and I paused. He waited patiently for me to continue, so I took a deep breath and forced myself on. "You don't know what happened... I..." I stopped short, the tightness in my throat choking out all further speech.

"Kassia, don't..." He pressed his finger to my lips. "There's no need. It's no secret what goes on behind prison walls." I nodded and looked down at my hands. He may have guessed at the source of my shame, but he didn't know that the seed of it had taken root and now grew within me, that it would soon be the most tangible result of what had happened to me. How would he feel then? Would it change anything? I wanted to find a way to tell him, but he spoke again before I could find the words. "It's no matter... not to me... because it doesn't change who you are." He kissed me lightly, this time with gentle affection devoid of the flame. I was suddenly overwhelmingly tired; the moment of my courage was gone, and I allowed him to envelope me in his strong arms. Within this circle of security, I finally relaxed enough to sleep.

◆ ◆ ◆

"Kassia, what do you want?"

I was awake now, but the luxury of our journey's respite kept us from moving. Our traveling companions seemed no more eager than us. I could have answered Jack's question any number of ways. I could have said that I wanted to make it to our destination alive and well, because it was true. I could have said I wanted to join a band of circus performers and learn to juggle flaming torches. Somewhat appealing, but not entirely true. I also could have said that I wanted to marry a prince and live out the rest of my days wealthy and in luxury, but he would have known I was lying. While I could have answered him any number of ways, I knew what it was he asked so answered accordingly.

"It probably sounds silly," I paused and looked down at my hands somewhat embarrassed at the admission I was about to make. There was a tiny purple wildflower blooming near the toe of my shoe, so I plucked it gingerly from the spongy earth as an aid to my thoughts. I wasn't sure if I wanted to go on, but when I noticed that he watched me with sincere earnestness, I continued. "I hate the city. I've never liked it. I always loved it when my mother would take me and my sister out of the city, to a place far outside the walls where we spent hours playing barefoot and carefree." My sight turned inward, and the forest faded in favor of an open field filled with wildflowers. "We gathered flowers." In my mind's eye I saw a basket in my hand, filled with the blooms of larkspur, harebell and coneflower. "My sister, Irisa, would put the blooms in her hair and carry them about, pretending to be a princess on her wedding day." I smiled at the memory. "I never played at such things, pretended instead that I was simply harvesting my crop for market."

"You never speak of your sister." Jack's question was innocent, not probing.

"No." How could he fully comprehend the burden of guilt I carried because of her? He knew she was a prisoner of Casmir, but could he understand that while I remained free I would always feel responsible? Another memory stirred, this one of a broad-shouldered man with long, fair hair and eyes the color of a storm-tossed ocean. Thinking of Issak and what had happened to him because of me made my stomach churn, and I fought back against the queasy feeling threatening to overtake me.

I didn't want to dwell on those thoughts, so I swiftly steered the conversation back to safer waters. "When we gathered enough flowers and returned home, the women living near mocked us, thinking that what we had done was foolish, that it served no purpose, and that our time would be better spent working to earn money because we had so little of it." I smiled at the memory despite its harshness at the time. "It's true. There certainly is no purpose in a flower, not really... except to bring beauty to life." I remembered the smile that always lit my mother's face as she surveyed the interior of our small home, wildflowers filling every empty receptacle. A fragrant aroma filled the air, perfuming our very life. "My father didn't understand why we did it either. He seemed irritated with my mother every time, but he never scolded her because he knew she wouldn't have cared, would have continued to go without his approval."

I stopped talking for a moment and forced my attention back to the present. Jack had watched me tell my story, patient and intent. He was a good listener. "So what do I want? I want to live a simple life, far from the city, in a wide open field with fresh air and flowers."

Anywhere I can find peace and security, I added in my head, but I didn't say it out loud. Jack gave me a gentle squeeze and I smiled, suddenly remembering one of my most frequent dreams, adding "...and some day a brown pony for my children." Though in reality, all of the things I had just told Jack were dreams. Did I truly believe that any of it would come to be?

As he so often had the ability to do, Jack read my thoughts. "Do you think you'll find these things where we're going?"

I had no answer for him. The tumult of the past week had all but consumed me, effectively stifling any thoughts about my future. No, I didn't know if I would find what I wanted in Islay Bay, nor did I know if I had any right to, because to find these things would be to find happiness. Was such a life meant for me? When I didn't respond, Jack pulled me into a fierce hug that I feared would reopen his wound, a hug made uncomfortable for me because of the dagger tucked into his belt and now digging into my ribs.

The dagger reminded me of something I had wondered about but never asked, and now seemed as good a time as any to ask.

"In Lynchport, when you freed Swine... You were quick. Very quick."

I didn't have to elaborate. My meaningful look and weighted words were enough to ask the question without asking -- how had he approached the guard with an amiable smile, casually and self-assuredly, until the tip of his blade bit through flesh and muscle as though through butter? Jack didn't flinch, kept his arms tightly around me as he considered his response. When it came, his words were soft, measured.

"Survival. Kassia, you have lived it yourself." It was true. I had. And I knew the cruelty of humanity, knew the dark passions lurking beneath the surface despite the veil with which polite society tried to cover it. On the mean streets however, it was given leave to come out more readily, if only because there was no check. Most people simply looked the other way when evil reared its head, preferring to move along and pretend not to see. Cruelties are inflicted in one of two places: under the cover of absolute secret, or out in the open with the approval of the masses and the power of public opinion for support.

"But what has been necessary at times comes at a greater cost than you know," Jack continued.

His eyes looked haunted. It did bother him, and knowing this gave me the comfort I sought, the reason I had asked him, even though I knew his skill was so deadly accurate that it had to have been honed through practice. At least now I knew that he counted the cost and that the skill did not own him; he carried it as a tool, but he was its master and not the other way around.

"Kassia..." I looked up at him, into his face, into his eyes, "...I will keep you safe," he whispered then brushed away a small leaf which had drifted down from the trees and landed on my hair. His fingers lingered and he twisted a loose strand of hair around his thumb then brushed a kiss onto my upturned face. I didn't know how he would keep his promise of protection, but right now it didn't seem important. It was a hope I needed to cling to despite my doubts.

The moment seemed right to try to tell him again what he would find out soon enough. What everyone would find out soon enough, because the passage of time would make my secret visible. "Jack, there's something I need to tell you."

He kept twirling my hair with his fingers, and the light sensation sent shivers down my back. "Whatever it is, can you tell me later?" He had nuzzled his face into my hair and his breath was tickling my ear, but I didn't want to be distracted away from telling him. He needed to know.

"Jack, you need to know..."

"Hmmmm?" His face was still buried in my hair and he was tracing a line with his finger, down my arm, across my palm and back up to my shoulder, to my neck. I wanted to wriggle away even while delighting in the sensation.

"Jack, listen..." He wouldn't stop, and in truth I didn't want him to. I tried again, somewhat feebly, "That night in Mosrad..." I gasped. Jack had just kissed the sensitive spot behind my ear. "...there is more you haven't guessed..." I squirmed. "...about what happened to me..." He kissed my earlobe, brought his hand up from my waist to trace the outline of my curves. "...you need to know..." I was losing focus as well as any desire to keep it. Getting lost in the moment was all the more appealing than conversation.

Whether or not I would have been able to tell him what I had intended, or even whether I would have been able to continue to talk at all would never be known, because just then we were interrupted by shouting that pierced the haze of intimacy swathing us from reality: "Jack! Kassia! They come! Quickly, we have to go!" Any heat kindled between us melted away instantly, like snows on the Plains of Oesk in the height of summer.

I had never seen a man like Swine clamber up onto the back of a horse so quickly, hedgepig that he was, but within moments we were flying along the forest trail, crashing through the thick undergrowth with such heedless haste that our flight was as likely to kill us as our pursuers.

It was only now that I finally heard the sounds of pursuit from somewhere behind us. They too were on horseback and likely rode singly, meaning that they would more easily out-distance our overloaded horses, particularly in open country if we were lucky enough to make it so far. We needed to make a move soon, and I hoped that Buran or Jack had a plan.

Eria sat behind me and held on with all her strength. She, more readily than I, knew what would happen if we were caught, if the Swamp People were more likely to kill us outright or take us back as prisoners. No matter. I didn't intend to be captured. Not again. Not ever again. I would die first.

We crossed a ditch filled with water, more quagmire than stream because it was choked with leaves and other decaying debris, then climbed a low rise on the other side, the horses' sides heaving with the effort required to lurch with an almost leaping gait up the loose dirt and rocky graveled side. Once we reached the top, we continued on as before. The trees of the forest thinned, becoming as sparse as the undergrowth had previously been thick. Cover would be more difficult to find here. I wanted to look back over my shoulder but didn't dare, not wanting to see just how close our enemies were. We would go on. For as long as we needed to.

Nothing happened for some time, and despite all evidence to the contrary, I felt the stirring of hope. The feeling was short-lived however. Rather than the simplicity of rushing wind, I began to feel the very air around us come alive, rapidly dissolving my embryonic hope and replacing it with a panic more primal than the hope had ever been. Small disturbances in the air close to my skin overwhelmed with small tingles like the exhale of tiny puffs of hot breath. Buran was in the lead and must have felt it too, for he urged us on, surging to a pace that would either free us or kill our horses.

A rock formation loomed up ahead, and Buran steered us towards it. We swung our stumbling mounts around the first outcropping and into a sheltered cove within, all but falling from our horses.

Without being asked, Cai vaulted from the back of his horse and ran towards the rock wall, scrambling up its side to a ledge high above, kicking loose bits of rock and scree as he went. Jack fell from his horse, but before I could cry out he recovered himself, drew his sword and flew to the mouth of the outcropping along with Buran.

Then silence. Absolute and complete.

I fought to steady my breathing, and we waited.

When it seemed as though time had stopped, that we had somehow become rock statues in a horrific garden of terrors, when it seemed like nothing would happen, it did. Baleful shrieks pierced the illusory calm, and Buran and Jack bolted, like arrows from the bow, around the corner and off into the forest to confront the demons of the swamp, the Children of the Yðir, our enemies.

Swine cowered on the far side of our cave, looking as if he had just swallowed a wild turkey and covering his ears with pallid hands. Eria huddled not far from him, curled into a tight ball on her side, facing away from me. I merely collapsed where I landed near the horses just inside the lip of the cleft. I sat silently with my knees drawn up to my chest, hugging them while keeping my eyes open and listening intently to the sounds of the battle just out of sight, of demons shrieking, of steel clashing, of flesh tearing, of bone cracking.

Then everything went still again. I straightened my spine but remained where I was, and what seemed like yet another eternity passed before I heard the sound of heavy steps approach. Much to my relief, Buran and Jack rounded the corner, shoulders heavy with fatigue, barely able to keep their swords from dragging on the hard-packed, rock-strewn ground. I locked eyes with Jack, questioning. He shook his head and I knew that we were free. Finally and fully.

The two men sat down together to clean their blades, and I did my best to pretend not to see the blood and gore. They spoke quietly with one another, and I found myself wondering if this shared experience would erase the antagonism that Jack had felt towards Buran. Cai returned too but said nothing. His sling was tucked into his belt, and he made his way over to Swine, ostensibly to see how his new friend fared. The boy was more sympathetic than I, it seemed. My thoughts turned away from them and to Eria. She had not moved since we arrived, was still curled into a ball.

I went to her and knelt down, thinking that perhaps emotional exhaustion had finally wreaked its havoc on her body, that perhaps she was finally overcome by it and that a good long rest would do her good, that it would do us all good. I reached out a hand to touch her shoulder, but before my hand even made contact, I felt the heat radiate from her small frame. I couldn't account for her fever; she was fine only moments before. I shook her, but she remained unresponsive.

"Buran!" I yelled with frantic fear. "It's Eria, something has happened!" Buran dropped his work and leapt to her side. He rolled her over, and we all sucked in our breath at what was revealed: a tiny dart, no larger than a common fly, had imbedded itself into Eria's neck. It was likely propelled there by blowguns, explaining the lightening-charged air during our flight, and likely tipped with poison, a suspicion confirmed when Buran turned his haunted eyes to stare at us.

"Elder flower, feverfew, belladonna leaf, yarrow... see what you can find. Quickly." He instructed us quietly and calmly, but I could see that his eyes were hard and unyielding, were windows to the anger that boiled just beneath the surface. He was determined to do what could be done.

While the use of these herbs was the most common way to bring down a fever, I also knew that using them was a vain hope; only an antidote to the poison would help her. Buran was grasping at straws, but what more could be done? I nodded my understanding and dashed away with Cai at my heels. Both of us were glad to do something, anything, whether or not it was likely to help.

I knew we wouldn't find feverfew in the forest, but elderflower and belladonna were readily available. The berries of belladonna, also known as nightshade, were fatally poisonous when used in abundance, but the leaves of the plant could bring down a fever when brewed properly. Life and death in one plant.

When we returned, we found that Swine had made himself useful, was heating water over a small fire. Whether he did this at his own initiative or under instruction was not clear. Buran was still huddled over Eria, doing his best to soothe her brow with the water he carried in his pack. I prepared the leaves we had found as best I could, cutting them with a knife to expose their insides to free the juices which would infuse the water with their medicative goodness. It was quickly finished, and once allowed to cool, I handed the concoction to Buran who propped up Eria enough to encourage her to drink.

I let him tend to her, comforting and soothing her as best he was able. There was nothing more I could do, and the heavy weight of my ever-present fatigue was settling over me with familiar ownership. I made my way over to Jack who was still cleaning his sword despite his own obvious fatigue. I collapsed down next to him in companionable silence, watching him work. He was nearly finished but his motions were slowing, becoming more lethargic. He must have been more tired than I realized. It was only when I saw a sheen of sweat gathering on his brow that I became worried. I sidled in closer and looked more intently, noticed the rosy hue of his cheeks, the red rimming his eyes.

"Jack?" He looked up at me then, his eyes glazed and blank. This alarmed me immediately. I reached for his cheek with tentative fingers, nervous at what I might find, not at all surprised when my fingers met fire. "Cai!" I called, urgent and pleading. He came rushing over. "Get more of that brew, and hurry!" He scampered over to retrieve it as I had asked. I took the sword from Jack's shaking hands, lay him down gently. "A dart got you too?" He nodded weakly, making a feeble motion with his hand as though he were brushing an insect off his neck. "And you didn't think it important to tell me?" I bristled with anger bolstered by fear.

Cai returned with a small measure, and I made Jack drink it down, all the while fighting against the subtle thought which sought entry into my consciousness, that perhaps the messengers of Swamp People were about to extract the payment that the Yðir required, despite the fact that they too were now dead. It seemed so unfair to have come this far, to have survived all that we had, only to see it end in this way.

The next several hours found us trapped in a cycle that seemed endless. Buran tended Eria, I tended Jack, and Cai kept us in supply of herbs. While Swine had kept the fire blazing, important for brewing the herbal mixture, he was in all other respects useless. The quailing rump-fed pignut hadn't even managed to poke himself with a stick in the process.

Clouds moved in to cover the star-crusted sky as dusk fell. A hush descended over the vivacity of daytime's birdsong, and I was grateful, for it ushered in the arrival of subdued, lulling night sounds.

"Kassia," I looked up to see Cai's sweet, expectant face. Lines of worry creased the corners of his eyes. His mink-soft blonde hair was more dulled than usual from the ordeal of our journeys. Poor, dear Cai. He had mostly been a silent participant, always busy, always helpful, always knowing what was needed nearly before anyone else, acting before being asked; highly indispensible and exceedingly courageous. When life settled itself I would find some way to thank him. For all the pomp and blather of the noble class, Cai was true nobility, worth his weight in gold in triple measure.

"Kassia, give him some of this." Cai held out several small lumps of charcoal. I couldn't hide my skepticism. "It helps draw swallowed poisons," he explained. "I don't know if it will help what's in his blood, but," he shrugged, "the... women..." He never met my eyes when he spoke of his mother, but I knew that's who he meant. "...The women say it works."

I didn't want to know how the temple prostitutes back in Corium knew about poison, but at this point I was willing to try anything if it gave Jack a fighting chance. Even if it did nothing to help Jack, it would bring Cai comfort to know he had done all he knew to try. I did as he instructed and placed two small pieces of the black lumps on Jack's tongue and made him swallow with sips of the herbal mixture before settling back into my vigil.

Jack had only recently begun to heal from his injury, and I didn't know where he would get the strength to recover from the poison that now flowed through his veins. Thinking back to the moment I found him pinned to that tree by the bolt of a crossbow, it occurred to me just how strong metal-smiths were. Almost immediately, a flood of images of Issak taking his beating surfaced, but I quickly dismissed them, not willing to allow complicated emotions to cloud the moment.

I was brought out of these meditations by the slowly arising awareness that Buran appeared more agitated than normal. I rose up quickly and motioned Cai over to me. "Cai, stay by Jack." He nodded silently and I moved to Buran's side.

Eria was tossing her head from side to side, and her movements were getting more agitated. Within moments she was thrashing violently, her arms wrapped around her stomach. She sat up in a frenzy with a howl of agony, and as she did so spewed a mixture of blood and bile. She collapsed to her side, rolling in her own filth, but Buran pulled her from it, doing his best to calm her with desperation. I shrank back as the image of Eria became my mother on her deathbed, convulsing and screaming that dark night in Corium so many years ago. I turned and ran.

Cai found me a while later down by the stream, hunched over and heaving. He touched my shoulder gently, and I wiped a shaky hand across my mouth but remained as I was. When he didn't speak I knew what had happened; there was no need for him to tell me. I rose slowly, dried my tears with my other sleeve, and followed him silently back. Swine had also fled the gruesome scene and was seated next to a tree, staring blankly into the shadows. As I approached our rock cove, Buran appeared, his face ashen, the pallor clear to me even in the dying light of the day.

"We must bury her." His tone was flat, defeated, as if this latest trauma in his life had taken everything, leaving him with no hope of ever finding joy again. I could only guess at how he felt, knowing that Eria was all he had left, and now he didn't even have her. Weariness clung to his frame, and he wandered off alone. I nodded, setting aside my need to ask questions, to attempt to understand the people that did this to her. I hated them, and rage seethed within me, though it coexisted with grief and filled the ragged hole her death had created. I barely knew Eria, had only heard the smallest portion of her story, but she was a friend, and she had saved us by her courage and swift action. For that she had paid with her own life. Full mourning would have to come later, for now our friend must be buried.

It was then that Swine did something that surprised me. He left us and went out into the forest to dig a grave for Eria. When he was finished, he returned for us and we went silently with him, to bury our friend. I stood dry-eyed, but Buran shed tears, telling the story of two deaths -- the poison had taken Eria's life, but it took Buran's too, though he still breathed and walked and ate and slept. He would remain a participant in the world he walked, but I doubted at that moment whether he would ever truly live again.

Deep night was upon us. Rooks and jackdaws roosted in the treetops overhead, and their chattered "kaahs" seemed a declaration of finality over what had just happened. A breeze picked up unnoticed as we stood near Eria's grave and I pulled my cloak around my shoulders. Casting an eye to the trees, I left the feathered sentinels to watch over Buran as he remained near Eria's grave. Cai, Swine and I returned back to our rock shelter.

I found Jack sleeping peacefully, his fever broken. His ending would not be like Eria's, and I was grateful. There was no peace for me however. I feared sleep, expecting the dark memories of my mother's pain-wracked body, her convulsions and screaming, to haunt me with terror all through the night, but once I stoked the fire to a full blaze, settled in next to Jack, and pulled our cloaks over us, I fell into a deep sleep devoid of dreams.

◆ ◆ ◆

Dawn came earlier than normal, I knew for certain. A single shaft of sunlight poured itself through the cleft crack, spilling its cheery brightness directly onto my face. I cracked my eyes and cursed it. Didn't the sun know that we were a party in mourning? Couldn't it see the evidence of a recently dug grave, the scattered remnants of medicinal preparation around our now cold fire? Today was not the day for the bright warmth of its rays. More likely was it that the skies should have rained, poured and showered us with depressing discomfort. That would have more suitably matched my desultory mood.

We each arose, and without need for speech assembled our paltry gear, packed and mounted. Jack was weak and tired, but like the rest of us wanted to leave this place as quickly as possible, letting the Yðir triumph in their victory, in the life they had taken.

We didn't know where we were going. Westwald was on the west side of Allmor Lake, but since we had raced headlong through the forest in our escape from Porpio á Fen, we had no true notion of where we were or how to find Westwald. The best we could do was ride north and east and hope beyond hope that we would eventually make it to the shores of the lake.

We rode for several hours, and eventually it became clear that we had been descending for some time, though subtly and not noticeably until the forest thinned and we could see a panorama of landscape around us. The air was clearer, cleaner, carrying less of the woodsy smells of mushroom, rotting logs and decaying organic matter, replaced by the more fragrant scents of open meadow and wildflower. When finally we came to the forest edge, a vista of inspirational beauty arrested me from the introspection that generally accompanies mundane travel. Off in the distance lay a vast lake, its open waters bright with myriads of diamonds glinting in the sun's rays, breaking them into millions of reflections on the dancing waves. Progress and hope also glinted in the lake's depth, for far across the expanse of this water lay Islay Bay, a city that promised me refuge, a new start, answers to mysteries.

It was only midday, but an afternoon's rest was much needed

for Jack's weakened body and Buran's weakened spirit. Now that we had gained our bearings, the idea of stopping was easier for everyone to swallow.

Cai, ever the provider, scampered off wordlessly in search of game from the ever-boundless provision of the forest. It seemed to me as though Cai truly enjoyed the freedom life on the road had given. Like me, the confines of the city had been almost like a prison. By contrast, Swine was out of his element, for his language was commerce, and the forest held nothing for him; therefore, as was his way, he found a tree under which to nestle and fell instantly asleep. I disregarded him as usual. Buran moved off in a trance, seeking a place to wrestle with his ghosts.

Jack and I found a place to settle down together where we could have a bit of privacy. We said nothing for a long while, simply enjoyed a quiet companionship, but eventually gave ourselves over to light conversation. Both of us were in need of distraction away from all that had transpired the day before. To look at Jack now it would have been difficult to guess he had been pinned to a tree and pricked with a deadly poisoned dart, each within days of the other, for he was calm and seemingly at peace as we talked of his father and his hope that the people had made it safely to their hidden mountain refuge.

Eventually our conversation stopped, and I dozed, awakening only when an insect buzzed with vexatious insistence near my ear. I swiped at it with an irritated flick of my hand and cracked open one eye to see Jack watching me.

"What are you thinking?" he asked me, his voice filled with the warmth of contentment.

I closed my eye again and said with feigned distaste, "I'm thinking that once we get to Islay Bay I will be happy to be rid of you and all the trouble that seems to surround you."

He pinched my arm and I yelped. "No, I think you have it backwards. I think I've been saving your skin most of the time." That was hardly the case since he hadn't actually saved me even once, but I wasn't about to argue with him when there was no logic in either of our comments. "Kassia," he began in a serious tone, all traces of our easy conversation gone. "You experienced a lot in Corium. I told you that I would keep you safe and I meant it." He put one arm around my shoulder and the other around my waist, a waist which had subtly begun to thicken, though it was likely not visible to anyone but me. I felt my palms grow icy cold despite the warmth of the sun. "Kassia, when will you learn to trust me?"

I have heard it said that to trust another person is to lay open your heart to them, to give them access to a part of yourself that few others get to see. Once they have that access, you hand them a knife, showing them the exact place and the exact way in which they can cut the most deeply, the most painfully, and with the most efficiency. Whether or not they strike however, is completely up to them; you have yielded control.

Did I trust him? I thought I did. I had decided as much back in Tóka's sick room, yet I hadn't had reason so far to act on my decision. My determination hadn't been tested. Now in this moment I questioned myself. It had been easier to decide to trust, to yield to my need for another when I was at a weak point, when circumstances were dire and I had nothing else. An honest look revealed that I was still afraid, but I thought I was still willing. If not Jack, who else? Rather than respond with words, I kissed him lightly then put my head on his shoulder.

My attention was distracted by a pair of squirrels racing down a tree, tumbling into a head-over-tail roll as one caught the other before the captured squirrel escaped and ran up another tree, the chaser close at his heels. My thoughts drifted, and I thought back to that night in Lynchport, at the Buxom Maiden, when Jack had introduced me as his new bride. I laughed a little at the memory and the sound disturbed Jack's thoughts enough that he asked me again what I was thinking. I told him the story of my bath and how he had fallen asleep sprawled across the bed, of how distraught I was at the notion that there was only one bed and that he slept on it. He laughed at my tale of how he grabbed me as I leaned over his prone figure, how he had flung me down on the bed next to him and embraced me like I was someone else he knew, how he had whispered... a name...

"Jack?" I lifted my chin and looked up at him, asked uneasily,

"Who is Nairin?" The muscles in his arm tensed, but his face remained passive. When he kept silent I prodded him, suspicion growing that I wouldn't like his answer. "She's the girl from your little hut back in Mercoria, isn't she?" The suspicion kindled only moments before was growing steadily, and I pulled away from him slowly, warily, looking him full in the face to gauge his answer.

"No," he said softly.

I didn't believe him. His face had clouded over when he answered, and now he didn't look like he was going to say more without being prodded. I pulled away from him farther, and he looked up at me with misery in his eyes, confirmation that my suspicions were correct. He had a secret, and he was pained that I had uncovered it.

"Who is she then?" I didn't want to know. I needed to know. All of it made me confused and scared and angry all at once. "You thought I was her. You wanted me to be her that night." Jealousy, plain and simple. I was jealous, and the unreasonable rage that is oftentimes jealousy surged.

He shook his head slowly in denial. "No... yes..." he faltered. "Kassia, I don't even remember saying her name!" He was panicked now, looked at me with confusion. I shoved away from him with my hands and stood. My heart had already begun to harden towards him, the familiar anger and defiance had returned, though I wasn't ready to run from him, not yet. I needed an explanation, even if it killed me.

He heaved a big sigh and gently took my hand, pulling me back down next to him. I allowed it, but sat rigid, at full alert. "Kassia, she was my wife. Once." He glanced at me to see if I was listening, willing me to understand. For now he had my attention, but my eyes blazed heat at him from across the gulf that was now looming between us. I had found him out, though I didn't yet know what I had found out.

"It's not what you think," he offered, and I challenged him with a glare, so he continued. "Kassia, she died, two years ago." I wanted to be relieved at that, but there was more to his story; there had to be or else he wouldn't have reacted so guardedly. I knew there was more he had to tell me from the weight he still bore on his frame. I was ready for the rest and urged him on with the fire in my eyes, daring him to hold anything back, no matter how unsavory it was to either of us.

"It was a sickness. It came on like a wildfire, consuming and wasting her pain-wracked body in a fortnight. When she died suddenly, we were all bereft, her family was devastated. But then the inevitable responsibility fell on my shoulders, to marry her younger sister, Mairona." Fire Woman. It had to be Fire Woman. And she had a name. Mairona. "It was tradition. Kassia, I didn't want her. I don't want her. But it's a tradition fiercely held to by a small portion of people from Agrius, including Nairin's. Once married, if the older daughter dies, the younger one takes her place if still unmarried. It preserves the union intended between the families." He was pleading, willing me to understand, his tone broken, painful to hear. "But I knew my duty and accepted it, whether I wanted to or not. I just thought that maybe... with everything that has happened..."

"So you *are* married?" I squeaked incredulously.

It had all been too good to be true. I had been right to question my decision to trust him. As I had come to know all too well, things that appear to be too good usually are. I should have known that happiness was not a permanent state for me. He was not mine; he belonged to another, and there was nothing I could do about it. I was crazy to have even hoped for it. If it's possible to feel your own heart break, I felt it now.

"No, Kassia, not *married*!" He said as his fist pounded the dirt. He was determined to make me see his side.

"You are betrothed..." I whispered, mostly to myself, studying the trees in the distance. Then I looked back at him, a heated challenge in my eyes. "You thought it would change? The fact of your betrothal, it's binding nature? Just because you are here and she is... somewhere... not here?" The words tumbled out of my mouth in an incoherent stream. I was confused, muddled by the brokenness that had reasserted itself. "When did you plan to tell me all of this? You were planning to tell me this, weren't you? Maybe once you got what you wanted from me? Perhaps a good tumble?"

I stood again, my rage numbing me to all else around, making my thoughts, my words, illogical, and though I could see that I had wounded him, I didn't care. Perhaps I wasn't worthy of love after all.

I turned and fled. I didn't want him to know how he had broken me, for him to see that I had changed back into a Kassia I thought I would never be again. He had taken the knife I offered him and struck where it did the most damage. He didn't follow me and I didn't look back.

10

VAPOR. LIFE IS vapor. The substance of a thing can change in a moment, in a heartbeat. What was once fixed and absolute is transformed into something entirely different upon the breath of the wind. The sea mirrors life this way. In a breath, all that was calm and blue and crystalline turns angry and gray and clouded. Squalls rise up, tossing and turning a vessel, and without a lodestar, it is all too easy to lose sense of place and time. The last leg of my journey was no different...

We entered the town of Westwald on a miserably cold, wet day, each of us equally miserably wet and cold. Even Cai's normally undaunted cheerfulness was dampened. Once leaving the forest edge we trudged on, mile after mile, following the contour of the lake's shore, past fertile fields covering the hills to the west of the road overlooking the lake, and past the small farmsteads which were home to the families tending those fields. The weather turned inclement on the second day, and we encountered few people, only those whose tasks required them to be out in the rain. Those few we met were courteous if not unequivocally friendly, a nice change from the furtive, evasive people of the marsh. Finally we reached the walled town of Westwald.

The citizens of Westwald were similar to the farmers we had encountered -- courteous if not overtly friendly -- as we entered the gate on the west side, descending through levels of cobbled streets to the harbor below. The rain had tapered off to nothing by the time we left our horses with a farrier. I sent Cai and Swine in search of food and a few other necessities while Buran, Jack and I searched out a boat for hire, to take us across the lake to Islay Bay. The decision of which boat to hire was instantly made however, since after a quick survey of options, there were few to be found, and only one of these was large enough to carry us and our horses.

Its captain was easy to locate, for he was speaking with the harbor master not a stone's-throw from his ship. The man had the appearance of wealth rather than that of the swarthy, sun-kissed, deck-dwelling sea dog I had expected. I gave him greeting and presented him with our proposal for passage. I did so without flourish, figuring that he would take us or he wouldn't, and no amount of floridity on my part would change the nature of my request. He took a careful look at our small party, his face devoid of expression. His eyes flicked from person to person, taking in every detail about each of us, spending the most time on Jack, and for a moment I was sure he sensed Jack's compromised health, feared immediately that he would deny us out of uncertainty over Jack's condition. Perhaps it had been unwise to allow Jack to accompany me. To my surprise however, the captain nodded his agreement and we shook hands. He informed us that he was leaving the next day at dawn, and if we wished to be on the ship, we should arrive slightly before, that he would sail with or without us, then gave us a suggestion of where to stay the night. With our purpose accomplished, we left the quay in search of Cai and Swine.

Jack and I had still not spoken since our argument in the forest; at least not beyond the most absolute and necessary of comments like "move your horse, it's in my way" or "I want to slap you, you dissembling puttock." Perhaps not the latter, though my thoughts mirrored the sentiment constantly. I avoided him as much as possible, a miraculous feat considering the fact that there were only five of us. Jack had hurt me before on our journey, wounding me with an arrow of damaging words, but this last rending of my heart, the revelation of Mairona, was irredeemable. I had committed myself to the vulnerability of complete trust, and he had wounded me irrevocably in repayment. Though he seemed miserable because of it, seemed to want to discuss it again, to convince me that the situation was not as dire as I believed, I could not, would not allow myself to trust so easily again.

Cai and Swine materialized out of the crowds, having found success in their assignment, and led us to a small cook shop where we found a small table just outside the door, and ordered the first real food we had eaten in many days. Sitting around the small table with a flagon of weakly watered ale shared among us and a platter of food, we spoke little, each of us lost deep in thought or in the throes of avoidance, respectively. After some time Buran announced that he planned to stay in Westwald until he could figure out a way to get back to Pania and any family he may have left there. None of us was surprised, and we accepted this without ill-will. When our meal was finished, I offered him a heartfelt hug and good wishes, all of which he accepted and returned in equal measure before leaving with little ceremony. We saw no more of him.

Morning arrived as it is wont to do each and every day, and we made our way from our inn to the quay. We boarded on time, and despite a critical look at the storm clouds gathering overhead, the captain ordered our departure.

Vapor. Changeable. Life and the sea. We were not far out from shore when the winds picked up, turning very quickly into a squall and then a storm, and I was seized with fear. I had never been on a boat, so my experience was lacking; however I imagined that lake storms could kill as effectively as sea storms, and my stomach clenched with threatened upheaval as I hastened to the railing to retch. A passing sailor forestalled me and firmly guided me safely away from the side with a bucket in hand. He left me there in my misery, his scolding words echoing with a reminder about the pitching deck and strong winds that could easily send me headlong into the tossing waves.

The captain was beset by the duties of piloting his ship through the weather, but after a while he took it upon himself to send a man who was quick to assure me that storms of this nature were all too common on this lake and that his ship was well able to ride it out. Being a novice to such things, I accepted his knowledge as superior to my fears and sought a place to sit in continued discomfort, waiting out the storm. I could not however, no matter how hard I tried, dash the hope that perhaps Swine would be swept overboard. This hope came to nothing when the next day the storm abated as quickly as it had come, Swine still securely aboard. The waters calmed and became clear again, crystalline and brilliant, melting away my fears and bolstering my composure if not my appetite.

I did my best to occupy my mind with happy memories, and thoughts of my sister immediately surfaced. Irisa. My sister. My sweet, innocent sister. Was she still innocent? I shuddered to think about it.

Had Casmir treated her the same way he had treated me in Mosrad? My heart went cold, and it took every ounce of my will to focus my conscious attention on the wood grain of the ship's railing under my hands, to concentrate on the feel of the wood, so smooth and polished with care. Despite my efforts, memories of Mosrad seeped in, and I imagined what my sister might be experiencing, angering me anew. Rage filled me, and I groaned at the sky. My travel companions likely misread my misery as having to do with Eria, and the sailors cast me backwards glances, walked more paces around me than were entirely necessary. I was past caring. I rammed my fist down hard onto the top of the railing and the resulting pain sent shock waves up my arm. I watched the water glide by, far below the railing on which I leaned. Somewhere behind me one of the sailors had pulled a small pipe from his jacket and played a doleful tune composed of haunting notes, mellow and breathy. The notes filled me, resonating so perfectly down to my core that I wondered if perhaps the man played it purposely for me.

My despondency was broken by a discreet clearing of a throat from behind me. I turned to find the captain there, recovered from any stress the storm may have given him and dressed smartly in a fine coat and polished boots. I had not seen much of him since the storm had abated, for he had been content to stay in his cabin. He stood before me now, his back straight as a lance, his hair clean cut and neat under his hat, his eyes piercing and direct. I doubted they missed much. He acknowledged me with a deferential nod before telling me that we would arrive in port by nightfall. I acknowledged what he said, then he turned retreating back to his cabin, speaking softly with his men as he crossed the deck. From the beginning, he had not met my preconceived notions regarding what a ship's captain should be. It seemed unlikely that he often took on passengers, so why he had agreed to take us on was a mystery. But whatever his reasons, I was thankful and would not prod him for answers. We could have been weeks waiting in Westwald for another suitable boat, so the serendipitous meeting with this ship's captain could not have been any better planned.

I retreated from the railing and found Cai sitting with Swine, playing the same game they had played at Tóka's house. Jack sat nearby but separately, leaning against a barrel, his eyes closed. I let the two know of our impending arrival, but if Jack heard me he gave no indication. I returned to the railing and remained a fixture there until we arrived at our destination.

◆◆◆

If I thought Corium was a jewel of a city, I had formed the opinion before ever having seen Islay Bay. This jewel truly took my breath away. The streets and bright white buildings gleamed with a warm radiance, reflecting orange as the evening sun began its descent towards the edge of the lake's farthest side. The temperatures in Islay Bay averaged mild and were moderated by lake breezes which blew constantly, though the radiance of the plastered white exteriors gave everything a warm glow, making it feel hotter than it really was. My troubles were momentarily forgotten as I wondered how anyone could ever be unhappy living in a place such as this.

Our vessel docked at an immaculate jetty where we were greeted by an efficient dock crew who helped to moor the ship. Once he had finished his business, I paid the captain our agreed price, though he seemed unconcerned with it, taking the coin I offered him without a glance and pocketing it as he studied me. I was tempted to be unnerved. It had not occurred to me to question the man's loyalty, but perhaps he had ties to Casmir? Everyone had a political affinity of some sort. It seemed unlikely, I decided, in a town so far from Agrius. Though I had not asked, he again suggested a small inn where we could find comfortable lodging. I thanked him and we moved off, echoes of all that had unnerved me about him reverberating in my bones. I did not turn around, but I could feel the man's eyes on me until we melted into the crowds, out of his line of sight.

While crossing the sea, we had passed out of the Empire of Mercoria into the Kingdom of Elbra. While Mercoria was ancient and vast in size, containing many and various people groups, Elbra was smaller, younger and more cohesive in its culture. It had once been a part of Pania, the home of Eria, Buran and my mother, but it had experienced a secession of sorts, though a bloodless one, the result of a shift in economic and political power that had allowed the nobles of Elbra to do as they pleased without the expected political reprisals, the protestations of its former king rendered effectively impotent. Elbra had simply acted as a separate political state, and because of Pania's inability to keep it, Elbra became its own nation-state. The Elbran noble house was younger, but what it lacked in age, it made up for in wealth, the main catalyst for its independence from Pania. For this reason it had been courted throughout its fledgling years as a strategic ally by kings and rulers all over the known world. Alliances were made and broken constantly, as was the way of the world, but none had yet been successful in making a strategic alliance of blood outside of those already existing with Pania.

We navigated Islay Bay, its wide lanes lined with beautiful merchant booths hung with decorative awnings to keep the sun and glare off merchant and shopper alike. Beautiful people were everywhere, men and women alike dressed in draping robes of exquisite material, fine jewels hung on chains of gold, and rings adorned fingers in brilliance. Never before had I experienced this level of wealth and opulence, and I felt somehow diminished by my own shabby appearance, despite having changed into the finest dress I owned before disembarking for Islay Bay.

Eventually we made our way into another district of the city, one that was decidedly less gleaming yet equally as neat and tidy. The inn the captain had suggested was easy to locate, and we arranged for lodgings for ourselves, opting for private rooms rather than suffer a stay in the common sleeping room in the eaves of the building. Thanks to Figor's largesse, we could afford it, and I preferred to keep our business secret until we knew more about what that business was.

This part of our journey was at an end, and now it was left to us to decide what to do, where to go, how to solve the mystery. But first we needed rest. It was late, and there would be plenty of time to start tomorrow. Cai, being Cai, immediately made friends, moved off to watch a game of knucklebones in the corner. Swine made no apologies about leaving immediately for a room upstairs, undoubtedly to sleep. That left Jack and I standing alone in the middle of the room. I felt awkward, but since we had practical matters to discuss I turned to look at him full in the face. Since I had been adept at avoidance for so long, I had not observed his fatigue and was alarmed at what I saw on his face. He was drawn and pale, and there was no light in his eyes. He wavered where he stood, threatening to collapse, so I grabbed his arm and steadied him, ignoring the heat that flooded my insides as I touched him.

"I guess you're not as recovered as we thought." He said nothing, simply nodded his head and allowed me to lead him upstairs to one of the rooms we had rented. I forced him to lie down on the neat straw mattress in the center of the small room then pulled up a small chair, sat in it to make sure he stayed put. I was still miffed at him, but I couldn't stand by and do nothing with him in such a state. I comforted myself in this seeming irony by the fact that I would do as much for a sickly dog. When I was sure he slept, I slipped downstairs and commandeered a loaf of bread and a small jug of ale from the kitchen, ignoring the shocked look of the serving girl at my brazen trespass into her domain. I returned upstairs to find Jack still sleeping. With nothing more to do until he awoke, I took a few mouthfuls of the bread then leaned my head back against the wall just to rest my eyes for a moment.

It must have been far more than a moment, for I was startled awake by the sound of an efficient, crisp rap on the door. It couldn't have been Swine or Cai, for neither of them would have knocked. I rubbed my eyes then the corded muscles of my neck. I glanced around the small room and saw that Jack still slept and daylight streamed through the small window, indicating that it was morning and I had slept all night upright in the chair. The knock sounded again. Curious yet cautious, I stood and silently cracked the door just enough to see who was outside, not wanting to wake Jack.

A man stood in the dark hall outside the door, dressed in an opulent coat of satin, embroidered at the neck, down the front and around the bottom hem with gold stitching. A decorative dagger hung in a sheath at his belt, but other than that, he was unarmed. As I studied him to make up my mind what to do, he watched me in return, his cultured politeness overriding any irritation he may have felt at my lack of hospitality or greeting. Having decided he was neither footpad nor mercenary thug, I put my finger to my lips to indicate the sleeping form behind me and asked, "Can I help you with something?" The man glanced briefly behind me and tried to hide a twitch of amusement. I wondered why he would be so cheeky until I sensed movement behind me, turned to see Jack sitting up on his mattress. His cheeks had the warm flush of sleep and his hair stuck out at awkward angles, while I myself looked no better, being quite rumpled from travel and a night's sleep on a chair. "You may as well come in and tell us what you want." I should have moderated the rawness of my words, but I was tired and it was early. I turned without ceremony and eyed the loaf I had confiscated the night before but decided I should wait. I returned to my seat on the chair, Jack remained as he was on the mattress, and since there was no other place to sit in the room, I didn't invite our guest to be seated.

"I have been sent to welcome you to Islay Bay and to pass along an invitation to you and..." he looked to Jack "...your companion, to join my lord for dinner this evening." His message was short and to the point, stated in such a way that brooked no disagreement because it was assumed the receivers of such an invitation would have nothing to consider, would accept with gladness and joy. Likely in his world, the invitation could not be refused.

I glanced at Jack, but the look he gave me was devoid of nuance, so I turned back to our guest. "Your lord... He is?"

"Serdar Janko Barbaros," he said with habitual nod of deference in honor of his better. A serdar in Elbra ranked akin to a count, and likely the man being referenced here was the local noble ruling Islay Bay. "His illustrious family holds vast tracts of land in the north but the Serdar resides most often in Islay Bay, overseeing matters of trade. For you see, the Barbaros family has connections all over the world."

When Elbra freed itself from any sovereign ties to Pania, it created a new state, but it also revolutionized a new approach to aristocracy. Wealth had been created through trade, therefore trade was power in Elbra, and most of its nobility had no need to adhere to antiquated notions of what the noble class should and shouldn't do in regard to it. Though this system worked well for the Elbrans, it was still often misunderstood by other cultures who maintained the traditional separation between aristocracy and the trades. Though he kept his tone bright enough, I sensed a hint of defensiveness behind his words. Little did he know that I cared not a whit for any of the social niceties that made his world turn.

I didn't respond to his tidbit of noble trivia, instead got right to the heart of things. "So why would this Serdar Janko Barbaros," I drawled out his name, "want to have dinner with us? How does he know about our arrival, and why does he care?" The answer was obvious; the captain was this man's source, though I had no idea why our presence was noteworthy except that the Serdar was somehow involved in the mystery.

The man looked at me as though he also wondered why. "I am afraid that is something you will have to ask the Serdar." He smiled smugly. "Someone will be sent to collect you this evening." His cultured politeness neared exhaustion, and it seemed as if he was straining to reply levelly to my caustic tone.

Collect us...as if we were chattel... "And if we don't want to come?" Of course we would come, but I couldn't help the urge to tweak Lackey Man.

He flicked a quick look at Jack as if challenging Jack's decision to leave all the talking to me then looked back at me and gave a slight shrug as if to say that there was no reason why I would even consider not coming. I brushed past him, opened the door and held it there as if I was ushering him out. "Well, if I am to be received by a Serdar, I should probably find somewhere to wash up first." There was no mistaking the acerbity in my voice but the man still managed to maintain his mask of politeness.

He gave me a deferential bow. "Kveðjum. Farewell," he said thin-lipped.

"Kveðjum," I replied as I shut the door on his retreating figure.

When the sound of his steps had receded, Jack spoke.

"Kassia, there was no need to be so rude to the man. He was only doing his duty. And likely he works for the man that sent you that book. Tonight you may have all your answers." I retreated into silence, but I knew he was right. "You have so much anger inside you. I worry for you. Not every aristocrat is a bad person."

His tone was very placating, gentle, but still I said nothing. Just like me, his life had been affected both directly and indirectly by the games the ruling class played. Jack and his father had lost everything because of it. Either he ignored this fact or had come to terms with it. I had lost more, and I would never come to terms with it.

I was suddenly tired, my heart heavy. "I don't need to explain myself, to you least of all," I said wearily then left the room.

◆◆◆

Despite the smoke and bluster of my attitude toward Lackey Man's invitation, I fully intended all along to attend the dinner that night. Answers would be found there and I knew it. Regardless of the identity of my dining companions, whether I was to dine with the Emperor himself or just a lowly cook shop owner, I was in desperate need of a bath and my scalp itched. And since my body was going to be clean I decided it wouldn't hurt to have my clothes washed as well, so I searched out a public bath and sent my dress off to a laundress.

After I had enjoyed an uncharacteristically and thoroughly luxurious day, I returned to the inn to find my room empty except for a new dress laid out carefully on the straw mattress. I was relieved that Jack was not there but curious about the dress.

These thoughts had no more than formed in my mind when a soft knock sounded on the door. I turned and opened it, discovering a young girl standing there with an open, curious expression on her face. She dropped her direct gaze and bobbed a quick curtsy before announcing, "M'lady, I was sent to help you, to arrange your hair and help you prepare for tonight."

I frowned and without thinking reached back to feel my freshly washed hair which was plaited down the middle of my back in a very simple braid, thinking it was suitable. While I was still considering the notion of having this anonymous girl rearrange my hair, she fluidly stepped around me and into the room, unconcerned by my confusion. "Oh, I thought maybe you would have dressed by now. Here, let me help you."

"I'm not a lady, and as you can see, I *am* dressed." She pretended not to hear me, lifted the new dress to shake out the folds, so I added, "...and my hair is fine."

The girl turned back to me and tilted her face up to meet mine. She was a study in heartbroken fallenness, her pert little lips forming a perfect pout, her neatly manicured brows drawn closely together. "Oh, but you must! You are dining with Serdar Barbaros!" As if that was supposed to change my mind. "And your friend, Jack... he asked me to shop for you, gave me a pouch of coins." Before I had a chance to reply, she continued, "He is very handsome, don't you think? Are you two lovers?"

My face flashed a brilliant shade of crimson but she didn't notice, had pulled off my old dress with the deftness of one who was used to tending to ladies at court. She spun me to face her, and I saw her eyes drift to my waistline as she did so. She said nothing, but I saw a flash of understanding flit across her face, though it was gone as quickly as it came. I didn't protest as she slid the new dress over my head, for I wanted nothing more than to be covered again.

"If you are not lovers, you should be." She met my eyes. "I would be, if he asked." She winked and a smile quickened her lips. She was under a false impression. About many things. But I didn't have a desire to set her straight, not right now. She didn't give me a chance to, even had I wanted to. "Now for your hair. How should I do it?"

I was at a loss. Thinking back to how my mother used to braid my hair in elaborate plaits woven in an impossible way on my head, I explained to her how it was done. She listened without comment and then let her fingers fly. She was very adept, and I wondered where Jack had found her.

When she finished she spun me to face her, hands on hips, a brilliant smile on her face. "You are beautiful." It was a pronouncement which brooked no disagreement and I blushed. The girl truly was a force of nature.

"What is your name?" I asked, trying my best to hide my embarrassment.

"Lidia," she beamed, but dismissed my curiosity about her with a flick of her hand. "Just wait until he sees you!"

"Who? The Serdar?"

"No, silly! Jack, of course!" She took my hands in hers and leaned in, lowering her voice to a whisper, "If he's not your lover yet," she purred, her eyes hooded, her voice knowing, "he will be after he takes one look at you." I felt heat blaze over my face, so quickly changed the subject.

"Thank you for your help, Lidia. I hope Jack paid you well?"

"Jack? No, Jack didn't hire me to help you. I was sent."

"But you said he gave you coin..."

"Yes, the dress was his idea. But I was sent here to see that you were ready, to help with your hair and to make myself useful by..."

Before she could say anything more another knock sounded on the door. My audience chamber was a busy place. Lidia opened the door and there stood Jack. He too had washed and changed into new clothes, and I felt a deep pang but was determined that it would not move me.

"Kassia, a man has come for us. We should go." Without saying more, he turned and left. I stared after him.

"See what I mean?" It took me a minute before I could look at Lidia. I questioned her with my eyes. "He's smitten. As you are with him. I give you until tomorrow morning, if it's at all necessary." Her eyes narrowed with a mischievous twinkle, and I gaped at her, but she turned, swept up the items she had used to arrange my hair and was off like a puff of wind.

I glanced around me, taking note of the ordinariness of the room, wondering if things would be the same after tonight. I noticed my medallion necklace on the bed and snatched it up quickly, put it on, then followed in Lidia's wake.

11

THE SERDAR, BY way of his messenger Lackey Man, was true to his word. An escort waited for us just outside our modest inn as promised. It was early evening, and the bright sun of day had faded; the brilliant jewel-blue expanse of sky was now washed out, was now nothing more than the watery pigment of a painter's canvas, with color running towards the edges to the lake, following the sun and leaving streaks of memory behind. Casting my gaze lower and out over the city below, I observed the tops of buildings stair-stepping down as they sloped to the edge of the lake where the water itself caught and held the dancing reflection of the retreating sun, illuminating the water with streaks of orange, red and carnelian, pink, yellow and gold.

I caught a flurry of motion out of the corner of my eye and turned to see two swallows chasing each other in and around the rafters of the building's overhang next door. Everything around me was normal. Life continued. Was I the only one to know that the entire world was about to change?

Most of the citizenry was home for their dinner, but enough foot traffic yet remained to provide an audience for our going as we boarded the lightweight, wheeled and enclosed coach. A servant in an immaculate yet simple robe of light blue cotton assisted me into the coach. Once we were seated comfortably, the door was closed, leaving me alone with only Jack for company. I gave him what I thought to be a stealthy glance and found him watching me openly. Not knowing how to respond, I turned again and looked out the window, keeping my gaze firmly fixed on the passing scenery rather than on the man sitting next to me, the merest handbreadth of distance between us a deep and precipitous cleft.

Eventually the density of the city thinned, structures became more widely spaced, and the road ascended a gentle slope nestled between carefully tended fields, vineyards and an orchard or two, until finally we turned into a narrow lane lined by curiously shaped poplar trees leading us to a gate and a waiting courtyard beyond.

Carefully mannered grooms helped me descend the short drop to the ground, and almost immediately we were greeted by Lackey Man who offered us a tepidly banal but polite greeting before ushering us into the elaborate manor of Serdar Janko Barbaros.

I have encountered more wealthy homes in Corium than I care to remember -- from the outside. They are opulent, usually in very gaudy and overly resplendent ways, designed with the sole purpose of providing anyone with eyes to see a measuring stick with which to gauge the weight of the owner's purse. The house we entered now was nothing like those houses. That this house was a grand one was not in doubt; it was grand and then some, but it was grand in a simple and elegant way, as if the owner had the confidence born of an inherent rightness about his station in life that need not be enhanced by artificial means. The owner of this home knew his worth and cared little if anyone else agreed with him or not.

After passing through a simply adorned and colonnaded antechamber, Lackey Man ushered us into a hall larger than any I expected to see in a private residence. How anyone could be comfortable in such a room as a part of his daily life without being suffocated by space itself I would never know. The Serdar was a prince of his own domain, and I shuddered at the idea of living in such a public manner every moment of every day. Generally no one cared about my daily comings and goings. I had never experienced the Serdar's world and I meant to keep it that way.

Before leaving us, Lackey Man directed us to a table set with wine and a platter of tidbits of food, telling us to make ourselves comfortable, for the Serdar would join us shortly. At his insistence I took a little of the wine, thinking that it might calm my nerves, but didn't touch anything else.

Waiting had never been a strength of mine. After quaffing my wine, I paced up and down the length of the hall, picking up items at random, touching tapestries and fingering furniture. In contrast to my nervousness, Jack simply sat watching me, though eventually he gave up doing even that. I was edgy; an edginess born out of lack of clarity because I knew that events were careening off in a direction I could neither foresee nor anticipate. I wasn't creative enough for that. My future was as uncertain as the night was dark.

"Kassia, you'd put a caged bear to shame."

His voice was quiet, his irritation thinly veiled. I chose to ignore him, pretending instead to be fascinated by a pile of logs stacked neatly in a shadowed corner of the room. It was a nice shadow, deep and gloomy, and I decided that I would fulfill the rest of my sentence hidden there in the security of obscurity.

A door softly opened and footsteps crossed the room. I kept to the shadows but turned to see Lackey Man escort another man towards Jack. That I wasn't with him seemed to surprise both Lackey Man and the new arrival, for as he walked he searched out the empty spaces of the room. I pulled back more deeply against the wall, not yet ready to cross the abyss separating my past from my future, holding to the shadows for just a little longer.

"I am Serdar Janko Barbaros, and this is my home. You are most welcome here. I hope that your needs have been attended to, that you have been made welcome?" I couldn't hear Jack's reply, but likely he assured the Serdar we had been well attended. The Serdar once again quickly scanned the room. "Kassia, she is here, yes?" He was confused but too polite to say more.

Once again I couldn't hear Jack's words in reply, but as he spoke he turned and casually waved in my general direction. The moment had come; the abyss must be crossed. Like a condemned prisoner walking to her death, I put one foot in front of the other, willing myself to cross the room. This was the moment I couldn't be patient for, yet at the same time feared with every fiber of my being.

As I entered the light of the room more fully, the Serdar transformed. Originally a picture of reserve, he now looked as if he had come face to face with a specter from his past. The fact that this man, who was likely practiced at keeping his thoughts masked, now stood as a picture of mute disbelief disconcerted me, and the fragile grip on self-composure I had managed to pull together was in danger of shattering. Uncertain of myself and not knowing what to say or do, I dropped my gaze to the floor, clasping a fold of my dress with one hand, and reached for the space where my medallion lay hidden under my clothing with the other.

"By the gods, if you aren't the very image of Naria," he croaked while reaching out to grasp the table edge for support.

At the mention of my mother's name my head snapped up and my eyes locked onto the Serdar, my mind wiped utterly clean of all conscious thought.

"Your hair, it is more the coloring of your father, but you are Naria in the flesh, may she live on in our hearts," he added quietly. "But I forget myself..." He seemed to shake himself out of whatever had entranced him. "Pú ert velkom ingað, heiður dama." At that last phrase he gave me a slight bow. I glanced at Jack, but he was looking at the Serdar. "It is Panian," the Serdar said, when he saw me glance at Jack. "For come with me, my lady," he continued, motioning with his arm. "Come with me."

While it was a simple command, I could tell the Serdar was used to being obeyed. He turned and began to cross the room with a confidence that brooked no disagreement. Knowing I wouldn't move on my own, Jack took my arm in his and gently led me across the room, in the footsteps of the Serdar, to answers and the culmination of the waiting.

◆ ◆ ◆

The Serdar's manor was bright, airy, and open to light. The room to which he took us, by contrast, was dimly lit. Whether this boded good or ill I couldn't tell. We paused just inside the door, and I took in what I could of the room, which wasn't much. Not that it mattered, for almost immediately my attention was arrested by a figure sitting on a padded bench on the far side of the room directly across from me. My feet were in motion almost before my mind had an opportunity to process the movement or the fact that I was now unaccompanied. It seemed that this particular meeting was for me alone.

As I drew closer I could see that the man watched me with dark, shadowed eyes rimmed with dark circles and deep grooves. Limp hair, despite being neatly trimmed, together with skin that hung loosely on his frame worked together to give evidence that he was or had been quite ill. All of this consideration happened within the merest of breaths, but that brief moment was enough to unleash a torrent of understanding. I sank to my knees before him, taking his hand in mine as tears spilled freely down my cheek.

"Katava..."

It was enough. Through tear bleared eyes I looked up at his face -- the face I had known all my life, the face that I had longed to see these past three years, the face that I thought was lost to me. I was orphaned no longer.

"Father..." I said and stopped. There was a stream of words wanting and waiting to come out, all blocked by the constriction in my throat. I fell forward, resting my head on his lap while he brought his other hand to lie on my head. The tears turned into a deluge, but eventually I calmed and they slowed to a trickle. After a time my father patted the bench next to him, so I unfolded myself from my kneeling position and took a seat on the bench next to him.

Like the force of nature that emotions can sometimes be, my sadness turned instantly to anger mixed with defiance and guilt and insecurity and bewilderment all at once. "Why... How...are you here? Why have you been away for so long, and where have you been, and why didn't you send me word?" The words tumbled out of me. I wanted to hug him and throttle him all at once.

He waited out my mercurial mood, and when I finally fell silent he spoke. "Katava, mine is not an easy tale to tell. There is much you need to know, and I promise I will tell you everything." I looked into his eyes for confirmation and found it there. "But first I need to know that you are sound in body, that your journey was not more than you could bear?"

"I am well." This was not strictly true, but my full tale would be complicated and none to his liking, assuming I decided to tell it to every last detail. "I didn't come alone. I had help from many sources, some known, others not." I said this last part with emphasis, my eyes pleading, doing my best to let him know that I didn't want to talk about me, wanted to know everything there was to know about why events had led us to this place, to the here and now.

"You are so very much like your mother, a picture of her when she was your age."

"That's what the Serdar said too." I fell silent for a moment, then, "Father, who is he? How did he know my mother? Did you work for him before moving to Corium?"

He didn't immediately answer, averted his eyes momentarily in equivocation before returning his steady gaze to me, saying, "Ah, my dear, that is part of the long tale I have to tell. Trust me when I say you will be told everything, but not just yet." My heart sank. I had come so far and waited so long only to be told I couldn't be told. There wasn't a reason I could conceive of which would keep the story from being told, yet so it was. "The young man with you, he was on your journey from Corium?"

I nodded that this was so and he motioned towards the place the Serdar and Jack waited. Jack followed the Serdar with hesitancy, stopping next to, yet slightly behind him. I watched Serdar Barbaros closely as he locked eyes with my father, gave him the most imperceptible of nods, his eyes bearing a message of significance that I couldn't quite comprehend.

The Serdar remained silent, and my father turned his attention to Jack, studying him before speaking. "You are Jack, the smith, this is so?" Jack met my father's gaze with a steadiness that impressed me and nodded. "I thank you for your service, for your help in seeing my daughter safely here."

Jack's steadiness dissolved and a tremor passed through him as the significance of what my father had just said sank in. He looked to me then back to my father and back to me once again. He needed to sit but did his best to remain standing.

"Our friend here is only recently recovered from a serious wound and illness." Serdar Barbaros slipped in helpfully. "May I suggest that we have dinner served?"

Before acting on his suggestion, the Serdar waited for my father to acquiesce. My father immediately did so, and the Serdar clapped his hands, briskly signaling servants to enter the room. Within a short time tables appeared and a veritable banquet was laid out. Someone took me by the elbow and ushered me to a seat next to my father.

The table before us was opulent - goblets of thick crystal filled with ruby liquid were set at each place, and the center of the table overflowed with food. Meat piled atop platters, baskets overflowed with bread made from fine white flour and lay next to bowls of creamy butter. Many dishes were yet covered and others contained exotic foods for which I had no name. My already overwhelmed senses reeled at the delectable aroma tempting my nose; never before had I seen a feast of such magnitude.

A host of servants lined the room, and each of us had a personal server, to select appropriate dishes and heap portions onto our plates. Before I had taken in everything fully, my young serving boy had already filled my plate with a wide selection from various parts of the table. My nose wanted to eat, but my stomach was too overwhelmed by novelty and threatened to rebel.

The Serdar and my father engaged in polite conversation, and every so often a question regarding my opinion of Islay Bay was asked. I got the impression that topics were kept purposefully light, and I had to work hard to stuff my rising anticipation that we get on to the important matters.

"Kassia, my dear, you are pleased with the meal? Is there nothing more we can get for you? Another bit of stew or another portion of roast pork perhaps?"

I shook my head and remembered almost belatedly to say, "No, thank you." He seemed satisfied, and I switched my attention to my father, noticing that his plate remained relatively untouched despite the conservative amount of food he had been given. I wondered then about the nature of his illness but knew I would have to bide my time a little longer. Answers would come soon enough.

Without even the hint of a signal, servants appeared and replaced our plates with small dishes of sugared plums as well as large goblets filled to the brim with a honey-colored liquid. Once everyone had been served, the Serdar raised his cup in the air, and with a single finger raised from the rim in salute, offered this toast: "Mi anlit áhveum góðar fréttir, aftur ad hver slamer fréttir að vera að okur."

It was lovely, but I had no idea what it meant. Even so, I raised my goblet in recognition of the sentiment and took a tentative sip. A wave of sensations erupted on my tongue, honey and wildflowers and bright sugary notes of life itself all wrapped into a gentle blanket of warmth. My pleasure must have showed on my face, for the Serdar smiled his infectious smile once again.

"Kassia, you approve?"

I nodded without speaking, took another delightful sip, giving myself over to the sensations whole-heartedly this time. He beamed his approval.

"This is a very special drink that comes from my estates up north. We save it for the most special of occasions, and as you are about to find out, this is one of them." He smiled knowingly, mysteriously, and somehow I wasn't bothered, so caught up was I in the drink and the sweetened plums as the Serdar continued. "The toast I just gave is roughly translated from the Panian as: 'May the face of every good news, and the back of every bad news be toward us.' From this night on, we carry this maxim as a banner!"

He looked utterly triumphant, but the deeper meaning still made no sense to me, so I simply smiled pleasantly in return then looked to my father to gauge his reaction. He was triumphant as well, but his face registered something deeper, more complex.

Next I looked at Jack and wondered what he made of it all. He returned my gaze with a look that made my limbs melt like butter, so I dropped my eyes to study the tablecloth.

It was with enormous relief that I realized the Serdar had begun to speak again. "Kassia, it is time we would hear your tale, from the beginning, if you please. Leave nothing out." All signs of the congenial host were gone. He was a man of business now.

I wanted answers, but it seemed as if I must follow the Serdar's rules. So I began.

At the beginning.

With Figor and how he had approached me, armbands in hand, asking me to work on them. It had seemed so ridiculous at the time, and now that the episode was a distant memory, even more so. How touched in the head he must have been to ask me to do such a thing! But no matter - the coin to pay off Swine was the best thing to have happened to me in years. Or so I thought at the time, thinking then that Irisa and I would be able to start a new life. It was ironic, but just how ironic I still didn't fully understand. Despite the Serdar's instructions, I skipped over the part about Issak and continued on to tell of my journey to the abandoned forge in Heywood and how I encountered the band of exiled Agrians.

I watched my father and the Serdar closely as I told them about my return to Corium only to discover that Irisa had been kidnapped. Neither of them appeared to be surprised, and I suspected that they knew all about it already, so I continued on to tell about my arrest by my slimy landlord, Swine, the corpulent little bug-eyed ninny we had left back at the inn.

I remained vague on what exactly had happened to me in prison after my interrogation, but told them about Liri and praised her care of me. They listened in silence as I related the story of our escape and journey to Lynchport. My revelation that Irisa was being held by Prince Casmir was met with nothing more than a subtle glance between the Serdar and my father, so I moved on to explain about Jack's injury, the Swamp People, our escape and encounter with Eria and Buran, followed by everything else up until the point Lackey Man found us.

Now my story was told, my part of the bargain fulfilled. When my words had faded into mere memories of echoes, we sat in silence, but I was neither satisfied nor happy. Now I wanted answers. I wanted all of them.

The Serdar considered me with serious eyes for a long while before he spoke. "Kassia, you have been very patient, and I know how much indeed you desire to solve the mysteries surrounding all that has happened to you."

After so many years of habit, it was difficult to bite back the caustic comment that came naturally to my lips in reaction to his statement of the obvious, but considering the circumstances, and mostly for the love of my father, I behaved. Instead, I gave him another pleasantly bland smile certain to please his cultured senses along with a very proper and polite nod of my head. Jack seemed to know the precise line my thoughts had taken and coughed a laugh into his cup. The Serdar never noticed.

With a meaningful and acquiescent look to my father, the Serdar addressed me again, "Kassia, you remember your father's departure from you and then his failure to return?" The question was a rhetorical one, so I said nothing. "While on that trip, your father sustained... injuries... which have taken a very long time to heal, and as a result he has dealt with weakness ever since. He has been here with me, recovering for some time now."

I flicked a glance at my father, but he wouldn't meet my eyes.

The Serdar took a deep drink from his cup and turned his attention back to me, changing the direction of his narrative. "You are to be applauded for discovering the small clue I left for you in the book, the clue that led you to Islay Bay. I admit that I did not know for certain that you would find it, and even then had no idea how long it would take you to reach us, but reach us you did." He took another drink. "As you will come to understand, it was too dangerous to give you more direct help. At the very least, I was assured you had been given sufficient money, and that Liri had tended you well enough."

The book from Liri, back in Corium, the one she gave me from an anonymous benefactor. Serdar Janko Barbaros of Islay Bay. "So Liri is your woman?"

The Serdar smiled widely, his eyes crinkling at the corners with creases that were not new, had been long etched into a face used to smiling. If I hadn't been so exasperated by the circumstances, I'd have formed a more immediate affinity with the man. "No, not mine." He grinned widely again, as if the very notion secretly amused him. "Liri serves the House of Sajen, has been faithful in her devotion these long many years."

"Sajen," I repeated after him, tasting the name on my tongue. I had heard it before, around a fire one night while on the road. Swine had said it while looking at my medallion. Bellek Sajen? No, Bellek was the name of the current Agrian king. The usurper. The father of Casmir who held my sister. Casmir... "Serdar, why would Prince Casmir want my sister? Why did he take her? Does it have something to do with my father? Something he discovered in his work as a scribe?"

The smile left his face instantly, as if it had never been, and my father began to cough violently. "Aren," the Serdar said, turning to address Lackey Man who had stepped instantly to my father's side, "would you see to his medicaments?" Lackey Man, or Aren as I now knew him to be called, did as he was bid and soon returned to administer a draught of something to my father. His spasms soon passed.

"Now, where were we? Ah, yes. Liri."

No, Irisa and Casmir. But I let it go for now. The Serdar had an agenda to get through, and I would let him get on with it at his own pace.

"It was necessary to get you out of Corium, but it was equally essential to be as cautious. Liri has had a long and faithful service. Helping you heal from your ordeal was merely the last of a long string of helps she has given. Miarka and her husband as well."

The last? I wondered at that, but asked instead, "So they're all spies?"

The Serdar seemed amused by this notion. The same twinkle I was beginning to admire appeared in his eyes again. "Yes, I suppose you could call them that." I opened my mouth to ask another question, but he raised his finger, signaling his request for my silence. With uncharacteristic acquiescence, I obeyed, surprising myself greatly. "Kassia, all in time. You will have all your answers, this I promise."

"Serdar," my father interrupted. It seemed that he no longer wanted to sit back and let the Serdar tell all the news. The Serdar dipped his chin in wary deference, and my father began with a trembling voice full of emotion. "Kassia, I must apologize to you, my youngest daughter."

He paused to search for the right words, but I interrupted him. "Father, there's no need. I know your injury is what kept you from me for so long. There's nothing to forgive."

He shook his head and continued, "No, you misunderstand." He seemed frustrated, so I settled myself and waited for him to continue. "Kassia..." His use of my full name signaled that whatever it was he had to tell me was serious. "I have lied to you all your life. Your mother and I..." He paused for a drink, and I remained still. "Nothing about your life, about my life, is as it seems. Nothing!" His voice rose as he spoke, and as his agitation increased, he fell into another coughing spell.

Giving my father a chance to recover, the Serdar took up the story: "Kassia, let me interrupt for a moment and tell you my part in your story." It was all I could do to restrain an eye roll out of exasperation that they both get on with it already. "I am indeed a Serdar of Elbra, this you know, but I am also cousin to your mother."

Nothing about the evening had been or could have been dreamed up by me. But had I dared to try, this piece of news would not have been a part of my imaginings.

"You know of course, that Elbra was once a part of Pania, that the two lands were once under the same sovereign." I nodded mutely that indeed this was all known to me, so he continued: "It should also be no surprise that the two lands share close ties between noble houses, ties of blood and kinship..." He looked at me weightily, as if willing me to comprehend the implication of his words on my own, but I remained clueless and waited patiently for him to continue. "...that the two sovereignties share close ties of royal houses." I blinked. "Kassia, your mother..." He paused again, his eyes darting through the room as if his next words could be found somewhere along the columns supporting the roof beams. "...your mother," his gaze rested back on me, "was Princess Naria of Pania, youngest daughter of King Aleksandar. Naria is... was... my cousin. You, Kassia, are my cousin... and are a blood member of the royal house of Pania."

He stopped speaking, letting his words hang there in what felt to me like a hovering cloud of doom. My father had long since stopped coughing and sat motionless, watching me from behind hooded eyes. There was much to be read in their depths if only I was to search them, but I was too stunned to do so. My pulse raced, and my heart pounded in my chest. Perhaps it was the wine, but I thought not.

My mother, daughter of King Aleksandar of Pania. Princess Naria. The weight of it was too much to comprehend. The mystery of my life was about her after all. My beautiful, sad mother. How did she end up living a life of poverty and want in the slums of Corium? My mother, for all her beauty and strength, for all the love that she had given to Irisa and me, had always been a mystery to me. While I knew she loved me, there was a part of her heart that she kept curtained off, guarded and safe from the world. Now I understood why: she had a dangerous identity. Had she kept this from me by choice or by force? Should I be saddened or angered? Did she not think me capable of keeping her secret? And my father! What role did he play in this, and why did he never tell me even after she died? All of these convoluted thoughts and feelings assailed me at once, and I was at an utter loss to know where to start making sense of them.

"Katava, we wanted to tell you, and so many times we nearly did." His voice was a whisper, a puff of smoke on the wind, so light and ethereal it was. "But we decided that the burden of it could be a danger to you. When I would have told you, after the death of your mother, matters quickly complicated themselves, and I had to travel. While I was gone, it seemed best to keep you in the dark a while longer, for your own protection, you understand."

I didn't fully, but could see some sense in what he said. When a person doesn't know the truth of something, it's hard to give away any secrets. All of this was good and well, but there was a lot that had yet to be told. Such as how it was that my mother came to be married to a mere market scribe.

"Katava, there is more," my father continued, his voice and tone gaining strength, as if the very message he had to relay to me was carried along on its own power. To me it seemed another pronouncement of doom, and I didn't know how many more revelations I could handle despite wanting so badly to know. He glanced briefly at the Serdar then continued again. "There is more to the mystery of you than just your mother." He was suddenly very uncomfortable, as if he wanted to stand and pace the room, knowing however, that he was too weak and unsteady to do so. His reprieve came from an unlikely source.

"You are a Sajen." Every head in the room snapped to the speaker. "Your father," said Jack, indicating my father next to me, "is Bedic Sajen, rightful heir to the throne of Agrius." My father was stunned into silence by Jack's perception.

I was also stunned into silence. When I first learned of Issak's murder, I claimed that the world had gone stark raving mad. I knew nothing then. Now the world *had* gone stark raving mad. The room tilted ever so slightly, began to spin, and I feared it would spiral like a top, flinging me off the edge.

Without warning, a vice clamped down on my back in a spasm, and I choked back a scream. Anyone who noticed my distress likely passed it off as shock. I grabbed the edges of my seat with hands to steady myself, fighting off dizziness as the band of pain around my midsection eased ever so slightly, like a wave that had pulled back a bit from shore. Disregarding my discomfort, I forced myself to concentrate, to breathe. There was too much at stake to give in to fatigue or illness, to my rebelling body.

"Kassia, don't you see? Your mother Naria is the Naria that wed the heir to the throne of Agrius." My mother and father, their wedding day interrupted by a little matter of an overthrow, chaos, death and destruction. Jack let that thought sink in and then continued, "The medallion your father gave you to keep, the arm bands from Figor, the interest Casmir showed you... " He looked to my father for confirmation and I took a deep breath, rubbed my hand over my eyes. "My father suspected who you were, I think, but he wasn't sure so kept the secret close."

"You mean Rem knew?" I asked through clenched teeth.

My father perked up at the name and looked to Jack. "Rem? Your father is Rem, the metal smith?"

"Yes... my lord..." Jack said, somewhat uncertainly. All the rules had changed. Nothing was as it seemed, as if all of us were in a dream, following a path covered with swirling fog, unknown terrors lurking in every shadow.

"So you are young Jack..." He smiled, looking inwardly through the mists of time, to a distant memory which seemed to rouse a warm fondness for him. "You were usually found sitting as near your father as you could, on a small stool he made especially for you, so you could watch every move he made, every strike of the hammer, taking everything in like a sponge. A small mite you were. Your father was a good friend." If Jack was surprised by this last statement, he hid it well. With a shake of his head my father came back to the present, and his voice and posture regained a certain augustness reminiscent of his former life. "Jack, now is not the time for titles. For now I am Bedic. Just Bedic. We will work out the proper niceties at a later time."

Bedic. I had known my father as Amion Monastero all of my life. But he was Bedic, Prince of House Sajen of Agrius. And I was his daughter. My father was meant to be a king, which would make me... I felt sick. I stood hastily and stumbled away from the table seeking the oblivion of a shadowed corner. Acting on instinct, Jack followed. The Kassia that had been hurt by Jack in the forest near Allmor Lake would have shoved him away; the newly stunned Kassia needed him, welcomed his strength.

I was grateful when no one said anything for some time, left me to my own thoughts. Even Jack kept his silence, but he had always been subtle in his perception of my moods and needs. When the narration of my new reality continued, I was ready to listen but not to move.

This time the Serdar took up the story. "Kassia, your father has been quietly working for the last several years to actuate a rebellion, to build support for his cause -- to regain his lost throne. A quiet network is in place, led by those who have never accepted Bellek, the usurper. Your father has a great deal of support, and there is a plan forming to use the levies of the Agrian lords who support him as well as soldiers of Elbra. These forces will be the impetus of our plan, emphasizing your father's claim to the usurper." The Serdar laughed again as his own understatement. "Your safe arrival here was the last piece of the puzzle, for we feared to act upon our plans publicly before you were safe. That Casmir took your sister was... unfortunate."

Another knife lanced through my midsection, but I ignored it and turned on the Serdar with fury burning. "Unfortunate?" I pulled away from the shadows with a single step towards the table.

"Kassia..." Jack warned, his voice a low rumble, loud enough for only me to hear.

I ignored him. "Unfortunate? If he had taken me as well, would that have been a setback?" I was furious. "Cause to pause and consider matters? A bump in the road, an obstacle to overcome, a bit of a blow, a delay, a misfortune, a mishap, a hold-up, an impediment..." With each phrase I took another step towards the table. I searched for more words but Jack came alongside me and put his hands on my shoulders. I took a deep breath and steadied myself.

The Serdar sat unmoving, stunned by my tirade, but my father appeared amused, even approving. When I said nothing more, he stood, filled with a strength he hadn't yet shown, reminding me again of the father I had known all my life. He exuded the casual confidence that only those steeped in power and authority from birth would ever know.

"Kassia, be still." It was simple but heartfelt, a phrase I heard so often as a child, yet it was all that was needed. I ceased my protest and allowed Jack to lead me back to the table, though I didn't sit. "There is so very much more to explain, but I think we have put enough on your shoulders this night. It is late, and we all need to go to our rest."

The Serdar stood and came to my side, taking my arm. "Yar Hátin Kassia, if you would allow me? I will see you to your room."

"Yar Hátin?" I wondered at the phrase. "Miarka and Liri both used it when addressing me."

"It means 'Your Highness' in the Panian. Elbra and Pania share a common language, as you know. It is the form of address for you now."

They had both known who I was. There was so much to take in, too much, in fact. My head swam in the confusion of it all. I wanted to argue, to push back and demand to be told all the rest, hoping to make sense of it all. There was so much more to learn, as my father had said, but my back protested; I was infinitely tired. I wasn't sure I would be able to hide my discomfort for much longer, so with a nod I turned on my heel and allowed myself to be led away.

The room to which I was taken was exquisite in quality yet simple in taste. I was glad, for I wasn't sure I could handle elaborate or ornate. I was left alone and was grateful. The Serdar had any number of servants who could have attended me, but whether an oversight or a conscious decision, leaving me to my solitude was the most merciful thing he could have done.

I made a cursory circuit of the room, taking in my surroundings before I returned to a small table I had seen upon entering, drawn by a small hand mirror laid out along with other personal care items. Mirrors were in common use by ladies of means, but I had never actually seen one close up. Despite my shaking, I reached out and grasped the small, silver-plated handle worked with a very delicate pattern on the surface. The pattern on the back held my gaze, for I was not yet willing to turn it over to see my reflection on the other side. After some moments, without thinking what I did, I turned the mirror.

The Serdar was right about me. The eyes meeting my gaze were the color of dusky winter moss. It was my mother, Naria, daughter of King Aleksandar of Pania.

Another sharp pain knifed through my midsection, but this time I couldn't ignore it as easily as I had done in the dining room and dropped the mirror in agony. It crashed to the floor, breaking the glass into thousands of tiny shards, shattering in every direction. In my pain I doubled over, doing my best to take deep breaths.

The door flew open and before I knew it, Lidia was by my side. I tried to push away from her, frantically backing towards the bed, but her grip on my arm was too strong and she held me as the pain slowly eased, leaving only a dull throb in my lower back.

"My lady, I will get help."

"No, don't. I'll be alright. Please... please don't," I whispered as I finally pulled away from her and scooted back to the far end of the bed, not stopping until I ran up against the pillows. Lidia dared not countermand me, but she gave me a look that said she was none too pleased. "Please, leave me," I said with more conviction, and she finally obeyed, leaving me in darkness. All alone and hidden there in the shelter of my bed's overhang, I lay down and curled into a ball, remaining thusly into the earliest hours of the morning.

12

THROBBING, PULSING BEATS... Piercing stabs of pain gored like a superheated pike thrust through my skull... Eyes gauzy and weighted with lead... Swirling noises dancing in my head, some voices and others meaningless sounds...

◆ ◆ ◆

Half-dreaming, half-awake I lay in my cocoon of luxury, soft coverlets of exquisite fabric draped over me in a manner at odds with the state of my suffering. Though I wasn't entirely sure, I may have succeeded in getting a little sleep just before the sun rose. The lingering effects of the heady wine from the night before combined with a heavy dose of shock made my entire body heavy and aching, and I was determined not to move for at least the next week. Or so I had determined until someone drew back the bed curtain then peeled away my coverlets. A rush of chilly air washed over my exposed flesh, and I reacted by sitting up, instantly regretting the rashness of the move. I realized that I was quite naked, having somehow managed to remove my clothing in the early morning hours before burrowing into bed.

Hot color rose in my cheeks and with frantic fingers I sought back the bed sheet to cover myself. When I couldn't find it, Lidia materialized at my side, and I noticed that the other two women in the room paid no heed to the royal guest they had been sent to tend.

"My lady, you need to rise. I have hot water for you to wash, and you will feel much better afterwards, that I promise you."

I very much doubted it but rose carefully, despite misgivings about ever feeling better, somehow managing to forget that I was fully exposed. The other women had already slipped out silently, making it easier for me to act on Lidia's request. I crossed the room, delighting in the feel of the soft woven fabric of the rug under my bare feet. A tub full of steaming water awaited my use, and along the way I took in the sight of a soft towel, lavender-scented soap and a new gown Lidia had laid out for me.

I dipped a hesitant toe into the water before allowing myself to succumb fully to the therapeutic bath. Lidia handed me a cup of warm liquid claiming that it was filled with herbs sure to ease my throbbing head. The thought of ingesting anything made my stomach churn, but I did as I was told, knowing Lidia wouldn't take no for an answer in this. Once I had relaxed enough to suit her, Lidia washed me. She remained silent all the while, but her patience lasted only as long as it took to get me out of the tub and dried off. She had something on her mind.

"My lady, I don't mean to intrude upon your thoughts, but..."

I looked at her with the same doubtful look I had given her upon rising from the bed. For the first time since meeting her, she looked abashed, dropping her gaze to the floor momentarily before continuing, a bedeviled smile returning to her face.

"You are somewhat of a surprise. Your identity, I mean." It was hard to argue with her, so I didn't. She picked up the new gown, its softness unfolding like a waterfall, a color akin to the color of Allmor Lake, between blue and green but not true to either one. "I hope you like this gown, my lady, for I picked it out especially for you." I nodded that I did, and she continued, "When I was first asked to attend you yesterday, back at the inn, I had no idea that you were the daughter of Bedic Sajen of Agrius. Who would have had reason to suspect that you would suddenly show up here, in Islay Bay?"

Who, indeed.

"Had I but known..."

Had I but known... but I probably would have run screaming in the other direction if I'd been given any tip-off prior to arriving at the Serdar's. I was uncertain enough about my own feelings and didn't want to burden this well-meaning girl with my own doubts. While Lidia had come across as a breezy, confident girl yesterday, sure of her actions and certain of her own charm, today she seemed somewhat flustered. The facts were all new. I was no longer a visiting mystery, someone preparing to dine with the Serdar. I was now the daughter of a prince. How was a girl, how was anyone, supposed to come to terms with that?

"My lady, I am truly sorry if I offended you yesterday." She paused as the garment slid over my head. "I didn't mean to say those things I said, about Jack being your lover. It wasn't my place to speak, but..." I saw her involuntary gaze flick to my waistline. Before she could say anything more on the subject, a wave of pain overtook me again, leaving me breathless. Lidia was alarmed and took me by the arm to lead me to a seat. She knelt down before me, and in a tone heavy with deep concern, pleaded, "Won't you let me get help? It's clear there is something wrong with..." I had closed my eyes and was trying to breathe deeply but held up my hand to silence her before she continued. The wave of pain only just passed when the door swung open and two women came to remove the bathing tub and other supplies.

I was relieved when Lidia didn't resume our previous conversation after the girls left. Instead she remained silent as she busied herself making sure that each lace, each cut and fold of the cloth was perfect before starting on my hair. I hoped she wouldn't mention Jack again.

"Your Highness..." she started hesitantly, "I should call you Your Highness, or Yar Hátin as we would say..." she paused briefly, uncertain before proceeding, but I cut her off.

"Kassia. My name is Kassia." I did my best to be kind, but it was hard to take the edge completely out my voice. Lidia noticed and recoiled slightly as if slapped, though she was quick to recover. I felt a stab of guilt, but it was hard enough to keep a lock on my own emotions without taking care to be careful with those of other people.

"Kassia," she said, with a thinly veiled hesitancy, not at all comfortable with using such a familiar name with the daughter of a prince, "the Serdar has given me freedom to enter your service, as one of your maids... and I would like to, very much, if you would have me."

Not more than a day ago I was an orphan, running for my life and subject to the whims of fortune, my entourage nothing more than an exiled metal smith, an overweight lump of misbegotten hedgepig, and another orphaned boy. That anyone should defer to me or pay me any heed other than common courtesy due any other human being made me entirely uncomfortable. However much I hated it, I had a new reality to adjust to. There was no sense in denying it.

"I would like that too, very much." I gave her the most convincing smile I could, and she beamed back, her smile revealing a perfect line of pearl white teeth. I had previously discovered Lidia to have an irreverent streak. If I must have a maid hovering about me, I may as well enjoy her company.

Once all the pins of my hair and folds of my gown were arranged correctly, Lidia brought out a pair of soft leather shoes for my feet, and I was ready to depart.

"Lidia, you said I was to rise and get ready, but where Am I supposed to go?" Clearly I had a lot to learn about the business of noble life.

She giggled, receiving my question with a fair dose of humor, never once considering that I didn't truly know. Lidia had discovered my true identity only last night, but she had no notion that I had as well, that there was much more to my story. As far as she was concerned, I was the daughter of a prince, and though I may have fallen on hard times, I had been raised with this knowledge. Yesterday's revelations had been for her benefit alone.

"You are to meet with your father and the Serdar this morning."

Hopefully it would be another day of revelations. Lidia opened the door and walked with me to the same room we had dined in last evening, though nothing about the path we took seemed familiar; everything last night had been fogged over with shock and wine. The room we entered did look familiar however, and my father's warm face very much so. Despite what Lidia had told me, the Serdar was not with my father. Lidia paid him a brief obeisance before turning and leaving the room, closing the door quietly behind her.

My father watched me with a broad smile on his face as I crossed the room into his open embrace. "Katava," he said, speaking into my hair, breathing in its clean smell, "you look absolutely beautiful, the very picture of your mother when she was your age." This made me smile inwardly yet left a deep pang at the same time. "If only she could see you now, she would say the same, would be very proud."

He released me and turned to a table behind him, plucking a bloom from flowers in a glazed pitcher. Turning back to me once again, he deftly entwined the stem into the plait on the side of my head. "There. Just as your mother would have done."

I smiled at the memory of my mother and her flowers. "You slept well last night, father?"

A cloud flit briefly across his features and was gone. I knew then that his sleep was disturbed by demons just as my own was. "Yes, it was the best sleep I have had in a very long time. My heart has more peace with you here now. Turn for me, Katava, my little flower."

I spun in a circle, my skirt twirling about my ankles, in the same manner I had done so often as a child. My father clasped his hands together before gently grabbing me under the elbows and drawing me near him again.

"You are well? Truly?" He searched my face, looking for any hint of darkness there. He didn't find it. Right now I felt none. Relieved, he drew me over to a chair near the hearth. "Let us sit for a while, before the Serdar joins us. There is more I would tell you of your mother."

The morning had dawned with sun, but dark rain clouds had since moved in. Just as we settled in, rain announced its arrival by pounding with fury against the windows. It seemed as though the weather wanted to show me its other face -- that it wasn't always bright sunshine, gentle breezes; sometimes it was dark and sinister with a chill lurking in the shadows.

"Katava, I wanted to have time this morning to explain more of the things that have been kept from you. First, about the death of your mother and why I began to travel so much afterwards." He picked up his cup and took a delicate sip before continuing. I looked at my own cup, but I couldn't bring myself to drink it so left mine largely untouched.

"We hid in Corium in plain sight in a way, your mother and I, because who would suspect a royal household living as wage-earners in the marketplace of Corium? Had anyone known who we truly were, it would have meant our discovery by Bellek and instant death. My father hadn't escaped, but we were lucky. I used my education to serve as a scribe for hire in the marketplace."

It was a demeaning profession for this man who had been born in a palace. But I saw the wisdom in it. He couldn't hide his education any more than a peacock could hide its colorful feathers. At least by serving as a scribe he could hide behind his skills and never draw curiosity.

"Kassia, when you were a little girl you nearly begged me to enter the private service of a lord. As much as I wanted to, for it would have brought a better price for my services, I dared not for fear someone would recognize me, a very real and very dangerous possibility. This is why we lived as poorly as we did.

"We had hidden from Bellek for so many years," he said the name as if it was a brand on his tongue, "and had been successful, but success oftentimes breeds complacency. When your mother died, I feared that complacency had brought her death, and though I had no way of knowing, the risk of staying where we were was too great. We moved to an even poorer district, and I became more careful about what work I took."

I cried out inwardly at the memory of leaving behind all the memories of my mother and the home we had shared together. Our new home was hardly more than a hovel and was the place Irisa and I shared after my father left us, never to return.

After taking a restorative drink he continued, taking a new tack, "In the few years right before your sister was born, I made contact with a few men I knew had remained faithful to my house, starting with my friend, Figor. He had aided our escape you see, at risk to his own life." My father's eyes glazed over, as if he was bearing witness once again to all the terror and turmoil of that day. "Figor survived and managed to earn the trust of Bellek," he said sourly, as if the idea left a bad taste in his mouth. "He has been vital as the nexus of all my plans ever since because of his position on Bellek's Council.

"While many of my lords have maintained their status since the overthrow, their influence has been greatly diminished. It has been essential that they maintain the protection of anonymity else they would have been immediately punished. Building up a broader network of support has been slow going because we've had to be so careful.

"Your mother's death heightened my need for caution. I determined that certain matters needed my personal attention. Some of the lords demanded to see me in person before they would be convinced our plans were legitimate. Not all of them believed I was still alive, you see. I needed to prove otherwise, so was required to step out of obscurity and reveal myself to them. Even so, it was not yet safe to bring my daughters along. Anonymity remained your best protection."

A crack of thunder boomed near us, shaking the windows with a rage that seemed likely to crack the pristine glass panes. I swirled my cup and took a deep drink, allowing the liquid calm to penetrate.

"Figor is a dear friend, and a better man you could not find. He has been the key to everything these years, the linchpin keeping all of my hopes alive. I owe him everything."

"So when he came to me in Corium, he knew who I was?"

"Oh, yes. Most definitely! By that point the groundwork had been laid well enough, a strong enough system of allies and supporters established, that it was time to actuate everything." His eyes sparkled when he said this, a passion and intensity flaring, revealing the prince he once was. "Figor's initial contact with you, using those armbands, was merely the tool to establish a believable reason for his visits to the marketplace. That you would take them out of the city and disappear for so long was not part of the plan."

He gave me a disapproving look then, but I merely looked back at him with a smirk and said, "Had I known that my father, the rightful heir apparent to the Sajen throne, was trying to use it as a means to contact me after having been presumed dead for three years, then no, perhaps I wouldn't have left." My father smiled. "I would have thought that a more straightforward approach might have been a bit more, well, straightforward."

"Kassia, it couldn't have been that easy. He is a royal advisor. His comings and goings are known and he is watched, is always with others. Anything as blatant as showing up at your door and announcing your identity and his plans for you would have been noted. It would have resulted in your death!"

He had a point. I was no more a fan of my death than was my father.

"The fact that Figor was in Corium at all was fortuitous, an event not likely to come again for some time. He needed to proceed as cautiously as possible.

"Once he established contact with you by hiring your services, future visits would not be suspect. Arranging to get you and Irisa out of the city was to be the next step, but it had to be done with delicate care. When you disappeared, Figor feared for you. He arranged to have Irisa hidden, at least temporarily, but the interference of your landlord complicated things. Once Figor discovered that Casmir knew who you were, he arranged to get you out of the prison and forced Sviene to take Irisa out of the city. The rest you know."

Indeed, I knew it well.

"So you have been in contact with Figor all this time? You knew what happened to us?"

"I have heard from Figor only once since he arrived in Corium. He was able to send me a detailed report at great risk to himself. Other pieces have been filled in by the others you met in Corium. Once you left the city, however, we lost track of you."

I considered all of this for a moment before changing topics. "After mother died, you knew we'd be safe. How?"

"Jeah. She was with you, and I trusted her to watch out for you."

"Jeah knew who we were?"

"Yes, of course. She was one of your mother's ladies. She came from Pania when your mother and I were to be married then fled with us from Agrius. Once we carved out a new life, she married. A person doesn't always have control over how or when their heart is stolen, it seems." He shrugged as if the notion was a mystery to him. An image of Jack flashed before my eyes, but I quickly snuffed it. "Jeah married her merchant, but she was always devoted to your mother."

The next question I asked cautiously, for I had sensed a vapor of agony shrouding the topic. "Father, who hurt you? How did this come about?"

He studied me heavily for a moment, pain radiating from behind his eyes, offering a clear view into the conflict raging in his soul. "On the last foray to meet with my men, I was captured, taken by a group loyal to Bellek, or so I initially thought. I expected to be handed over to Bellek, or that perhaps they might kill me outright." He paused for a moment and then continued. "They should have handed me over to Bellek, but they didn't. Bellek was never told."

His memories appeared to have slowed his speech, as if in recalling the horrific experience he had been weighted down with bonds. I remembered my own dismal prison cell and shuddered. My father and I had a shared experience. If only we could manage to share the full terror of it, we might begin to bring healing.

He remained silent for a long while, and I thought he might end his narrative, but after what seemed like an eternity he took a long drink from his cup then continued. "I found out only later that their lord, a man named Taibel, wanted information from me, about the plot to overthrow Bellek, in order to use it in his favor, against Bellek. He was a greedy, ruthless man." He quieted to a whisper, and I had to strain to hear him over the cataclysm raging outside. "I was held for two long years in their prison, enduring... torture... so they could learn as much as they thought they could get from me. But they did not count upon my ability to resist." A small shudder washed over him, and I felt a prick of ice threaten my spine.

As if written specifically into the script of a guiser's play, the storm ceased its raging and a quiet calm descended over the room. I didn't know the specifics of what they had done to my father, and hoped that I never found out. "How did you escape?" My words were no louder than his had been.

"Janko Barbaros, the Serdar. He knew I had been taken but it took him that long to find out by whom and where I was being held. It was no small task to get me out, but he managed it and made it look like a traitorous job from the inside. He brought me here and I began my convalescence. But now you are here, and you are safe at last." He was tired, yet his eyes were bright as he surveyed my face.

His tale was a big one, nearly as big as my own had I decided to tell him the full version. He held back his own demons as did I, and for now it seemed as though it would stay that way. I unconsciously pulled the medallion from under the fabric of my gown and fiddled with it, drawing my father's attention.

"You still have it then? After all these years?"

I dropped my gaze to look at the surface of the metal in my hand. "Yes. You told me always to wear it, to trust no one with it, to keep it safe. I always have."

My father nodded his approval.

"Father, what is the picture here?"

He smiled warmly before answering. "That is a bennu." When I remained uncomprehending, he continued, "A bird. They are mythical birds associated with rebirth, renewal. Quite brilliant birds in their splendor. They regenerate through fire, or so the story goes. I took it on as the symbol for my new house the day of my marriage. Those medallions were made in advance, but they were never given out. There hadn't been time."

I wondered what part of the bennu was significant to him, the splendor of the bird or the rebirth from fire. Considering what happened during his wedding ceremony I thought it a rather poignant sigil. I knew nothing of his father, the former King Nikolas. I didn't know what form of man he was and wondered in that moment if my father's choice of the bennu had anything to do with him. There would be time enough later to explore all of this, so for now, I kept these thoughts to myself.

"Why did you give me this medallion all those years ago? If you intended to keep our identity a secret, giving me the medallion seems a rather negligent thing to do." I thought back to the careless accusations Jack had made about my father when we were fighting over the events in Lynchport.

My father looked evasive for a moment, as if a near-lifetime of keeping his identity a secret was a hard habit to shake, but then continued, "Your mother thought it best if there was something to connect you to your identity. In case something ever happened to us. It was her idea, for the medallions to be an identifier, just in case... Figor knew where we were, but he did not know you in those early years."

I accepted his answer as reasonable. One more mystery explained, even if I did not yet fully understand the bennu.

My father's vigor had been renewed as he explained about the medallion, but suddenly he looked immeasurably tired again.

"There is so much more to discuss, one thing above all that is vital for you to know, but... Katava, I am tired. It is enough for now. You understand?"

It was hard to say whether the telling of his tale had taken a toll on him or if his remembrances of the horrors he had endured had done it. In either case I was happy for a reprieve, for I had much to think on. Even his ominous warning about one more vital thing to be told wouldn't hold me here. I stood and kissed him on the cheek before making my way towards the door.

"Kassia, wait." His words were merely whispered, but they stopped me and I turned back to face him again. "You are beloved, my daughter. And I am very proud. Always remember that."

My throat constricted and I couldn't speak. I knew my father loved me, but I wasn't sure he had ever said the words. Funny that they came now, but perhaps his ordeal with Taibel had changed him, made him more introspective. Impending death tends to order one's priorities. Perhaps I had always undervalued my worthiness to be loved, and now in this moment, to know he was pleased with me, it was enough. I nodded a quick understanding and left.

◆ ◆ ◆

It was only midday when I left my father, and I had no desire to go back to my room. In fact, I had no desire to be anywhere within the walls of the Serdar's home, wanted nothing more than to find Rose and ride off as fast as I could towards the horizon. I wanted the freedom of obscurity again, wanted the freedom of disappearing into the markets, hidden in my cloak of anonymity, a penniless orphan attracting no more attention than a mouse. I knew my new life would overwhelm me if I let it, if I couldn't find strength from somewhere.

I was not feeling well. While the pains of last night had come only briefly this morning, I knew it was only a matter of time before they returned, and I wasn't sure how long I would be able to resist Lidia's suggestion that I seek help. This only added to my despondency so that as I wandered the Serdar's manor, anyone I encountered gave me a wide berth, both because they were trained well and knew who I was, but also because my countenance did not encourage their friendliness.

Making my way towards the outside I encountered an outdoor garden lined with columns and trellis, thick with trees and plants, all protected by a densely grown arbor overhead. I was intrigued by this so began to wander about, thankful for the distraction and a reprieve from my troubles.

So caught up was I in the discovery of this place that I almost didn't see the figure seated on a bench hidden in the deep shadow of a far corner. He was seated in a forward position, his elbows on his knees, head bowed to look at the ground, and I was nearly on his toes before either of us realized it. He startled and stood quickly, nearly knocking me over. He managed to recover quickly enough and caught my arm to keep me from toppling backwards over a potted plant.

"I didn't mean to frighten you." Jack's words were solicitous, though awkward, as if he was speaking to a stranger. I couldn't find my voice, so he offered, "Let's sit for a bit?"

The rain had picked up again, though this time it maintained a softer cadence, far from the violent storm of earlier. Though we could see the rain, here in this outdoor garden that was not quite outdoors, we were protected. It was difficult to read Jack's expression clearly, though I thought I could imagine the conflicted emotions warring within him, because I felt the same way now that I was face to face with him. My fingers fidgeted with my gown, wrapping folds of cloth from the skirt around my hand then releasing to repeat again. How did one even attempt to make sense of everything that had happened in the last day, much less be able to make a plan for the road ahead? I imagined that the roadmap for my life had already been determined for me, but where did that leave Jack?

"How is your father this morning?"

It was a safe place to start.

"He was much rested. We had an enlightening conversation

this morning, but afterwards he seemed very tired. Considering all that has happened to him these past few years, I can well understand." I went on to summarize all that my father had told me, stopping short of sharing the details of the horrors of his imprisonment. Jack listened carefully in the gentle way he always did, and I sensed rather than saw him nod his head in understanding as I spoke.

When I couldn't hold back the emotion any longer, I gave in. "Oh, Jack," my voice cracked, "if only you knew what he went through. His torture and illness..."

Jack took my hand in his, held it while I continued to process my thoughts, content to give me time to begin again. If he had learned nothing else about me over the course of our long journey together, he knew that despite my desire to appear strong and capable, independent and well able to take care of myself, there was still a scared and vulnerable girl inside that I didn't often show to others. I leaned into him, resting my head against his shoulder and he stiffened initially, surprised. Eventually he relaxed and pulled me close, as if nothing had ever happened between us, as if the existence of Mairona was irrelevant despite the fact that she was extremely relevant.

"So have all your mysteries been solved?"

I laughed, bitter and humorless though it was. "Yes, for the most part. Other than the mystery of what is to become of me."

"They haven't told you what happens next?"

"You mean beyond an all-out rebellion? Bloodshed and violence, the deaths of thousands?"

He squeezed my hand. "I meant for you personally. I don't imagine you'll be forced to take up a sword in your father's name." I could hear him smiling.

"No, I imagine that news is yet to be sprung on me. My father seems to be able to handle only so much at a time before he tires. It happens so easily for him. I expect that the details of the vast conspiracy to regain the throne of Agrius will be revealed to me soon enough, though to be honest with you, I'm really not all that interested. I never asked for it, don't want it."

"Kassia, this is your life now. You have to find a way to come to terms with it, whether you want it or not. Besides, what other choice do you have?" He was doing his best to lighten the mood despite the consequences to himself personally. He knew this new life of mine could not include him. "Running away is hardly the answer!" He said this last part with irony as an afterthought, but when I did not laugh along with him he stiffened again. "Kassia, I mean it." He pulled back and turned to look at me, searching my face as best he could in the dim light of the cloudy afternoon. "You have just found your father again, and he needs you."

I nodded miserably, hating to agree because it went against everything I thought I wanted for myself. I tore my eyes away from his face to look down at my hands and he pulled me back to himself as we sat in silence again for a long time.

"I'm not sure I'm strong enough," I whispered, nearly inaudibly.

"What did you say?" he asked incredulously.

I didn't repeat myself.

He lifted my chin with the crook of his finger, forcing me to look at him. His eyes were hard, his mouth frowning and angry. "You, Kassia, are the strongest person I have ever met in my life. Don't ever say that again." I wanted to look away but he held my chin firmly in his grasp. "If you could see yourself the way I see you, then you would know how strong you truly are. How beautiful you are, how treasured," he whispered. I dropped my gaze. "Do you remember all the spitting and fire you unleashed on me when we first met? You were defiant and angry, strong and determined."

"And you were amused." I looked up again, scowling.

"No... I was... intrigued. You were a little slip of a lass, and yet you raged at me, like a snared wildcat hungry for freedom." His face softened and he smiled his half-smirk, one side of his mouth curving up in mischievous remembrance.

The dark shock of hair which habitually fell over his right eye was combed neatly into place now, obediently staying where it belonged. I took one look at it and grinned back at him before reaching up to dislodge it. "You were kind of a rake."

He caught my hand, held it to his cheek, and I made no move to pull it away. When he turned his face into it, planting a kiss in my palm, my insides melted and I could no longer form a single thought in my brain. My stomach turned to jelly, my toes curling inside my fancy shoes. His other hand came around behind my head, and he pulled me to him.

Dangerous. What we were doing was dangerous. Things would only spiral into complication if we continued, resulting in even more misery.

He kissed me anyway. Softly at first until the fire took hold. Gentleness was replaced with ardency, very quickly becoming urgency. But as quickly as it had begun it was over, for Jack stopped short, broke off his kiss, and ended his embrace with a deep growl of frustration, standing so quickly that I nearly toppled off the bench. I propped myself up on my elbows to regain my balance, panting for air. He moved away, into the deep shadow behind a column, his back turned towards me.

"No, this can't be."

I sat up fully, took in my disheveled state, felt my hair, noticing that several tiny braids had slipped from the restraint of the pins holding them. He spoke true, no matter how much I wanted to disagree with him. I said nothing, merely straightened my clothing as much as possible then replaced my wayward locks, trying all the while to regain my breath. Jack hadn't moved, seemed to be nothing more than a statue in the garden, his jagged breath the only evidence that he was a sentient being.

I stood and he turned to me then. "Kassia, I'm so sorry," he whispered.

I looked down, fighting the bevy of emotions I felt at that moment. He reached out and plucked a leaf from my hair and I grasped at his hand, brushed a gentle kiss onto his fingers then released it and turned to leave the garden. Jack followed several measured paces behind.

As we passed back into the house, I nearly ran into the Serdar who was strolling down the corridor at an unhurried pace, Lidia in tow just behind. He took in my flushed appearance, looked to Jack and then back to me, vaguely disconcerted yet doing his best to keep a disapproving look from his face, if not entirely successfully. Recovering quickly, he greeted us politely then added, "Ah, Yar Hátin Kassia. Your woman," he gestured behind him to Lidia who looked relieved to have found me but was equally dismayed to see me with Jack, "has been looking everywhere for you. There is much work to be done for your new wardrobe. We will be leaving for Brekkell in a few weeks and everything must be ready prior to departure."

I looked at him blankly and then to Lidia who noticed my confusion.

"Dear lady, Caelnor in Brekkell is where my lord, Prince Isary lives," he began cautiously. My face still didn't register understanding and his smile wavered. "The Prince of Elbra, your future husband?" I think it took no more than a heartbeat for my face to drain of color and he immediately realized his blunder, horrified by his misstep. "My lady, I am indeed sorry! I assumed your father had told you this morning as was his intent!"

The last vital thing my father meant to tell me.

He took a step towards me, reached out his hand to steady me and I recoiled, spun to look at Jack. But Jack was gone, the corridor behind me empty and silent save for the sound of the pouring rain echoing in from the garden.

The pain I dreaded pounced again, but this time it wracked my entire body, and I doubled over as I had done last night, this time spewing the contents of my stomach all over the marble floor. In the midst of my pain, I realized that a warm wetness seeped down my inner thighs, though neither the Serdar nor Lidia knew it. My legs began to shake so violently that I could barely stand on my own. The Serdar turned and looked helplessly at Lidia who rushed ahead to steady me. I could tell she knew instinctively what was happening while mercifully the Serdar remained mystified.

"Shall I send for a physician?" he asked, looking so uncomfortable that he might well melt into the floor tiles if not given a reprieve.

"No," Lidia said quickly, offering up as genuine a smile as she could. "She is still feeling the effects of last night's wine." It was a lie and the Serdar knew it, but he wasn't about to press the matter, happy to leave matters vague. "I'll see her to her room," she added quickly.

Instant relief flashed across the Serdar's face and he offered, "My pardons, ladies." Bowing quickly, he turned and fled down the passageway.

"We must get you to your bed," Lidia entreated, her voice a raspy whisper. I merely nodded in between the waves of pain that constricted my abdomen in waves of fire, my teeth gritted as I did my best to take soundless gasps of shallow breath. A loud clap of thunder rolled just then, rattling the walls. Lidia looked frightened but whispered a silent prayer to whatever gods she knew.

◆◆◆

The fire had long since died out, leaving only an orange glow that illuminated the hearth with the merest suggestion of spectral heat. The rest of the room was cold now, and dark. Lidia slept next to me, curled up onto her pillow, her breaths deep and rhythmic. I lay draped in a light woolen sheet, though it clung to me, conforming to my sweat drenched body beneath it. Lidia had done her best to clean me after my body had finished its rebellion, doing naturally what Böðvar had tried to do in Porpio á Fen, but a fever still ravaged my body and I could not stop the chills which alternated savagely with flashes of heat.

Before falling into an exhausted sleep, Lidia changed me out of my sodden garments and removed the bed's bloodied linens, burning both in the fire lest they be discovered and my secret revealed. No other ladies had been allowed into the room in the long hours of my ordeal, and likely rumors were spreading though they would never be substantiated as there was no proof. Lidia had simply informed everyone that I was merely ill and that she was tending to me herself. My fever would be discovered in the morning, but that was easily enough explained away.

Now as I lay here in a semi-stupor, my fever raging mercilessly, one thing was clear to me: I was now just Kassia. One only, and no longer two. The seed of my abuse had been expelled, and I was free. My future was not my own any longer, but I was free of my shame and could put the past and its defilement as far away from me as my innocence.

13

As MY FATHER stood on the raised forecastle at the bow of the ship, tall and confident, like a king finally coming into his kingdom, the wind whipped at his mane of white hair, swirling it as the foaming froth along the ocean's rocky shore. His dream propelled him, a dream finally emerging as tangible, the reality of which was mirrored in the ease and confidence of his stance, his chest puffed out with pride, his frame arrayed in the finest cut of cloth the Serdar's money could afford. The Serdar's purse was quite large, so this was saying something.

Never before had I seen my father dressed in such finery, and the image of him standing on the deck stirred fear, pride and anxiety in equal parts within me. He was my father, and yet I didn't know him. Not really. Everything I had known about him all my life was a lie or a half truth; my own life as I had known it was also a lie. I had awakened into an existence unlike any I could ever have imagined, and even after many weeks of wearing it like a new gown, testing its feel, its drape and cut, its warmth or lack thereof, I found it wanting. It was not tailored for me and never would be. Once again I was at the mercy of external events, in control of nothing. My waking hours were more dreamlike than the demon-wrought visions that frequented my nights, visions which had changed in subtlety since that fever-wracked night at the Serdar's house.

Neither Lidia nor I spoke afterwards of what happened that night. Not the next morning, and not in the days that followed it. We simply continued on as if nothing so emotionally scarring had occurred. With each passing day it became easier for me to deny that it had ever happened, for to give voice to the trauma would have allowed it to take a foothold in my heart, and I would not allow that.

Now that I was aboard ship heading south along the Elbran coast en route to the city of Brekkell, home of Caelnor Palace and the waiting arms of my betrothed, those memories were left even farther behind.

Once again I found myself in the care of Captain Eckroth, the same man I had hired to transport us across Allmor Lake from Westwald to Islay Bay in what seemed to be a lifetime ago. I had suspected early on that this all-too-easily discovered captain was somehow involved in my story, but it was only later that I learned that he was indeed the Serdar's man, that he had been sent to Westwald to wait for us in case we showed up. When we boarded the flat-bottomed merchant cog for this present voyage, Captain Eckroth greeted me with a deferential nod but couldn't hide the gleam in his eye. The wink he gave me just as I turned away was unmistakable.

Leaving Islay Bay, Captain Eckroth turned inland, away from Allmor Lake, navigating the fast-flowing Isle River until it emptied into the Elb Inlet, which in turn emptied into the Eastmor Ocean where we now hugged the rugged coastline in this vessel not meant for deep water sailing. Early autumn had turned to late autumn during the weeks of our sojourn in Islay Bay, and here aboard ship I was getting a foretaste of the months to come, when winter would pierce its icy talons into land, man, and beast alike. The weather had been seductively mild in Islay Bay, but now that we had entered the colder, rougher waters of the Eastmor Ocean, the approaching winter announced its coming by harrying my flesh with bitter winds that blew down from the northern coast.

Winter as I had known it in Corium was a minimalist affair, nothing more than a milder version of summer, usually requiring the addition of an extra layer of clothing to keep the drop in temperature from raising gooseflesh. Corium lay to the south and faced west, its prevailing winds sweeping across the vast continent to the east so was warmed by the dryness of the Sidera Mountains; Brekkell, by contrast, faced east, exposing it to the prevailing winds of colder climates much farther north.

Lidia had done well dressing me for my arrival at the residence of my husband to be, choosing one of the finest of the new garments prepared for me in Islay Bay. The over tunic was deep blue velvet similar in color to my father's own coat, slit through at the sleeves to reveal a silk undercoat of deep gold. While plain in decoration, the wealth of the garment was demonstrated by the volume of material used, my skirts taking up nearly an entire bolt of fabric, or so it seemed to me. The velvet was slit around the skirt at intervals to match the sleeves, revealing even more of the golden silk which was further adorned with tiny gems up and down the length of each slit. Complementary gems inset the necklace I wore and also trimmed the delicate ribbons woven throughout my hair. I felt like a walking treasury, and indeed this is precisely how my father and the Serdar hoped me to appear.

It was now late-afternoon and we were fast approaching our destination, would soon see the city as we rounded the narrow pointed headland just ahead. The sun angled sharply, setting the mottled clouds on the horizon ablaze with deep orange and pink hues. I shielded my eyes with my free hand to stare at the palette of colors overhead, thinking it a better way to keep fear at bay. I had learned many things during my weeks of residence with the Serdar, not the least of which being how to keep my thoughts and emotions contained behind a court mask. It was a skill still in its infancy, but I hoped even the most basic mastery of it would serve me well this day. My fear was very real, and I hoped it wouldn't be obvious to those awaiting our arrival in Brekkell.

Jack however, had noticed. Sidling over to me with a stealthy grace, he grabbed my hand, quickly concealing the move by pressing our joined fist into a pleat of my voluminous skirt.

While the excitement of our circumstance was wasted on me, it wasn't wasted on Cai who came rushing up close to my other side, pointing wildly with his finger. "Kassia, look!" His enthusiasm was infectious and I couldn't help but smile, if only for his sake. High above us on the promontory of rock that was the headland stood a large tower, tall and forbidding, a sentinel guarding the approach to the city. As we rounded the jut of land, more details of the tower came into focus, like the brightly colored flags emblazoned with the image of the bennu, the herald of the House Sajen. These flags alternated with the herald of the royal house of Elbra and hung on tall poles, silken material snapping smartly in the crisp wind.

When a blast of trumpets sounded from the heights of the

promontory, a line of gleaming helmets appeared all the way around the topmost reaches of the tower and the wall lining the edge of the sheer rock face. Spears snapped to attention, flashing sparkling sunlight off the razor-sharp tips. My father stood a little taller and his hands grabbed the deck railing, a broad smile spreading across his face. He saluted the men, arm held aloft and straight as a rod.

I shrank back a little, wanting nothing more than to run from the ship's deck, to hide in the small cabin below. Jack would have none of it, gripped my hand more tightly, nearly stopping all blood flow. It was the pain of his grip that stayed me, fixing me firmly to the planking at my feet.

"Kassia, it's for you! It's all for you!" Cai's face beamed up at mine, the brightness of his eyes matched only by the brightness of his hair. I reached out and tousled it. While the Serdar and my father had insisted we leave Cai behind in Islay Bay, I insisted equally as strongly that he come along. I was glad to have won this small victory if nothing else. While all the fanfare of our approach was not necessarily about me, as Cai had declared, there was some small truth to it nonetheless. A sharp gust of wind whipped up, and I pulled my soft velvet tunic more tightly to myself, hoping that the redness in my cheeks would be attributed to it rather than to my discomfort.

I had never craved attention, finding in the obscurity of poverty a freedom that most of my betters would never understand. My newfound identity made my former world of obscurity a lost civilization however, and while Lidia sensed this inherently about me, she didn't fully understand its cause, for she did not know my true story. She had become quite adept at my daily appareling, because she discovered early on the extent of my distaste for all things extravagant and gaudy. She knew too however, the importance of appearance to members of high estate and had gently sought to win me over from my preference for plainer things towards a more tasteful selection of gowns. Everything was made from costly fabrics, though she saw to it that they were adorned simply in order to appease me. My father had disapproved at first but then agreed, likely thinking that I would ease into my new role as time went on.

In an ironic twist of fate, the hall of Serdar Janko Barbaros which had at first seemed cavernous and unfit for private human habitation, a place I couldn't envision any one person abiding with any comfort, had become the scene of my daily lessons. Every step, every turn, every sneeze and breath of air was a matter of observation and then of discussion. While my father's court was purposefully small, it was still vast to the eyes of a former street rat such as me.

I also had a hard time trusting those who surrounded my father, for behind every pair of eyes I envisioned minds that plotted and schemed, men intent on grasping for position, prominence and any scrap of favor which would result in a better situation when my father finally achieved his life's goal -- sitting the throne of Agrius.

My convictions about the divided motivations of the courtesans were only peripheral at best early on, but as the weeks progressed I observed more and more which brought these convictions to the forefront of my consciousness, and even more as word of my arrival spread. Up to this point my father had managed to remain in the shadows of anonymity. As news of him spread, my father suddenly acquired a base of support much broader than it had been. I suspected that most of the people who showed up daily had likely been living life indifferent to the fate of House Sajen, but now that there was a chance for benefit, whether financially or politically, it was time to reconsider loyalties. The time was ripe it seemed, for my father's plans to move forward. Bedic Sajen, rightful heir to the throne of Agrius was alive and intended to make his presence known. King Bellek was now on notice. We would soon have a civil war whether it was good for anyone or not.

◆ ◆ ◆

Our ship rocked gently in the sheltered waters of Brekkell's harbor, an artificial haven built behind a massive stone breakwater on the south side of the promontory that guarded Brekkell's northern approach. A deputation awaited us on the quay, and when it was time for us to disembark, my father lifted my hand and placed it over his as we descended from the ship to the awaiting crowd. Jack, Cai and Swine (whom Cai insisted we bring along as much as I had insisted we bring Cai himself) were left aboard until our party had departed, their presence having been deemed too insignificant to be included in this exalted bunch. I felt Jack's absence immediately, realizing how much his calm and reassuring presence had supported me during the last several weeks; but I was now beyond his help and had to trust instead in my father's time-tested care, a habit now several years out of use.

After the formal introductions were over, a man whose name I immediately forgot stepped forward, and with a practiced smile informed us that Prince Isary sent his deepest apologies, but that he had been called away on an urgent matter and could not meet us personally. We would be conducted to Caelnor Palace where the prince would join us as soon as he was able. I couldn't say that I was terribly disappointed, though it did only postpone the inevitable. My father pretended not to notice the slight, but I could tell from the tight set of his jaw that the incident would not be forgotten.

Possibly I hadn't over-awed the officers of Isary's court as we processed from the harbor to the Palace, but out of sheer dumb luck it was safe to assume that I had succeeded in the most basic skill required of me -- carrying myself with a haughtily aloof pride. Life on the streets of Corium had focused this talent well, for the confident bravado necessary to survive as an orphaned girl was closely akin to the haughtiness the court seemed to love so much. That and I was so petrified that I couldn't do more than stand stiffly erect as we progressed up the hill.

The painful presentation duties over, we were allowed to settle into a set of apartments prepared especially for our use. If I thought Serdar Janko Barbaros was a wealthy man, I clearly had no experience with wealth. Even the Elbran court rats it seemed, were housed in gold leaf and gilt. This ignited a new fury within me, for on the road to the palace, amongst the clean streets, cheering crowds, and immaculately adorned vestments I had noticed a single pair of eyes watching me. The same eyes followed along, dodging and weaving through the crowds; a face that could have just as easily been another Cai. There were children like Cai everywhere, in every city, in every kingdom, representing a world of poverty and misery hidden away in the shadows of the back alleys and muck encrusted corners. It was to this citizenry that my heart was instantly aligned, and I decided then and there that if I was forced into a new life of luxury, I would do everything within my power to help the powerless and poor, whether it was fashionable or not.

"Where is Jack housed?" I asked as casually as I could. "...and Cai?" I added quickly as an afterthought.

Lidia smiled at me, her eyes flashing with a knowing. "I'm not sure, my lady, but I can find out for you?"

I nodded and she left me, silent as a cat except for the rustle of silken skirts on the wind of the door closing behind her. As soon as she was gone, I pulled the pins from my hair freeing my braids to fall as they would. I took off my jewelry and dropped it all on the bed, removed my over-tunic of velvet, and wandered over to the window dressed only in the lightness of my golden-silk gown.

Caelnor Palace was set on a rock overlooking the city below, and the view from my room faced out towards the sea. High overhead the gulls circled and cried out to one another with deafening shrieks. I closed my eyes and tried to imagine how I would summon the energy to continue to act out my role with conviction. I certainly had no desire to be the wife of a prince of Elbra, but neither did I want to return to my life as an orphan on the streets of Corium, even if that was an option, which it wasn't. I found myself inside a living conundrum, caught between my former life with its simplicity despite its struggles, and my present circumstances, surrounded by ease and comfort but ever a living prison. Old versions of Kassia had been created and cast aside with so much frequency during the passing of the last many months, and I had yet to discover the definition of the present Kassia.

My ruminations ripped away at Lidia's return. "Jack is here."

He looked well, and I smiled as he crossed to me. Dressed in clothing more finely made than anything worn by any metal-smith I had ever met, he could easily have passed for my Elbran betrothed. I blanched at the notion and pushed it aside, took several steps towards him to embrace him but was stopped with once glance at a wide-eyed Lidia who was shaking her head ever so subtly. I stopped myself and realized that I could no longer be so familiar with him. I didn't care for my own sake but realized Jack's precarious position. The only reason he was tolerated now was because I wished it, and because he had been instrumental in bringing me safely to my father.

I directed him to a seat and Lidia summoned servants to retrieve wine, quickly whisking them away when they finished so that she could serve us herself, allowing us space for freer conversation away from listening ears.

"You are well? They are treating you well?"

He answered quickly, that yes, he had been shown nothing but respect and that his lodging was adequate. Everything imaginable had been done to make him appear a little less metal-smith and a lot more courtier.

We continued in light, rather meaningless and utterly unsatisfying conversation for some time until Lidia indicated that it was time for me to begin preparing for the evening meal. Jack rose, offered a decorous farewell, and left.

Later that evening, after the meal, my father summoned me to his room.

"Katava, come, sit with me." He was seated in a large cushioned chair very near a large fire that crackled over aromatic logs. While the day had been crisp, the night air was positively chilly. I pulled a large blanket from off a chest in the corner and placed it on his lap before sitting. He smiled at me gratefully. "Oh, daughter... you did well tonight."

I frowned, thinking that it was easy to do well enough when one was not addressed in conversation. It was fine by me to have been all but ignored. I had nothing to say to anyone anyway. Most people were uncertain of me because no one really knew much about me. Our host remained absent, and until that time his household was only required to be accommodating. The few times I was addressed directly, people were polite enough to speak in my own tongue, but it resulted in shorter conversation. No, my role this night was purely decoration. My time as the center of attention would come when Isary arrived. The evening had simply been a space-filler.

"You entertained a guest this afternoon, I understand." He

asked the question casually enough, but his eyes studied me over the rim of the cup he held to his lips. I nodded that it was so, keeping my gaze steady, giving away nothing of my thoughts. He slowly lowered the cup to his lap, his hand shaking ever so slightly. Today's events had tired him, though he did his best not to let it show. His eyes were alert but rimmed with fatigue, and I wondered if he was truly ready to return to his place on the world stage.

"Kassia," he said, his voice more firm than his appearance would suggest. "I am grateful to Jack, for the assistance he provided. He is to be rewarded greatly for the service he performed for our family." I could hear the but coming and wasn't disappointed. "But you must remember that you are born into a different life. It may not be the life you ever imagined, yet it is where you belong, and there is no going back from it."

A servant entered quietly, refilled the wine flagon and left as unobtrusively as he had come. My father's eyes barely registered the action, his gaze remaining steady on my face. It took all of my effort to remain calm.

"It will not be easy for you, I will not lie. You lived a life very much apart from anything these people could even begin to imagine." He lowered his voice at this last part. "It was an upbringing no daughter of mine should ever have had to endure. It was not meant to be this way, and certainly not these last several years for you. For that, I blame only myself." His voice dripped with regret, but I swallowed back my sympathy because he was right. I had been an impoverished orphan and did many things that would scandalize the court because I was forced to do so.

My father went on to explain how we would account for my life up until my arrival in Islay Bay. While we wouldn't hide the fact that I grew up ignorant of my identity but we would gloss over the meaner aspects of my experiences, creating a mixture of truth and fabrication turning me into a more palatable version of myself. As long as no one probed too deeply, all would be well. The fact that no one would want to dwell on that much discomfort practically guaranteed our success, my father assured me. I wasn't so sure but offered him no argument.

I was under no illusions regarding my role in my own future. My marriage to Isary was an essential part of my father's plan -- one of his daughters was to marry the second-born of Elbra's king because this prince had much to gain by the match and would be grateful in return. Isary's older brother was heir to the Elbran throne. For Isary to gain a crown of his own, ingenuity would be his savior over birthright. A tie with the House of Sajen offered him what he craved, assuming he was willing to use his vast wealth to help my father regain his own throne. In this, I was told, he was more than willing, for he would then be next in line to rule Agrius. My father also gained in that he would have a strong ally for the rest of his reign and a secure heir afterwards. Everyone came out a winner.

Except me.

"Kassia, you are to keep your distance from Jack in the future, is that understood? There cannot be even a hint of impropriety. None. You will be married, and then we will begin our war." His face hardened to granite as he spoke those last words, revealing the prince he was, not the father I knew. Gone was the gentle scribe I had known in my youth, replaced with a political force, a man schooled in the machine of war and diplomacy, politics and game-playing, a man set on a course and who would not be diverted. When I said nothing he asked, "Do you hear me, daughter?"

"I hear you just fine, father." Without another word I stood and stiffly walked from the room.

◆ ◆ ◆

Three days passed. My father never said as much, but I could tell that he was not pleased. Certainly Isary could explain away his absence, though I suspected that it was a play on his part calculated to send a clear message that no one but Isary himself commanded this aspect of the throne-regaining enterprise.

I didn't see Jack in all that time. It was just as well, and I knew it. What I did feel most keenly was the loss of Cai. My father was of a mind to eventually take him into his own household, but for now Cai trained with Isary's men. He was a cheerful boy and had taken to his duties with great enthusiasm, enough of a recommendation for his peers to accept him despite his questionable background. I saw him occasionally, but all he saw before him was novelty and possibility with little time for me. In happier news, Swine was out of my life for good, had been paid off with a bag of coins and subsequently slithered away into the business districts of Brekkell. I rejoiced at his going -- though certainly not to his face, which I hoped never to see again, the mewling joithead.

I remained companionless and felt it keenly. Certainly I had Lidia who was close enough in age to me, but there were enough differences between us, the primary one being our understanding of the world and our respective places in it. While Lidia was not a royal daughter like me, her early years had been spent in the house of a minor lord, being the child of a minor lord herself. She had grown up with an inherent understanding of the world in which I played my part with merely a novice ability, and she had no comprehension of what I lacked or why. Any shortfall she perceived in me though was too polite to give voice, she likely attributed to eccentricity. For this reason we were not destined to become intimates.

Early on the fourth day, I received notice of Isary's impending arrival, giving me time enough to prepare my appearance appropriately, though it would take several lifetimes to prepare my attitude. This was not, and never would be, my first choice, or even my second choice. I did it for my father. Rebellion wouldn't work; the price was just too high. I determined to play my new role even if it killed me. Jack claimed that I was strong, and now I needed to prove it to myself.

My mind made up, I descended into the abyss. My father was already present, talking with a man. A tall man. A man who filled the room with charisma alone. A man confident in his own physical prowess. His motions were liquid, his smile flashing, and when he turned to look at me his face took on a new light.

I bowed a deep obeisance, saying nothing and nearly grazing the cold tile floor with my knee. My eyes remained downcast, not out of docile demure but because I didn't trust myself to look at him. He had nice shoes made of soft kid leather, and though they were trimmed with fur and silver fittings, they were entirely more practical than I expected a man of his rank to wear. I knew nothing of Isary the man, but perhaps his predilection for these shoes augured a more practical nature than I was prepared to give him credit for?

I didn't have long to dwell on this before he took my hand in his warm and gentle grasp and raised me to standing.

"My lady, the reports of your beauty fall far too short of reality." He bowed low over my hand then kissed the back of my fingers with a flourish. I sighed inwardly with resolution and looked up.

He wasn't necessarily handsome in the classical sense, certainly would never be made the subject of a bard's tale of romance, at least not in a truthful manner -- his eyes were too close together and his nose was a bit too pointy -- but his mouth was full and symmetrical, the teeth behind his smile white and even. Olive-toned skin paired nicely with chestnut hair, and when he smiled, his eyes crinkled at the corners making him seem warm and benevolent. With a surge of irritation I felt a flush threaten to rise to my cheeks, and I fought it off for all I was worth. I wasn't a flighty female by any stretch of the imagination, and it troubled me that this man, this prince, my betrothed, had such an alarming affect on me. I wondered if other females felt this way around him.

He made more light talk and I responded in kind, remembering none of it immediately after. I was too caught up in trying to remember to stand straight, to smile, to look him in the eye as I spoke -- in other words, to remember all the things I had been taught. The few memories I did retain had no more real substance than a phantasm, were merely snatches of things, of faces, a word spoken here and there, a smile, the flash of perfectly white teeth, light shining off of gilded surfaces, my father's laugh.

I returned to my room in a daze, completely oblivious to the ladies scurrying around my room, doing what was necessary to prepare me for the welcome banquet that night. Lidia tried to engage me in conversation but I heard next to nothing of what she said. It was as if I was a puppet in a play, my strings being pulled while I was powerless to engage on my own terms. I had checked out.

"...in a dark room," someone giggled.

The tittering drew me out of the insubstantial world into which I had retreated. "What did you say?" I asked, equally disturbed and embarrassed.

Lidia grinned at me impishly, a dimple appearing on her cheeks. "I said, you two are nicely matched, will make beautiful babies. Just put you together in a dark room..."

I flashed Lidia a look and she silenced. I swallowed hard and closed my eyes, trying to imagine anything other than what I know the girls had just suggested with their giggles, beginning instead to recite the Laws of Rondle as best I could recall them from my father's lessons when I was younger:

First, every particle of matter in the universe attracts every other particle with a force that is directly proportional to the product of the masses of the particles and inversely proportional to the square of the distance between them...

I stopped, deciding that perhaps this principle relating to particle attraction was not the best place to start. Lidia giggled again and gave the lacings of my bodice an extra tug for emphasis. I frowned and made a mental note to replace her with a less saucy maid later, knowing I never would.

By the time Lidia had finished, I begrudgingly admitted that she had done her work well. I was dressed in an emerald green gown fitted with enough jewels to catch the light no matter how I stood. It was the most extravagant thing I had ever seen, much less worn, and surprisingly I found it exhilarating, a notion that unnerved me enormously.

I was met downstairs by Isary who, with an air of possession, took me on his arm and introduced me to more Elbran nobility. Eventually we found ourselves seated at the table in full view of everyone, and the evening progressed with alarming speed. Isary did his job well as host, directing everything with skill and efficiency, from food and drink to music and conversation. He was gracious and engaging, and I found myself quickly relaxing under his gallant attentions. By the time it was over, I was nearly breathless from the whirlwind, despite my paltry expectations. If nothing else, at least one thing was accomplished by the evening: it was now possible for me to envision a life with the man who was to be my husband. I remembered how it had been with Issak even though I had made a conscious effort to spurn him. This time I determined to make the most of the opportunity. I would choose to be content.

The hall was mostly cleared out by the time I submitted to the late hour and allowed Isary to escort me away. We progressed through the corridors and finally out into a small garden courtyard. The sky was blanketed in deep purple velvet, scattered points of starlight puncturing it with even strokes across its entire expanse. We were out of the wind, but the air was bracing and I began to shiver immediately. Isary wrapped his cloak around my shoulders as we walked together enjoying what was left of the late autumn foliage. In the summer months this garden would have overflowed with scents of moonflower and lavender, honeysuckle and jasmine. Now there was only the smell of deep earth, and it reminded me of the deepest forest.

It was also quiet and solitary. Only the crickets watched our progress.

"My lady, I have been given an education today." He flashed a smile at me, his teeth reflecting the light of the moon. I slanted a questioning look at him with my own half smile, all the while keeping my face turned enough to prevent him from sensing the fiery blush in my cheeks. He continued, clarifying, "I was prepared to do my duty, to take to wife a lady of House Sajen for political reasons alone, playing the part of martyr if necessary." I smiled to myself, recognizing the cynical admission for what it was, simultaneously amused by the fact that it mirrored my own thoughts precisely while also wondering if he was being entirely truthful. I hoped he was.

We stopped near an elaborate topiary and I studied it admiringly, astounded by the artistry of its construction. It was getting late, and I was very tired, but Isary clearly had more he meant to say so I waited patiently for him to continue. He remained silent for a moment longer as if looking for just the right words. "Kassia, I have found that I will not make my oath to you as a martyr..." he caught my hand in his, lifted it to his lips, "...but rather as a willing participant..." He brushed a light kiss on my knuckles. "...for I am hopelessly enchanted by my bride-to-be." Now he turned over my hand, pressed a kiss into my palm, and my knees threatened to give way.

The moment was interrupted by a small noise, the scraping of a shoe on stone. I glanced away from Isary instinctively to find the source of the sound, saw the shadowed figure of a man melting into darkness. Just before the figure edged completely out of the light, he turned and looked back over his shoulder. Isary's back was turned to the retreating figure, but he turned in response to my reaction. If Isary saw the man's face as I had, if he had reason to recognize him, he gave no indication. But the man was known to me -- Jack -- and the look he gave me bore into my soul, a look full of enough pain and sorrow to leave me feeling cut off and empty.

Isary turned back to me, noticing that my face was bleached of color. "It is late." When I didn't react, he tipped my face up towards the softness of the moonlight so that he had my full attention. He brushed his thumb across my neck as he brought his face close to mine then murmured softly, "I should take you to your room, to your bed."

His words dripped with honey-warm seduction, and he knew full well the effect it had on me so smiled lazily, satisfied with the result. He grazed my lips with his own then pulled back a little, taking my arm in his, the proper courtier once more. "Come, we should get you back to your room, safely back to your ladies."

14

"IRISA, HOW WILL you last the day, now that you have no bread of your own?" My sister isn't looking at me. I see only her back, and as she shrugs her shoulders in reply I think she is stubborn. What a foolish thing to do! Why does she not see that if she eats her own bread, she will stay healthy enough to find more useful ways to aid the muddy little beggar-child? Sickening, dying of starvation, what good will it do anyone?

The streets here stink. Kitchen scraps and urine-sodden refuse clutter the narrow lane between toppling buildings, and as we walk, Irisa and I keep one eye to the sky, watching for falling pieces of siding, and one eye to the ground so that we don't step in something overly obnoxious. Irisa is wearing her most recently sewn gown fashioned from scraps. It looks remarkable on her. I glance down at my own shabby skirt and wonder if I will ever be like her.

"Kassia, you needn't worry. I ate yesterday."

How this is supposed to appease me, I have no idea. Rather than continue to argue with her over the issue, I tear off another piece of the heavy, black bread I carry in my tight grasp and pop it into my mouth. It makes me want to choke, but I chew it anyway. I bite off another portion and nearly scream as I bite into a large piece of stone. My teeth rattle. I wonder if I have cracked one of them? I mumble curses, but my sister isn't listening. She is looking at something else. Before I have time to react, the bread I held so securely only moments before is snatched away. Irisa took it from me and has handed it to the dung-encrusted, one-armed man sitting in the shadow of a horse's trough. I am pretty sure that her tendency towards compassion will someday be the death of us both.

◆ ◆ ◆

As I studied it more closely, the pane of glass in front of me transformed into a block of ice, solid and unyielding, its uneven surface distorting the feebleness of reflected light into strange images. My palm pressed flat against it, and as I stared, I imagined it to be part of the wall of the ice palace of the Ice King Petri, ruler of the mythical kingdom of the Snow Dwellers.

Each night at dusk, the kingdom of the Snow Dwellers froze before full dark fell, and each morning as the new sun rose, the ice imprisoning the inhabitants of the kingdom melted, waking the citizenry to a new world of light. None knew what darkness was, and none remembered the day before. Each new dawning of the sun brought confusion and mystery so that by the time the sun sank below the horizon again, ushering in a new dusk, the people had only just begun to remember who they were. Their world was nothing more than a mirror of the day before. They were condemned to live a life of repetition and drudgery, yet none of them knew it.

Life at Caelnor Palace flew by in a blur, days turning inexorably into weeks. The crispness of autumn dissolved, and trees which were once bright with the colors of burning coals lost all vivacity, were now brown and bare. While it didn't snow here on the coast, the winds battered and bludgeoned man and beast, buildings and landscape alike without discrimination.

No responsibilities had been placed on me beyond the expectation that I be a student. Each day brought more lessons in living my new life, and it was relentless. Hours were spent learning faces and recalling names, or working tirelessly on embroidery and needlepoint, two things I neither had interest in nor skill.

When not forced to think about matters of court, I spent my time daydreaming about the life I had escaped, nostalgia having edged out memories of the harsher realities of life on the streets -- being dirty, hungry, alone except for my sister, and always living in fear. As an escape, I dreamt of roaming the markets of Brekkell, dissolving into the citizenry where I belonged, overlooked as I once had been.

Isary had taken me to the market himself, once in the early days, and he made a big show of purchasing an alarming amount of fabric, jewelry and other items of frippery. I suspected that not only was it to curry my goodwill, it was also a show meant to demonstrate to his people that he understood their common ways. His interactions were received with politeness, but I could tell most people wished he would finish his errand and leave them in peace. Not everyone welcomed him with open arms, it seemed.

Wherever we went, a large entourage consisting of a bevy of ladies who had been attached to me, several courtesans of generic stripe, and a contingent of guards followed us. It was exceedingly uncomfortable for me, as all eyes watched me, taking note of how I carried myself, how and when I spoke, to whom I spoke, etc. No matter where we went, it was always with great relief on my part that we returned to the palace.

I pulled my hand from the frozen pane, leaving behind an outline where it had melted the ice. I felt entombed here. The day was unusually bright, reminding me of Corium and signaling a deep pang within me.

Before I had time to think better of it, my feet moved. Crossing the room with purpose, I retrieved a fur-trimmed cloak from the peg in the corner and swept out the door.

"My lady, where are you going?" an anxious Lidia asked.

"To the market."

"But... But..." She rushed to keep pace with me, barely remembering to grab her own wrap before following. I heard a muffled twittering behind me and assumed the other ladies were following Lidia's example.

A groom jumped to do my bidding when I asked him to saddle my horse. Two of Isary's men noticed what I was about and scrambled to get their own horses ready. With Lidia and several of my ladies following in addition to the two guards, I knew I wouldn't be alone, though anything was better than staying in the palace. Perhaps I'd encounter Swine then could find a good stick with which to poke him. The thought brought a rare smile to my face.

Ignoring the icy winds that whipped like a fury, I kicked Rose's flanks and she shot across the open courtyard, under the arched gates, and out onto the road beyond. The two guards followed closely behind Rose's streaming tail, a small band of ladies in comical disarray at various points behind them.

The road was a fine one, laid with tightly knit cobbles the color of warm sun-baked stone, as high in quality as any in Corium. The morning sun pierced the cloudless, watery blue sky deep in the southern half of the horizon, radiating an illusionary heat. It did nothing to warm my skin, yet it warmed my heart immediately.

Crowds choked the wide avenue between the palace and the town, so with some resignation I slowed my pace, not wanting to trample any of the people I so wished to be a part of. Some of them looked at me with indifference as I passed, some with hastily hidden scowls, while many others looked up with awe. No matter the reaction, not a single one of them had any idea who I truly was. I thought back to that morning long ago in Corium when I sat on the edge of a marble pool in the garden of a wealthy aristocrat and saw a girl reflected back to me from the surface of the placid pool. Her eyes were green and closely set, framed by long lashes over smudged cheeks displaying a smattering of unfashionable freckles. Her hair was an equally unfashionable copper brown, and her dirty clothing hid a scrawny, unappealing frame. She was poor, hungry, and worthless. But she was free. Yet these people -- the crowds, Lidia, my ladies, the guards, even Isary -- knew none of it. Only Jack knew.

Unconsciously I gripped Rose's side more tightly with my knees, and in response she arched her neck then brought her mouth back to nip at the toe of my shoe. With a yelp I released the pressure and pushed aside my morose thoughts.

Eventually I found the market and dismounted, pushing my way through the crowds on foot and bypassing the finest stalls of the street-front merchants in favor of those deeper into the warren of streets. Lidia took my arm in her own while the rest of the ladies followed closely behind, wide-eyed and clearly ruled by both confusion and fear. Wary even as they resigned to go along with this crazy, spontaneous act, the guards maintained a close vigil, alert to any sign of trouble, hands hovering near the hilts of their swords.

Most market-goers gave way as we passed. I wasn't known readily enough for immediate recognition, but the appearance of Isary's household guards alone would have been enough cause for us to be noticed even had we not been trimmed in regalia. The reactions of the onlookers varied: some pretended not to notice, flicking us furtive glances only; some watched us with muted curiosity; but most others stared openly, causing a ripple to run through the crowds.

I tried on multiple occasions to stop and admire the wares of several merchants, wanting nothing more than to give them my good will and encourage their trade. Despite my best intentions, it seemed my actions were counterproductive. I wasn't welcome here. Contrary to my desire for them to know I was one of them, these people held for me the same wary caution as they had held for Isary the day he brought me here. With horror I realized that I had crossed over the class divide, likely never to return.

Just as my spirits were descending into misery, I heard a wail from somewhere behind me and turned to find its source: a young mother with an infant. The infant was clearly hungry, but from the looks of the mother, there was not much help to be had from her, so thin and impoverished was she. Her eyes were darkly shadowed, hollowed from both fear and hunger, and my heart instantly went out to her.

Pulling aside one of my ladies, I gave her some hastily whispered instructions. She listened, speechless, then bobbed her head with a mixture of understanding and disbelief. Soon she was back with a bundle: a bag full of last season's apples, a loaf of hearty bread, and a blanket. Before anyone could stop me, I approached the young woman who stood frozen as if being approached by a wolf on the prowl. When I gave the lot to her, explaining my intentions, she accepted without a word. It was only when I reached out to pat her infant on his soft, fuzzy head that she smiled. On instinct I pulled a small, delicate band of gold from my finger and slipped it into her hand. At this, she collapsed to the ground and wept.

All was quiet; so quiet you could have heard the nail of a horse's shoe drop.

"That is the Lady Kassia!" The shout rang out from somewhere in the crowd. "She is to marry our Prince!"

A low rumbling of murmurings stirred, followed by open talk, all of which grew with ever increasing volume until the crowd worked itself up into a boiling sea of excitement. Very soon bodies pressed up around me, eager hands reached out, and for the first time I felt afraid. Regardless of the intentions of the majority, my guardsmen moved in, one behind and one before, edging the people away in an attempt to pull me down the alley and back to the main street where I would be safer and in the bailiwick of a gentler class of people.

They weren't very effective. Fortunately for them, it didn't matter.

A shout rang out, and I heard a clatter of hooves in the distance, the clash of metal, the jostling of crowds. The latter soon parted and a contingent of immaculately dressed palace guards shoved their way through and encircled me.

The leader of the group gave me a crisp bow. "My lady, will you come with us?" It was not a question.

◆ ◆ ◆

The pane of glass in my room was frost-free in the late afternoon. The sun had long since moved across the sky, hung now over the western sky as a pale yellow orb, leaving my rooms gloomy and shadow-filled. The view out my window, over the city to the harbor below, was clear, and my eyes sought out the quay where our ship from Islay Bay had docked weeks before. A lifetime before. I turned my back and walked away.

Lidia ordered a bath and a tray of food and drink. I took the bath but ignored the food. My mind fixated on the memory of the young mother and her infant. I knew that the food I had given her would do her immediate good, but the truth of the matter was that unless she had reliable help, there was no future for her or her child. I didn't know her story and likely never would, and instead of anger I felt nothing. It was obvious to me that despite my new rank and resources, I was powerless.

Lidia helped me out of the bath and dressed me in a sheer robe of fur-lined silk. Sitting near a brightly burning hearth to keep warm, I relaxed as Lidia combed out the long waves of hair falling down my back. She had only just applied oil of jasmine to the comb when our quiet retreat was invaded by the arrival of Isary. Lidia was the only other person present and startled at the invasion, but did her best to hide her chagrin, backing away to find other duties to occupy her.

Isary spared the merest of glances for her as he crossed the room in several quick strides. I stood to meet him, wary of the stern look in his eyes. He stopped before me and took in the sight of my hair as it hung loose about my shoulders, lingering where the firelight took hold, enhancing it to look like burnished copper. His gaze strayed lower, to the lightness of fabric draped loosely over my shoulders, making me distinctly uncomfortable. I wanted to grab the blanket from the chair behind me to cover myself, but I stayed my hand and remained passive instead, waiting for him to talk.

"Why?" The question was simple and spoken softly and calmly, but the leaping flames behind me illuminated his face, chasing away some shadows while creating others, making his eyes appear hard, cold and thus investing his words with menace. I did my best to appear unmoved, and when I didn't answer, he continued, "Do you have any idea what might have happened, the danger you were in?" His eyes flicked back and forth between mine. Grabbing me, he pulled me tightly against him, so close that I had to arch my back to look up at him. "Kassia," his voice now solid as granite with not even a trace of softness left, "that was a very foolish thing to do."

A stab of fear pierced me, but I dismissed it. Isary would never hurt me. I lowered my lashes and looked straight ahead, at the rise and fall of his chest and the glint of the ruby set into the broach at his neck.

He released me with such suddenness that I swayed as he turned and paced the room. Running his hands through his hair in thought, he turned back to me. "Do you realize the position you could have been placed in? If you have a need for something, tell a groom to fetch it, send a contingent of your ladies! This is their purpose, their sole reason for existence, to serve you, to do your bidding!" He wasn't yelling exactly, but just on the edge. "To mingle in such a way with that kind..." He waived his arm dismissively. I bristled with anger.

"With that kind?" I asked in mimic of his tone.

"Yes, with that kind. The urchins, the filth, the street rats.

They exist as a rule of society, but their province is their own. They choose to live where they do, let them take care of their own!" He returned to face me, his eyes blazing, and I returned his look, my initial stab of fear solidifying into glacial ice.

"What do you know of their plight?" I spoke with quiet caution, but there was no mistaking the firmness of my conviction.

He narrowed his eyes at me. "And what do *you* know of their plight?" he returned, then smiling, added, "Ah, yes, I forget. You were raised in humbler circumstances, to a king without a country." I thought I saw mockery for a moment, but it was quickly replaced with a softness that countered the evidence. "Kassia, it is admirable to have a weakness for the dire circumstances of the less fortunate," he paused and smiled a cat smile, "but you can do so without endangering yourself in the future. Send your women with alms next time you feel weakness at their plight, and have them delivered at the gate, where that kind expects it." He paused again, his smile waspish. "And in this way more people can see your largesse."

"So that we reap the benefit, my lord?" I asked, my voice soothing and honey sweet.

"Yes," he said, satisfied that I was finally beginning to see it his way. "And to think that you actually touched that whelp! You may have become infected!" He chuckled at his own wit. "What did you hope to accomplish?"

"She was hungry. Her infant was hungry. And she could have easily been my own mother!" It was a careless thing to say, and I realized my mistake immediately.

"What do you mean?"

What was the use in pretending? My full story was bound to come out sooner or later. The explanation we had given Isary was a version of the truth anyway, merely enough facts pieced together to make my story believable yet easy to navigate, all concocted in such a way to distract him from the more distasteful parts. It was flimsy, easily dissected and could readily be disregarded as falsehood if examined too closely. I told him all, leaving out the most private things that needn't concern him, and he listened quietly, his demeanor uncharacteristically stoic. Even his eyes were unreadable. But with each part of the tale I told, I felt increasingly smaller and more exposed, as if I stood before him naked.

"I am Sajen. Of that there is no doubt," I finished in a hushed voice. "No matter what my life has been up till now, I am no less valuable to you than would be a diamond cut from the earth, waiting firstly to be shaped and honed before it is made brilliant. Gaining your throne depends only on my birth, not on how I lived my life up till now."

"I see," he said in a murmur, dangerously. With nothing more, he turned, walked across the room and closed the door quietly behind him.

"No, you don't," I whispered. But no one heard me.

◆ ◆ ◆

"Kassia, I need to tell you about our plans. Come, sit here by me." My father indicated a chair near to him which I dutifully took and sat quietly, waiting for him to continue. It was early morning several days after my escape to the market. I hadn't seen Isary much since his visit to me, for I had intentionally tried to avoid him, though I suspect he had done the same. Publically it was a simple enough excuse: he was planning a war, and such a thing tends to take up a lot of one's time, with all the marching, charging and sieging plans to establish, the bloodletting to be envisioned, the warriors to be provisioned...

"I need to show you these maps so you can understand what we plan to do. I did not teach my daughters to be ignorant of strategy, after all."

The room was large, tall narrow windows faced west, allowing the late afternoon sun to spill in. My father sat before a large, heavily carved mahogany table. Spread across the vast surface of the table lay a large map, intricately drawn and shaded with vivid colors from corner to corner. Lines and symbols crisscrossed the face of it, and I reached out a tentative finger to touch what appeared to be water, thinking that my hand might come back wet, so real did it appear. My father watched me with wry amusement and proud approval. He gave me a moment to take in all that I saw before beginning his instruction.

I could tell my father had long been closeted behind closed doors. His face was drawn with lines of fatigue, but as he began to talk about his plans, I sensed a new energy about him.

"Brekkell is here," he pointed with his finger to indicate the port city in Elbra, "and Agrius is here."

I had never really known where Agrius was, but now I saw a vast land mass far across the Eastmor Ocean. Because of their relative positions, it was easy to see the great political advantage in being allied with Elbra and Pania. Agrius and Pania had a clear advantage when it came to trade routes across the ocean, but with the addition of Elbra, control over what passed into Mercoria could be greatly enhanced. While Elbra may not have needed the enticement of wealth, the offer of a throne was something this younger son of the Elbran royal family could not pass up.

My father went on to explain that Prince Isary was to provide the majority of the funding for the military campaign against Agrius, and that he would be providing half of the troops necessary while Pania would provide the other half. He continued with more details about routes, the strategies behind which cities to attack first and why, but I had long since stopped listening. I had never cared about such things, finding the contents of the map itself, the locations of various cities and mountains and bodies of water, far more evocative. Despite my inattention, I maintained myself as a study in concentration, doing my best to pretend that I hung on every word.

"Kassia, do you understand all that I have told you?"

I lied by nodding my head and he smiled, stood slowly, using the table for support.

Isary was present but hadn't spoken once all the while my father unveiled his plans. His casual pose -- leaning against the far wall with arms crossed -- spoke volumes: it was a waste of time, he thought, to explain anything to me. It wasn't women's work to go to war, and my input and understanding was irrelevant. But my father thought differently, had always known that a daughter of his would rule in his stead when he was dead and buried, and that be it a he or a she, any ruler needed to have a thorough understanding of the politics of governance as vital to the success of Agrius.

Despite this forethought, my father had raised us ignorant of our heritage. While our obliviousness all but guaranteed our anonymity and therefore our preservation, it had one serious consequence: we had known nothing of the main purpose behind our education and therefore couldn't associate a single practical application. Neither Irisa nor I cared about politics or military strategy, and neither did we have any reason at the time to believe that the knowledge was relevant to our lives. What good was political strategy when one lived in a back alley? Now, of course, I knew that my father intended me or Irisa to be queen of Agrius after him, with Isary as consort. But perhaps it was too late. Perhaps Isary was right after all.

I endured until my father was satisfied. When he finally dismissed me to my ease, relief washed over me like a raging current. I wanted nothing more than to change out of my self-important court attire into something more practical and comfortable. Sighing inwardly, I knew it wasn't to be. This was now my lot. Instead I went to find Lidia, telling her I wanted to walk. She jumped at the chance, happy to get out of her other duties in exchange for some fresh air.

While I was no prisoner, I knew better than to leave the palace precinct, having learned my lesson after the market incident. It wasn't for Isary's sake that I now refrained, but rather for the sake of my father and the love that I bore him.

Lidia and I walked a circuitous route around the inside edge of the outer curtain wall. There was little enough to see except for empty kitchen gardens. During the summer months these empty beds would be hives of activity, but now in the winter months, the ground lay dormant, sleeping until the new season brought warmth and bright sun and the hope of a new harvest. The only eyes on us now were those of the bored guards watching from high up on the walls overhead.

We had just rounded the corner when we encountered a raucous group of young men engaged in a friendly competition astride horses. The horses and riders didn't capture my attention, rather one particular observer leaning up against a makeshift barrier protecting the onlookers from the racing combatants.

Jack didn't notice as I approached him from behind. In fact, no one really noticed our approach, so enrapt was the gathering with the antics of horseflesh and steel. Lidia kept several discreet steps behind me, giving me the opportunity for private conversation with Jack. It was several moments before he turned and looked at me. He didn't immediately speak, and neither did I. What was there to say, after all? We were worlds apart, and it would be difficult to pretend otherwise.

It was all I could do to keep from reaching out to sweep back the hair that habitually fell over his right eye.

"You look well."

I snatched a quick look at his face. His expression was flat, his tone, while warm, lacked both the cadence and rising tones of sincerity.

"As do you," I replied with the same flatness, but unlike him I waited a beat then released a brilliant smile, triggering a returned smile from him.

"I heard about what happened in the market." His voice was pitched so that I alone could hear him over the exclamations of the crowd, and as soon as he said it he turned away from me, fixing his gaze back on the antics of the men in front of us.

I pretended to be interested in the newest contender, a sleek youth astride an equally sleek horse who together performed a feat of athleticism infused with such supple grace as to throw the onlookers into a clamoring frenzy.

"I was duly chastised," I replied, my eyes hard, my tone unyielding, determined.

Jack flicked me a sideways look, and a smile quickened at the corner of his mouth. "Kassia, don't let him change who you are. You've been given a gift of position. Use it. If you can't change the tide of your life, go with it. Use your position to do good and never apologize."

I wanted to counter him, explain to him what it was like to be around Isary, that Jack was wrong and I didn't have it in me, but what difference would it make? His assessment of my quality was rock-solid. We had argued this in the past, and he would not be moved now. My face must have betrayed some doubt.

"Kassia, I'm serious. You have steel in your spine. The quality of a person does not depend on the definition another has imposed, and I know you are strong enough to resist. You are no more or less valuable because of Isary's opinion." Jack whispered this last part to be certain no one had overheard him, and I had to strain to make out his words. He turned to look me full in the face then, and I saw behind his eyes the fire that fueled the passion of his words. In that moment I knew he was right, however much I wanted to deny it. Jack alone had this influence over me. How to find this reservoir of resolve on my own, without his abiding companionship? I simply would. There was no other way. There were worst fates in life, and perhaps there were aspects of being Isary's wife, as Jack pointed out, that I would come to realize, even appreciate, if given enough chance. Time was all I needed. It would be enough.

He must have seen the subtle shift in my countenance, for even when I said nothing in reply he turned back to the exhibition in front of us, satisfied but closed to me again. It had been a brief exchange, far from satisfying in its brevity. The moment was gone, and though I longed for more, it was no matter; I had been given a gift -- a glimpse of the Jack I knew before everything had become as it was.

♦♦♦

Sleep escaped me, so I lay in the darkness, listening to the softness of breath rising and falling as one of the younger maids slept soundly on her small mattress near the door. I thought about the afternoon's short encounter with Jack, remembered all that we had shared, knowing nothing would ever be the same again. My father and Jack's father had somehow managed to strike up an unlikely friendship in the happy days of their youth back in Agrius, but that was different. Any hopes of maintaining a friendship with Jack were dangerous ones and required exorcism. I would soon be married, and it was paramount that I maintain the strictest appearance of fidelity.

Growing impatient with my sleeplessness, I rose from my bed and crept out into the dark, empty halls. The flagstones were cold on my bare feet, and I wished immediately that I had bothered to put on a pair of shoes. I had no desire to go back lest I wake anyone, so setting aside my discomfort, I made my way to the cavernous kitchens and slipped out a side door and into a small courtyard which contained a dormant herb garden to find a lonely bench, hoping that solitude would help to clarify my wildly rampaging thoughts.

Once again, I miscalculated. Rather than clarity, I found cold and misery instead. It was winter, and not only had I neglected my poor feet, I hadn't brought a cloak. The bitter temperature mocked my mistake.

I was here, I decided, and it wouldn't do me any harm to make a quick circuit of the garden before retiring back into the warmth of the kitchen where perhaps I might find a leftover tart or pudding to satiate the rumbling of my stomach which I had neglected during the evening meal, choosing to brood in my room rather than eat.

The head cook insisted that a fountain operate year-round, despite the coldness of winter. It benefited the birds, she argued, keeping the surface of the water from freezing over so that they would have a place to drink and be refreshed. I suspected that her motive had more to do with the fact that luring birds to a working fountain made simpler the catching of a partridge for the pot rather than because of any interest in animal husbandry, but it was none of my business. Regardless of her motives, I was thankful, finding the musical cadence of the bright waters pouring over the edge of the fountain's terraced edges enjoyable, so slowed my pace to listen.

My listening produced another result. In addition to the sounds of murmuring water, I picked out another kind of murmur, not water but voices. I knew that the slightest sound of crunching gravel under my foot would announce my presence, so I backed up and edged my way over to the soft grass at the garden edge.

From here I was nearer the source of the murmurs coming from behind a thick hedge. The voices quieted, followed by the rustle of clothing along with breathy sighs, silencing after an urgent gasp. All went still once more.

I was distinctly uncomfortable, deciding that my discovery was no more than two star-crossed lovers catching a fleeting moment of passion away from observation. It was a very odd place for a coupling, cold and awkward, but not everyone was privy to comfortable and private lodgings.

My fingers had lost all feeling, and I was just about ready to turn and leave, when something I overheard froze me to my spot: "...Kassia..." I hadn't been addressed; I was being discussed. The whispering continued, and though I couldn't make out the words, I strained to hear more. "...your news will be rewarded... because of her father...will have to wait, but then I can..."

It went quiet again, and I thought that perhaps they had finished. Nothing I had heard made any sense, and I was frustrated. Was this a plot of some kind?

"...her only purpose..." There was more laughter, and I grew increasingly impatient. Just when I thought there was no hope of discovering what I was hearing, the voice speaking grew louder, the speaker revealing himself. "Royal marriages are made for alliances only, after all. Nothing more. I will do my duty to her, and she hers, but then I will free myself of her." It was Isary.

◆ ◆ ◆

I tilted my face to the sun, closing my eyes while taking a breath of the sweet earthy scent in the air. Winter waned, the coming of spring promised in the song of a single songbird, its beautiful and melodic tune decorating the otherwise lonely landscape with delicate notes of joy. Hints of green things peeked out of the brown loamy earth all around. In the coming months farmers would venture out to plant their crop in hopes of another productive growing season.

I sat astride Rose, riding next to Isary, and we rode on a circuit of his lands near to Brekkell. The unrest that had taken Isary away from the city when my father and I had arrived from Islay Bay was still an issue in Elbra. I hadn't concerned myself with the details of the unrest, and Isary had never bothered to enlighten me, but I knew it involved farm laborers' disgruntled attitude towards Isary's management of his father's taxation policy. Since my arrival, Isary had taken several similar journeys to provide support to his tax men, and in a gesture that shocked me, he asked me to accompany him as he rode out on another survey. While I didn't necessarily enjoy his company, I did enjoy the escape from Caelnor Palace and the relative freedom of horseback, so agreed to go along.

I was delighting in the rarity of oblivious daydreaming on this journey, having no need to converse with anyone much less continue on with lessons. After two hours of bliss, Isary took it upon himself to break into my luxury, thinking it far more stimulating to provide me with a detailed analysis of soil management in addition to many not-so-subtle descriptions of regional fertilization techniques, tongue firmly in cheek all the while. His tiresome commentary was thankfully interrupted by the arrival of a messenger, his beleaguered horse tired and lathered despite the coolness of the season. He reined up hard next to Isary, his mount shuddering to a stop, the whites of its eyes showing as wide orbs, its mouth grimacing in pain. Whatever the news, it was important.

I pulled my gaze away from the animal to watch Isary as he read the letter the messenger had handed him. He scanned it quickly then gave a curt nod and spoke a few words to the man who gratefully dismounted his horse now that his mission was complete.

Isary turned to me and said simply, "I am needed." Gesturing towards a broad meadow just a short distance from the road, he added, "There is an old manor in that clearing. Wait for me there." Without another word, he signaled several of his men and took off at speed in the direction from which the messenger had come.

It was indeed an old manor, sturdy and well-built, though derelict, and I was immediately drawn to the mystery of the place. Distracting myself with exploration, I investigated the yard around the manor, poking my nose into outbuildings and delighting in my finds, for it appeared as though the inhabitants of the place had left suddenly, evidence of daily life left in place exactly as it had been the day they had departed.

With a smile I was reminded of the last time I poked my nose into abandoned buildings -- the abandoned mining camp outside Heywood. That exploration resulted in a lump on the back of the head, and without realizing what I did, my hand found its way to the back of my skull where I massaged the memory of my head wound, smiling as I thought of my first sight of Jack.

My musing was interrupted by a cloudburst which broke open just above the quiet meadow. The deluge was so sudden that it caught everyone off guard, sending people scurrying for the nearest shelter. I happened to be nearest the manor, so followed several of my ladies inside where we found refuge in the darkened, dusty hall.

Layers of dust coated the surfaces of tables and chairs, yet everything was undisturbed as though the residents had left things without notice in the middle of the day. I wondered again at how and why the holding had been abandoned, wondered even more how it had managed to evade pillaging by the locals.

Leaving my ladies to themselves, I made my way to the upper level, finding a small room, likely the domestic space used as a private retreat for the masters of the place. There were no linens or bed hangings, but using a little imagination, I could easily imagine how the room would have been cozy, comfortable, and peaceful.

On the far side of the room, near the window overlooking the wide plain just below the hill, stood a richly carved table, its surface polished like glass underneath the film of dust. I stood next to it, admiring its smooth surface then moved my gaze to the window. High overhead I spied birds of prey circling, hunting in the meadow. A pang cut at my stomach as I watched those birds, admiring their beauty all the while envious of their freedom. I swallowed hard, not wanting to descend into a state of misery over my dismal future. I had promised not to do that again.

My attention returned to the table's surface, and without thinking what I did, I wrote the letters of Jack's name in the dust.

He entered silently, the soft soles of his leather riding boots muffled in the closeness of the room. But I felt his hand on my arm before he spoke, as he turned me to face him.

"I'm sorry that you had to wait so long for me." His face was a study in polite sympathy. "But you will be glad to know that my duties are finished in the village. It was a simple matter really, and I'm not sure why the reeve was not able to handle it. But alas, not all are as gifted in such matters as should be expected. He will be educated."

Isary's last phrase chilled my heart. I didn't know what he meant by "educated", yet it in that moment I was glad not to be the poor reeve. Isary's face remained passively pleasant, yet he maintained a coldness about him which was indefinable. My eyes flicked to the far side of the room, creating a flutter of alarm when I noticed that we were alone.

Isary lifted his hand, put out a finger and twirled a loose strand of my hair around it. The sensation was slight, but even so it set off a shiver. I dropped my gaze to try to cover my disconcertment.

"You are nervous around me. I would know why."

There was nothing in his stance or his actions that should give me cause to be uncomfortable, yet uncomfortable I was. The man was a tempest and I a sparrow. How was I to fly in the face of it? I had no words for him, no explanation that would make sense to him, for I had no understanding of it myself. How to explain powerlessness to a prince? Even if I was able, he would have no comprehension. The misery I tried so hard to keep at bay stabbed a cold finger into my heart, and it was all I could do to keep it from getting a hold. Summoning up courage, I remembered my resolve to remain unmoved by his opinion of me and looked up at him.

"You are quiet. Do you have nothing to say to me? Kassia, we are to be married. You will learn my ways and you will become comfortable around me, that I promise."

I nodded, and he moved closer, sending my heart into such violent palpitations I thought he would hear.

His eyes narrowed, locked on to me, penetrating, yet cold and distant. I couldn't begin to fathom what was in their depths.

With a swipe of violent swiftness, he grabbed me around the waist and tightened his hold so that I had to bend backwards as he forced my face up to meet his gaze.

He took my cheek in his palm and brushed his thumb across my lips. A callous smile spread his lips thin as he said, "My closeness affects you. Your cheeks are colored with a hue I would not expect in the virginal daughter of a king."

Was there a hint of mockery in his tone? I flushed with anger.

He smiled a cat smile then brought his mouth down to mine, kissing me with a force brutal enough to leave me breathless and sending the heat from my cheeks through the rest of body. He released me then, and I caught my breath, trying to do so without him noticing that he had taken it from me to begin with.

His gaze flicked down to the table, but only briefly, and I couldn't be sure if he noticed the writing in the dust, the letters of the name I had written so hastily only moments before. His demeanor didn't change, but his attention did. Disregarding me momentarily he looked out the window, studied the sky before turning back to face me.

"You are mine. I bought you as the means to a throne." He spoke in a matter-of-fact way, as a tutor would instruct a pupil on the follies of his waywardness. It was a startling shift of conversation, and I was caught off guard, had no idea where he intended to go with it. To suggest that I was a purchase, no better than chattel, was an insult, yet this man was a prince and the taking of wives was in the nature of a business transaction to him. This should not have surprised me.

He paced away from me, across the room, fingering the hilt of the dagger at his waist with one hand and swinging his other arm as he walked. His path was meandering but the firmness of his steps was purposed. I took an involuntary step backward, willing myself to disappear into the very stones of the wall behind me.

Turning after reaching the far side of the room, he came back to me. This time there was a dangerous glint in his eye, and I set my face, determined not to let him shake me despite my fear of him.

"Kassia," he purred, "I could take you now. Right here." He flung his arm around him carelessly. "In the dust of this filthy room. No one would care. No one would stop me." He traced a line down my throat, down the hollow between my breasts, all the way to rest at my hips. "I have a right to you, and I can take whatever I want, whenever I want it."

My eyes welled up, and I bit my tongue to distract myself from the fear that was crowding out my strength. "But I wouldn't be the first, would I?" His smile was serpentine. "I would only plant my seed where others have been before. It would be a favor to you, would it not?" He stroked my cheek, my neck with casual intimacy. I wanted to scream, knew it would make no difference. "My use of you would hide the fact that you come to me, not a virginal bride, but a spoiled one, stained and used."

I fought against the weakness in my legs which threatened to collapse under me. Isary knew what had happened to me, and I could only surmise that he knew it all. My mind raced as I considered my defense. Before coming to court I carried a small knife in my sleeve, but I had long ago abandoned it. In this moment I wished for it with all the longing of a beggar for coin, could imagine plunging it into the spot in his neck where his blood surged. With equal conviction I knew that I never would. Isary's men would find him here, drowning in his own blood and the reprisal would be too costly. Not only would it mean the end of my father's alliance, it would likely herald my own death.

His hand swept out with suddenness, and I flinched, thinking he would strike me. Instead he brushed it across the table behind me, cleaning off a swath of dust. And like the sun emerging behind a cloud after the storm, his mood changed again. His voice was light and carefree as he said, "Terribly dirty, this room, yes?" I couldn't be certain, but I suspected Jack's name was now gone.

His demeanor turned yet again, turning feral as he thrust against me, shoving me back against the wall and pinning me so that I couldn't move. I feared he meant to follow through on his earlier threat, so I cried out and slammed my hands against his chest in protest, to push him away despite his overwhelming strength.

Rather than be angered by my struggle he smiled, a picture of princely charm. "You have spirit, I'll give you that. Should make things interesting on all those nights you warm my bed." Then, taking a long, slow, salacious look up and down, he added, "This throne of yours..." He placed his finger under my chin again, forcing my face up to meet his gaze. "...is it worth it? Is it worth the price I have paid for it?"

My face hardened, and with ill-concealed contempt I whispered, "It's not mine, it's my father's, and I never wanted it, will never want it."

"But it will be yours regardless. That I vow."

The exchange had been so draining, had required me to maintain such masterful control over my emotions that when he released me from his grip I sank to the floor. I closed my eyes and did my best to control my breathing. It was some time before I focused on my surroundings enough to recognize the silence and stillness of the room, the cool refreshing breeze which blew in from the window and the open door of the room. Isary was gone.

Eventually I stood and navigated outside, discovering immediately that Isary had left me. A small escort remained, and though I had no reason to believe any of them knew what had happened between Isary and me, the furtive looks they cast me indicated that they had devised a truth of their own making, my dirty dress and disheveled hair offering evidence to support their fiction. Even so, they knew well enough to keep their mouths shut. I was still the daughter of a king, misplaced throne or not.

Holding my head high, I mounted up and we rode silently back to Caelnor Palace. It was only upon my return to my apartments that the shock set in. Lidia helped me change but said nothing. Once I dressed in a comfortable gown of soft wool, my composure slipped and I wept bitterly. Taking me in her arms, Lidia held me closely. When I could no longer stand, we sank together to the floor, and Lidia cradled my head in her lap as she soothed back the hair from my face. I felt nothing save for the cold, hard stone floor, mirroring my heart precisely. Never once had I thought to wonder at Isary's accusations, how he had discovered my shame; never once did I connect the fact that Lidia had been the only one to know my secret.

15

I SIT ASTRIDE the brown pony. It is raining and my skin is turning blue and icy from the cold, wet conditions, yet I smile. Kicking my pony's flanks, she takes off like an arrow shot from a bow. Just ahead is a door, and it is ajar. Light is spilling out from the wide crack, and I know that whatever is on the other side will offer me security if only I can reach its protection. I near the door and stop my pony, get off her back and pat her nose, telling her that everything will be fine. We will be fine. She blinks at me unconcernedly. I tiptoe towards the door as the rain continues to pour over me, running in rivulets over my hair, down my face, over the edge of my nose in a constant stream.

The sounds from behind the door are unfamiliar. This is not what I expected. My heart beats loudly, the blood pulses in my ears. I am afraid. Everything is different. I place my hand on the door's rough wood and push...

◆ ◆ ◆

A knock sounded at the door, heavy and booming, reverberating throughout the entire bedchamber. I had slept in late hoping to find in sleep the peace that had eluded me last night. Lidia had neglected to wake me on this miserable morning, and I was grateful. I sat up and rubbed my bleary eyes, noticing that apart from Lidia's ever-present company I was alone, for my other ladies had somehow known something was afoot and stayed away. The present intruder knew no such sensitivity and announced his arrival with the insistence of a hungry woodpecker.

Lidia rose hastily and opened the door, blinking back the light which poured in from the passageway outside my door. Standing there, hands on hips and scowling like a mother scolding a wayward child, was one of Isary's men. "My lord has summoned you. You will present yourself immediately."

I blinked several times in an attempt to comfort my dry eyes which were red and swollen from a late night marked by tears and despair. My efforts were unsuccessful. Now there was nothing to do but rise and dress, face my *beloved* with all the respect due him regardless of how ill the thought made me, puffy face and all. Isary would not be contravened.

The corridors of the palace near my room were deserted this morning. I saw no one until I passed down a tiled and open passageway along the main courtyard inside the bailey beyond the great arch. The courtyard was a beehive of activity, and with curiosity I stopped to watch, Isary's demand temporarily ignored. Another few minutes wouldn't hurt him I decided, even better if it did.

A bevy of men waited around packed horses while others dressed for a journey prepared to mount. None of this was unusual, yet something kept my feet frozen in place. It was when I noticed Jack amongst the group that my interest heightened. I caught the sleeve of a passing servant.

"What's going on? Do you know where everyone is going?" I asked, pointing to the gathered assembly. The man looked at me as though he had been touched by fire. I realized my breech of protocol and released his sleeve then repeated my question. His eyes were fearful and he said nothing, merely shrugged and hurried on as if a hound was on his trail. Seeing no one else, I moved on to find Isary, making a mental note to pursue this further when Isary was finished with me.

I found him in a small room off the main hall. Servants scurried about, setting out food and drink. My stomach rumbled when I smelled the freshly baked bread but turned instantly with disgust once I saw Isary seated casually and comfortably at the table in the center of the room. This man who had attracted me with magnetic appeal when I first saw him was loathsome to me now, and the very thought of sharing the air we breathed was enough to make me want to vomit. Surviving a lifetime of marriage to him would require that I daily plumb the depths of my acquired survival skills, seeking out all the steely traits a lifetime on the streets had forged in me, the traits Jack insisted that I had and that I had only recently come to recognize in myself. I put one foot in front of the other.

Lidia had done her part well, dressing me in a gown of the most feminine drape, clinging to my form yet cut generously enough not to distract. It was a cool day despite the bright skies, and I wore an outer coat of soft wool patterned with embroidered flowers along hem and neckline. My face remained blank, schooled into a mask of cool detachment, though inwardly I was fuming. The grief I felt last night had changed, morphed into a vastly different emotion. With my back straight and chin high, I approached Isary, offering him the briefest of acknowledgments by way of a bob of the knee and head then stood, every inch the princess he thought he had purchased.

Isary sat unmoving, neither speaking nor acknowledging my obeisance as he watched me, his indifferent expression mirroring my own. How long we would have remained this way wouldn't be known. Our mutual stare-off was interrupted by the arrival of my father.

"Ah, Kassia..." he said, breaking the tension of the moment. With the tentative steps of one living in a constant state of convalescence, he made his way to me and embraced me, an embrace with no more substance than a puff of smoke. A seat had been prepared for him at the table, and he sat down, leaning back against the chair while immediately focusing his attention on the food, oblivious to the frosty atmosphere of the room.

Isary studied me for several more long moments before a humorless smile played at his lips. I stared at the tip of his nose to keep myself from spitting in his princely face. My father was already helping himself to breakfast when finally Isary stood and offered me his hand, leading me to the seat closest to him. I resisted the urge to bite his hand off, taking it gently instead and settling myself decorously next to him.

Make it through the meal, Kassia. Then you can ignore him for the rest of the day. You have endured worse. This roguish lout can't do any worse than what has already been done to you, and you survived that, are stronger for it. It was a pathetic pep-talk, but what else did I have?

My father and Isary ignored me, caught up in a bout of meaningless conversation, their words swooping and swirling around me in a cacophonic spiral. I sat silently, picking delicately at my food, powerless to concentrate on their words. Isary's urgent summons this morning served no purpose other than to prove that I was under his control. He didn't need me here, had just called me because he could. I forced myself to empty my mind of conscious thought, concentrating on the pins holding my hair, bringing to mind the image of their sharp ends piercing into my skull, using the pain as a focusing lens. This was my life now, just as Jack had miserably suggested.

"...found Jack a position there..." My ears perked up. "He will be settled well." I cursed my previous lack of attention. Isary watched me carefully, a mocking smile on his face as he added, "...repayment for services to my *beloved*."

His mocking smile turned evil, twisting into a contorted image of what I imagined his soul to be. *Services*. I knew full-well what sort of services Isary thought Jack had done for me, and I hated him for that and for so many other things. Even so, there was nothing I could do. My toes danced on the slippery line that was politics and power, a delicate game which I had come into as a novice but which had been the mother's milk of Isary's entire life.

I couldn't control the rage that surged through me, suffusing my face with blood and ire. Isary pretended to misunderstand the intensity of my reaction. "Why, Kassia, what might people think if he stayed here?" He sounded thoroughly and convincingly scandalized by the picture he painted. "...to then remain at court, and us to be married?" Oh, how reasonable he made it sound. "We wouldn't want anyone to question the fidelity of our marriage, would we?"

I looked to my father for help, but he avoided my eyes, instead picked up his goblet and drank.

"Father, did you know about this?"

He continued to avoid my eyes as he replied, "Yes, I knew about it." He paused for a moment then met my stare with a look that was unfathomable. "And it is a good plan." When I remained unmoved, he continued, "Kassia, he will have a better life there than he ever could here. Isary promises his patronage and good word." I repaid him his betrayal with a look that spoke of my deep hurt. He melted a little. "Kassia, you must see that this has to be."

I did, but I wished it could be otherwise. My life had fractured yet again, another piece of my heart torn away with ferocity.

There was cruelty in the way Isary had pulled it off. The group of men in the courtyard, the horses packed...it all made sense now. Jack was being sent away today, this very moment, and I wouldn't get a chance to say goodbye. By calling me here so urgently, there was every reason for Isary to believe that I would be kept from Jack, maybe even hoped I'd see his going but wouldn't comprehend it until it was too late. The man was calculating and vengeful, and my father wished me to marry him. His dream for Agrius was too big, his price too high, and I was the one to pay it.

"...outing yesterday was most enjoyable... Kassia?"

Belatedly I realized that my father had changed the subject, pulling me back to reality. Likely he had no notion of Isary's dark machinations or the threats he made right before the abrupt end of our journey, so it took me a moment to grasp about for an answer containing any degree of believability. I needn't have worried.

"Your highness..."

A man handed Isary a letter affixed with a wax seal. He broke it with delicately manicured fingers and scanned the contents quickly. Though his face changed little, I sensed a subtle shift in the light reflected in his eyes. He glanced briefly at my father then turned his attention to me.

In a voice overly loud, he declared expansively, "Kassia, beloved, you must have a multitudinous amount of work to do in preparation for our most joyful event."

Joyful event nothing, you sack of viper dung. My gut bound up, and I wanted to fling the dregs from my goblet onto his richly embroidered vest, but I held my hands firmly in my lap, digging my nails into my palms.

"Why don't you get started seeing to your affairs while your father and I discuss some important matters?"

He stood, led me to the door with impeccable manners, then raised my hand to his lips for a parting kiss. I felt maggots crawl where our skin touched. Rather than release me to go on my way as I expected, he pulled me closer, leaning in to whisper, "You and I still have unfinished business."

His hand tightened around mine until I felt he would crush my bones, but I refused to cry out in pain, bit the inside of my cheek instead. He noticed and laughed, releasing me with relish.

I fled the room, passing along still empty corridors until I came to the courtyard which now stood empty. Jack was gone.

◆ ◆ ◆

I was a non-person, a pariah. I found my room as I had left it, empty except for Lidia. It was unusual not to find a flurry of activity here, my women busy keeping my little corner of the world running smoothly. But none of them came today, and that only furthered the loneliness which had settled in more deeply the longer I lived in Caelnor Palace. Lidia had been my only source of comfort, but our relationship had facets which I still did not comprehend.

I wandered about aimlessly, my mood gloomy and petulant, a lost soul. There seemed to be little point in preparing for a joyful event that I wasn't joyful about. Isary gained everything; I lost everything.

Lidia sat still, uncharacteristically subdued. Since I felt nothing but my own misery, I wasn't motivated to ask if she was feeling well.

This sullen scene came to an end when a soft knock sounded on the door. Lidia sought my assent before opening it.

My father stood in the doorway, shadows hiding his expression. He took several shuffling steps inside, and when the light of the room filtered over him he appeared drawn and pale, an apparition of the man I had eaten breakfast with only hours before. Lidia reacted quickly, reaching out to take his elbow to lead him farther into the room, but he would have none of it, shook her hand away with a force of effort incongruous with his appearance.

"Kassia, there is news."

He spoke as one blind to his surroundings, his mind's eye far away, captured by whatever it was he had come to tell me.

"Your sister... she is to marry..."

Of all the things he could have come to tell me, this was the last thing I expected to hear. It wasn't the most shocking thing, however. There was more.

"...Prince Casmir."

Now my knees felt weak and I took hold of a chair to keep from falling over. Irisa. My poor sister. She would be forced into marriage with a monster, another blood sacrifice to a cause which was not her own. Isary for me, Casmir for her. I shuddered a little for her sake, but my father's thoughts were not on Irisa.

"The rebellion is over."

I hadn't thought of it that way. A tiny jolt of thrill rippled through me.

"Father," I began. I wanted to tell him that it didn't matter, confess to him that I never wanted to rule Agrius after him anyway, but he cut me off before I could say more.

"The ruling nobles of Agrius feel his claim to the throne is legitimized now. Sajen blood will sit on the throne in Irisa, and for them it is enough. They truly did not want to work so hard in the first place. This war I was to bring... it would cost them dearly in gold and blood."

Grabbing the nearest piece of furniture for support, he worked his way to a chair and sank down, willing his very essence to fuse into it, trading its lifeless nonexistence for his broken heart of flesh so that he would feel nothing ever again. I saw the dream of a man die as if it was a physical thing, and it pierced my heart to its bloody core. I went to him.

Agrius, Elbra, thrones, crowns, princes, power, wealth... none of it mattered, not to me. But it was my father's world; it had sustained him even while it consumed him, to the point that he was willing to sacrifice his own daughter. For this reason I was glad it was over.

Did I begrudge him for it? No, in all honesty I did not. He was my father, and my love for him would take me to the underworld and back. Yet his dream was a double edged sword: life for him and death for me on one side, or life for me and death for him on the other. So far we had seen the first side, but now the sword had turned, the edge piercing in my favor.

"I must go to her." It was utter nonsense, of course. I almost laughed until I saw he was serious. "And you must come with me, we must..."

He tried to stand, but I put my hand on his knee. It took no more than that to restrain him, a disheartening demonstration of how weak he really was. "Father, there is nothing for us there, or here for that matter. Not anymore." I peered into his eyes, looking in vain for any remaining hint of fire but was left wanting. He remained detached, separated from his present reality.

Easing myself onto the small space left on the chair next to him, I lifted his arm and put it around me then leaned my head against his shoulder, sheltering there under a blanket of memories of better times. After a while I felt a wetness dampen my hair, realized that my father wept. I joined him, but not for myself. I had given myself up as lost long before.

◆ ◆ ◆

We are told stories when we are young, stories meant to entertain and delight, to encourage us to dream dreams and fantasize about a world that could be -- an idealized world that the teller of the tale knows is unattainable yet still weaves and spins the fantastic threads simply to keep the listener enthralled. When a child grows up without the proper balance between truth and illusion, great damage can be done when it is discovered that the world is not as ideal as it was supposed to be had the stories been true, that real life often mirrors nightmare over fantasy.

My fantastic tale found me wandering a dark, lonely road astride a horse and leading a small sumpter pony. It was raining.

Bedic Sajen, rightful king of Agrius rode a mild-mannered mare alongside me, his head bowed, his chin bobbing against his chest in rhythm with the horse's slow gait as he slept. Had the heavy woolen mantle wrapped around him and the soft leather boots not been of the finest cut and quality, he could have easily passed as a mindless, drooling old peasant, for nothing about his bearing right now suggested his true identity. It was just as well. I didn't want anyone to know who we were.

I wiped a damp sleeve across my face in an attempt to wick

away a tickling drop of rain from the end of my nose. A loud boom of thunder reverberated overhead and Rose shuddered beneath me. Had I not been holding her steadier than I was, likely she would have bolted. My father's horse was benign enough not to offer even a hint of protest at the foul weather, simply plodded along steadily as if the weather was bright and sunny.

Cold and wet and fighting the gloom in my heart, I glanced around in yet another vain attempt to find shelter. All around was empty landscape, fallow fields still awaiting the spring planting, and solitary copses of trees standing away from the road. We had encountered one or two settlements already this day, but up until now my desire to put distance between us and Isary had proven a stronger motivation than getting out of the foul weather. Now I just wanted to be warm and dry, cursing Isary and my fear of him under my breath.

It was nearly a week ago that we departed Caelnor Palace at Brekkell, on a night that imitated too many nights from my past, punctuated as it was with urgent whispers, hurried feet, and a covert escape under cover of darkness.

Initially the news of Irisa's impending marriage to Prince Casmir had devastated my father and his grand scheme to regain the Agrian throne. It seemed futile to commence a military campaign designed to rescue a people who didn't want rescuing. Yet after a time of consideration, he decided that there was some merit to their plans. There was still hope, he argued, that his supporters in Agrius could be swayed to see the advantages in returning him to his throne despite Casmir's marriage to his own daughter. Because he wanted a throne so badly, and despite his disdain for me, Isary allowed himself to be convinced by my father. And so we stayed the course. Things were no longer dire for my father, and the life slowly seeped back into his bones.

All of it came to a screeching halt when Serdar Janko Barbaros, the largest financier of the expedition after Isary, distanced himself from my father citing eleventh hour regret. Seeing it as an easy way to get out of doing what their hearts were not fully convinced of in the first place, most of the Elbran nobility threw in their lot with the

Serdar, abandoning my father en masse. This was the final death blow.

Very late in the night shortly after, Lidia came to my bedside.

"My lady... are you yet awake?"

I was. Most nights I was, in fact. I worried about my father, worried about my future. My father was a king that no one wanted, a very precarious place to find oneself -- more threat alive than dead. Yet what could be done? We were without help, had nowhere to go, and were always watched. Our prospects were hopeless.

When she sensed my wakefulness, Lidia crawled into bed with me, pulling the bed curtains tightly closed so we could converse in the relative privacy of our silk canopy.

"Everything has been arranged," she whispered, her words melodious despite the context of her message.

"What has been arranged? What are you talking about?"

"Tomorrow night, you and your father will slip out of the palace by a small gate. Horses and supplies have been gathered. I will have you packed -- clothes, money, food -- so you can escape, start over somewhere."

I considered all she had just said. It was what I wanted, but so far had no notion of how to achieve it without help. Lidia was offering me the help I needed, but I had no idea why she would do this.

"Why?" I asked, suspicion coloring my tone.

She was quiet for a while, and when I didn't think she would reply, she said quietly, "Isary means to end things soon. In a matter of days. He is finished with your father, with you." She didn't elaborate on what end things meant. She didn't expound upon how she knew, and I didn't ask. I knew Isary's methods well enough to dread the answer. Lidia said nothing again for some time then added with a rippling murmur, "And I do it because I owe it to you, have a debt to repay."

Rippling murmurs... like the waters of a fountain... Then the truth hit me like a mountain of rocks rolling over my heart, crushing and bruising. Thinking back to that night long ago, out in the kitchen gardens, the coupling I had encountered, the "news" that would be repaid, the fact that Isary knew my secret and Lidia was the only other person privy to it. Lidia had betrayed my secret to Isary. I had always known. It was too obvious not to have known. I just didn't want to admit that the only friend I had at court would do such a thing to me. It explained the facet to our relationship that I couldn't comprehend.

It was my turn to remain quiet. I could hear Lidia fidget with something in the darkness, clearly uncomfortable with her veiled admission, though I felt no compunction to alleviate the tension for her.

Finally, she continued, "My lady.... I... it was..." she stuttered. Still I kept my mouth shut. "I'm sorry," she said finally, so faintly that if I hadn't been listening I would have missed it.

I rolled over and pulled the covers up around me. She took this as her dismissal and left.

The next night she was as good as her promise. Waking me in the darkest hour of the night, she helped me dress, gathered up a few last minute belongings, and we were away, down to the cavernous kitchens and through the garden, out to a courtyard behind the laundry where we found a small postern gate. I heard the snuffling of horses and the stomping of a foot in the soft earth, didn't see but sensed someone else there, assumed it was my father waiting for me.

I turned to Lidia. "Come with us," I whispered hoarsely. I don't know why I said it. Impulse made me do it. Impulse brought on by the desperate isolation and loneliness fostered in me during the long months at Caelnor. Lidia was the last person I wanted to go with me, but something compelled me to give her the chance.

The moon cast a faint enough light to reveal the instinctive move of her hands to her abdomen as in protection. The action told me all I needed to know as if she had spoken aloud -- She had no intention of leaving Isary, for she carried his child.

"I see," I said flatly. She may have felt guilt over her betrayal of my secret, but not enough to end her liaison with him. So be it. They deserved one another.

With nothing left to be said, I took Rose's lead, and as we passed out of the gate, I noticed another figure holding the door, waiting to close and latch it behind us. "Cai...." I almost choked his name. He looked somber, but Cai was never good at being serious for long. I threw myself at him and he embraced me in a fierce hug.

"Kassia, you will be safe. The guards will sleep well tonight, and you will have all the time you need to make a start if you go quickly." He smiled when he said this, and I almost laughed at his implied complicity in the guards' sleep. Dear Cai.

"What about you?"

"I'm happy here, Kassia. I have a good place with Isary's men. For now it is enough."

And I believed him.

◆ ◆ ◆

All my friends were gone. Now as I rode in the rain, cold lodged in every crevice of my body even down to my bones. We were loaded down with food and clothing, jewelry and heavy bags of coin, and I hoped that all the work of my conspirators, whatever their motives, wouldn't be for naught. If we were taken ill and died out here in the wilderness, none of it would matter.

My nose caught a faint whiff of smoke and I looked up, awakened out of my reverie. Rose sensed the same thing, for her ears suddenly perked up, and she tossed her head, jangling her harness. Smoke meant humans, and humans meant fodder and a warm bed. I clicked my tongue, urging my father's mount forward, for his docile mount hadn't noticed what Rose was straining to get to. Just ahead, above the line of trees atop a bluff, I saw a pillar of smoke ascending in a lazy spiral against the angry gray sky. We could be there by midday if I was gauging the hour correctly on this overcast, wet day.

In the end I was wrong. What else was new? It wasn't midday when we reached the source of the smoke, it was midnight, and what I thought was a single settlement was a town on the bluff. We were still in Elbra, still in Isary's lands, and the thought of stopping in a town made me nervous, yet I decided I was beyond caring.

Through a narrow window fronting the muddy street, I spied a light still burning inside a small inn with a steeply peaked roof in the center of the town. If nothing else, we would be out of the rain tonight. After finding a sheltered byre in back for our horses, I pushed open the front door and led my father inside.

The room was clean, orderly, and smelled of last night's meal.

My stomach rumbled. Crossing the planked floor to a serving table, my heavy booted feet sounded out my steps, alerting the innkeeper that someone had arrived. I heard a noise, soon saw a sleepy face appear.

Had it been me in her place, I would have ignored the approach of a new lodger in favor of my warm bed. But fortunately for us she was not me. "Can I help you?"

"My father and I, we would like a night's lodging, if space is available?"

The woman yawned and looked at us, saw our cold, wet state and took immediate pity on us. "There are no rooms left, but if you are content with a blanket and a spot over there by the fire, you are welcome to stay the night, and at a discount." It may have been pity, it may have been laziness. I didn't care why she offered us a discount; I was grateful.

I paid her a coin, she fetched us some blankets, and as she turned to leave, I thought of one more thing, asked her, "Please, if I may ask? What town is this?"

"This is Belbourne, on the edge of Greenlaw." And with that, she left us.

Belbourne. My heart sank. I knew nothing of Belbourne except that it wasn't Dawick, the town to which Isary had sent Jack. There hadn't been any reason to believe that we had found it by sheer luck, but I had dared to hope.

We would try again tomorrow. Maybe someone could direct us.

◆◆◆

The sun had a way of waking me up in the most inappropriate of ways – piercing with cheery beams of light on the wrong mornings. Thankfully this morning was not one of those times. Since I was still wet from last night's rain, I wouldn't have had the energy to fight off the optimistic urges that sunlight tends to encourage.

My father still slept, and I decided that there was no reason to wake him. He needed the rest more than I, and a longer dalliance near a warm fire would only improve our chances of success with another long, hard day in the saddle. I was very tired, weakened from lack of food resulting from my desire to keep moving, and my father was worse than I was.

I stood, doing my best to shake off the dizziness that overcame me, and looked around. The room was empty except for a serving maid who was just making her way back towards the kitchen from a table where sat a single patron huddled with a decided slump over a plate of food. He looked nearly as rumpled as me, and though I hadn't noticed him last night, it was fairly likely that he had slept on the floor as we had done.

There was no one else around to ask about the location of Dawick, and I figured he was as likely as anyone else to know. "Excuse me," I began as I approached the man. "I'm looking for Dawick. Do you know where it is?"

The man didn't move. I wasn't sure he had even heard me. Finally, in a voice so soft I had to strain to hear him, he said, "Dawick would be a very dangerous place for one such as you just now". His voice was deep and raspy, as if he had fallen asleep in his cups after taking a file to his voice box. I hoped he wasn't a professional thug or a horse thief.

"Why?" I asked cautiously, taking a step closer. The man stood though he didn't turn around. Alarm bells went off somewhere in my head. Now that he was standing, I could see that his clothing was finely cut and expensively tailored. If he was a hired thug, he was paid well. Something screamed at me to turn and run, but I knew I could never get to my father quickly enough, and even then we'd never get past this man. I would have to tough it out.

"Sir, I'm only looking for a man. I don't want trouble. Can you tell me where Dawick is?"

Desperation clawed at my insides. My inner common sense told me to turn, irrationally suggesting that there was still time to escape even though I knew better. Ignoring all of that I took several steps closer so that I was just behind the man with the rumpled yet exquisite coat. My gaze flicked to the man's waist to see if he carried a dagger featuring a sun emblem. There was nothing.

He turned.

292

"Kassia," he said, and I fainted.

◆ ◆ ◆

I tiptoe towards the door as the rain continues to pour over me, running in rivulets over my hair, down my face, over the edge of my nose in a constant stream.

The sounds from behind the door are unfamiliar. This is not what I expected. My heart beats loudly, the blood pulses in my ears. I am afraid. Everything is different. I place my hand on the door's rough wood and push...

This is not what I expected. It is something better.

◆ ◆ ◆

The bed was comfortable. While nothing like the bed I had occupied in Caelnor Palace, the lair of my former beloved, Isary, Prince of Elbra, this bed was my own. For that reason alone, no overstuffed mattress of feather and down could ever take its place.

If I was to rise from my comfort, if I was to stand and cross the room, look out the window, and had it been daytime rather than night, I would have viewed a small meadow, wildflowers blooming in their spring splendor, surrounded by a deep, thick wood sloping up the side of a steep foothill. It wasn't a broad meadow, and it wasn't a mountain -- it was a perfect compromise between them. I smoothed the linen coverlet over me as I leaned against the pillow at my back, my eyes lazing shut in contented peace as I thought over the events that led me to this place.

Yes, I had fainted at the inn in Belbourne. I am not proud of it. But I awoke within minutes, finding myself lying on the floor under a warm blanket and looking up into the face of the matron of the inn who held me securely in her arms.

Anxious feet shuffled from somewhere behind the woman, and without success I tried to turn my head to see who it was.

"I'm fine!" I said to the woman, more politely than I felt. "Please, would you let me up?" She was very strong, probably as a result of a lifetime of lugging barrels of ale.

"Are you sure you're alright, dear? You gave us quite a scare."

293

"Yes, yes," I began, more impatiently this time, brushing aside her effort to help me sit up. I smoothed out my damp skirt and pulled my legs under me to stand. "I didn't bump myself on the head, I don't think," I said as I swiped at the back of my head, feeling no blood and finding no lump. I straightened and turned, continuing, "Trust me, I've taken a worse blow than this..."

It couldn't be. But it was. Jack. Shock and surprise mingled with anger and embarrassment, warring for dominance over my features.

He must have thought I would faint again. Before I could say anything more, he grabbed me around the waist and lifted my face towards his, searching my eyes. "Kassia, are you sure you're okay?"

"Yes!" I said indignantly, irritation winning out over the competing emotions. "Being the new-found daughter of a king doesn't mean I'm all fragile and delicate and...." I stopped, realizing that the inn's matron was staring at me wide-eyed. I had said too much and snapped my mouth shut.

"Kassia," Jack said, grabbing me by the hand and pulling me over towards the fireplace near where my father still slept. He looked back across the room towards the matron who watched us sidelong. He smiled broadly and with an uncomfortable laugh waved her away good naturedly. Just then another group of patrons entered, sending her off into a flurry of activity; hopefully she'd soon forget all about us.

"Jack, why are you here? How..." I whispered urgently.

"Kassia, I have been searching for you, ever since the news got out that you had escaped." He flicked his eyes towards the door nervously.

"Escaped?" I shrieked in exasperation, immediately lowering my voice again. While I had not officially been a prisoner of my former fiancé, an abusive, treacherously manipulative egomaniac, it was true that I hadn't exactly been free to leave as I had done. Escape was the most accurate word to describe what had happened, particularly when one considered a middle-of-the-night flight with horses packed and loaded by stealthy means. "Is that how they are spinning this?" I asked as quietly and calmly as I could, shaking my head. "My father... he's no good to anyone now. Why should they care?"

I said it half to myself, but Jack looked at me as if I should know better. It was true, I did know better; I just hoped he would give me the courtesy of lying to me about it.

"Let's wake your father, and I'll take you someplace safe. We're not that far, really. Another day's ride."

We left within the hour. It wasn't raining.

"Why aren't you in Dawick like you were supposed to be?" I asked him as we rode along. "I thought Isary had made provision for you?"

He gave me a limping look as our horses splashed across a stream and up a short bank on the far side. "Kassia, Isary never intended for me to go to Dawick. Or if he did, he intended me to have an 'accident' shortly after arriving. I didn't give him the chance. Let's just say I 'persuaded' my entourage to let me go." I had seen Jack's methods of persuasion in Lynchport; I didn't ask him to spell out the details.

"So where did you go then?"

"While we were in Brekkell, I used our old friend Swine. Ever the man of business, he had reestablished his network of contacts pretty quickly after setting up shop. I simply asked him to do me a favor -- search out news of my father. It seemed like a hopeless thing to ask, but I didn't know what else to do." I raised my eyebrows but said nothing. Cai, and even Jack to a certain extent, had made peace with Swine, but I would never forgive the ill-faced botch of nature. "Believe me when I say I was shocked when Swine actually found something."

"He did?" My jaw dropped open like a flapping barn door in a gale of wind. We had emerged into a clearing, and further questioning was unnecessary. Across from us no more than an arrow's flight was a stand of leafy bough-covered huts. Jack led us over to them then stopped and dismounted, helping me down after him.

"Kassia!" It was Rem, emerging from the hut. I embraced him. Once my father and I were settled, we sat down for a meal and a long conversation.

Rem had indeed taken his people to their mountain refuge as had been the plan all those months ago. There was every reason to believe that they would be safe upon arrival, and for a time they were, but disaster soon struck, though it wasn't Casmir's men that had been their undoing. A mysterious sickness caught and spread, possibly from contaminated water, though no one was sure. It took all but five of the people. Rem gathered up the few that remained and they headed for Islay Bay, hoping to hear news of Jack. Upon arrival they caught wind of the political crisis looming and left town, settling here in obscurity, at least for a while.

As casually as he could Jack asked after Mairona. I admit that I had already scanned the camp and hadn't seen her, feeling a bit triumphant until guilt overcame me when Rem broke the news that Mairona had been one of the unlucky ones. I pretended to be sad, but when I saw jubilation on Jack's face it was hard for me to keep up the farce.

Jack was a free man. Everything else said that night became a swirl of noise and blather.

After several weeks in the little camp, and after a good deal of conversation and planning our next step, we left Elbra for good. Following the advice of my father, we went to a place he knew of in Pania where we could live in anonymity. The land of my mother. I had always wanted to see it.

Rem was skilled in a trade that was easy enough to set up in our new land once the village discovered how talented he was. They were in need of a metal-smith and welcomed him with open arms.

My father had a harder road ahead. He was a different man after the events in Brekkell, a shadow of his former self, never really finding a new identity when his life's dream was taken from him. The few Agrians who remained with Rem knew his true identity, though no one ever spoke of it aloud. They enveloped him as their own, and he never lacked for comfort. I could not be certain but always wondered if he hadn't fully given up his dream, that he always harbored a secret desire to advance his case for the throne of Agrius. Sometimes a certain gleam would shine in his eyes when he spoke of former days, and I wondered in those moments if he still hoped.

For myself, I was finally free to be a new Kassia; not a Kassia whose birth determined her fate, or a Kassia forced to conform to the expediency of circumstance or to the dictates of a label that had been placed on my life by someone else. My life was now my own, truly and for the first time. I was free to be the Kassia I chose to be. I had uncovered my identity slowly over the past year through the fires of appalling experiences, and though once I doubted it, now I knew that I was redeemable and I was worthy of love.

As tended to happen on the most momentous days in my life, it rained the day Jack and I were married in a tiny stone chapel near the outskirts of the village, with Rem, my father, and the other handful of former Agrians to witness. Jack took up work in his father's shop, and we purchased a small cottage from which to mark out the rest of our life's journey together.

As I lay in my bed, the warm linen coverlet fine and clean under my fingers, the chill of the night air settled in around me. I noticed that the window was open a crack so rose from the bed to close it, stopping to stoke the fire afterwards.

He came in silently, on cat's feet. Before I had time to react, his hand was on my shoulder, and I turned.

"You should do something about your chilled flesh. What good will you be to me if you sicken and die?" He reached out and took hold of the lacing at my neck and pulled, loosening the strings so that the fabric freed up, sliding off one shoulder. He helped the rest to the floor himself.

"That won't help," I replied, flatly.

"No..."

His smile was half-cocked, reminding me of the self-satisfaction he had paraded after I kissed him that day in Corium, when we had seen Figor in a passing parade of guards. Which reminded me: I never had called him to account for that.

"...not if we continue standing here," he offered impishly.

He flashed a wicked smile, and I returned it before breaking my gaze to take in his face, his hair. His hair... it was perfect, every strand in place. Even the stubborn lock that habitually fell over his eye.

"You look like a wanton," he continued, taking in the

disheveled state of my hair, his voice deep as he reached out and stroked my flesh. I shivered.

I reached up towards his perfectly groomed hair and knocked it down over his eye. "And you look like a rake."

When he moved to grab my hand, I snatched it away quickly and spun away from him, racing to the bed before he could catch me.

He followed to the other side, stood over me looking down. I pretended not to notice him as he undressed and slid into bed next to me.

As he rolled over to face me, my fingers sought out then brushed lightly at the scar on his side, remembering the bolt of the crossbow that had pinned him to the tree. He brushed the hair away from my forehead, lingering over the scar where I had bashed my head against a crate in Mosrad.

Each of us was imperfect, flawed, broken and messy. But there was no pretense between us. We were comfortable with the knowledge of our past, knowing that the very threads which caused us to suffer in the moment had now come together to form a tapestry that was a work of art.

"You heard that Bellek is dead? ...which means Casmir will be king? And your sister..." His eyes searched mine, his voice quiet.

I nodded. My sister, beautiful Irisa. I had never wanted any of the things my father meant for me or for his own future. I was now free, secure, and more alive than ever before. But Irisa's story was on a different path. I prayed that the gods would give her the strength to do what I could not, would never have to. I knew that I was the daughter of a scribe. Irisa would have to make her way as the daughter of a king.

"Let's not talk about Casmir right now?" I asked, looking up at him through half-lidded eyes.

Jack smiled silkily and my insides turned into molten lava. Reaching behind him, he snuffed out the candle, casting the room into pitch darkness. Darkness free of shadows.

❖ ❖ ❖ ❖ ❖

About the Author

Stephanie is a mother of two and a recovering paralegal who never in a bazillion years dreamed of becoming a writer. Why? Because only authors become authors. Don't you have to be initiated beneath the light of a blue moon and learn a secret handshake? She had no such credentials. But when a very well-respected author of *New York Times* best-selling books casually asked her "Have you ever thought about writing?" she took the hint.

Her other hobbies include tea and coffee drinking, knitting, armchair traveling while dreaming of doing the real thing, watercolor painting, and spending time with her husband and kids. The rest of her time is spent trying to survive the murderous intentions of Minnesota's weather.

Website:
www.stephaniechurchillauthor.com

Facebook:
https://www.facebook.com/StephanieChurchillAuthor

Twitter:
https://twitter.com/WriterChurchill

Manufactured by Amazon.ca
Bolton, ON